# *DEDICATION*

For my husband and sons.

You have always believed in me.

# Chapter 1

## September 1870, Brighton, England

The loud and, if Rebecca was going to be honest, hideous clock ticked and whirred, giving fair warning that the wretched bird inside, more spectral raven than cuckoo, was about to burst on-stage. The bedraggled little thing made two shrieking appearances before she stilled the Air around it with a sharp pull of her fingers, muffling its third cry. Offended—no, it was not sentient, and unable to take offense, but it was gratifying to imagine it was—the bird returned to its hiding place within the old Gothic clock.

It would stay there for another hour, only to repeat the cycle, demanding to be silenced by her Skill once again. Noisy, disruptive, dreadful little contraption. She ought to pull it down, get rid of it, and be done with the disagreeable thing.

The customers of Fuller's Fix-All wouldn't mind. More than one feared it would be the death of them, the way it screamed every hour like the harbinger of death.

Rebecca Fuller leaned back on her stool near the workbench and removed her wire-rimmed glasses to glare at the intricately carved, dust-collecting tribulation. It was not as if there were any other family around to care if Father's Master-Wright project were on display or not. Her customers did not, and could not, ever know its precise nature. Father was always the one who insisted it be front and center, a memento of his proudest achievement.

Who would not want such a reminder staring at them when the debt collector came calling?

Gracious, what had rendered her such a crosspatch this afternoon? She laughed to herself as she wiped her glasses along the shoulder of her practical, drab work dress. Forever dusty and dirty, they were.

It had been a long day, part of several long weeks. The pressure of the coming debt payments must be getting to her. Best not continue on with such a sour disposition, lest she earn a reputation as a bitter old spinster. No, focus on remembering that the lockbox upstairs now contained nearly enough to cover the moneylender's demands. And he would not be calling for another week. All would be well. She settled her glasses onto her nose and blinked the cluttered—no, not cluttered, it was busy—shop into focus.

Tools, great and small, hung along the back wall, all worn, but well cared for, and mostly for show. She managed the actual work in the cellar workroom, away from prying eyes, not at the front-of-shop workbench where she did small manual tasks to remind customers their beloved items were in expert hands. Wood-paneled walls, dust-free through no small effort of her own, made the broad space homey and smell just right, like Father. Shelves lined the left wall and glass-fronted cabinets on the right.

Some of Father's works still lingered on those shelves, waiting to find homes, but these days it was her work that filled them. Bits and bobs fashioned from scraps and discards that made their way into her hands. A novel means to supplement her stretched-too-thin income, and draw in customers, both curious and sentimental, when they had an idle hour and spare coin in their pocket to spend. Perhaps it was time to rearrange those displays.

Father had hated it when she did that. A complete waste of time, he said. But it helped sales—her records proved it, even if Father had never believed her.

With his passing, the shop was hers and hers alone. She could do anything she wanted with it. And now that the new laws had passed, she might even marry and retain ownership of it all. Married women were now permitted to own their own property! These were heady days indeed.

Not that a potential husband lingered in the wings. It was the principle of the thing that mattered.

She parked her elbows on the worn wooden workbench and leaned her face into her hands. She could do anything she wanted. Anything within reason. Even sell Fuller's Fix-All and move to the country, or at least to a town more proper than Brighton. There were moments when being out of Brighton seemed the best thing in the world. The Guild here was ... ugh, impossible, simply impossible.

But selling the shop would require finding some manner of a job. There were several alternatives that might support her with no one the wiser about her Skill. Assuming, of course, she was frugal, and dull and proper and boring, and willing to give up her fondest hopes.

Not yet.

As encumbered by debt as it was, Fuller's Fix-All challenged her, gave her purpose, community, and the hope of becoming a Master Wright. The shop was Father's pride and joy, almost like a child to him. It was a son to replace the one he had lost, to carry his name in the future.

After Joseph died, Father insisted she should let Fuller's Fix-All pass into other, more capable hands than hers when he shed his mortal coil. After all, what would, what could, a mere journeyman, much less an unorthodox female journeyman, do with the shop in the first place?

When the Guild revoked his training credentials, Father gave up all hope the Guild would recognize her as a Master Wright, enabling her to carry on his legacy. Everyone knew women did not possess the Skill, and even if they did, training one was unheard of. What matter that her very being contradicted all they 'knew?'

Still, he had a point. If there was no chance of attaining Master's status, what point in holding on to the shop?

She pounded the workbench with her fist. Dash it all! They were all wrong, and she would prove it. It might be too late to prove it to Father, but she would prove to the Guild, and to Brighton at large, maybe even to England as a whole, if it would pause and take note. She was not a mere journeyman, but Master Wright, no, a Full Wright, as Skilled as the Royal Guild Master himself. Someday they would recognize it.

Yes, yes, they would. She thumped the workbench again.

Ouch!

Such hubris! Served her right.

She rubbed the side of her fist, then pushed herself upright. Enough of the mulligrums. Most definitely time to start some proper work—the sort that made her lock her doors and put up the '*Repairs in Progress—Do Not Disturb*' sign. She pushed back from the workbench and hopped off the tall stool. Its wooden feet squealed along the wood floor, protesting as it did when she left the front-of-shop. It would recover from its disappointment; it always did. Debris, wood shavings, metal filings, bits of thread and fluff cascaded from the leather work apron that covered the wholly impractical, ruffled and bustled brown dress she had to wear to keep up appearances. Some things could not be helped.

She ought to sweep up, but her fingers tingled and ached with Skill waiting to be applied. Sweeping would wait until morning. As soon as she locked up, she would—

The front door flew open, slapping the brass bells, which sweetly announced visitors, against the wall with an angry clank.

"Miss Fuller! Miss Fuller!" The rumpled boy, not more than ten years old, clutched a rough cloth bag to his chest. His dusty, dark brown knickerbockers were well made, though the elbows of his jacket showed a little wear. Big brown eyes completed his boyish features and a crooked, dusty cap topped off a shock of unruly sandy-blonde hair. "Oh thank St. Peter, St. Paul, and all the angels. You're still here!"

"That is quite the entrance, young man. Who might you be?" She folded her arms over her chest as she came around the workbench toward him.

"Fletcher, my name is Fletcher, and you are my only hope, Miss Fuller."

"Rather dramatic, aren't you? I'm about to close up shop for the day. Why don't you come back tomorrow, with your mother or your father, and you can tell me what you need then?"

"I can't! I can't! She will kill me—they both will. If you don't help me, I'm done for!" He looked over his shoulder as though one of them might appear in the doorway.

"I see." She slipped past him and turned the window sign. "You have five minutes to tell me why you are here. Then I must get to work."

"Thank you, Miss. They said you were good like that."

"Who said?"

"My mates, Jeremy, John, and Robert."

Three of the clumsiest boys known to man. "Have you broken something?"

"It weren't my fault, Miss, truly, it weren't. Ma and Pa are away, due to be home tomorrow. I was minding my own business, reading a book, and the cat—"

"The cat? It's always a cat to blame!" Why were boys ever blaming innocent cats? Balthazar knocked nothing off the shelves when he made his daily rounds, prowling across every horizontal surface in the shop.

Granted, there was the occasional item that got pitched off the shelf intentionally, but it was because Balthazar detected some flaw in the workmanship. He had an uncanny knack for that.

And he was always right.

"Honestly, it were the cat this time. She was sleeping in a sunny window when she took off like the devil himself was after her, she did. Tail all poufed, eyes as big as plates, she tore off running around the house, and knocked this off the top shelf in the parlor." He held out the coarse bag, pulling it open.

Broken porcelain. Shards and shards of it. Whether the cat or the boy were to blame, the bag contained a right mess.

"Come." She led the way through the shop and poured out the contents onto a soft leather mat near the middle of the workbench. With the tip of her finger, she sorted through the debris. That bit looked like a base, and there were two faces, some leaves. "Staffordshire?"

"I dunno, Miss." He wrung his hands, shifting from one foot to the other. "All I know is that my Pa gave that to my Ma as a reminder of them courting or some such thing. She likes it ever so much. They'll be no convincing them that the cat were the one who broke it. They will kill me. Please, Miss, you have to help me."

"This is well and truly smashed." Such an unfortunate end for what seemed like a sentimental piece. Not the first such item she had seen. "What do you think I will be able to do?"

"Me mates said you can fix anything like new. They say you gots a trade secret glue or some such that mends everything. Can't you do something? Please?" He turned up puppy dog eyes at her, the sort that were the reason she could not keep a dog herself.

His friends were right; she was able to do the work. They were the sons, nephews, or grandsons of important Brighton Wrights, just starting their own apprenticeships, and understood exactly the nature of her Skill. If only their elders appreciated her abilities the way the boys did. "You have the means to pay for the repairs?"

Fletcher reached into his pocket and pulled out a few coins. "This is all I have, Miss."

Despite the puppy dog eyes, it was not nearly enough to justify the time away from working for clients who had already placed a down payment with her and had proven they would pay their bills in full.

"You can take it all, and I will pay you the rest over time, yes? My father lends money, and I know how important it is to make good on me debts. Please, I'm desperate. I need it before my parents come home."

"You realize it will cost five times this much for the repair."

"Five times?" He swallowed hard, tears welling in his eyes. "Please, you are my only hope."

There was something about the look in his eye. Oh, merciful heavens! "Who is your father, lad?"

His cheeks colored. "Dick Mallory."

Bless it all. Why did it have to be him? That name alone had her searching for ready avenues of escape. The back door wasn't far...

"Miss?"

Could she allow the poor child to face the wrath of a man like that? She rubbed her left forearm, the bump in the bone there still a tangible reminder of his parting gift to her. Blast and botheration. "What useful tasks can you do?"

Fletcher sucked in a breath, like a drowning man breaking water. He dragged his sleeve over his eyes. "Anything you want, Miss, anything." He glanced around the shop. "I can sweep. I can dust. I can run errands for you. Deliver things, pick things up. I can read and write, too. Would that be helpful?"

Actually, it might.

"I can work for you every afternoon after I finish working for Pa."

"And your parents will approve?"

"Pa'll be happy that I have a proper job to do, and Ma'll be happy to have him happy."

No doubt the poor woman would be. "Come tomorrow, and we'll discuss the terms of your employ here."

"Oh yes, Miss! Yes. I'll work ever so hard. I promise you!"

"Go on, then, and let me get to my business."

"Mightn't I watch you? Me mates all say you do amazing things but they ain't never seen you do it. Can I watch?"

Rebecca stepped back and stared at him, restraining the urge to brush away the chills running down her arms. What was he about—asking that sort of question? "No, that is my first rule. Trade secrets I will not violate. If you aren't willing to abide by that, then take this, and we'll go our separate ways."

He jumped away as though he'd released a mad dog. "No, no, Miss. You can work in whiteface dressed as Clown himself, for all I care. I won't intrude on your secrets!"

Blasted puppy eyes! "Scamper off, then. I've a great deal to get done tonight. I will see you tomorrow, then."

He bobbed 'thank yous' as he backed his way to the door. and she locked it behind him. So many clients waiting on repairs. Why had she agreed to take on the boy's troubles, too?

Apparently, she was still in the habit of cleaning up after Dick Mallory's wrath.

# Chapter 2

SHE LEANED BACK AGAINST the front door and blew out some of the bitter weight accumulating in her chest. The brass bells hanging from the doorknob tried to ring against her skirts, but only managed a muffled sigh. Breathe, yes, that was the thing to do—especially now that the door was locked.

One day, the mention of Dick Mallory would not turn her into a frightened fawn. One day.

But enough of that.

She scrubbed her face with her palms and pushed upright from her slump. Not a ladylike recovery from a swoon, but what was to be expected from a spinster in the world alone, running a shop that was—

Enough!

Self-pity was well and truly a waste of time and strength, something she could hardly afford.

She dusted her hands together and smoothed her leather apron. Door locked, now all that remained was to pull the window shades and get to work. With the aid of a stepstool, she wrestled the heavy canvas shade down behind the big shop window. The other two windows' shades had the good sense not to fight her so much. Almost as if they could detect her frayed temper, knowing she could pull them to pieces and rebuild them any time she so desired. A lesson she had taught Mrs. Stephens' heirloom music box, which she had dissected with great satisfaction and rebuilt it into the obedient beauty that waited in the glass-fronted cabinet to be reunited with its owner.

With the bag of young Fletcher's distress tucked under her arm, she walked past the workbench as she fished out the long chain that held the Chubb key to the cellar from under layers of ruching and decorative trim that polite society deemed to be the appropriate uniform for women in every profession.

Habit required her to take a backward glance across the quiet workshop, now lit only by the late afternoon sun as it forced its way through the canvas blinds. Yes, everything was in place, as much in place as it ever was, at least. It seemed so peaceful like this, free from the angst and storm that customers often brought with them, and the tortured agony of the pieces that required repair.

Was it odd that some days she could sense the pain of broken objects—especially those that were victim to some sort of violence? Father thought it both impossible and sentimental—the ridiculous romanticism only a woman could come up with, and a solid reason women should not be Wrights.

He was probably right, at least regarding the former point.

She slipped the key into the Chubb detector lock and it gave way to her. There was something oddly satisfying about knowing no other person could get into the cellar workshop. It was her space and hers alone.

Cool, damp air rushed up the stairs, carrying the smells of stone and Earth. Unwelcoming to some, the sensation soothed her, steadied her, called her to the one place she was safe to be who and what she was.

As always, the candle in its iron holder waited for her in the niche by the door. She pinched the wick and snapped it through her fingers. It brightened, then glowed, blooming into a polite little flame that illuminated the first three steps of the narrow wooden staircase. As she turned the lock behind her, the scents of dust and damp and the base Elements: Fire, Earth, Water, and Air— embraced her. She closed her eyes and reveled in her connection to ... everything.

Each Element, its every flicker and movement, she felt in her fingers, her skin, every part of her being. When she listened, she could hear them whispering and groaning against each other. In the near dark, the waves of Air shimmered against the candle's Fire, dancing like ballet dancers on the stage, complete with fluffy skirts and graceful arms. Fortunately, in the light of day, such things were nearly invisible, or she would never overcome the distraction.

No time to indulge in unfocussed romanticism now, though. So much work to be done.

The cellar had been dug extra deep, without even the usual narrow windows near the ceiling to bring in some measure of light from the street level. Father had been very cautious about security that way. It was inconvenient, to be sure, but the yellow-orange flames of gas lamps drove out the otherwise perpetual darkness.

The workshop still felt like Father, organized as he had it for the whole of Rebecca's life. A corner devoted to each of the Elements, and a central worktable where one could work surrounded by them. Between the corners, shelves of tools and materials that might be necessary to accomplish the work when hands alone would not do.

Fire first, always first. Start with your native Element, or so Father insisted. His had been Earth, the strongest, most stable, the most common for Wrights to be attuned to. Some said the easiest to manage.

The opposite of Fire.

She stopped at the base of the stairs and placed the candle on a small shelf under the gaslight mounted on the southwest wall. Father had made the glass shades himself, a special design that hinged open, allowing for an easy reach inside. She fingered the narrow brass pipe, cool and smooth, with the stability of Earth, but an affinity to Fire.

With her left hand, she pulled the chain to open the flow of the gas as she snapped her right-hand fingers in the surge of Air through the lamp's mantel. A spark and the Fire bubbled and blossomed, filling the lamp with brilliance. She borrowed a flame petal and held it in her palm.

Such a complicated dance, exotic and entrancing. One could almost hear the music it followed, if she but listened carefully enough. But now was not the time to play with her Element. She returned it to the lampshade and closed the glass. Yes, she could have allowed it to die in her palm. The flame was no living thing. But the niggling sense of despair it caused proved unconducive to her work.

The warm glow of gaslight bathed the workshop as she turned to her left, to the room's southeast corner where a pair of bare pewter shutters hung, each the length of her forearm and half again as wide. Air. Slippery and capricious, wild, like Fire, but with greater freedom to course where it would. She opened the matching shutters to reveal a pair of shafts that led to the street level, in the mews behind the house. The vague scent of roses wafted in. Several large and especially thorny rose bushes grew around the shafts' opening, protecting them from unwelcome attention.

Air was like breathing, in and out. All dealings with Air must come in pairs, breathing out and breathing in, breathing in and breathing out. She placed an open spread hand in each of the openings. First in, then out. She only had to make the mistake of reversing that order once.

In through the left. Street air, warmer than the cellar's, tickled between her fingers. Fire might be the hardest Element to control, but Air was more difficult to gain purchase on. Thin and filmy, with so little substance to grasp. Held too tight, it slipped away; too loose, and it did the same.

The promise of rain today made the humid Air heavier and more substantive. She caught it through her fingers and pulled it into the room in a great whoosh that felt louder than it sounded. She pushed the flow across the back wall, beckoned it along the far wall, around the corner, past the stairs where it fed Fire into a brighter glow, and back to her hands again. By now, though, it had gained speed and a mind of its own. With both hands, she tried to push it through the right-hand shaft.

But Air was true to its nature, slick and capricious, demanding its own way. Whirling around the workroom, it gained speed and shape. A whirlwind—why did Air always seek to become a whirlwind?

"Ruddy, stubborn blowhard!" She muttered through her teeth, a trickle of sweat burning her eyes. "You will do as you are told." No, the words made no difference, but they reminded her she was indeed in charge, something which Air encouraged her to forget.

She reached her hands into the whipping wind, tangling it in her spread fingers. It slowed, but fought her all the way. She dragged it back to the shaft and jammed both hands in. Releasing one finger at a time, the Air reluctantly followed the path she set. She tucked the last tendrils of the Air stream into the vent. A windy whistle danced around the room. Still too fast. She slid both hands into the inbound stream and squeezed down until only a soft breath remained.

Blast and botheration! It felt too much like strangling a cat when she did that. There was a reason her relationship with Air was love-hate on the best days. Something Father never allowed her to forget as Air came easily to Joseph. At least until it turned on him that day.

She moved left again, now cross-corners to Fire, Water needed to be the farthest away from Fire. Carried by Air, it was close to Air, but at odds with Fire.

Or so the Aristotelian tradition that dominated the Guild's Theory of Elements argued. Father had his own ideas, and she agreed. Not that it mattered to the Guild.

A small pewter sluice, the size of her hand, jutted from the stone wall with an earthenware basin below. She opened the sluice gate and laid her palm against the wall above it. Reaching past the wall stones, she searched for the cool smoothness of Water. The recent rains had left their gifts near the surface. She gathered them and pulled them through the sluice. Spitting and splashing, a modest stream trickled out, covering the bottom of the basin. There, that was enough, just enough for the crisp smell and the smooth slick sounds of Water to echo in the room. She closed the gate, shutting off the flow, but a few obstinate drops forced their way through and plopped into the basin. Best allow that for now. The Water had a sharp, stubborn attitude today, the kind it was best not to force.

Moving to the left once more, she approached the Earth corner. No, there was no magic in the soothing habitual order she followed when rousing the Elements; there was no magic to any of this, contrary to what some members of the Brighton Guild were pushing members to believe—all that mysticism nonsense they were trying to bring in left a bitter taste on her tongue. Another point Father knew better about.

Two rocks jutted from the wall plaster—the only plastered wall in the workroom. Not an aesthetic choice; it helped her isolate those specific stones, helping her avoid the entire wall responding to her. Her facility with stone had always irritated Father. Earth was his Element and it should have been as difficult for her as Fire was for him.

She laid her hands on the two contrasting rocks set into the wall and framed by the white plaster. One rough like sand, the other deep black, glassy and sharp. One formed by Water and eroded by Air, the other made by Fire. The Elements, no matter how disparate they seemed, always connected; but that was Father's teaching, not the Guild's. Why were they so enamored of Aristotle's model that they could not see what was clear, right in front of them?

She caressed the sandy stone with her right hand until it became soft and malleable under her fingers. Coaxing it with smooth steady strokes, she drew it out like clay, into half an arc. With her left hand, she drew out the residual flame of the other. As most things connected to Fire, it resisted her at first, until she convinced it that cooperation was better than shattering. At last, she pulled it into the other half of the arc, connecting the two parts of Earth and finishing the circuit of Elements that assisted her focus on labors.

She moved to the worktable in the center of the room, braced her hands on it and closed her eyes. The Elements swirled around her, singing together in a pleasing harmony she felt as much as heard. More perfect than any man-made music in a concert hall, her every sense awakened under its touch. The thrill along her skin, energizing, electric even. So soothing after a day filled with customers and disorder.

If only she could bathe in the melodious order a little longer.

But no, the hound of work worried at her heels. Tame that first, then she could bask in peace.

She lit the lamp above the worktable, adjusting the brightness until no shadows remained, then removed the leather blanket covering the projects awaiting her touch. Two pieces of silver hollowware that had gotten caught on the wrong side of a drunken dust-up; a broken rocking horse made by a long deceased relative; pocket knife, bent and rusted, that had belonged to a beloved uncle. All previously taken elsewhere for mending, to metalsmiths and toy makers, but declared not worth the blunt to fix; the sort of things that often found their way to her.

But first she would start on the figurine. Mostly Earth, it would help her stay focused. She pulled a high wooden stool to the table and sat down, absorbing the wobble as the barely uneven legs settled on the hard-packed dirt floor. One day, she would have to fix that. What was it they said about the cobbler's children going shoeless?

She removed the larger pieces of the figurine one by one from the coarse bag and laid them out on the table like an anatomist laid out body parts. Heads, hands, arms, legs, a pair of torsos, eerily disconnected from all other limbs.

A shudder ran down her spine as she pushed her glasses higher on her nose. Do not read more meaning into that than there was. Nothing more than a broken piece of bric-à-brac here. There were no such things as omens or auguries. Just clumsy, frightened cats, which brought her enough business to warrant her feeding the stray ones that ran the mews behind the shop.

When only dust and shards remained in the bag—Fletcher had done well by bringing all those bits to her—she laid it aside and stared at the puzzle before her. The Elements did not have feelings, but if they did, the Earth before her would have been sad. Aching with the force of the destruction, it cried out to be mended and molded back into its original form.

Or at least that was what her romantical female imagination told her.

She sighed. She really needed to stop allowing Father's voice to echo in her mind.

The breaks between heads and torsos were jagged, but well matched. That was the place to start. The female figure first, for politeness' sake, of course. Inspecting the head close to the lamp, a few bits of carpet fuzz and cat hair became obvious. She brushed them away with a fine, soft hair brush. Few might notice the sloppiness they would bring to the join, but why practice work she would not be proud of?

Once clean, she cupped a piece in each hand, eyes closed, feeling the inherent movement in each. Earth moved slowly, deliberately, but it moved. One had to get quiet enough to find it, sense it, direct it.

There, a slow, halting step, stumbling because of the break. Yes, it was something she could work with. She stroked the broken surfaces with callused fingertips. Rough, jagged, disordered. Earth did not like to be disordered. That's what made it easiest to tame. It embraced structure and order as no other Element did. She beckoned the tiniest bit of Fire to her fingers, warming the edges only enough to increase the motion within them.

Earthenware needed only a slight coaxing. Too much and it would lose form and slump into a shapeless heap not worth mending. Too little and the joint would not be complete, with tiny gaps and thin connections that would be prone to break again. There, barely warm enough to detect through the calluses. Now to join them.

Pressing head to torso, the pieces rasped together, sighing as they found their proper fit. Such a satisfying sound. She pinched the spot where the fragments met. Two separate motions tickled her fingertips.

This was the fun part, finding the patterns in each and how she might urge them to merge into one.

The Earth of the head swirled in dizzying twists. A determined folk dancer resolved to prove his endurance. The torso swayed in easy motions, like an audience entranced by a soothing flutist's skill. There! Yes, there! They both danced in the same underlying beat, the frenzy and the sway meeting in soft, predictable ways. Now to build on that.

"Behave. Listen to each other." How silly to talk as though it could hear her. But it helped her focus on what she needed to do. Pull the motions together at the points they met.

But they were stubborn, as Earth usually was. Three fingers on each hand pulled, directed, pinched, and pushed until the two motion streams collided. Confusion first. The joint quivered, threatening to shatter, but then caught hold, like dancers coming together on the floor, turning together and catching other dancers as they went. Tiny shockwaves rippled through the joint and across head and torso, slowing, stopping, as the earthenware fragments finally moved as one.

She dabbed sweat from her forehead with her sleeve. The first bit was always the most difficult. The motion from the joined pieces would be stronger with each one added, making each join easier than the last. With the remaining dust and fragments to smooth over any imperfect joints, she would be able to start her paid work in no more than an hour.

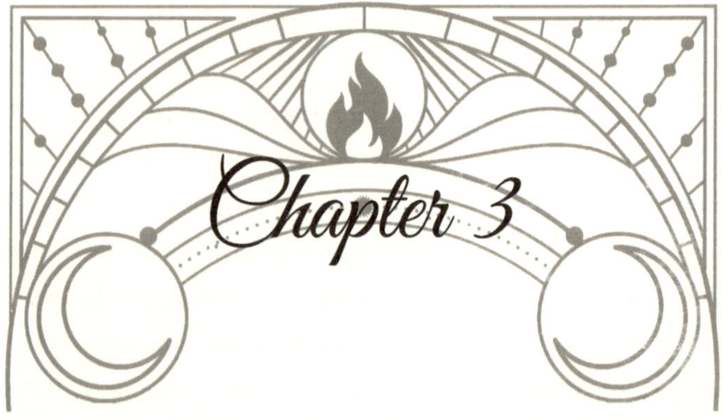

# Chapter 3

THE NEXT MORNING, A warm, grey, furry body, with sharp claws and a purr that could be felt from across the room, landed squarely in the middle of her chest. Thankfully, there were enough blankets between her and Balthazar that his claws did not leave their mark on her flesh. He pressed his face into hers and breathed his distinctive cat-breath into her nose.

Ugh! What had he been eating?

"Mrrrow." Fuzzy goblin was as predictable as the day was long, waking her every morning to fill his not-so-little, greedy belly.

"Yes, yes, you are starving and might well waste away to nothing if I do not provide you sustenance immediately." She sat up and rubbed grit from her eyes and perched her glasses on her nose.

Plain, tidy, and a gentle meadow blue—not that fashionable Paris green which made her headachy and sick to her stomach—her little room slowly came into focus. Though Father's room was half again as large, she still could not bring herself to move into it. Neither silly, nor superstitious, she simply preferred to claim the warmest chamber in the house as her own.

Balthazar nosed her until she pressed her feet into the thin carpeting and wrapped her dressing gown around herself against the morning chill. All told, he was an attractive creature-except first thing in the morning, when he was a demanding nuisance. The size of a beagle, with long grey fur which tufted atop his ears, and a dignified bearing, he was the sort of cat one might expect to accompany a grizzled old wizard.

"Can't you see? I am indeed awake." Granted, she would much rather be asleep, and would be, if not for the hairy glutton rubbing himself around her ankles. "I swear, one of these days I am going to lock the door, bolt the window, and sleep as long as I like."

Such a look of disdain! One only attainable by a cat. Quite motivating in the morning. One of the reasons she kept the annoying little furball employed. He was also an excellent listener, too. But that was later in the day, after he was fed.

She dressed as quickly as her corset would allow. Living alone gave her some excuse for lacing it only tight enough to provide a secure grounding pressure instead of the rib-crushing waist-nipping that fashion suggested was best. It did not hurt that spinsters were not expected to be fashionable. There were a few advantages to her independent lifestyle.

Balthazar led the way downstairs and through the mews behind the house to the pub next door. Dewy morning air, kissed with smoke and saltwater, caressed her face, as though trying to apologize for the abrupt awakening she had endured.

The tradesman's entrance to the pub stood barely open, the signal that she should come in. Delightful scents wafting from the kitchen made the invitation irresistible.

A wooden trencher overflowing with scraps for Balthazar waited inside the door. With something between a growl, a warble, and a purr, he pounced on the offering, relishing them as one should delight in a well-earned meal. No doubt, Birdy had discovered more rats in the cellar and was bribing Balthazar to stay about and take care of them. Hardly any need for that, as he considered it his sworn duty to protect anyone who fed him from vermin of every kind.

Beside the trencher, a battered wooden box marked 'Fix' overflowed with bent hollowware, hard-worn pewter plates, and two flour sack bags that contained the remains of something well and truly shattered. At least Birdy was getting fair value for their trade today.

The pub kitchen boasted an oven with hob and an open fire, and Birdy made use of them all. Wood smoke mingled with the mouthwatering smells of her morning offerings. A deep sink, under the window facing the mews, was piled high with potatoes and some other veg that would no doubt grace customers' plates later today. Shelves piled with pots and pans and pewter dishes, all of which had passed through Fuller's Fix-All at some point in recent memory, lined the far wall. The rest of the cramped space held busy worktables covered in bread, stews, and puddings in various stages of preparation.

Plump and jolly, with rosy cheeks, deep bronze skin, and a stained apron, Birdy, owner and proprietress of the Bird's Nest Pub and Inn, shuffled in. "I see de cat brought you with him dis time." Her warm island accent sweetened every word Birdy spoke. For all her sweetness, she was a shrewd business woman and had taught Rebecca more about how to keep Fuller's Fix-All afloat than her father ever had. Birdy leaned back, crossed her arms over her ample bosom, and cocked her head to study Rebecca with a maternal eye.

"I suppose he decided I needed one of your fine meals, too." Rebecca gestured toward the box. "Looks like you have had an interesting week."

"Ya might call it that, lass. But the names I would use for it are less proper." She rubbed her hands down her apron, her prim lips pressing into a wrinkled frown.

"Dockworkers and the gas workers at it again? Or was it the railway workers this time? As I recall, none of them seem to get along very well."

"All o' 'dem last night. I dunno. It's a full moon, and that makes 'em all crazier than a bag o'cats—not minding present company, of course." She curtsied to Balthazar.

Did he acknowledge her with that mew, or was his belly full? One never knew with that creature. "What makes them all want to sup together under one roof?"

"It's my cooking, dontcha know? I had a line waiting outside here last night 'cause they all want to sit at me table." Birdy snorted and rolled her eyes. "It don't look like nothing among them got settled, though, so it wouldn't surprise me if the box were full again in the morning. Go on and take that basket with you when ya go. I put in a cake, some extra pies, and a few other oddments for you. No doubt you have earned it dis month."

Rebecca licked her lips. "That's most kind of you—"

Birdy held up an open hand and pointed to the nearest worktable and a stool. "I don't give away nothin' fer free. You be working for yer keep, same as me." She shuffled to another worktable and dished up a plate of sausages, eggs, beans, toast, and rich red preserves whose fruit Rebecca could not name. "I don't know how you eat like a bricklayer and keep looking as you do, but good on you. Here ye go. Eat up, you gotta keep up your strength if you're to chase down some sort o' man."

Rebecca laughed, mostly because she was supposed to. "As busy as you're keeping me, there'll be no time to chase anything."

"There's always time to chase a man, dontcha know! I'm considering it myself! Might settle the pub down to have a man to contend with." She flashed her brows and winked.

No doubt she was joking. Birdy had outlived three husbands. The first kept bad company and met his end at their hands. She had lost the next two to typhoid and consumption. She had not gotten around to marrying her most recent beau, which was just as well when he up and left without so much as a backward glance. Word had it he boarded a fishing vessel to avoid outstanding debts of honor, and he'd never come back. They were all better off without him.

"You've got your eye on someone new?"

Birdy dismissed the notion with a wave. "Not today, anyhow, but a lady must keep her options open, yah?" Heavy footfalls pounded down the stairs. "An innkeeper's work is never done. That lot will be wantin' victuals now. Eat up, lass while I tend to them that pays the bills." She laughed and lumbered out of the kitchen.

Thank heavens she left. No one needed to watch Rebecca wolf down food like a starving man. She was starving, though. Working into the wee hours raised up a ravenous hunger that no proper lady should ever display.

Balthazar batted his empty trencher about, but gave up with a snort a few moments later, when it became clear she would not share her breakfast. He trotted off towards the cellar. No doubt he expected that presenting Birdy with a rat might produce another serving on his platter. He could be right. And if not, he would still have the rat.

Rebecca finished her breakfast and hurried back to the shop, with Birdy's basket of all things delicious, hanging in the crook of her elbow, and the box of mayhem in her arms.

Fuller's Fix-All would not be open for some time yet, but that did not stop the impatient and the hopeful from trying to peek through the windows. As long as she made a good show of unlocking the door for them and telling the customers she was not open, but was willing to do them this favor, there was little to lose and much to gain from allowing her patrons to feel special and cared for.

And that made her more likely to be able to pay the bills. Maybe one day there would be more on her mind than keeping customers happy, paying off her father's debts and the Guild's dues, and managing the shop. But that would not be soon.

The horrid little clock whirred and clicked—warning of what was about to come. Rebecca dropped the box and basket on the counter and covered her ears. The mangy black bird appeared to shriek eight times. Somehow, Father had crafted the clock so that its morning voice was more shrill and demanding than its afternoon voice, almost as though the clock got tired during the day. He was forever tinkering with the thing. No telling what its full range of tricks might be.

Sunlight peeked around the shades and brightened slivers of the busy—no, it really was cluttered—shop, not quite reaching to the wide workbench and counter along the back wall, behind which she spent most of her days. If she had her druthers, the shop would have been neat and orderly, with shelves in tidy rows, labeled with the nature of the repairs done and the cost of said services on one side and the odd and sundry items for sale on the other.

But most people found that arrangement far too cold and unfriendly. Brighton shoppers, many of them on their holidays, preferred to explore and discover the secrets the shop had to offer, especially the neatly penned notes attached to the items she sold, describing their former existence, how she had found them, and the repairs they had been given. Somehow, knowing the history of the pieces made them more interesting, and most importantly, more likely to be sold. And for the most part, the little notes were not complete works of fiction, so her conscience could be clear. It was not as if she claimed any of the mended teacups had been owned by royalty or anything so far-fetched.

She tucked Birdy's box under the counter with the other pending projects. Thankfully, most of the work Birdy sent was quick and easy—and in steady supply. Life would turn decidedly more expensive if Birdy's customers became more genteel and their food-for-mending barter was no longer a fair trade.

The basket went under the counter, too—after she plucked a heavy hand pie from under the napkin. Last night had taken more from her than she wanted to admit. She opened the bulky ledger that she kept out for show. There was something official and businesslike about it that men seemed to like—as if it meant she was indeed serious about her business and not playing at it like a child might play with dolls.

No, she was not at all bitter about being dismissed as frivolous and even stupid because of her gender.

If only they understood the craftsmanship required to do what she did! Even making Father's silver fountain pen work was a triumph of her Skill that none would ever recognize. Father refused to acknowledge it, even though he regularly asked her to cajole it into proper behavior.

She removed the filigreed pen from the drawer and held it out over a blotter. Finicky, but useful little item. Running her fingers over the length, she found the Water in the ink and coaxed it into order. No, no leaking or spotting, A nice steady trickle through the nib. Temperamental though it was, it was still better than dipping a pen into ink, which inevitably would be spilt at a most inconvenient time. Most often, thanks to Balthazar.

Not to mention, having a working fountain pen and declaring it a trade secret was also good for business.

She updated her ledgers and set last night's work—both bespoke repairs and her own craftings—on the shelves for customers to admire. Except for Fletcher Mallory's piece, of course. It would not do for one of his neighbors to discover the piece here and mention that to his father. She wrapped the figurine in brown paper, tied it securely, then tucked it under the counter.

Time to pull up the shades.

Wind and Fire!

Fletcher Mallory's nose pressed to the window glass greeted her. The still-rumpled child was nothing if not persistent.

He met her at the front door, bouncing on his toes, as she unlocked and opened it.

"I suppose, then, cleaning the front glass will be your first task for me. Nose prints are most unsightly." She crossed her arms and tapped her foot.

He slipped in, barely missing her toes. His hat sat askew and the buttons on his shirt were misaligned, leaving his shirt collar on the right side pushing up toward his ear. Scamp should not have been here before afternoon. "Were you able to fix it, Miss?"

"The name of the shop is Fix-All, is it not?" She led him back to the counter and pulled out the bundle. "All is done and dusted. No more worries."

He felt the figurine through the wrapping. "You did it! I cannot understand how, but you did it." He swept a dramatic arm across his forehead and heaved a heavy sigh.

"As requested. Now about the charges."

"Yes, yes, whatever you require. Please, let me take this home first, then I will come back and work for you every afternoon, and as many as you say. Just let me put this back so me father won't chance to find it missing."

It was a recipe to be cheated, to be sure, but the spark of genuine fear in the boy's hazel eyes, that she could not ignore. "I expect your return in a quarter of an hour. If not, I will be speaking to your father about this."

He flinched, the color fading from his cheeks. "Right, Miss. I will be right back, I promise." He tucked the package under his arm and dashed away. The tinkling bells on the door wished him godspeed.

At least he believed her threat. Following through on it would be at least as bad for her as it would be for him. Would it be worth the trouble if he did not return?

She blew out a rough breath through puffed cheeks and trundled to the door. She'd sort that out when she came to it. Best lock the door, though, before—

Mrs. Helma Lackwood, short and sharp, all snoot and bluster, pushed her way in before Rebecca could turn the lock. She wore a fur wrap, though it was not the season for it, and a huge hat that all but touched the doorframe as she sauntered through. "What is that little scamp doing here?"

"Good morning, Mrs. Lackwood. What brings you in today?"

"That child is nothing but trouble. If I were you, I would not let him set foot inside. And where he wanders, his good-for-nothing father will follow." Mrs. Lackwood shed her wrap and handed it to Rebecca.

If she didn't have a reputation as a customer who paid well and on time, Rebecca would have dropped it on the floor and walked across it like a rug. Even so, she was sorely tempted. "Have you something in need of repairs?"

"Indeed, I do, but I could not possibly bring it with me." Mrs. Lackwood did not deign to look at Rebecca, instead browsing the shelves of repaired items waiting to be picked up. No doubt spying on her neighbors for bits of juicy gossip. Mrs. Lackwood seemed to know something about everyone in a five-mile radius of her posh Montpelier Crescent home, effectively most of Brighton.

Rebecca steered her toward the curio cabinets of wares she might buy instead. "What is 'it' that you speak of?"

"I am sure you will have no troubles with it. You have quite the reputation." Mrs. Lackwood opened the nearest glass door and removed a pair of steel and onyx earrings crafted from broken bits of mourning jewelry, and studied the tag with their story. "I will have these, I think." She dropped the earrings into Rebecca's outstretched hand.

"I do not do work outside my shop. If you want something repaired, you must bring it to me."

Mrs. Lackwood turned to face her. Though she was a handspan shorter than Rebecca, and thin as a waif, she had this way of looking down on one that made her seem far bigger than she was. "But that is not possible."

Rebecca drew herself up very tall. "I am not a doctor, Mrs. Lackwood. I do not make house calls."

"I insist. You must."

"I am firm in my policy."

"I will double your fee."

Interesting. "I don't charge much for fixing bric-à-brac. Double that is hardly an enticement."

"This is not bric-à-brac, as you call it." Mrs. Lackwood tapped her foot in a loud staccato. "Triple, then."

Heavens! "What do you need repaired?"

"Can you keep a secret?" Such irony coming from a woman who never met a word she did not repeat.

"You know my reputation for discretion. If you cannot trust me, then it would be in your best interest to find another who will better suit your needs." Rebecca turned aside and headed for the back counter. "Shall I wrap the earrings for you?"

Mrs. Lackwood followed with sharp, echoing steps. "The stone mantel in my drawing room."

"The white French marble one, well known in the Seven Dials as being valued upwards of a thousand pounds? I have not seen, it of course, but I have heard of it." Heard that it was gaudy and ugly, and an ostentatious show of wealth that no one understood how the Lackwoods came by.

"Yes, that one." Mrs. Lackwood edged back half a step, bit her lip, and looked at the floor. "It has come to some mischief."

"Would you care to be more specific? In what manner was it damaged?" What secrets was she hoping to conceal?

"With an iron poker," she whispered.

Rebecca winced.

Her husband and eldest son no doubt had another drunken row, with the mantelpiece suffering most of the damage. Those rows were a well-known secret—the neighbors' servants often heard them. Did Mrs. Lackwood know that? If she didn't, Rebecca wouldn't be the one to tell her. "How extensive is the damage? Should not a carver or even a stonemason be called? Could not Mr. Enright, the stonemason, help you? I understood he was the one who installed it."

"I am quite certain we are beyond that point. Well beyond. If you cannot repair it with all your special trade secrets, then it will be a total loss." And that meant a complete loss of face in society, something worth more to her than even the mantelpiece.

Rebecca laid the earrings on the counter and leaned back against it. “This is most irregular, to be sure.”

“You can see why I require discretion, no doubt.”

“I do, indeed.” And she needed to stop wasting her time with this busybody and return to paying work. “I will make a house call—”

“Excellent, excellent. You may call—"

Rebecca stepped forward, nearly treading on Mrs. Lackwood’s toes. “I will examine the damage when it is convenient for me. And yes, I will use the tradesman’s entrance, but I will deal with you, not the housekeeper. And you will pay me for my time. Should I decide to take the job, I require quadruple my usual fee. There will be a strict set of conditions under which I will work. These will be nonnegotiable, and if you do not meet any of them, I will cease work and nothing will persuade me to continue.” Surely, that would be enough to dissuade her.

“Excellent. I knew you would have your price. Everyone does. I will expect you later this week. Do send word of the time you are coming. I have an active social schedule.” Mrs. Lackwood trundled out, as pleased as Balthazar with a rat. “And send the earrings to the house, along with the bill.”

The bells clanked flat notes as the door shut behind her.

That was not what was supposed to happen. Not at all.

# Chapter 4

FULL WRIGHT DAVID ENRIGHT, undersecretary of the Brighton Wright Guild and designated Guild legal counsel, tugged at the not-quite-long-enough sleeves of his coat as he hesitated at the edge of the street. This was the sort of assignment he detested but was invariably assigned, primarily because the Guild Secretary detested it even more than he did, and the Guild Master could not tear himself away from more important things to be bothered with it. More important things like taking his afternoon nap. One day, he would have to confront the Guild Master about his work ethic, but not until he got other matters in order.

In the meantime, he would continue juggling Guild matters that ran him like a ragged scullery maid through a house falling apart at the seams, and rendered him not half so much respect. So much disorder and blatant disregard for procedure and protocol. How could he not?

Secretary Cinderford, though, insisted exhaustion was only to be expected when trying to deal with so many issues all at once; he should slow down and deal with one matter at a time. But if David did that, nothing would ever change. How deftly Cinderford ignored the fact that those concerns would have been much easier to address if any other officer were willing to lift a hand to help. But no, those things were beneath their dignity, outside their expertise, or more than they could add to their busy schedules.

He had expected to pay his dues as the only junior officer of the Guild by the sweat of his brow. Still though, that rationalization had its limits.

Then again, even knowing what the job entailed, David would have taken it on, anyway. Someone had to save the Brighton Guild from itself and he had the skills to do it. That was why Uncle Rutter had ensured that David inherited not just his property, but his office as well. Uncle was the only one who admitted to the shabby state the Guild was in.

And it wasn't only the Brighton chapter. Wrights were fading into obscurity throughout England. He might be the youngest Full Wright in England, but he would do anything and everything in his power to ensure their survival into the new century. Like today's rather dreadful errand.

This new era of industrialization brought with it the death throes of the old apprenticeship models; whereby nascent Wrights were most often identified. With fewer and fewer up-and-coming young Wrights, extinction was in the offing. For now, at least, if the Wrights were to survive into the next century, they could not afford to disenfranchise anyone with the Skill. Even if they were irregular, irresponsible, and difficult.

Luckily, that was something he knew how to do. Thank you, Uncle Cresswell. At least something productive came from that debacle.

He huffed out a sharp breath, squared his shoulders, and stared at the squat little three-story building across the street. All he had to do was deliver the request for payment of Guild dues. What was so difficult about that? Just hand *her* the past due notice and leave. That was all he had to do.

Oh, there was a pleasant thought. It was nearing midday. The shop might not even be open, and he could be justified in dropping the notification in the mail. Perhaps he would be so lucky.

He dusted his sleeves and forced himself to cross the bustling cobblestone street, avoiding the horses and their leavings, the careening children in their mother's tow, and the street peddlers. The broad front window of Fuller's Fix-All had its shade drawn up and the sign on the door read 'Open'.

Bollocks.

At least its Guild affiliation badge was properly displayed in the window. Including the caveat that only journeyman level work was done there. He'd half expected to find that requirement flaunted as fragrantly as her dues.

He tugged his jacket until the collar pulled against the back of his neck. Why was it he had nothing that properly fit his lanky frame? Perhaps a visit to the tailor... stop fiddling with things and get on with it. The sooner he did, the sooner it would be done.

He opened the door and strode in, brash brass bells clanging to announce him. Almost simultaneously, a grotesque cuckoo clock screamed a full dozen times.

So much for a genteel, even discreet, entrance.

The smells of dust, polish, and the faint, lingering aroma of wright-work, damp and minerally, like limestone, hung in the air. Stuff. So. Much. Stuff. Shelves everywhere, except for the open bit of the wall behind the counter where a hodgepodge of tools and items that did not display well on a shelf hung, including an intricate framed mirror, with a scrollwork pattern etched in the glass. Cluttered and distracting.

An old, stooped woman in black stood at the counter, dabbing her eyes with a handkerchief.

"Feel free to have a look around. I will be with you in a moment," Miss Fuller called, then turned back to her customer.

She removed the etched mirror from the wall and laid it before the old woman. "I hope it is to your satisfaction, Mrs. Gilroy."

"I don't know how you do it, Miss Fuller, but it is like the day my dear departed Frank gave it to me." Mrs. Gilroy sniffled. "It is like I have a little piece of him back again."

"I am glad you are pleased. I'll have it wrapped up and ready for you to take home in two ticks."

Mending a broken mirror was tricky work—not the kind that a journeyman could generally manage.

Interesting.

David wandered toward the displays.

An odd assortment of articles, each with a detailed handwritten note, populated the shelves nearest the window. Apparently, Miss Fuller was apt to ply her journeyman skills upon used and broken items crafted specifically for sale, drawing attention to their repaired nature with little stories about them on their tags. Her penmanship was lovely. He had to give her that. But the stories were utter poppycock, for ignorant bleeding hearts who wanted sentimentality with their possessions.

Annoying, but not as problematic as the way it skirted the strict Guild rules about revealing the nature of their trade. Rules which she had agreed to uphold when she was granted journeyman membership, despite her unfortunate father. Did she realize how many were prepared to deny her membership on the basis of either her father, her sex, or most often both? Perhaps if she did, she would be, should be, a bit more careful, more conventional.

If only she had been an Earth Wright. They were solid, dependable sorts, if immeasurably stubborn. Or even a Water Wright like the precious few women Wrights had been. The Royal Court Guild histories noted two such women since the Guild formation in 1736. The documents were silent about their Skill, though they did mention that the ladies laughed and giggled like babbling brooks, and were temperamental and sometimes angry.

"Sometimes angry" was nothing to the temper of a Fire Wright, though. Flame-tamers were mercurial at their best, and at their worst—there were reasons most of Brighton's Master Wrights avoided Fuller's Fix-All.

Interesting how Fire Wrights were virtually the only Wrights who ever tamed the other Elements. The Wrights most likely to attain the rare and exalted rank of Full Wright. David, like Morris Fuller, her father, was a rare exception to the rule, a low earth-mover who dared reach beyond his station to become a Full Wright. None of the local flame-tamers liked that much. Including Miss Fuller, who, unfortunately, aspired to the Full Wright title herself.

But it was time to put personal issues aside and get on with his day. He tugged his sleeves again. Stitches popped on his left shoulder. From the corner of his eye, a little hole opened in the seam. Dash it all!

Miss Fuller, wearing a heavy leather apron over her drab brown dress, walked Mrs. Gilroy to the door, then strode toward him, the heels of her half boots clacking on the wooden floor. She was one of those women who could have been pretty had she wished to, had she put any effort into it at all, with large hazel eyes and a turned-up nose. But she did not. Her hair was drawn back in a tight serviceable knot, with no curls or plaits or decoration. She wore no jewelry, only a pocket watch pinned at her waist. From the look of it, it might have been her father's. Her hands bore the trademark calluses, cuts, and scaly skin patches typical of Wrights.

Some men found her carelessness toward her appearance offensive, but truly, it made her easier to deal with. No distractions from a pretty face or figure to be bothered by.

"Are you here on official business, Mr. Enright?" Why did she have to say his name as though it were some sort of rotting vegetable?

He glanced around the shop.

"No need to worry, only Balthazar is about to overhear us, and I have sworn him to absolute secrecy."

As if on cue, a huge grey cat appeared and rubbed himself around David's ankles. David sneezed several times. Why did cats always seem drawn to him? "Doesn't he have a mouse or something to catch?"

"He prefers rats." The look in her eye—what did she mean by that? "On you go, Balthazar. I am sure Birdy has some work for you."

Balthazar trotted off as David fumbled for his handkerchief.

"What may I do for you, Undersecretary Enright? I expect your visit is official, no?" She crossed her arms over her chest and leaned back a mite, like a schoolmaster looking for an excuse to apply his cane.

"Ah, yes, that. I have a notice of dues—" He reached for his pocket.

She raised an open hand. "I am well aware of what the Guild is trying to extort from me, sir."

"Extortion? Hardly, Miss Fuller. You knew full well what the dues would be when the Guild explained the implications of operating a shop as a journeyman without a Master to cover your work."

"You mean when my father died? You can say it. I am not going to dissolve into some little quivering puddle at the reminder." She crossed her arms over her chest and glowered. "Interesting how you do not mention that I was told about the dues at the same time I was promised a fair chance at consideration as a Full Wright, which I have yet to see happen." She tossed her head, flames dancing in her eyes—not literal ones, though they did not need to be literal to burn through him.

He edged a step back.

"I don't have time to waste. You have delivered your message and you may inform the Guild that I have paid enough dues to show my good faith in following their rules. It is time for them to do the same. I will attend to their demands when they have fulfilled their promise to me."

And this was why he dreaded this errand. Stubborn, arrogant creature without the sense to be grateful for the Guild's indulgence that permitted her to keep her shop after her father's death, or had she forgotten that journeymen were not generally allowed to operate independently? "I am not privy to—"

"And my tomcat, Balthazar, is going to deliver a litter of kittens." She sneered, barely, but enough to make her point. "You are the undersecretary. Of course, you are well aware of who is going to be considered and when."

Best not dance around the real issue. "You do not have a Full Wright to sponsor you."

"My father was my sponsor and put me up for consideration before he died. I had a sponsor."

Just walk away. That is what he should do. Simply walk away and leave her to the auspices of the Guild Master and the Secretary. They would handle her, and he could be done with it.

He looked over his shoulder, around the shop. Condemn it all, every shelf, every cabinet, even the walls gave testament to her Skills. Skills that went beyond the Fire Skill she was born with.

"There is nothing in the Guild bylaws that says a sponsor has to be living at the time of consideration, only that they must present a journeyman for the office. Which my father did." She cocked her head, daring him to challenge her.

Morris Fuller had submitted her application for consideration almost four years ago, the day before the accident that nearly burned down Fuller's Fix-All and besmirched Morris Fuller's standing with the Guild, costing him his training credentials. Prior to that, he was a Master in good standing, with the right to present a journeyman.

He closed his eyes. Section one, section two, section three...paragraph... Oh, damn it all, she was right. According to their own rules, the Guild was obligated to consider her. Dash it all. These were the kinds of technicalities that drove David mad and forced him to take unpopular stands. "It would be far easier to push the matter through if you had a current sponsor."

"Which my father's reputation—ill-earned, I might add—makes nearly impossible. There is not a single Master Wright—much less a Full Wright—in Brighton who will deign to greet me on the streets these days."

There were few of them to start with, and she had driven them off with persistent requests to sponsor her. But best not mention that.

"You are the first to speak to me in months, even if it is only for official business." Her rapier-sharp glare challenged him to an affair of honor.

Earth-Air-Fire-and-Water! What was she suggesting?

"Just as I thought." She turned her back and headed toward the counter. "You're nothing more than a lackey with no more backbone than the rest of them. Show yourself to the door, or do you need an escort?"

A lackey? Had she any idea of what he was trying to do here? The magnitude of the situation facing the Wrights? If she were not so crucial to his quest, he would turn on his heel and be done with her. "Do not be hasty, Miss Fuller. I made no answer to your crudely implied request."

That stopped her. Good.

She glared at him over her shoulder. "That suggests you have an answer—do you care to express that, or shall I guess?"

"I don't know yet. Sponsorship for Mastery, much less as a Full Wright, requires many standards of consideration." David snorted into his handkerchief, loudly blowing his nose to cover it. By Jove, what he had gotten himself into? "Would you do me the honor of showing me the lock on your workroom?"

"Interesting that you would begin with security concerns. You're the rulebound sort, eh?" She pinched her temples.

He was a barrister—what did she think? That he would willingly ignore any provision of the charter and bylaws because it was convenient?

"Fine, come. You will find nothing to fault." She took him to the door behind the counter and pointed to a well-maintained Chubb detector Lock.

Only the most skilled lock picks had any hope of opening such a device, and the polished brass plate surrounding the keyhole scratched easily, giving ready evidence of tampering even if the detector mechanism were not triggered. Subtle and clever. Probably installed by her father before her. David crouched near the door and placed his hand on the lock.

"Don't you go meddling with my lock, now! I expect the Guild to pay to repair any mischief you wreak!"

"I do know what I am about, Journeyman Fuller." He tried to glower, but her furrowed brow and narrow eyes drove him back to his examination of the lock.

"Father had other metal-molders at this door before, and they made a right jolly mess of the lock." Her tone softened.

"You mean Earth Wrights?"

"Yes, them." There was that horrid sneer, returned to her voice. "They were not master locksmiths, only Master Earth Wrights. Just because you master an element, it doesn't mean you are also master of all the mechanisms made from it."

"An astute observation." And one that Wrights often forgot, sometimes with fatal consequences. But now was not the time to become distracted by that. The lock; he was here to examine the lock. Without proper security in her workshop, consideration as a Master would be a moot point.

Tracing his fingers along the brass faceplate, he reached for the lock mechanism within. Forged properly, all the components resonated with the smooth flow that marked superior quality metal. Intricate form and fit, it was the work of a master, though not a Wright. Still worth admiring. "Yes, it seems in excellent order."

"Exactly as I told you." Did she huff at him? Insolent.

He stood and dusted his hands together. "And your workshop?"

She closed her eyes and shook her head. "If you are asking if it is secure, yes. If you wish to see it, then the answer is no. No Wright invades the workshop of another without an express and willing invitation." Her posture dared him to push the point.

"Tell me of it. That will be sufficient." Any claim she made could be readily verified with a quick inspection if necessary. But he didn't need to say that now.

"There is no door from the outside, only the one from the shop, and no windows. A single vent the width of your arm brings in Air, and it is hidden in the mews, behind a rather formidable rosebush. You may check those things in the mews if you like."

"There is a gas line in the cellar?"

"Yes, though I don't think it large enough to invite any intruder larger than a cricket. Do you consider that cheating, as it makes Fire more readily available? Do I need to resort to candlelight? Or perhaps build a wood fire. Would that be better? Did you know it is actually easier to create fire with wood than it is with gas?"

Best ignore that bait. "Have you also a water pipe to your workshop?"

"Hardly necessary." This time, she actually rolled her eyes!

"You are that fluent with Water?"

"Regardless of what the dashed Guild recognizes—"

He winced. Such language from a woman!

"I am in full command of all the Elements. At all times, Mr. Enright. That is what it means to be a Full Wright, is it not? It hardly takes a master water-wringer to pull water from the ground."

Actually, it did. Water was fickle. Perhaps that was why the very few female Wrights were more adept with it. "Boastfulness is unseemly."

"So is willful ignorance, stupidity, and arrogance, Mr. Enright. Do stop wasting my time and show yourself out." She pointed at the door.

He hesitated. Surely, there was some solid reason the Guild had ignored her application for Mastery. They could not have been so petty as to hold her father's peculiarities against her. It would be a favor for all involved to find it and make the reasons explicit instead of smacking of procedural failure. He was not leaving until he found it.

"You are not finished insulting me? How kind. What else would you like to examine?" She clenched her fists and paced a tight line behind him.

His shoulders twitched. Allowing a flaming woman to get behind him seemed like a poor idea. "Whatever you believe would support your claim to Full Wright status, Journeyman Fuller."

"Fine! I have nothing to hide, absolutely nothing. What you evidence do you need to deem my Skill is sufficient in all fields? What does the Guild need to be satisfied?" Her face turned ruddy and the flecks of gold of her peculiar hazel eyes all but sparked.

He squeezed his eyes shut. "If one were to sponsor you, evidence would have to be provided to support the application." If, that was the key word, and surely, he would not have to.

She stomped toward the shelves.

Best not inflame her temper further. He followed at what should be a safe distance.

"Examine it all. All the repairs are complex, and flawless. Handle them, touch them, but do not break anything or I will see that you remain here until you have repaired the damage to my inventory. Those items represent a substantial portion of my Guild-limited income, so treat them with respect. If you have any questions, I will be at the counter." She turned in a tightly controlled tempest of skirts and fury and stalked to the back of the shop.

He dragged in a painful breath. Good, good. She was not going to hover over his shoulder, telling him the conclusions he should draw. That was something. It should not take long to find something to indicate the true limits of her Skills.

So many items on these shelves. But very little dust. Was she merely scrupulously tidy—probably. Flame-tamers tended to be—or did her products sell quickly enough not to gather dust? But if they did, how did she have time to maintain such a stock? Wright-work took time, and energy. She must work like a cart horse and eat like a dockworker and railway hand combined, despite her petite figure.

He reached for the first item on the nearest shelf. Brass candlesticks, a pair, perfectly polished and identically matched. The note read: *The only remaining pair from a set of eight, the remainder lost in a tragic house fire. The last relic of an old and noble family.* Interesting and sentimental. He ran his fingers over the length of the candlestick. There and there, the faint traces of disruption in the metal, barely noticeable. More hints along the length—these had been well and truly mangled, to a point that most Earth Wrights, even Masters, would have simply melted them down rather than bother with a repair.

Beside the candlesticks, a porcelain goose, the sort of thing old women collected and displayed in an overfull house where one could not breathe without risking breaking something. The note read: *Owned by the daughter of a daughter of a daughter of a woman who kept geese, a symbol of the family's source and supply. Good fortune and plenty had been brought by those geese.* What a happy little history. He stroked it with three fingertips, from the tip of the long beak, down the neck, across the back, over the tail.

He shuddered and winced. Beneath the smooth finish and perfect curves, a disorder in the Elements that none could have erased. There had been some extreme violence done to this piece, not a simple fall from a shelf, but shattering, crushing ... He pulled his hand away and rubbed away the phantom pain in his hand. Interesting, the happy little tale she had fashioned around an item that probably had not experienced a peaceful existence.

A child's rocking horse looked up at him from a low shelf. Crouching, he lifted it for examination. Wood, a bit of metal, fabric—fabric was an exceptionally difficult substance to wright. The fibers, the weaves. It required a delicate touch to bring a fabric back to whole.

With only those three pieces—no one could challenge her skill with Earth. But a Full Wright had to be able to bring all those Elements together. Perhaps those lamps? Brass, made accommodating to gas flame, did that hint at a skill with Air? That was closer. The hourglass that dripped oil instead of sand, Water and Earth, that, too, brought several Elements together.

A clockwork figurine, no. Crystal chandelier, no. Sword cane, no. Interesting and flawless pieces, but not works that joined all four Elements. Perhaps that was all he needed, to demonstrate the absence of all the Elements working together, then he could be done with this exercise in diligence—

Wait! There, on the other side of the shop.

On a table, just out of direct sun, a Wardian case containing several pink orchids and a small fern. He crossed the room in purposeful steps and knelt beside the finely crafted, rectangular glass box.

About a foot wide, two feet long, and a foot and a half high, it rested on a dainty carved table, wood with an intricately wright-molded marble top. Brass strips rose from the marble base. Lined with a material he could not identify, they contained a shallow layer of soil. Glass panels that appeared to be joined by brass strips walled in the tiny garden, but feeling beneath the decorative brass revealed perfectly formed seams in the glass joining the panes together. Why would she obscure such impeccable work?

The glass panels enclosed the blooming orchids and sprawling fern in a miniature world of their own. Beads of moisture gathered along one of the topmost glass panels, dripping down on the plants, in a tiny little rain shower, and flowed down into a minuscule stream that fed into a tiny pond, perfectly clean and flowing. What was that?

The faintest of movement in the leaves. Did a whispering breeze blow through that other-world as well?

Though a hand-printed sign read 'Do Not Touch', he ran his hands along every inch of the Wardian Case. This was no repair. This was original craftsmanship, bearing the same unique signature that marked all the items in the shop. Each piece resonated with order. Even the water inside hummed in perfect pitch.

"Remarkable." He sat back on his heels, jaw gaping.

"I am glad you think so. Few can truly appreciate it."

He jumped and looked over his shoulder. When had she sneaked up on him? He clambered to his feet. "It is a precise balance of all the Elements. Subtle as well. The craftsmanship is remarkable. Is it for sale?"

"No. If the Guild wishes to examine it, they are welcome to come and study it for themselves." She rested her hand on the glass and a tiny storm cloud formed above the fern.

Only a Water Master could manage such a feat. "Your Master's project?"

"Nice of you to notice. It has only been sitting here for three years, waiting for the Guild to decide to judge it."

"And you have maintained it all that time?"

"It would not be much of a Master's project if I had to tend it, no matter what I tell those who ask about it."

Great Scott, what a feat! "It is a shame they have ignored it."

"Yes, it is. Especially since in doing so they are refusing to abide by their own rules on the issue."

The cuckoo clock on the wall over his head screeched once, and thankfully only once.

Unfortunately, she was right.

And the Guild wasn't going to like it. Dash it all.

# Chapter 5

Mr. Enright tipped his hat and hurried for the door, striding out like some ridiculous seabird, with legs too long for his body.

Insufferable, arrogant man. Coming in like some sort of schoolmaster, evaluating her work, looking for imperfections. What right did he have? Did he consider himself special because he was one of only two mud-men—Earth Wrights, he would rather have been called an Earth Wright— who had become Full Wrights?

Hardly.

She had seen his Master's project, displayed in the Guild Hall the year he had first arrived in Brighton. While it qualified, it was nothing to what a Full Wright who began as a Fire Wright could accomplish.

Nothing to what she could do.

She leaned against the back wall and huffed out the tension from her chest.

At least he had the decency to recognize that, even if he didn't say it directly. The way he looked at her Wardian case. He understood the expertise it had taken to craft that. Perhaps even appreciated it.

But appreciation alone wasn't enough. How much authority did he wield?

His stated purpose was to remind her to pay her dues. A simple, straightforward task.

He hardly appeared prepared to judge her quest for Master status. He seemed surprised when he heard himself offering to sponsor her. And even that wasn't straightforward, only implied in an odd sort of way.

Why would he do that?

The quality of her work had never attracted attention before ... was it her appeal to the rules of the Guild itself? He had been particularly attentive when she reminded him of the Guild's failures.

Pleasing, but would he do anything about it? That was the real question.

Would he, could he, get them to pay attention to her this time?

How many times had they turned her down already? She had so many marks against her. She had a flamer's temper, but she had gotten better at controlling it. And every other Fire Wright had one, too. Most with far less control and decorum than she.

Then there was the issue of her sex. She was too female. The rest of the world might finally start to recognize women as actual intelligent, contributing members of society, but none could accuse the Guild of innovation or forward-thinking. Over a century of depending on the apprentice system, which included only men, to identify nascent Wrights had left them assuming that female Wrights were impossibly rare, mythical creatures, curious, but useless. If the Guild could have returned to medieval times, they probably would have. How easily they forgot they would more than likely have all been burnt as witches in those days.

Even if they stopped being stupid about women, they still wouldn't want Morris Fuller's daughter. Father had been ...peculiar... that was the kindest word for it, in everything he did. Including his wright-work. Especially his wright-work.

And Wrights did not like peculiar. Did not like anything that deviated from their traditions, their hidebound ways, even if it worked.

Especially if it worked.

If there was anything the Wright Guild liked less than change, it was being proven wrong. Or maybe it was being asked to consider new ideas. That stirred them up like a hive of angry bees.

Mr. Enright had shoved an envelope into her hands before he left. Probably ought to see what it contained, even though chances were good that she would not like it.

An invitation to the next Guild Assembly. She had skipped the last three—what point was there in attending when she was either ignored, belittled, or outright condemned depending upon which member took notice of her at the time?

But this was the kind of meeting during which Journeymen hoping to advance to Master were presented, their projects displayed, and their achievements considered. Did she dare attend and demand the right of evaluation, insist that the Guild follow their own rules?

What would happen if she made those demands in a public forum? Would it shame them into doing the right thing, or would it get her thrown out on her bustled arse and banned from wright-work entirely?

It would be a bold move, even for a flame-tamer, and it could cost her everything. But with debts, dues, and limits on what fees a journeyman could demand for their work, the possibility of losing everything was already looming like a vulture perched at her doorstep, summoned by every shriek of that dashed cuckoo clock.

She blew out breath through puffed cheeks, filtering out the vitriol that fought to escape. She had been skipping the meetings—what point to being there? But this one, she would attend. Whether or not she would go through with her wild-hare notion—she didn't have to decide that now. Not yet.

Later. She would deal with that later. But even the possibility—

The bells rang as the door swung open and slammed into the wall. She shoved the invitation into her apron pocket.

"Miss Fuller!"

She winced. No one forgot a voice like that. Loud, drunk, and dangerous, Dick Mallory marched in, dragging Fletcher with him by the ear.

Mallory hadn't changed since she first knew him. He had been marginally handsome then, marginally. But the distinct planes of his face had hardened into angry, chiseled features, and the scowl he had perfected while he tried to cow her during their blessedly brief and failed courtship had deepened into a permanent expression, blending anger and disgust into something altogether worse. Marriage to the woman Rebecca had discovered in his bed days after he had proposed to her left him with a paunch, poorly-maintained clothes, and a step-son whom he probably treated worse than he had Rebecca. Poor child.

"Mr. Mallory, how may I assist you?" She stood her ground against every better instinct to flee.

He released Fletcher, turned to the nearest shelf, the one laden with glass and porcelain, and raised the coarse bag he held.

No, he would not destroy weeks of her most profitable work. She clenched her jaw and gathered Air around open fingers held near her waist. Slippery, temperamental stuff, almost as difficult as Fire to coax into obedience. A sharp pull with one hand and push with the other brought in a gust just powerful enough to knock Mallory off-balance.

He cast about, as if looking for the source of the wind, and stumbled toward her. Was it possible to smell his gin-addled breath from across the room?

"Get out of my shop. I have no business with you." She flung another gust of Air as she pointed to the still-open door, gathering another ball of Air behind her back.

"Then what do you call this?" He dumped the bag, filled with shattered porcelain, onto the floor. "My property, my business."

She allowed the Air to wriggle through her fingers, as it begged to be set free. It would not stop him, but it would buy her time. "The boy brought me that object."

"You saying you didn't know the boy were mine?"

"It is not my practice to turn away customers—"

"I don't give a damn about your so-called practices. I don't want my family associating with witches." His eyes darkened like a mad dog's. The spittle on his lips seemed to foam.

"I have told you before, it is trade secrets, not witchcraft. This is the nineteenth century, sir, not the seventeenth. In case you are not aware, the Witchcraft Act of 1735 declared that witches were, by law, not real. Only charlatans and cheats. My work stands for itself. I am neither charlatan, nor a cheat. If you did not want to associate with me, then you should never have lent my father money in the first place." She released the ball of Air. It rushed past him toward the door. Perhaps he would take the hint.

"I should whip the boy here and now for associating with the likes of you." He grabbed Fletcher by the collar and shook him.

The look of terror on the poor child's face... "You will do no such thing. Get out!"

Fletcher wrenched himself from his father's grasp and dashed away, slipping in the pile of shattered porcelain. He fled toward the nearest door. Botheration! Terrible time to leave the stairway to her home unlocked. Hopefully the child would simply hide and not get up to any mischief.

"Don't talk to me that way, witch—" Mallory wheeled on her, fist raised.

"As of 1735, it is a crime to so accuse me. And if you do not cease and desist, I will not hesitate to report it to the local constabulary." And it would not hurt that a certain constable owed her several favors for repairs made without his wife's knowledge.

"Do not threaten me, woman." He stomped toward her, snorting, eyes flaring, a raging bull ready to attack. "Or have you forgotten how much you still owe me?"

Tiny movements of her fingers on both hands drew Air along the floor, sweeping porcelain dust into this path. "My father incurred those debts, not I, and only because he thought you were a different sort of man altogether."

"Don't think you can get out of—"

"I have never missed a payment and until I do so, hold your peace. You will get your money and the pound of flesh that goes with it. I need to return to my work. Leave now."

"Don't you forget who you're dealing with, 'Becca. It didn't have to be this way, if only you'd been reasonable..." He reached for her.

She dodged away. "If only you had been honorable!"

He lunged her direction, but his right foot skidded sideways, his left foot went back. His arms windmilled like a panto clown as he fought to keep upright.

"Do be careful, sir. If you break my wares, you will have to pay for them." She should not have taunted him, but he really did deserve it.

Huffing and staggering, he shook a finger at her. "I don't know what you did to me—"

"You are the one who threw debris on my clean floor and both you and your son tripped on it. Now get out and don't come back. Out!" Heat gathered in her palms, and she smacked them together in a thunderous clap that rattled tiny things on the shelves. "Out!"

He covered his ears as he stumbled for the door.

A powerful gust slammed it behind him, hitting him right in the arse, shoving him out the last few inches. Skirting the slippery spots, she dashed to the door, threw the bolt, and braced her back against it.

Mallory pounded the doorframe with his fist, shouting profanities and inanities with each thump. The impacts rattled her spine as surely as the sound tore through the fiber of her soul. Why did he have to be so loud?

Palms flat against the door frame, she concentrated on wood's grain, pulled on it, tightened it, hardening it against his assault. If he kept to his fists, she could hold it. But if he found a stronger weapon, she would not be able to sufficiently harden the wood against the assault.

He began to kick. Each impact reverberated in her bones, her skull, a primal rhythm of war and destruction, trained on her.

Fingers spread, palms, wrists, and forearms pressed to the door, she whispered her words to help her focus. The words had no power themselves, but they helped block out the distractions—so many distractions—around her.

"I hear you, witch. Trying to cast some forsaken spell. It won't work. I got charms against it. How do you like that? You can't stop me this time." His growl was just loud enough for her to hear.

Fool. His little bag of herbs had nothing to do with anything. How much money had he wasted on the chicanery? His judgment was no better now than it had been when he loaned Father more than he should have thinking the gesture would bind her to him, regardless of what he might do.

Mallory's shoulder slammed the door, threatening to shatter the wood along the grain. Time for a different tack. She absorbed the chaos and reflected it through the door. One of the tricks Father had taught her—one the Guild insisted was impossible.

"Oof!" Footfalls suggested he staggered back.

Good, he felt it.

Crack!

Shock waves drove her backward.

Running up against the door now? Brute!

He should have stopped before it came to this. But he never was that smart. Feet and shoulders braced, she gathered heat into her hands and added it to the chaos, pushing it through the wood while pushing Air away to keep it from bursting into flame.

Another drive with his shoulder. Mallory cried out, cursing, as a thud suggested a man falling flat on the street.

Whistles and shouts! Was it possible?

"You there! Stop!" That was the constable? "Come away from there! Drunk already this morning?"

Mallory muttered and growled. "Witch. She's a witch I tell ya."

"I coulda let you go, but for that bit o' rubbish out your mouth, Constable Bragg'll be taking you in to the station. Don't give him no trouble now or you'll be extending your stay in the local gaol something considerable. Get on with ya."

Rebecca leaned back against the door, panting. Sweat trickled down the side of her face. Constable Moore had seen for himself what was going on. Good

"Miss Fuller?" A polite rap followed Constable Moore's voice.

She released the bolt and opened the door enough to peek through. "Constable, I am so glad to see you!"

"May I?" He stepped in.

Some found Constable Moore menacing, with his jet-black skin, close-cropped tightly curled hair, and large teeth that rendered his smile a little unsettling. The only Black man on the Brighton Police Force, he was fair, committed to justice, and a profoundly good judge of character. Unlike more than one of his fellow officers.

"Your timing could not have been better." She dabbed her forehead with her sleeve.

"Did he injure you in any way?" Constable Moore glanced about the shop, gaze settling on the broken porcelain on the floor.

"He did not lay hands on me, if that's what you mean." Few would include terror among injuries.

"But you feared he would?"

"Without a doubt."

The constable removed a notepad from his coat and began writing. "Can you tell me what happened?"

As she relayed the facts, the stairway door peeked open. "Is he gone now?" Fletcher scanned the room, eyes filled with fear, cheeks straked with tears.

"Yes, he is. You might want to stay out of his way for a while." Rebecca beckoned him out.

"I will." He stared at Constable Moore, as though afraid to move. "Kin I go, sir?"

The constable jerked his thumb toward the door. "Is that the boy who came to you for help, not Mr. Mallory? Is that common?"

"Yes. I had never met the boy before this. But this sort of thing happens from time to time. You are well aware of my reputation for being able to fix nearly anything, and that attracts desperate youths at least a few times a year." She winked.

Constable Moore chuckled and glanced aside, looking toward the shelf his wife's favorite hand mirror had occupied after Rebecca had repaired it. "I can imagine. Did the lad pay you for those repairs?"

"A bit of a down payment only. He was going to work off his debt to me."

"That is not your regular practice. Why?"

"I think it should be obvious."

Moore grimaced. "I am familiar with Mr. Mallory's reputation. Do you have prior history with him?"

"Everyone in the neighborhood has a prior history with him. There's not a one on this street that doesn't owe him money or favors in some form or other."

"Anything more personal than that?"

"I did not mistreat him, if that is what you are implying. Years ago, he courted me, but I broke off the connection when certain ... incompatible expectations came to light. Not long after, he married his current wife." She rubbed her upper arms and suppressed a shudder.

"I am not implying anything, just trying to understand the facts. Will you press for payment? I am only assuming, but it seems reasonable to expect that the boy will not be working for you."

"After that business, I would not want him to. And no, I shall let this go. You can see my efforts have been quite undone." She gestured to the rubble on the floor.

"That is beyond repair now, isn't it?" He crouched and fingered the dust. "Was this the only thing damaged in this episode?"

"I was able to distract him away from my shelves before he had a go at them." No need to explain how she had accomplished that. "And he brought this in already smashed, if that detail is of any use."

Moore stood and dusted his hands against his pants. "I do not generally encourage letting things go, but in this case, with the boy involved, it seems the wisest course. Mallory will face charges of assault, disorderly conduct, and public nuisance. And I will personally warn him to stay away from you and your shop, though if you owe him money, there is a limit to what can be enforced there."

"Thank you. I knew it was a risk to help the boy. I suppose I should have listened to my better judgment and not let the poor puppy sway me."

"I expect so, Miss Fuller. I don't generally give advice, but if I did, I might suggest that it would be wise to listen to that better judgment. As much as we like to ignore it, people are people and they aren't always good." He tipped his hat. "Good day now."

He let himself out, and she locked the door behind him. Constable Moore's timing couldn't have been better. But what about next time? Mallory would be back when her next payment was due.

But, if she got recognition from the Guild, as a Master Wright, they would be obliged to protect her from hooligans like Mallory.

Something she needed to seriously consider.

For now, though, she needed to eat. Mallory had left her too spent for much else.

Then there were windows to strengthen, a door to fortify, a stronger bolt to craft, and a mess to clean up. Then, perhaps, she could get to the work that actually paid the bills.

# Chapter 6

WELL, THAT HAD BEEN a surprise.

David Enright squinted in the bright sun and shaded his eyes with his hand, as he glanced both ways along St. George's Road, checking for the least filthy path to cross. No matter how useful they were, horses were rather a nasty, messy business, with minds and tempers of their own. He would not be sorry to see them replaced with something more scientific, more controlled, and the creatures relegated to the countryside where they belonged. One day... He picked his way across the street.

For all her independence and lack of manners, Miss Fuller had not been the pretender that Secretary Cinderford insisted she was. Yes, she was a flame-tamer, hot-headed as all of them were, but there was something more as well. What was it? Perhaps it was mastery over the other Elements that had changed her into—how did one describe a woman like that?

Highly skilled, to start with. He tugged his jacket straight, mindful of the torn seam, and he turned toward the Guild Hall.

That Wardian case, such a show of true mastery of all the Elements. Her natural Fire only came through in the subtlest of ways, in the even warmth throughout the case, but that was all. She allowed the other Elements to shine more clearly. Most Full Wrights—almost all of them flamers—relied heavily on their natural Element, using the others only when pressed, even in their Master's projects.

If he were to be honest, his own project was a showcase of Earth and as little of the other Elements as he could get away with. It had never occurred to him to do otherwise. What point in not relying upon one's strengths? It seemed wholly rational and reasonable, but damn it all, she offered him another way of thinking, never mentioning, much less forcing her perspective on him. He should resent it.

He'd rather resent it.

But no, a rational man at heart, he was out to save the Guild, despite all its faults. He had to consider the possibilities, thoroughly and without bias.

And he would have to ensure the Guild did as well.

But at what cost? To be perceived as her advocate...

It wasn't about her, though, not at all. It was a matter for the good of the Guild. If there was merit in her approach to the Elements, then the entire Guild could stand to benefit from it. And in its current state, the Guild could not afford to ignore it.

If only they could be made to listen.

He dodged an overburdened peddler trundling blindly down the street, followed by a pack of giddy young boys of an age when they should be doing something productive. Best not wonder why they were unsupervised. That train of thought never ended well.

A sharp breeze refreshed the scent of salt in the air, ever-present in Brighton. So much so, one mostly ignored it, especially when the smell of horse overwhelmed it here in the streets. College Road was ahead, and he'd be at the Guild Hall soon. Somehow, he would have to break the news to them that the Guild was obligated to follow their own rules. That would not be a popular sentiment, no matter how gently he broached it.

The greens in front of Brighton College called to him, tree branches waving at him, tempting him to cross the street to visit them and postpone the inevitable at Guild Hall. Something about the smell of all the green, a bastion of countryside in the middle of the seaside community. One could not ignore it. There was even a solid reason to visit the College itself. Several Guild members were teachers there, quietly watching for signs of Skill in the students there.

After all, at Cambridge, Earth Master McIntire pulled David out for special training, attentions that set him on his current path. But, then again, it was the cousin who had secretly begun instructing him, until Father put a stop to that, who enabled David to preserve his Skill until his fateful meeting with McIntire. Without that childhood practice, there would have been no Skill left in him for McIntire to nurture.

With so few apprenticeships these days, fewer and fewer Masters found young Wrights in those ranks, at an age where their Skills could be trained and developed, before they faded away to nothing as adulthood set in. The Guild desperately needed new blood, making the work at the Brighton College all the more important, even if most of the students there were too old to have much Skill left to train. At the very least, it was a place to start.

Checking in on those efforts made sense.

But no, putting things off would not make them any easier. He tugged his jacket and forced his feet down Clarendon Place, to the mews behind the terrace houses. A little bit of green in the mews tried to console him, reminding him that even though tucked into the cellar beneath the large terrace house, the Guild Hall was not so terrible a place to be.

The house above belonged to Hobson Ames, whose family had been among the founding members of the Brighton chapter of the Royal Court Wrights' Guild. The Guild had been founded in 1736, after a group of intrepid Wrights saw the 1735 Witchcraft Act passed, which made England much safer for the practice of their Skill. But the Brighton Chapter did not itself form until 1800, as Brighton's popularity was increasing.

Not very long really, not as guilds and their chapters went, all told. But long enough to be a grounding pillar in the life of both the local Wrights, the few that there were, and within the country as a whole. Wrights had to hang together, or surely, they would hang separately.

Cinderford did not appreciate it when he quoted Americans. Ah, well.

David trotted down the short flight of steps to the cellar entrance and knocked. Mr. Ames himself greeted him. A round, jolly, white-haired man, with absolutely no political ambitions either within the Guild, or without, he was the ideal, loyal-to-a-fault sort of man to act as host of the Guild Hall. Not that a proper rent wasn't paid in recompense, of course. Accepting large favors was never a wise thing for a body such as the Guild to enjoy.

"Welcome, Enright, do come in." Ames ushered him inside and bolted the door behind him. The habit was a little uncomfortable, to be sure, but utterly necessary. "Here to see Cinderford, I take it?"

"I imagine he has spread news of my errand to everyone in earshot?" David followed Ames downstairs.

Ames chuckled. "Well, it is an important one, no doubt. Proper respects to the Guild must be paid by all, no?"

"To the Guild its due, from the Guild, its grace, Mr. Ames."

Ames stopped at the door at the bottom of the stairs and fumbled for the key. "Was there something irregular in your errand?"

"Forgive me, sir, but whether there was or was not, is something I am not at liberty to discuss."

"Of course, of course. Just making conversation." Ames unlocked the door and shoved it open. The old wood squealed against the stone floor, ever so slightly out of proper alignment. Odd that a Master Earth Wright like Ames would not have fixed that by now.

At times like this, it was difficult to believe his pleasant-natured exterior was not a façade for something more ...well, sinister... But that probably wasn't fair. Ames had done nothing in anyone's memory to warrant such suspicion.

Unfortunately, the years working with Uncle Cresswell as a barrister to London's seedy and unseemly gentlefolk had left their mark. Somehow, the criminal element always made a deceptively good first impression.

"Secretary Cinderford is with the Guild Master at the moment. If he turns you away, come upstairs to my study and join me for a cup of tea while you wait them out. You know how they can go on and on." Ames gestured down the stone corridor, lined with polished wood doors and lit by glass and brass gas lamps along the walls. A long, worn carpet runner ran the length of the hall, softening the sound that bounced off the stone.

"Indeed, I do. Thank you for the invitation." David tipped his hat and slipped past Ames.

He walked past Secretary Cinderford's office. A sign hung off the closed door's knob. "Out." Succinct to the point of abrupt, rather like the man himself.

At least that gave David an excuse to detour to his office for a few moments. Fuller's Mastery application should be in his files.

The space he called an office had once been a box room at the end of the hall. But for the desk, bookcases, and file drawers, it still could have been mistaken for one. Standing in the middle of the room, he could touch both walls at the same time. Although he had an extra chair in front of his desk, the dance to get two people seated was awkward at best, more often embarrassing.

At least it would not be difficult to find those files. David sat in the chair opposite his desk and pulled open the file drawer nearest his shoulder. She said the application was filed four years ago ... no, only one application from 1866, now marked "Denied three times, perpetual journeyman". Poor sot! What a fate. The name didn't look familiar. Probably left Brighton altogether for more promising pastures.

"1867" held one application, marked accepted. Not in "1868" either, no applications in that file at all. There, "1869," the only one in the file. He pulled it, and the other accompanying paperwork, out and spread it on his desk.

So many annotations scrawled across her paperwork, red spiders scrambling in a mad dance. "Too young" dated 1866, "In mourning" dated 1867. "Too female—flaming temper" read 1868's note. Somehow, it wasn't surprising that none of those reasons were called out in the bylaws as accepted rationales for deferring an applicant.

"1869"—oh, heavens, who did she upset to warrant the pages of notes pinned to the application? Clearly, someone who had a bone to pick with Morris Fuller went out of their way to note suspected irregularities in her training and the loss of Morris Fuller's training credentials in 1867—all the complaints seemed to center around her father, not her. Telling.

More notes. Every Master Wright that had refused to sponsor her in 1868 and 1869, with supposed comments from each one, none complimentary, and a recommendation that she be summarily designated as a perpetual journeyman.

Mostly hearsay, and all of it balderdash. David slammed his fist on the desk and jumped to his feet.

No, not on his watch. The woman might be irritating, temperamental, and even rude, but she was due the same rights and privileges as every other Wright in the Guild. No wonder she was so bitter. Her temper might be unpleasant to be around, but he could hardly fault her attitude.

Master McIntire had paved a smooth path for David to attain Full Wright status—a great favor David had done nothing to earn. Dash it all! As Skilled as Miss Fuller was, she deserved at least as much.

Unfortunately, Secretary Cinderford seemed to share the sentiments that were noted in her files, and there was no way to know how Guild Master Allbright felt. Nevertheless, he had to do something.

Might as well save a few steps and head downstairs to Guild Master Allbright's office. That's where the conversation would eventually end up.

The stairs at the end of the hall bore Ames' signature. Even, regular stone steps and perfectly smooth walls that had never been touched by a mason's tool. But that wasn't the real craftsmanship here.

Multilevel cellars were difficult at best, dangerous at worst. Only a true Master Earth Wright could have crafted not two, but three levels of cellars, all safe and comfortable while the house above them stood, as firm as if solid bedrock lay beneath it. It was actually the work of both Ames and his father, also a Master Earth Wright. Several years of effort, as David understood, offered to the Guild Hall after both men were affirmed as Master Earth Wrights.

Interesting, and it would have been suspicious had the work not stood for itself. But it did.

David had once heard a rumor that the current Mr. Ames had tried to pursue Mastery of other Elements, but had no affinity beyond stone. That wasn't hard to believe. Precious few stone-shapers did. Which was why they usually resented David. Jealousy was an ugly thing.

Perhaps that was the vague discomfort he picked up from Ames. That would make sense.

Another long, door-lined corridor stretched out before David, marginally narrower than the one above, and the ceiling seemed ever-so-slightly lower. But with glistening gas lamps—such a pleasing, mellow light they offered—and more carpeting, it avoided the dungeon-esque atmosphere it could so easily have worn.

Light leaked out from below the Guild Master's polished wood double door. David paused, listening. Yes, that was Cinderford's voice, and he did not sound particularly annoyed. At least not yet.

David knocked.

Cinderford yanked the door open. Built like a stout, half-burnt candle, Cinderford matched his name, from the greying shock of sooty black hair, to the mustache that dripped down his face like melting candle wax, and a blazing flame-tamer's temper. "The Guild Master is busy now. Go away—oh, Enright, you have returned from your errand?"

"Yes, and I think it best I speak with both of you."

"Do come in, then." Guild Master Allbright's rich voice resonated from deep inside the office.

Cinderford grumbled under his breath as he pulled the door open and shuffled out of David's way.

The expansive office opened before him. Though two levels below ground, the clever use of light, false windows with painted landscapes framed by curtains, and a gentle fresh breeze—evidence of

Allbright's Air Wright heritage—made it easy to believe that one was in a ground-level room. Allbright sat behind a huge wooden desk carved with all manner of Tudor-style decoration, an old-fashioned behemoth that lent authority to anyone behind it.

Elbows parked on the desktop, fingers steepled, as though he had been listening to another of Cinderford's lengthy rants, Allbright's long beard almost touched the desktop. His frizzled, mousy brown hair ought to have been done up in a Georgian-style queue to keep it in some semblance of order. He only needed robes and a tall pointed hat to be the very image of an absentminded wizard, although he had one of the quickest, most brilliant minds David had ever encountered.

"I heard about your errand, Enright. I am eager to hear your conclusions. Do sit down." Allbright gestured to a pair of heavy wooden chairs carved to complement the desk.

Cinderford scurried back to claim his seat. Territorial little weasel.

David pulled the empty chair to the other side of the desk. It was not a good idea to crowd an irritable Fire Wright.

"I hope you disabused that woman of her unseemly aspirations." Cinderford's lips twitched in and out of a sneer.

"What aspirations might those be?" David crossed his legs and laced his hands over one knee. "My purpose was to remind her she was late in paying her dues."

"Surely that was not the only thing you discussed. We are all well aware of her reputation." Cinderford eyed him like a schoolmaster waiting for an excuse to apply his cane.

"What do you mean by that?"

"Every conversation with that woman ends in the same way. She demands to be considered for a rank and position to which she is not entitled."

"She has not been judged for the rank, so you cannot say she is not entitled." Quoting the exact section and paragraph of the Guild rules which supported him would have been unseemly, so David clenched his jaws shut.

Cinderford bristled anyway. "She is not entitled to submit the petition in the first place."

"I can understand why you might hold that opinion, but with all due respect, sir, you are mistaken."

"Mistaken? Mistaken?" Cinderford slapped the Guild Master's desk. "Not in the slightest. A journeyman must be sponsored by a Master in order to petition to be judged for Mastery."

"A Full Wright sponsored her several years ago, and she has been waiting ever since for the Guild—"

"Sponsored by a man now three years in the ground. A journeyman cannot be sponsored by a dead man. The petition is null and void."

"No, it is not." David started to stand, but straightened himself in his seat instead. He was not approaching the bench. He could, he should, remain seated.

"As our legal counsel, you should know the Guild rules better than that." Cinderford pulled back his shoulders and squared his chin.

Great Scott, the fool was looking for a fight! "There is no stipulation in the bylaws, explicit or implicit, that the sponsor needs to be living at the time the candidate is evaluated."

"That is ridiculous! I read them recently, and I am quite certain—"

"Section 2, subsection 2, paragraph 8 defines the qualities of a sponsor. Subsection 3 defines the process for sponsorship, subsection 4 outlines the process for submitting an application for advancement, and subsection 5 details the way those applications will be handled. In none of those passages is there anything which may be read as a requirement that the sponsor be alive at the time the application is considered."

"Common sense decrees—"

"I am afraid we are not governed by common sense, but by the Charter and Bylaws that we have written for ourselves."

"They need to be changed then."

"That may be so, and it is the right of every Master Wright to petition the Royal Court Guild for those changes. However, it might be worth noting that the Royal Guild Master's sponsor for his first Mastership died six months before his application was evaluated, so he might not be sympathetic to your arguments."

Cinderford's face turned an impossible shade of red. Heat radiated from his skin, noticeable even at David's distance.

"What is your professional advice as our legal counsel?" Was that a smirk under Allbright's untamed beard?

"While there is flexibility in many of our bylaws, the issue of Guild membership is so central to who we are that there is no room for interpretation. We must adhere to the exact wording of the text and not add to the requirements by our own interpretation."

"Then it is clear—" Allbright said.

"We still do not have to permit her application." Cinderford slapped the desk twice. "The bylaws are clear that if her work is judged substandard—"

This was getting tiresome. "It is not. I took it upon myself to examine her work while at her shop, including her Mastery project."

"She has one of those lying about, does she?"

"It was prepared when her petition was first submitted. And before you object further, I tested it and could find no traces of any other Wright's work upon it. Why are you so biased against her?"

Cinderford might have glared flame if that were possible. And from the look of him, he would dearly love to find a way. "Beyond the inherent instability and insufficiency of her sex?"

"Beyond that." David drummed his fingers on his knee. Perhaps he needed to remind Cinderford that the bylaws also failed to mention any requirement that Wrights be male.

"She is arrogant and unruly, with opinions of her own that are not in line with the Guild's."

Allbright chuckled. "You still resent her father."

"He was an annoying, debt-ridden little man—"

"And one of the most skilled Full Wrights the Guild has ever seen." Allbright rapped his desk, punctuating his point.

"Who flaunted your precious rules at every turn. Have you forgotten he began to teach her before the Guild had even recognized her?"

"I believe he had little choice. When a young hot-head—"

Cinderford winced. Few Fire Wrights appreciated that appellation.

"—has that much innate control over her Element. It is not only unwise, but dangerous, not to train them as soon as possible. For the safety of all involved, they must be managed early."

"Managed? You believe that woman is in any way managed?" Cinderford snorted. "That Fix-All shop of hers flaunts all propriety."

"In what way?" David asked. "I was just there, and am convinced it conforms to all rules of security and secrecy in the Guild. Going over and above on several points."

"Are you bothered because she took it over from her father, rather than allowing the Guild to take on its management?" The sharp edge to Allbright's tone suggested waning patience.

"That is what would have been proper under the circumstances."

"We have had this discussion before, Cinderford, and I still disagree with you. There was no reason to take her livelihood from her, especially considering her father's death was judged to be from natural causes, not related to his Skill."

"She could have been given an annuity and—"

"Your petty resentment over having a girl-child more adept than your own wolf pack of sons is unbecoming. I recommend you work on bringing that under better regulation before it hinders your objectivity and your office." Only a fool would ignore Allbright's warning.

"How dare you accuse me of such pettiness, all the while you are dancing around the actual issue?" Cinderford glanced from Allbright to David. "Given her father's unorthodox approach to the Skill, the one that led to one known death already—"

"I looked into that matter when I first arrived in Brighton, and no proven link between Fuller's non-Aristotelian theories and his son's accident was established," David said.

"Perhaps not in a court of law, but any fool could deduce that failure of proper training killed that boy of his, not to mention that fire in his shop—"

"Also judged an accident, from natural causes."

"And you believe that?"

"I have no evidence to support another conclusion." It would have been nice to take Cinderford's shoulders to shake some sense into him. David gripped the arms of his chair instead.

"I suppose that is to say that you intend to sponsor her yourself, and petition for her recognition as a Full Wright this year, despite all the irregularities and her outstanding unpaid dues." Cinderford turned his face aside and snorted.

"The unpaid dues are no small issue, but one could argue that the Guild is in breach of its contract to her." David offered the idea on open hands.

"Breach of contract?" Cinderford nearly spat. "This is what we get for bringing a barrister into our midst. Complicating and convoluting clear and simple matters until we can't tell arse from elbow and are convinced into all manner of stupidity."

"That is quite enough." Allbright rapped his desk. "The decision is mine to make."

"You are a sensible man, Guild Master. Expel her from the Guild, as you threatened to do with her father, and be done with it. We will all be better for having that family dismissed from our numbers."

"To do so would put us in violation of our bylaws, which will set a precedent that will lead us into dark and dangerous days. It is bad enough that we have ignored the bylaws on application for mastery this long." David stood. He probably shouldn't, but there was no helping it now. "If you will hear me out, Guild Master, I have a suggestion that might allow us appropriate middle ground."

Allbright's bushy brows shot up. "Go on, I am listening."

"Since her elevation to Master Wright—"

"Full Wright, don't forget she has the audacity to pursue that rank!" Cinderford looked at Allbright, not David.

"—is controversial, relying on an old, established precedent seems advisable. Our histories suggest it was once the custom for all Master Wrights to demonstrate their Mastery during a Guild Assembly. Should we consider her petition for Mastery, we might require her to demonstrate her Skill at the upcoming meeting and allow the Masters present to judge her work on its merits."

"That seems reasonable to me." Cinderford's slow smile resembled a predator's spotting its prey.

"I don't know," Allbright said. "No other Master, much less a Full Wright, has been asked to do such a thing in the last fifty years. I'm not sure it wouldn't send the wrong message. We do not perform our Skill for an audience."

"An excellent point, sir. But consider it might be in Miss Fuller's interest to do so. I am sure Cinderford speaks for a significant portion of the Guild, who still bears animosity toward her father and his unconventional ideas. Those men will not be satisfied to take anyone's word on her suitability. They will not support her as they ought if they are unconvinced of her qualifications. Does she not deserve the backing other members receive?"

"You know as well as I, men will believe what they want."

"For some, that is true, no argument. But there are others who trust their own experience more than the guidance of another's opinions. Is it not worthwhile to offer them and her that opportunity?

"I will consider it." Allbright nodded slowly as he stood. "I have much to think about, gentlemen, please leave me to it."

David gestured for a slack-jawed Cinderford to precede him through the door.

Cinderford strode halfway to his own office, then turned to face David. "You are a clever cur, Enright."

"What do you mean?" The hair on the back of David's neck stood.

"You do not want to see her succeed any more than I do. Not one of us is up to performing before an audience. She will fail, and we will not have to endure her voice among the board of Master Wrights. Clever."

"There is no guarantee she will fail."

"You go right on saying that and keep yourself in Allbright's favor, letting him think you are on board with his progressive ways. I didn't take you as such a crafty politician, but I am impressed. You've got the potential to go far." Cinderford sauntered away.

# Chapter 7

The Bird's Nest's kitchen bustled with homey activity. Pots boiled on the stove, popping and hissing. Burning coals heated the oven, humming and thrumming in almost musical tones only Rebecca could hear. And the smells—oh, the marvelous scents of breads and meats and so many other delights, provoking rumblings and grumblings in her belly.

"You've quite the appetite this morning," Birdy replaced Rebecca's empty plate with a full one, the third this morning.

"What can I say? You are an amazing cook." Rebecca laughed, and she reached for her coffee cup, rich with cream and plenty of sugar. It was true, Birdy's food was reliably good—plain, but always tasty, and homemade, not the adulterated stuff bought in a shop. One could not say too much in the praise of real food.

The hospitality didn't hurt either. A cozy kitchen filled with all manner of wonderful things; Balthazar, nose deep in a trencher nearby, purring for all he was worth; and a friend as steady as the day was long. What could be lacking in all that?

"How d'you keep dat pretty little figure of yours? No offense, to be sure, but if I ate like that, me poor corset could not keep up." Birdy parked her plump hip on the side of the worktable across from Rebecca, wiping her hands on her well-worn apron.

"When you do the work of three men in a day, I suppose you eat like three men." Rebecca laughed and tucked into her plate, avoiding Birdy's perceptive gaze. They both knew Birdy suspected something more to the story, but she was too polite to broach it uninvited. At least for now.

Rebecca's bloody appetite was the one aspect of her Skill that she could not hide, not when her work left her no time—nor inclination, to be honest—to cook for herself, and her budget did not allow for regular visits to the pubs, much less any of the nicer dining rooms.

Her stomach rumbled as she shoveled in another bite of eggs. Warm, salty, and fluffy, cooked in drippings from the bacon laid alongside them. Wind and Fire! So very good! But then, food always tasted better when she had been working longer than she should.

Though she had worked late into the night, the shop was not as well fortified as she had hoped. The door now had a heavy bolt across it, and the wood had been hardened, but strengthening the glass proved more difficult than she had expected. The sample of ironwood that Father kept in his collection had given her a pattern to follow in structuring the wood. But no such model existed for the glass.

Thankfully, she had practiced on an odd scrap of glass in the workshop first, otherwise the windows would have exploded in a rather spectacular, attention-drawing fashion. Exactly the sort of thing the Guild insisted its members avoid.

She tucked her scraped and scabbed left hand under the table as she reached for a sugar-topped scone.

“I expect your appetite might also have something to do with all the ways you seem to hurt yourself. I never seen a woman so apt to do herself damage the way you do. You sure you don’t need that latest one looked at by a doctor of some sort?” Birdy’s musical island accent softened her scolding tone.

“My father said the same when he was teaching me his trade. I’ve always been a bit clumsy.” The less said on that matter, the better. She adjusted her glasses.

“Perhaps you should take some time to heal up. Working bruised and bloodied can only make da clumsy worse.”

“If I did that with every mishap, how would I ever pay the bills? I have a big job today, and I dare not beg off ill.”

“I think you very well might.” Birdy’ air shifted from friend to wise mentor. “None other in Brighton kin do what you do. If a customer be desperate, they’ll wait for you, sure enough. You don’t give yourself enough credit.”

“While that might be true, making clients wait does not improve one’s reputation, and at the end of the day, one’s reputation is...”

“Yes, yes, you’ve said it a hundred times...as fragile as glass, as enduring as stone, and as deadly as fire if allowed to get out of control.” Birdy wandered to the far side of the kitchen and stirred a bubbling pot.

“Actually, it is a woman’s standing in this world that is as fragile as glass.” Stew, she was simmering a beef stew for supper. Rebecca licked her lips. “You can thank my father for that bit of wisdom.” She pushed back from the table. “And with that, I must be off to call upon my client.”

“Don’t forget the basket!” Birdy hurried to push a heavily-laden wicker hamper into her hands. “The fellows been gettin’ rowdy—there’s some more tension between the dock and the railroad.

Not sure I understand it apart from the damage that's been done to me poor pub."

Rebecca glanced over the contents. "Oh, heavens, how did this—" She pulled out a bent brass filigree-handled hand mirror, glass cracked. A very personal item to be caught in a customers' row. "—happen?"

"In the usual way such things do. I know it ain't the sort of thing we'd agreed I could send you, but—"

"Say no more. I am quite certain I can mend it, but it may take a little longer to get right."

A brilliant smile lifted the sadness in Birdy's eyes. "I'm glad to hear you can do somethin' wit' it. It looks quite the fright, don't it? Take as long as you need. I'll be grateful to have it back when you can." She held the door as Rebecca trundled into the mews with the hamper.

What was the usual way such fine items were damaged? And what did that mean for Birdy?

Rebecca locked the shop door behind her, adjusted her tool bag on her shoulder, and headed down the mews to the horsecar stop. She'd rather walk, but Mrs. Lackwood's house was in a posh area of town, an uncomfortable distance when she had her tool bag in tow. Toting the silly thing was annoying, but a necessary bit of disguise. What would it look like to show up to a job with no tools? No craftsman did that. The tools were a badge of professionalism, and she needed every advantage she could muster.

The horsecar stopped two streets from the Lackwood's townhome. Heaven forbid such a posh street be sullied with the presence of a horsecar.

Ah, well, it was just enough of a walk to remind those in the area of her presence, almost as effective as taking out an ad in the local paper—something she needed to consider doing soon. Word of mouth was excellent, but times were changing, and it behooved her to explore new avenues for the shop. She tucked her calling card into several hands on the way to her destination. That was one thing for the fix-it business; there would always be a need for it, especially if one were both skilled and discreet.

She ducked down the mews behind Montpelier Crescent. It would have been nice to be received through the front door, but that was really too much to expect from such a grand house. What a shock, scandal even, it would have been for the neighbors to have seen a mere tradeswoman entering where she could be noticed!

What would it be like to be front-door company at a first-rate house like this one? To have a grand front door opened for her and a posh butler announce her visit? Silly thing to wonder. That kind of thing only happened in fanciful novels that people like her did not have time to read.

She rang the bell at the tradesman's entrance. The cook, in her stained apron and smelling of roasting meat, ushered her into the bustling kitchen, and sent a girl for Mrs. Lackwood.

"You here for the mantel, I suppose?" The sturdy cook's greying hair pulled back into a knot so tight it stretched her forehead smooth and the edges of her eyes into a squint. She pointed Rebecca to an unoccupied corner, away from the bustling worktables with a glare that warned her to stay out of the way of the busy undercooks. And God help her if she were to think of helping herself to any of the tempting items left within reach!

Rebecca sniffed. To be assumed to have such bad manners was rather insulting. "I am afraid I am not permitted to say."

The cook guffawed. "As though Missus could keep such a thing quiet from the staff!"

Rebecca bit her lip while trying to look uninterested. Best not encourage gossip, no matter how interesting it might be.

"I haven't seen what 'appened, to be sure. Ain't none of us been allowed in that room since the row what caused it all. But we 'eard the commotion. I say it were a wonder none were kilt in the affair."

"Is that so?"

"It were the first time it come to blows with anything but a fist, you know. That 'appens regular enough—"

"That is quite enough, Cook." Mrs. Lackwood strode into the kitchen, face already turning red. A shade that clashed with the deep purple of her gown. "I will not have you gossiping in my own kitchen. And you, Miss Fuller, are hardly in any position to be found indulging in gossip. I told you I required discretion."

"Mrs. Lackwood, I resent the accusation. I am no gossip. I understand your need for discretion. If you feel that I lack that quality, you may find someone else to do the work. I am happy to leave now—"

Mrs. Lackwood harrumphed, "You are already here..."

"But it's clear you are not pleased by my presence. So, I shall go." Rebecca picked up her toolbag. "But as agreed, I will bill you for my time spent coming."

"I remember no such thing." Mrs. Lackwood's pale blue eyes widened. Such a funny look with her red, huffy cheeks.

"I do not quibble about my bills. They are all agreed upon before I begin. If you have already forgotten our terms, I will bid you a good day, madam." She curtsied and stormed out the back door. Wretched woman would probably not pay her for her time and trouble getting here, and Rebecca would be out the horsecar fare. But she would get the rest of her day back and could turn that into something productive.

"Wait."

Rebecca marched on toward the main street, past a modest carriage house and even more modest shed, the mews oddly silent around her. Was it possible to feel the cook's astonished gaze burning into the back of Rebecca's head? Maybe. The woman had probably often wished to do exactly as Rebecca was doing now.

Footsteps and swishing skirts followed. "I said wait!"

Rebecca whirled on her, pulse thundering in her temples. "I am not your servant, and I would thank you to remember that. I do not answer to you, madam. I shall go if I so choose."

"Please, wait."

"For what? For more insults to my character? For you to declare you will not honor your agreement with me? Or perhaps you intend to threaten me next. Why should I wait for that?" Rebecca's voice echoed off the back walls of the crescent's grand houses that she was not good enough to enter through the front.

"Lower your voice!" Mrs. Lackwood's eyes darted about—checking to see if any neighbors watched? "You cannot afford to deny me—you are a mere journeyman and should be honored by my patronage."

"How is it you are familiar with what I can afford or not?"

"You asked for four times your regular fee. That is too much to walk away from."

"What I cannot afford is to do work for someone who does not intend to compensate me for my time and my skill. Or have you forgotten you already intimated that you do not intend to honor that agreement?"

Mrs. Lackwood squeezed her eyes shut and almost stamped her foot. “But I need that mantel repaired.”

“And I need to be treated with respect. I need to trust in the good faith of my client.”

“Are you saying I am not trustworthy?”

“You claimed not to remember our agreement. What am I to think?”

“You made me angry—what do you expect when you behave in such a fashion?”

“Good day, Mrs. Lackwood, I wish you all the best finding someone better suited to do the work you require.” Rebecca turned on her heel and strode away.

“Wait, what will it take for you to do the work?”

Rebecca continued walking.

Running steps pursued. “I will pay you four times your rate.”

“That was what we already agreed, and what you do not seem to recall.”

“Five times.”

Rebecca did not turn.

“Six, then.”

Rebecca stopped but did not turn to face her. “You are eager to have this done.”

“I have a dinner party scheduled at the end of next week. I must have it completed by then.”

“You did not mention that before.”

“It’s no business of yours when I schedule a party.”

“I care nothing for your party, but if there is a deadline, then I need to know. This sort of thing takes weeks to accomplish.”

“But you said you could do it.”

"Of course, I can do the work. But these things take real time to accomplish. The physical demands alone—"

"Ten times, then."

Who was she entertaining? No, never mind that. She did not want to know. "You just claimed our first agreement did not exist. Why should this be any different? No, I will not enter any kind of engagement with you."

Mrs. Lackwood turned several additional shades of red—colors Rebecca had never seen before—and quivered. Who knew the human face could form so many expressions, so quickly, all of them ugly? "You cannot speak to me in —"

"Importune me no longer. There is a horsecar I need to catch."

"You are impertinent. Impossible! Arrogant! High-handed!" Now she was shrieking. No doubt there would soon be faces looking through windows at the commotion.

Rebecca kept walking.

"Come back here! I will not be treated in this way. If you do this, I will see that you never work again."

As if she had that kind of sway. Rebecca stepped out from the mews onto the busy sidewalk. If she hurried, she might catch the next horsecar home.

Warm rays of sunset filtered through the shop windows as Rebecca finished dusting the shelves and sweeping the floor. Despite the start to the day, she had still made several sales and taken in two new repair orders. Now, all was as it should be. All the shelves, all the cabinets, dust-free and at peace. The closing rituals might not have been necessary, but they were soothing and precisely what she needed after dealing with Mrs. Lackwood.

Horrible harridan.

Rebecca tucked the broom behind the counter and tossed the dust in the box with the others. As soon as she finished, she would lock up, head downstairs to the workshop, and lose herself in her Skill. Nothing could set her to rights like that did. And she desperately needed to be set to rights.

Ghastly arrogant woman!

She traded the shop apron for her heavy leather work one. The weight settled across her shoulders, a comforting, reassuring embrace. Now to lock the—

"Miss Fuller!" The front door burst open, bells jangling nervously. Mr. Arvid Lackwood entered, removing his hat as he crossed the threshold. Soft, round, and self-important, he was the physical opposite to his wife, tall enough to stand head and shoulders above Rebecca. He enjoyed looking down on everyone as much as Mrs. Lackwood did.

"I was closing for the day. Sir." She looked at the door. Perhaps he would take the hint.

The cuckoo clock shrieked six times, in its petulant, demanding evening voice.

Mr. Lackwood winced with each screech. "I realize that. I am sorry to disturb you. Have you a moment to speak with me?"

So polite. So different from his demanding wife. No doubt he wanted something very badly.

"I have work to do, Mr. Lackwood." She folded her arms over her chest and pulled herself up tall. Looking up at him put a disagreeable crick in her neck. She didn't need one more reason to be disagreeable.

"That is what I want to speak to you about." He adjusted his tie, faint color rising in his cheeks.

"I have already had a conversation with your wife."

"So I heard."

"I am afraid I cannot help you."

"About that." He reached into his coat pocket, handed her several coins. "As I understand, this is the amount you requested to look at the piece we need repaired."

She glanced at the coins. "It is."

"Will you consider doing the work?" That sounded like a statement, not a question.

The hair on the back of her neck prickled. "I am sorry, sir. I cannot. I require specific conditions to protect the trade secrets of my craft, which is why I do all my work here, in my shop. It is clear those conditions will not be possible at your residence."

"I can see to it that no one will bother you in the green drawing room."

"Green? Would that be Paris green, by any chance?"

"Yes, the room was recently redone—"

"I fall quite ill whenever I am near that color and cannot work in a room so appointed." It was a wonder they had not fallen ill themselves.

"I have heard of such things," he muttered to the floor.

"It is impossible for me to do the work you require under those conditions. That is not negotiable."

"I see." He turned the gold and bloodstone signet ring on his right small finger. "What if I brought it to you?"

"Your wife indicated that would not be possible."

"It is inconvenient and expensive, to be sure. But it is possible."

"I would need all the pieces, including any dust, everything." She squeezed her eyes shut. No doubt she would regret saying that.

"I understand."

"And I need an image of what it looked like before the damage."

"I have an illustration of the item. Will that do?"

Illustration? From where? That was most unusual.

"If it has sufficient detail." She pinched the bridge of her nose. Maybe that would stave off the headache that threatened. "You must understand, though, it is unlikely that I can restore it exactly as it was before."

"Even so, can you make it reasonably close? Will the damage still be evident?" Heavens, who were they trying to show off for? Perhaps more important, why?

"All repairs will be invisible and as much of the original character and detail as possible will be retained. That is more than anyone else could offer you, sir."

He looked away. "So I have discovered."

How many others had he approached this afternoon? Interesting. At least he would have learned no one else in Brighton would even attempt such a project.

"Can you get it done in time to be reinstalled by the end of next week?"

"Yes. You need to arrange for delivery and installation when I am finished. I must begin immediately. Tomorrow, the day after, at the absolute latest."

"Of course. I will make those arrangements."

"And I will not be responsible for any damage to the piece in transit or by the installers' hands."

"Naturally."

"I require our arrangement in writing, to be signed by at least two witnesses, and to be paid a cash deposit on the work when the piece is delivered to my workshop. And the cash balance is to be paid upon completion."

"Of course, that is entirely reasonable. I will have my solicitor draw up the contract first thing tomorrow, which will include a clause requiring your absolute discretion about the work. If you will, please make note of all your requirements." He withdrew a small notebook and pencil from his pocket and handed it to her.

"You realize how much this is going to cost you?" She wrote a number on the paper and flashed it at him.

"I have no option. And no, you may not ask why. That is irrelevant to you. Do we have an agreement?"

Firestorms! The amount could settle her father's debts once and for all! "As long as you continue to manage this affair, not your wife, then yes, I will do the work."

"We are agreed." He extended his hand.

She took it in a firm handshake. "We are agreed."

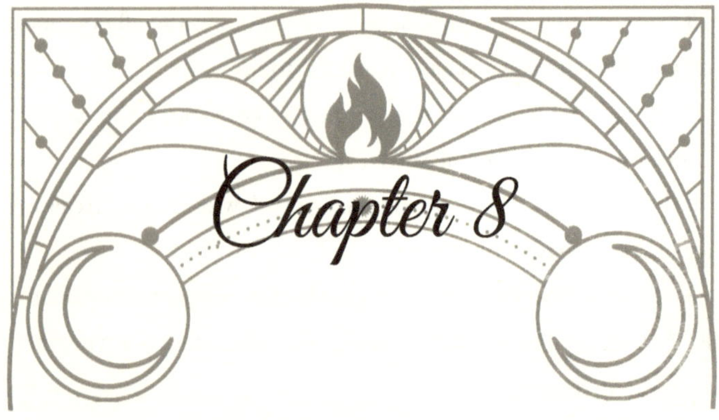

# Chapter 8

THE NEXT MORNING, DAVID trotted down Belle Vue House's narrow stairs, following the enticing aromas wafting up from the dining room. His stomach rumbled a warning. Odd, he didn't feel hungrier than usual. Was it possible his body already anticipated the drain he would put on it? Interesting thought, that.

He pulled out the notebook he kept in his breast pocket and jotted a note for future research. There was so much unknown about the Skill and the way Wrights used it, things that they really ought to understand.

Damn shame that Morris Fuller's son had perished in that accident. No reason that should mean Fuller's views on the Skill should be muzzled, though. Fuller's ideas might well be revolutionary—or utter hogwash. In either case, they ought to be fully investigated.

Confound it all. That only made the issue of Miss Fuller's quest for Mastery more complex. And compelling. And critical, considering how urgently the Crown wanted a better understanding of the kingdom's Wrights.

"Mornin', Mr. Enright." Mrs. Clara Gaskill, a cheerful sugar plum of a woman with grandmotherly grey hair, bright blue eyes, and enough spice to offset her sweetness as she ran the boarding house, nodded at him from her station at the door between the kitchen and the dining room.

No one went into her kitchen. No one. She guarded that space with the fervency of a Wright guarding his workshop. It made one wonder what she was hiding. But she was not registered with the Guild, nor did the records show that anyone in her employ was either, so whatever secrets she hid there were probably not as interesting as his overactive imagination suggested.

David hurried into the still-empty dining room. Long and narrow, with windows that opened to the lane behind the house, a table that would seat all her boarders, dressed with a well-worn cloth, surrounded by a few too many chairs, dominated the space. Along the near wall, hulking, dark wood sideboards held still-full platters of fragrant, fresh food. It paid to be an early riser. He filled his plate to heaping. Eggs, sausage, bread—not the pretty white kind, but the dark heavy variety farmers ate. Some of the other boarders grumbled about it, but the dense 'low-class' bread sat better in his stomach for all its lack of beauty.

"I still don't understand you," Mrs. Gaskill wandered toward him, hands tucked in her apron pockets.

"Who of us adequately comprehends any other, eh?" He lifted his fork in salute and shoveled a large bite into his mouth.

"How does such a long, skinny rail of a man like you put away so much food?"

"Father said I had a hollow leg."

"All boys do, but they grow out of it, you know."

"Then consider it a compliment to the fine cooking offered in your establishment."

Mrs. Gaskill laughed so hard she snorted. "You are a smooth one, shaping them words like you shape them headstones."

"An odd compliment, to be sure, but I will take it in the spirit it was meant."

"I don't understand you. None of us here do. You got the polish of a barrister, and could ply that trade if you wanted, yet you set yourself up as a common stonemason. It makes no sense. I worry about you, you know. You're one of the good ones, can't afford to lose boarders like you."

"Then let me put your mind at ease. I inherited the business from my Uncle Rutter and promised the family I would keep it going until a suitable cousin was installed to take my place. In the meantime, I am getting to know people here. It is difficult for a new barrister with no connections to get a leg up, as it were. I meet a surprising number of solicitors in my work, though. It is all part of my grand plan, never you fear." He filled his mouth with a plump slice of sausage.

"That makes as much sense as anything I've heard, I suppose. But..."

"What worries you?" He set down his fork and met her motherly gaze.

"That you got a worm or a cancer or something growing in your belly, taking up all that food." She looked him up and down, brows drawn tight.

"I appreciate your concern, truly I do. Would it help if I told you I have been this way all my life? The doctor pronounced me fit and healthy, if a little unusual." He reached in front of her to snare another sausage for his plate.

"As you will, then, I suppose. Good thing you pay extra for all the tucker, though. I wonder if I charge you enough."

She had a point. He ate for three. "But who else fixes the gas and the water for you when things go all pear-shaped?"

"Right enough! Go on and eat up before the others come down and harass you for taking all the best bites." She patted his shoulder and trundled back to her station near the kitchen.

No matter how much food was on the table, the other boarders were like jealous brothers, afraid they wouldn't have their fair share. Some days they could get truly surly.

David wolfed down the rest of his meal, tipped his hat to Mrs. Gaskill, and hurried out as the first of his fellow boarders tramped into the dining room.

The morning air struck him full in the face. Just two streets in from the shore, salty air always announced itself first. Then traces of horse, smoke, and daily life—all the scents that made up Brighton's very fiber. And the smell of stone. Not too many others noticed that in the background. Cool, and minerally, vaguely bitter and sharp. Not appetizing, but satisfying to his soul.

Recognizing stone-scent was his earliest clear memory, and the original demonstration of his inborn Skill.

An older cousin, a stonemason and Earth Wright, had noticed David's Skill early on, and began training him in secret. But Father did not want his son following in his mother's family business. No, his eldest son had to rise above manual labor and be a gentleman. So, David was packed off to boarding school to prepare for study at Cambridge. How ironic that it was there that Master McIntire recognized David's powerful innate Skills and introduced him to the secret world of the Wrights, taking him on as an informal apprentice.

What an apprenticeship it was! David's early training had been sufficient to strengthen his innate Skill enough that it had not faded away as David grew into manhood, as was usually the case for youngsters with Skill, but no Master to apprentice them. But that didn't mean it came easily to him. Pursuing academic studies during the day and wright training at night, he flourished as never before.

But those days could not last. Upon graduation, Master McIntire had patiently accepted David's decision to decline more formal wright training in favor of attending the Inns of Court and practice as a barrister with Uncle Cresswell. And even more patient when life with Cresswell fell apart and David showed up, hopeless and near penniless at his door, ready to embrace a new life as a Wright.

Master McIntire took him in and trained him, pushed him to his limits on the course to becoming a Full Wright. What was more, he introduced David to Uncle Rutter, an Earth Wright and officer in the Brighton Guild, whom, thanks to Father's prejudices, David had never known. Together, McIntire and Rutter acquainted David with Guild business, guiding him toward becoming a Legal Counsel to the Guild, and solidifying his passion to see the Wrights survive into the next century.

Unfortunately, Uncle Rutter had not.

David unlocked what had been Uncle Rutter's front door. The stone masonry business he'd inherited from Uncle was still a bland little place that looked like every other stonemason's storefront. With a somber air appropriate to the picking out of memorials for lost loved ones, sample gravestones lined one wall. Tall and short, dainty or massive, blank blocks of granite, marble, and limestone waited to be written upon with the all-too-brief details of lives lived and lost.

Of course, he did other sorts of work, too. Death could not be the sole support of his life. He had sectioned a part of the shop off as a barrister's office to give himself space to ply his first trade as well. Or at least attempt to. Even after nearly a year in Brighton, he had yet to bring in sufficient income from the law to pay for his keep.

That would change, eventually, as he made a name for himself among the Brighton community, a young barrister willing to get his hands dirty to preserve his uncle's legacy. Or maybe the pretentious stonemason with designs on a profession and life outside the sphere to which he had been born. It was hard to tell what people might think.

For now, though, he kept body and soul together with sufficient income from the memorials and from the decorative stone items that customers ordered from the heavy walnut desk in the center of the masonry shop. He displayed samples of those items on the other side of the shop: stone ornaments for gardens and doorways, custom fireplace mantels, keystones, and other such articles. Pretty ornaments were always in demand. Even so, as death was inevitable, headstones were the most reliable portion of his trade.

Surrounded by so much stone ready for work, his hands itched for the solace of his workshop. Sometimes it got that way, when he had been away from his true work for too long. Guild business—with only a small stipend in thanks for it—seemed to take up more and more time these days, leaving him less time to put his hands to stone.

Most stonemasons worked outside, in the open air. But Wrights could not afford that luxury. Their closely guarded Guild secrets had to be practiced under the tightest secrecy. Their finished products only unveiled in their final forms, to customers who either marveled at their brilliance or wondered if it was worth the price charged. More typically, the latter. If they did not see you sweat to bring it about, customers imagined that little to no effort had taken place.

Bah!

Uncle Rutter had tacked the wood-framed wrighting workshop onto the back of the shop, like an afterthought. The entire structure stood on a little plot on its own, sharing no walls with adjacent buildings. With a livery stable to one side and a bakery on the other, there was a little space to breathe. Space to add on to the building when his barrister's office needed to grow, and space to store the finished work outside to advertise his wares. That was an advantage of working in stone—difficult to steal.

He slipped the key in the Chubb detector lock—how many had been sold to secure Wrights' private spaces?—and opened the door. The narrow workshop extended the entire length of the building, with thin windows lining the top of the walls. He had etched the window panes in such a way as to prevent view into the shop without stopping the light from coming in. Took years to perfect that particular trick. It was time to talk to the Guild Master about offering it (at a fair price, of course) to other Wrights for their workshops. Good for the Guild and good for him. Though it would do little to cement his identity as the Guild's Legal Counsel, one could not have everything, could one?

He lit several gas lamps along the wall. The windows provided sufficient illumination, but it was best to have flame present as he worked. It was what Full Wrights did.

He never liked flame work, and wouldn't practice it unless he forced himself to. Another reason to visit each lamp and light it with a snap of his fingers.

Every other Element had come easily to him. He could catch the feel and flow of it, identify its character and coax it to do his bidding. Earth, his primary Element, was stable, cool, inclined to remain in its chosen form. Water was slippery and fickle, twisting and turning out of the way when one reached out for it, demanding a light touch and patience from all who handled it. Air, though, was exuberant, joyous even, distracting the Wright from his purpose, catching him up in its dance. Perhaps that was why Air Wrights were so flighty; pleasant folks as a rule, but unfocused.

Fire, though, it was the Element that fought back. If one did not manage it just right, it turned and bared its teeth. When one failed with another Element, one simply failed. The Earth did not take shape. Water flowed away. Perhaps the room might be mussed by a sudden gust of wind.

But Fire? Vindictive; vengeful, even. A mistake with Fire resulted in burns, to oneself, to the area surrounding. A whole house might ignite in a vicious conflagration if not handled properly. That was why Fire was supposed to be taught on rocky beaches, or barren fields, with buckets and troughs of water surrounding. Even then, there were those like the one McIntire often told him of, a young Fire Wright arrogant enough to ignore his Master's warnings. He drew the Fire too deep into himself for it to be extinguished. Poor sot. At least death came swiftly.

Though the Guild officially disagreed, nearly everyone acknowledged that only a born flame-tamer truly mastered Fire. What passed as mastery from those not born to it was a pale shadow of the true thing. And every Full Wright, who was not born to flame, hated Fire.

David loathed it.

Worse still, arrogance, the vanity, the self-righteousness of the flame-tamers—they brought the resentment on themselves with their intolerable attitudes. Especially when they became Full Wrights. Flaunting themselves and showing off their skill to remind everyone, at every turn, that the fire-folk were a special breed of Full Wright.

Would Miss Fuller become that kind of Full Wright, when—or if—she was given the title? It certainly would be interesting to see, given that her Wardian case proved she was more skilled than most of them. No, they would not like hearing that. Worse yet, seeing it demonstrated. That could turn the vote against her. But hers was the sort of Skill that they needed to bring in for the good of the Guild. If she were to go rogue—no, that was not a train of thought to follow now.

Rogue Wrights were dangerous, deadly, and met with extreme prejudice. Not something he ever wanted to be a part of. No, his plans would come to fruition. She would be safely installed as a Master Wright, maybe even a Full Wright, and the Guild and its members would all benefit.

That was how it would be. How it had to be.

Enough distraction. There was work to be accomplished. Mr. Penn's monument needed to be finished. He had taken a turn for the worse yesterday, and the family wanted it ready for his funeral.

He walked past the work-in-progress to the small sink at the end of the workshop, turned the tap, and let an inch of Water collect in the basin. Just enough. So what if Miss Fuller drew her Water directly from soil around her cellar? There was no shame in taking a bit of a shortcut. The critical issue was that he was able to work Water if he so chose. Holding his hand over the basin, he swirled the Water into a tiny whirlpool as if to prove the point.

He opened the transom window high above the sink an inch and coaxed Air into the workshop. Now he could focus on the task at hand. There was a certain conducive atmosphere, a harmony for wright-work, when all the Elements were present and active.

Where had he left that sketch? Ah yes, there. He trotted over to the far end of the worktable that ran the length of the wall below the windows and plucked up the drawing. With the lettering finished, all that remained was the relief of the avenging angel, wings extended, that was to grace the top of the stone. What exactly the angel was avenging was unclear, but Mr. Penn was a rather resentful man, with many grudges. Perhaps it was his hope that those grudges would see their fulfillment in that angel. Fanciful superstition and silliness, but one never knew what a customer was thinking.

He flipped the cover off the fine white granite block. Filtered light glistened off the shiny mica flecks in the squat and stubborn stone. He dragged his low wooden stool near and folded his lanky frame onto it, knees in his armpits. Where to place the image? He slid the paper about until the angel settled into the right spot.

Running a finger around the edges of the paper, he coaxed it to cling to stone. Earth to Earth connections required little effort. Not that granite was malleable—it was not. With its triune nature, it was a cantankerous stone to work with. Each of its components remained separate enough that he had to address them as individuals rather than as a composite. Annoying and fiddly, demanding patience that he did not particularly feel right now.

Perhaps it was not the best moment to work on such expensive material. He could at least get the outline on the memorial. That did not require too much finesse.

He traced the fingertips of his right hand along the boldest line of the figure and sought the stone beneath the paper. Hard. Sharp. The bits of black mica resisted him. Particularly stubborn they were. The quartz, too, felt ragged. Something was definitely off. If he continued to push the stone, it was going to misbehave, perhaps even shatter. He pulled his hand away. So much for mastering his distraction.

What was that? Someone was pounding on the front door.

He threw the cover onto the stone and pushed up against it to stand. A moment more to get the feeling back in his feet and his knees working, and he sauntered through the workshop, locking the door behind him.

The pounding grew louder. He jogged through the main shop to open the door.

"Good morning, Mr. Lackwood." He opened the door and ushered the blustery man inside.

One of the few men able to look David directly in the eye, Lackwood was not the sort of man one wanted to look in the eye. Left one feeling in need of a bath or a stiff drink. Or both.

"Good day, Enright. I have a job for you."

"Is your solicitor in need of my services?" A case heard in the Brighton courts—

"Solicitor, no. Oh, that's right, I had forgotten you were a barrister. I have no need for that. I need a piece of stone moved."

It had been too much to hope for. More and more, people were forgetting he was a barrister at all. Dash it all! "What do you need?"

Lackwood glanced away. "That mantel you installed for me after you first took over this shop. I need that moved."

Great Scott, that behemoth? Expensive and ornate, the piece had originated in Italy and come to the Lackwoods via some sort of relative—a gift? Yes, that's right, his wife said it was a gift. "Moved, sir? There is another fireplace on which you wish it installed?" By all that was holy, let him not want it dragged up another flight of stairs!

"No."

"Where do you wish it installed?" Why would one move a marble mantelpiece? Had his wife taken a dislike to it? Not that he would blame her if she had—far too fussy for David's liking.

"That is a matter of some delicacy. The mantel was ... damaged... and needs repair."

"Why did you not say so? You wish me to repair it?"

"No, we have another who has agreed to do the job." Mr. Lackwood ran a finger around his collar and edged back half a step.

"Another? Why? When I installed it, I told you if you found any damage to notify me, and I would repair it."

"Your installation did not cause the damage."

Oh. He had had another fight with his son, and one of them took it out on the stonework. "I see. Where do you need it moved?"

"Fuller's Fix-All."

Firestorms! "She cannot fix the piece in situ?"

"Miss Fuller has some sort of trade secrets to protect, or so she claims. She will not work in my home."

No doubt the problem was that wife of his. David would rather listen to Fuller's horrible cuckoo clock than that overbearing harpy. Lackwood might be one of his distant relations, but the choice to marry a shrew, not even ties of blood could overcome that. "It is a large, cumbersome piece. Perhaps I might address the damage without removing it."

"I would welcome that, Enright. Helma is certain Miss Fuller is the only one who can do the work. I'd much rather keep this in the family, as it were, if you're up to it. With that damned dinner party upon us, the wife is going twitterpated about the state of the house, and I'd just as soon deal with only one hysterical woman."

"Give me a moment, and I can come look at it."

"I will see you at the house shortly." Mr. Lackwood nodded once and left.

Interesting, interesting, interesting. David's skin prickled with the same sensation he had when working with Fire. That probably wasn't a good sign. Not at all.

Why was the party so important? Who were they trying to impress? Clearly, this was no ordinary party. Why had they not dropped names, though? The Lackwoods' climb up the social ladder had been littered with name-dropping and connection harvesting. Totally out of character to be so tight-lipped now.

Very, very odd.

At least as odd was that Miss Fuller had been approached for the repairs. Why? He was the expert in managing stone. He had installed the mantel, for heaven's sake. Why then would they approach her and not him to do the work?

And what would he do if he discovered he could indeed do the work himself?

David locked up his workshop, packed up his tools, and headed for Montpelier Crescent.

The housekeeper, a stern woman with glasses perched on her nose and a lace cap perched above her dark bun, met him at the service door and led him down a long, green hall to wait outside Mr. Lackwood's office. A faint scent of garlic hung in the air, one that only a Wright would notice.

Earth-Air-and-Fire! That was arsenic green—the paint still fresh on the walls! Was that why Miss Fuller refused to work in the house? No Wright, no matter how skilled, could work properly in such a poisoned atmosphere. The medical men might be prescribing the stuff as medicine, but to Wrights, it was toxic.

"He is meeting with the missus; you can sit here until they are done." The housekeeper rolled her eyes a bit as she gestured to the hall chair, her pointing finger implying he should not get up unless called by the master of the house.

David nodded and sat down, and the housekeeper trundled away. He might have wondered about the nature of the 'meeting with the missus,' but it was loud enough to be heard through the walls.

"Why was a crate of wine just delivered to the kitchen?" David struggled not to shrink at Mrs. Lackwood's piercing voice. She sounded quite like Mother.

"Because I ordered it. This is the usual reason such things arrive."

"I told you I did not want it."

"But I do." Was that Mr. Lackwood's fist on the desk? "I will not forgo my wine at dinner to appease your ridiculous notions of temperance. It is our guest's favorite and that should be enough."

"You are so blinded by your passion for drink that you cannot see—"

"I am blinded by no such thing!"

"You seem blind to the damage to my house caused by too much drink!" If her pitch rose any higher, her tone would be the same as the dreadful cuckoo clock in Fuller's shop.

"You have caused the damage by coddling the boy to the point he does nothing but drink. It's not the wine, nor the brandy, nor the gin. It is that lazy, good-for-nothing man-child!"

"You will not speak of our son that way."

"He is your son, not mine, and I will speak of him any way I see fit. Moreover, I will throw him out of my home if there is one more incident with him. Maybe sooner if you do not stop your hysterics."

Mrs. Lackwood screeched and stormed out of the office in a fury of feathers and lace.

Mr. Lackwood followed, shaking his head as he noticed David waiting in the hall. "Angel of the household, my arse. That woman is the devil incarnate when it comes to that worthless boy of hers. He's just like his father, who drank himself to death before the boy even walked. She thinks she can save him from himself. But we all know how that works, no?"

Learning all the family's dark secrets was not why he had come here. Of course, he would say nothing. Gossip was not David's preferred pastime. But to be burdened with secrets that ought to be kept? Was that a necessary part of doing business?

"Come, you know where the mantel is." Mr. Lackwood led the way down the vivid green hall to the drawing room, removing a key from his pocket to unlock the door.

So they were keeping the room locked now? Interesting.

Mr. Lackwood opened the door and ushered David inside. Shutting it behind himself, he made his way to the windows and tugged open the heavy ivory damask curtains. Sunlight poured in, bathing the new-looking, elaborate green wallpaper. More arsenic.

Fire-Earth-Water-and-Air!

David crunched his way across the marble dust that covered most of the floral carpet and stopped in the center of the room. His feet rooted in place, unable to take a step closer to the fireplace, the lingering shock wave from the concussive forces to the marble still lingering around it. All the fine cream-colored brocade upholstery wore a light coating of marble dust.

When he had installed the mantel, it had been a wonder of Italian craftsmanship, with carving so delicate and lifelike it nearly leapt off the creamy white stone. Perfect symmetry and balance working in tandem with the natural variations of the stone itself. An artistic masterwork, even if not to his taste.

But now?

An iron poker lay in the middle of the floor. Probably the tool which had pulverized the left-hand corner and caused the cracks that would split it into at least five large fragments and hundreds of small ones the moment David tried to move it.

"You don't look hopeful, Enright."

"No, I am not. It is beyond my ability to fix." Likely beyond anyone's ability.

Lackwood rubbed his chin. "Do you think that woman can do anything with it? You're the stone man, not her."

"Did Miss Fuller say she could do the work?"

"She said she would do it—I'm not sure she ever saw the damage. She took my money readily enough, though. But what do you think—can she really have some trade secrets that will turn the trick? Or do I need to cancel the damned contract she insisted upon?"

"I have seen her work and her reputation is sound. She would not have accepted the project without some certainty that she could deliver on her promises." It was the right and proper thing to say under the circumstances. But was it true?

"I admit I am relieved to hear you say that, since you know the business. I don't understand how anyone could make much out of this muddle. I'll leave you to it, then." Mr. Lackwood thumbed his lapels and sauntered out, obviously pleased to have made this mess someone else's problem.

David needed to get the job done quickly, though, before the contaminated air took its toll on him.

Bloody hell, where to start? Best collect all the dust he could sweep up first. There would be more of it as he made ready to move the piece, but the more debris he gathered, the better the repairs would be.

If repairs were possible in the first place. With so much damage, so many tiny pieces to fuse, much less to coax to resemble the original artistry, did Miss Fuller have, not only the Skill, but the talent to manage the task?

More importantly, would she permit him to watch whilst she worked?

# Chapter 9

A WORN, HORSE-DRAWN CART loaded with the remains of the rapidly becoming infamous Lackwood mantel rolled through the cool, afternoon-shadow draped mews, exactly as Mr. Lackwood had promised. Which, under most circumstances, would have been good, but something about this entire project did not make sense.

Rebecca bit back her sigh, pushed up her glasses, and forced her most polite, neutral expression onto her face. Best not dwell on that, not when this single piece of work had the potential to solve so many problems.

"Good day, Miss Fuller." Mr. David Enright, a fine layer of marbled dust coating his dark coat and nearly every other inch of his long, lean person, hopped down from the cart and tipped his hat. Sweat trickled down his cheek, carving a fine channel in the grime, as he waved to the driver to stay where he was.

"Good day, sir." Not really, though. His presence would complicate things.

"Perhaps we should discuss where you want this ... ah ... item set up before we start moving anything." He glanced at the tarp-covered mass on the back of the cart.

"Perhaps I should inspect what I am to be working with first." She slipped around him to the cart.

"Is it not unusual to agree to work you have not even visualized? Yet you took the job?" He cut off the end of his sentence as though he regretted giving the question voice.

"And yet, I did. Do you have a problem with my decision?" She glowered, struggling not to succumb to the temptation to add a bit of heat to the surrounding Air. He could use the reminder of the level of Skill he was dealing with. She walked around the cart, sensing the size and shape of the ruined stone from the Air surrounding it. "I wonder you were employed to move the piece. Wait—did Mr. Lackwood seek your expertise for the repairs?"

"No, not precisely. Since I installed the mantel in the first place, Mr. Lackwood engaged me to deliver it to you." He dodged her glower. "In the process, I confess, he asked me if I could do the work."

"And what was your response?" She tried to hide her clenched fists behind her back.

"I presume you are asking if I would have taken the job from you, madam. And the answer is no. I would not. That sort of behavior is, in my mind at least, unbecoming to Guild members. Cut-throat competition will only destroy the Guild from within, and I will not be party to it."

"You determined you could not repair it yourself."

"Even if I could have done the work, I would not, and that is the material point."

He was right, it was. "If that is the case, why did you examine it?"

"How else could I decide how to best move it?"

Clever way to evade the question. She cocked an eyebrow.

"And in answer to the question you seem determined to understand..." He shifted his weight from right to left and averted his gaze. "I am concerned you might have overpromised by taking on the job sight unseen. Simply trying to keep it from turning to dust on the way here has been a challenge." He dabbed his forehead with his sleeve.

"Your concern is touching." She reached around him and flipped up the tarp.

Great merciful heavens! She rocked back on her heels with the force of the violent energy radiating from the white marble ruins.

The legs had broken away from the mantel shelf and the corbel—probably in the process of moving it. Not at all surprising, but not to be blamed on Mr. Enright. The stone was cracked through by the time he went to work on it. The mantel shelf lay in three pieces—three major pieces—jagged and ragged. Even the most untrained eye could see none of those pieces would fit together. And that was without considering the carvings, which were barely recognizable.

At least that explained why no team of movers rode with him. No single piece in the wagon would be too much for one man to manage.

"Perhaps now you understand my concern?" He slapped the tarp back atop the ruined stone.

"It is not quite what I expected." Oh, it hurt to admit that. Considering the implications hurt even more.

"Where do you intend to do the work?" He glanced over her shoulder to the back of the shop, eyes lingering on the rosebush masking the workshop ventilation shafts.

Where indeed? "That is an excellent question."

"If I may venture an opinion." He edged back half a step. "Once you've completed the repairs, I expect it will take several men to move it. The stairs up from the workshop will be too narrow to accommodate it, and you might not wish your space invaded."

"Unfortunately, I agree with you." Ouch, again; but it was a considerate observation. "I suppose the storeroom is the only choice. I do not like to work there, but it has been used for that purpose before. It seems the most practical option."

"Shall I transfer it there?"

"Yes, do." She rubbed the back of her neck. It would take some effort to get the back room ready for wright-work again. "Did you sweep up—"

"Yes, there are bags of small pieces and several buckets of dust in the cart's corner."

"Excellent. I will make space in the back room."

He followed her in. Fire and Air! Could he not give her some breathing room?

"Pray forgive me, Miss Fuller, but there are several Guild-level concerns I would like to speak to you about."

She sighed and squeezed her eyes shut. "Might those concerns wait until we move the pieces?"

"I suppose, but no longer than that."

"Of course." She dragged her feet on the way to unlock the back room, guarded only by an ordinary lock, and enlisted Mr. Enright's help in moving the large workbench aside to accommodate the marble rubble. He made quick work of shifting the larger pieces while she managed the buckets and bags of smaller ones.

"That was quite the bit o'labor, wasn't it?" He dusted his hands along his pants.

And it was only the beginning of what looked to be a very long week. She scrubbed her face with her handkerchief.

"I imagine you would like to get to work, but..."

"Yes, yes. Would you care for a cup of tea whilst we talk?" She pressed a hand to her grumbling belly. Birdy's breakfast should have fortified her longer. These late nights were taking a toll.

"That is most gracious of you."

"Give me a moment." She locked the front doors and turned the sign to read *Please Knock,* then led the way to a locked staircase door on the far left-side of the shop.

Mr. Enright said nothing as he climbed the narrow wooden stairs behind her. No commentary about the Lackwood mantel or other mindless chatter. Which was a good thing, but it left her mind free to churn in anticipation of what concerns he would raise.

To be completely fair, he was right to be concerned. On many counts. But that did not mean she appreciated being called out. If only someone else had delivered the mantel. She would have had the project done and dusted and be on the way back to Montpelier Crescent, with the Guild none the wiser. It was not as if the Lackwoods were going to advertise the extent of the repairs she had made.

At the top of the stairs, she turned right into the narrow hall, then left toward the back of the house. A few more steps brought them to her compact parlor. "Pray sit down, whilst I make tea. It will only take a moment."

He nodded and did as he was asked. No commentary, no remarks on the size or decoration of the room. Should she be grateful, or was his silence ominous? Difficult to tell.

She filled the teapot directly from the faucet—running water was a luxury her father considered necessary, which she appreciated daily. She prepared a tea tray, added a plate of bought biscuits, forced a smile, and returned to the parlor.

The room's dark blue-green walls were better suited for a larger space, making the parlor feel cramped, as though it had been stuffed in a break of overgrown hedgerows. Heavy floral drapes and upholstery only bolstered the illusion. Two wing chairs covered in lived-in tan leather contrasted enough from the background to render them the most noticeable pieces in the space. Rather a shame, when they were far from the most attractive items within. But Father had the decorating of the room after Mother's death, and he could not do without his worn-but-comfortable chairs.

Mr. Enright perched like a hawk on the wing chair nearest the window, looking down upon the mews. Though his posture was relaxed, his eyes seemed to take in every feature, cataloging every detail. The gears of his mind made a nearly audible tick as his eyes moved from one spot to the next. What did he find so important out there?

"The tea will be ready shortly." She set the tea tray down on the small table between the chairs, nudged the other wing chair into a sunbeam, and settled into it. Wrapping her hands around her mother's pink rose-covered teapot, she felt for the Water within: cool, slick, deceptively simple, but not. She pulled Fire from the sunlight bathing the teapot and forced it into the Water until it boiled.

"There is no flame in the room. How are you doing that?" He gawked at her.

Good, better that than making noises about her practicing her craft in the presence of a guest. Perhaps there was something more to him than she had first believed. She shrugged and added the tea leaves to the pot.

"I am serious. How are you doing that? I have never seen a Fire Wright work without starting a flame first."

"It is not so great a thing. Having a flame gives one a point source to draw from. But it is unnecessary. My father called it lazy. According to him, the traditional Full Wright's workshop only has the four point-sources because it makes working there more efficient. Outside of that, he insisted a true Master Wright should draw upon the ambient environment for whatever he needed."

"Why? Wright-work is effort enough, why add to the difficulty?"

The ceramic grew uncomfortably hot, so she set the teapot aside and offered him the plate of biscuits. "Why indeed? I asked that often enough. He said doing things the easy way was no way to become a master of one's Element. Removing those crutches forces one to find the Elements more accurately, to gain efficacy in drawing them, accuracy in working with them. It was learn to do it his way or not at all." She drew her shoulders back and lifted her chin. If he was going to chide her for Father, then she would not give him the satisfaction of seeing her cowed even before he began.

He leaned back a bit and rubbed his chin with his fist. "You are testament to the efficacy of those views. I wonder he didn't hold office in the Guild."

Her laugh came out rather grim. "My father in such a political position? I hardly think that possible. He was not the sort to build consensus or alliances, not when he was certain of the way things should be done, and considered that the end of the discussion."

"Imagine what he could have contributed to not just our Guild, but to the Wrights as a whole!"

"And live in constant strife and conflict in every area of his life? There was enough of that when my mother was alive. She was a hot-head—"

"A Fire Wright? Another female Wright? Was she registered with the Guild?"

"Yes, though I am not sure she was ever given standing beyond apprentice. I am sure you could find those records if you are particularly interested. Father met her when she was but twelve years old and began training her himself. At sixteen, they married—he did not want to lose so promising an apprentice. A bad reason for marriage, all told. When one lives with that kind of flame-tamer, things are never calm or dull. Add a child with the same proclivities to the mix, and all a man wants is peace."

"Your brother was a Fire Wright as well, then?"

"No, my brother, rest his soul, was a wind-bag, if you will excuse the expression. And it made things no easier—Air only whips flame to frenzy."

"I can well imagine. Our Guild Secretary is a Fire Wright and our Guild Master a born Air Wright."

"Indeed, he is. I wonder he ever got that position—they are such a flighty lot. Excellent with ideas and getting things moving along, but those are not the qualities generally needed in a Guild Master. It seems to me Earth would be better suited. Is that what drew you to Guild service?"

He stared at her with the same detail-noting gaze he had trained on the mews below. "I suppose, after a circuitous fashion. I studied the law before becoming a Full Wright. It led me to see that we Wrights are nothing without a clear understanding of who and what we are, and a collective agreement regarding the principles that govern us. The population of Wrights has dwindled since our inception—"

"You mean the Great Volcanic Synchrony of 1680."

"Did your father not believe the coincidence of the Great Comet and the eruption of the Tangokoko volcano—"

"Father believed it was an eruption of Krakatoa that same year."

"But it was not as profound an event. Why would he—"

"If you are interested, I shall try to find the notes he made on the matter—the Guild would not permit those ideas to take up room in their library! He had reasons for the belief, though I confess my twelve-year-old self hardly followed his arguments."

"I can well imagine. I have read some papers written by the researchers in the Royal Court Guild, and I find them difficult to follow. Nonetheless, it does not change the fact we are a dying breed. And I want to change that."

"And what does that look like?"

"I am not quite certain yet. There are so many issues to address: how to identify young Wrights apart from the apprentice system, how to most effectively train Wrights—the recent interest in mysticism, in my opinion, is ill-guided at best, if there can be anything done to keep the Skill from fading without training... so very many things. Even so, I feel compelled to do something. Which is part of what I wanted to discuss with you."

"Of course." She poured the tea. Oh, the remarks, the questions on the tip of her tongue. But that would be her flame-nature talking, not her good sense, and right now seemed a time for sense, not sensibility.

"The work you are undertaking for Mr. Lackwood—"

Her hand trembled as she handed him a teacup. "I assure you, I will see to proper security in the back room. If you harbor any doubts about that, you are welcome to inspect my worksite."

"That was not my primary concern, but yes, it would allow me to stave off concerns from the Guild if you were to permit me to do so. Moreover, it would be instructive to watch you work." He cocked a hopeful eyebrow as he sipped his tea.

She grimaced. No, it would not be appropriate to boil his tea right now. The nerve to assume such an invitation—

"But the security of your worksite was not my primary concern, either."

"What then? I grant Mr. Lackwood is paying me well outside of Guild rates, but that is in compensation for the accelerated timetable and the adverse conditions presented by this particular commission."

"His wife?"

"You have met her, I imagine?" Rebecca nibbled a slightly stale biscuit. Bother, the store-bought ones always went old so quickly.

"The Guild has always understood surcharges added for those issues, so I have no qualms with whatever you are receiving. My concern is the scope of work."

"Do you think I am not up to the task? That I, a mere woman, will besmirch the Guild's reputation?"

"Hardly." He lifted open hands. "The bigger concern is the level of your success."

"I've no idea what you are talking about. How could that be a problem?"

"The level of repairs you've agreed to undertake are ... I don't even have the words to describe them. But they are absolutely impossible under any normal means. Even a Master Earth Wright, born to stonework, cannot return shattered and pulverized stone to its original state. The danger in demonstrating supernatural Skill—"

"I am aware of that. Never fear, though. I have a cover story already in mind." When one thought about it, his concern was something of a compliment, an odd one, to be sure, but a compliment.

"Do tell, Miss Fuller." He leaned forward, fingers steepled in front of his chest.

Was that a challenge? "I insisted on all the dust being swept up and brought to me. If asked, I will explain I developed a proprietary mortar I make from the marble dust that allows me to patch together the broken pieces and mold it like clay. With that substance, I can both re-create the damaged carvings and polish it back to the original luster."

"No one has heard of such a thing."

"What matter is that? The story is believable enough, and people are apt to believe the fiction that best suits their circumstances. My fix-all business is built on that principle." She shrugged. "As desperate as the Lackwoods are to conceal the damage done by their domestic disquiet, I hardly expect them to question anything I tell them so long as the work is done."

"Are you quite certain, madam? The risk of exposure —"

"I well understand the need for security! Better than you." She cradled her forehead in her hand. "Even the best security practices are not enough to shield one from scrutiny. Have you ever been accused of witchcraft, sir?"

"Witchcraft? I thought that ended nearly one hundred fifty years ago."

"Consider yourself fortunate. I have. Quite recently."

"Did someone see you working?" He almost dropped his teacup.

"If I were not a civilized woman, I would slap you for that accusation. I made my oath of secrecy before the Guild when I was recognized as an apprentice. I never violated that. Never." She stood and paced across the threadbare multicolored rug, lest she be unable to contain the flame rising in her blood. "No, my transgression was being more successful than a man of fragile self-worth. His ego bruised easily, especially when I refused his offer of marriage. His love of gin had addled his mind and led him to conclude I was a witch. You see, he is quite certain my ability to run a successful business without a man makes me a witch. Each piece of my work that sells only cements the idea further in his mind."

"It this that Mallory fellow, the moneylender to most of this part of Brighton? I have heard tell of him. Piece of work, that one."

"I reported it to the Guild, every time he has been troublesome. As required."

"And the Guild has not found some way to put him off you?" He cocked an eyebrow, but his eyes suggested he already suspected the answer.

"Oh, yes, of course, they have been ever so responsive. One can see that in the way they were ever so helpful when he tried to break down my door only yesterday." She drew a deep breath and chewed her upper lip. "It was the constables, not the Guild, who had my back then, and, in every other dealing I have had with him."

"Confound it all!" He slapped the arm of the chair. "That is unacceptable. I will look into the matter immediately."

Of course he would. The effort not to roll her eyes hurt. "Do not trouble yourself."

"I must. As legal counsel to the Guild in Brighton, this is exactly where I should trouble myself. I will return tomorrow and tell you what I have found."

"There is no need to put yourself to trouble over affairs I have well in hand."

"I insist."

Why would he do that?

# Chapter 10

THE NEXT DAY, A bit past noon, David sat in front of the Penn family's granite monument, muttering and cursing under his breath. Not that such language had ever had any impact on the stone before. There were some fanciful stories about Wrights so powerful that they could exercise their Skill with the use of their voice alone. But no one in the last several generations of Wrights had managed such a feat. It was probably more myth and wishful thinking than anything else.

But it certainly would have been nice at a moment like this.

The early afternoon sun struggled to find its way in through the narrow, frosted windows, bathing the workshop in a cool, grey light barely sufficient for the task at hand. Taunting him, somehow, reminding him of the lack of progress that seemed to dog his every recent endeavor. Silent blocks of stone, future projects standing in a silent line waiting for his touch, refused to come to his defense, resentful that they were being made to wait.

Mother always said he did not take frustration well. Perhaps she had a point.

For all its strength and durability, granite had a mind of its own. Sometimes it decided to be stubborn and resist the shape he sought to impose upon it. Often, he could trace that to a dense pocket of quartz in the stone. Something about the quartz crystal resisted rearrangement under his hand. He was not the only one to complain about it, though. Many Earth Wrights whinged about granite work. The way it responded to their touch was different to other minerals, but none could offer a further explanation why it seemed to fight back.

"Damn!" A hot shock resonated through his hands and he jumped away, shaking them as though to dislodge a live animal. An animal with rather many sharp teeth. He restrained the urge to kick the stone—barely. Broken toes hardly ever improved matters.

Throwing a heavy canvas cover over the monument, he stalked out of his workshop and locked the door behind him.

Maybe Comerford or Crampton would have some advice. There was just enough time to trot over for a chat on his way to Guild Hall to ferret out information that he suspected he did not want to know, then to Fuller's Fix-All for a conversation that was likely to go much like this session with the stone.

Condemn it all! Something really needed to work out right today.

Comerford and Crampton of C&C Stoneworks, a Guild-sanctioned and supported business, had no better suggestions on getting past that stubborn spot. Erasing his prior work and redrafting the design—an idea he had already toyed with himself—might be his only option. Unfortunately, it meant redoing hours of work. Frustrating, but not wholly unexpected.

The visit to the Guild office, though, that was surprising. Surprising in all the wrong and difficult ways. The disorder, and dare he say, even chaos, of the file room—no wonder Miss Fuller's grievances had gone unaddressed. Buried so deep in piles of paperwork, years might have passed before someone noticed them and months more before they got into the right hands.

Hers were not the only grievances lost in the avalanche of paper, though, which might suggest she was not being singled out. Until he went through and identified the sources of the other complaints that had received similar treatment, he could not be sure. The entire situation could simply point to poor management, but it might also be willful malice under the guise of ineptitude. The Guild would not be the first organization to capitalize on incompetence.

Either way, he directed the immediate matter to the proper Guild authorities and he could hope that Miss Fuller would receive the protection to which her (previously paid) dues entitled her.

He added several other irregularities to his list of matters to address, some of which might actually require his services as barrister to the Guild. He could not be happy with the difficulties members faced, but it would be nice to act in that capacity on their behalf.

But for now, there were other matters to attend. He pinched his temples.

What joy was his. His pocket watch declared it time to head to Fuller's Fix-All where who knew what fresh ordeal lay in wait.

Of course, he had not fixed on a time to meet her. She said she would not start work until after the shop closed. Which probably meant that the moment she locked the door and turned the sign to *Please Knock*, she would head to the back room. If he arrived once she had begun, there was every possibility that she would not hear him knocking. Or at least would have a plausible reason to ignore him.

To be fair though, when he was deep in wright-work, he often lost track of what was going on around him. And if it happened to him, then why should she not struggle with the same kind of enthrallment in her work? The grudging, even resentful, assent she had given to his request to inspect her security measures for the back room should not leave him questioning her integrity. That was not fair, though, no matter how tempting a conclusion it might be.

And considering his hope to glimpse her techniques, it seemed a bit hypocritical as well.

He arrived at Fuller's Fix-All at ten minutes to the hour, according to his father's pocket watch, which he always set about five minutes fast to help him be prompt. The shop bells chimed prettily as he pushed the door open and strode in. Had they sounded different the last time he was here? Was that clever wrighting of the bells or an overactive imagination? Both seemed entirely possible. "Good afternoon, Miss Fuller." He tipped his hat.

"Right on time, I see," she called from the far corner of the shop. The strokes of her broom threw up a fine cloud of dust that glittered in the late-day sun. "I am just tidying things before I close up for the day."

The ghastly Gothic cuckoo clock hung on the wall over her head, lurking like a gargoyle on a rooftop. Ten minutes and the shrieking would commence—best be ready to cover his ears. "Might I be of some assistance?"

"Are you in such a hurry?"

"Not at all. I can make myself out of the way if you prefer."

She rolled her eyes a little, but a tiny smile lifted the corner of her lips. She was the slightest bit pretty when she did that. "You see that shelf on the left there, rearrange the bits and bobs, switch them from one shelf to another, and back to front. Add the vase and other items from the counter among them."

"Give the customers something new to look at, eh?" He ambled toward the counter near the orderly workbench at the back of the shop.

"The longer they look, the more likely they are to find something that suits their fancy."

He gathered the objects from the counter and made his way to the shelves. So many odd sundries gathered there. A large hourglass, a ceramic figurine, a brass case with opera glasses, a fan. Nice that he had an excuse to handle them all, sense the craftsmanship that went into them. "May I ask, how much do these items resemble their original forms?"

"Only another Wright would ask such a thing." She chuckled with no trace of the acerbic notes he expected. "A customer generally asks what manner of damage was done to the original."

"And what do you tell the customers when they ask?"

"It depends on what they seem to want to hear. Many like the notion that they are rescuing a heavily damaged item, and giving it new life in some way."

"Interesting. I would have thought there would be a preference for items that were not too damaged in the first place."

"There are those customers, too, and I can tailor the story to whatever they need to hear." She propped the broom in the corner nearest the clock and pulled several dustrags from under the counter.

"Does that not bother you? It seems akin to deception—"

She sniffed, and the edge returned to her voice. "I am always very clear about the condition and quality of the item they wish to purchase. They understand how it can and cannot be used, any known weakness in the structure, anything which might affect the value or usefulness of the article. On those issues, I am completely clear. Far more so than any other shopkeeper I have encountered. So, before you render judgment—"

He lifted open hands. "I did not mean to imply criticism. Truly, I didn't. I find this aspect of your business so very interesting."

"You or the Guild?" Her eyes narrowed; their gold flecks seemed to glisten as her temper rose.

"The Guild has not sent me to examine your business, if that is what you are implying. The security of your makeshift workshop is my only concern, and I have been open with you about that from the beginning."

She lifted her eyebrows and cocked her head.

"Why are you so suspicious?" He crossed his arms over his chest. Bother, that made him appear defensive.

"You seem like an intelligent man. Can you not guess?"

"Why does Guild involvement bother you so much?"

Her laugh was more like the prelude to a growl. "What have they ever done for me? Their famed 'support for all members' does not seem to extend my direction."

"Ah, regarding the complaints you filed. I believe I located the source of that problem—a rather shoddily-kept office in which I found numerous mislaid items of business. I have made sure your complaints have been placed in the correct hands and hope to see your concerns addressed within the week."

"Mislaid forms, is it? And you suppose that all that is needed is to place them in the right hands and it will sort itself out? My, you are a hopeful fellow, aren't you?"

"I cannot make promises, of course, but I hope that by following the proper protocols—"

"That might work for some members, members like you, perhaps. But—oh, for the sake of Fire and Air, you have worked in law. You are well aware that there are two classes of people, those whom the law works for and those whom it works against."

David sighed and shook his head. Unfortunately, she was right.

"Do you believe the Guild supports my shop, sending business my way, as they claim they will do? Hardly." She threw up her hands and stalked across the wood floor, her heels clacking. "Why do you think I am forced to sell these wrighted-together scraps with their accompanying fictions? I am up till the wee hours nearly every night crafting these things because if I don't, the moneylender my father yoked me to will take everything I have. I cannot charge Guild prices on my regular repair work because they will not grant my store a charter to do so since there is no Master Wright present to verify it, making me the cheapest repair shop in Brighton. Which, I grant, brings in business, but every one of them is getting far more from me than they pay for."

"I can see where that could be a hardship in this case, but surely you can see—"

"What I see is that they have denied considering me for the rank of Full Wright every year since my father presented my application. And for reasons that have nothing to do with my abilities. Grieving? Being in mourning? Too young? Another candidate with a higher status sponsor? What other journeyman has been set aside for such trivial reasons? And now you are here snooping around, trying to find flaws that will keep me out yet again. You expect me to welcome this? I did not take you for a fool."

He rubbed the back of his neck. "I am not looking for fault in your work."

"Of course you're not." She snorted. "I dare you to justify the Guild's double standard."

"Your father was not exactly a friend of the Guild."

"He was a member in good standing."

"Good standing is a matter of opinion. I read one of his papers presented to the Guild—he argued with the fundamental approach to the Elements and refused to acknowledge the Aristotelian foundations we have long accepted." Those documents had been submerged in the file's bedlam room as well, not in the library where it should have been.

It was possible that space was maintained in chaos as repository for all things inconvenient for the Guild. Dash it all.

She stomped toward him. "Have you ever considered that perhaps, just perhaps, the Ancient Greeks did not know everything? Certainly, there were no Wrights then. So, why do we look to them for understanding? Might there be something the modern age can add to our knowledge? Even advance our craft in a way that those who follow the Ancient Greeks could not have foreseen?"

"Those are very strong ideas."

"Ideas which appear to threaten the very core of the Guild. Ideas too strong for a woman to offer, to be sure."

"I am not sure being a woman has that much to do with it. They did not accept those ideas from your father, either."

"They considered him a doddering old fool. I think they regretted giving him Full Wright status the moment it was granted, and he started voicing his philosophies. That does not mean he was wrong, though." She brandished her dust rag at him.

It did not mean her father was correct, either. "You never answered my question about how much the items resemble their original forms." He gestured toward the shelves she aggressively dusted.

"If you are the Full Wright they have acknowledged you to be, I am sure you can figure that out for yourself."

"I have your permission to examine them?"

"Go ahead." She turned her back on him. "Would you have respected it if I said no?"

It was a professional courtesy that one did not go poking around in another Wright's work without permission. But he wouldn't be able to convince her of that just now.

He removed the large hourglass and turned it in his hands. Glass, filled with tiny shiny beads, silver perhaps, held in a brass filigree frame, patterned much like fine Spanish lace. No manufacturer he knew of would use such a pattern in brass. That was entirely unique. It must have been her invention.

He closed his eyes and held the hourglass in both hands, reaching into the Earth elements within. Glass and metal were such pure forms of Element, they should be easy to examine. Traces of their original forms should be there, like shadows, evidence of the state they were in before they were last worked.

He ran his fingers along the edges. Edges usually held the strongest aspects of the past. There, the faintest trace ...

Earth-Wind-and-Fire! A mirror frame? This brass had been a mirror frame? And the hourglass itself had been the mirror. The beads within felt like silver—had that come from the mirror backing? Chills coursed from his neck all the way down his fingertips. "You call this repair work?"

"Is there a fault in it?"

"This... this is hardly a repaired mirror." He held out the hourglass.

"True enough. But a mirror is commonplace. With a little more effort, I have created something far more interesting, and saleable."

"A little more effort? This is remarkable, a feat worthy of—"

"The title which has been denied me?"

He shook his head and placed the hourglass on the most visible shelf. "You are not charging nearly enough."

"Indeed, but until I get Guild recognition, it is what I am limited to." She tossed her head and stalked to the door, threw a heavy bolt, and turned the door sign to *Please Knock*. "Come, you can confirm the security of my back room and then be about the rest of your evening. I am certain you have better things to do than look over my shoulder as I work."

No, actually, that was the precise thing he hoped for. "The stone is heavy. You will need extra hands to wrestle some of it into place. May I offer you that service?"

"Out of the goodness of your heart? Or will you be charging Guild fees for that assistance?" She put her hands on her hips and stared at him, an angry swan poised to attack.

He edged back slightly. One encounter with an angry swan—even if she was not of the feathered variety—was enough for a lifetime. "I would be interested in observing your technique. Consider whatever service I might offer in payment for that privilege?"

The way her eyes narrowed and the creases around her mouth deepened, she must think him sarcastic.

"I do not often have the opportunity to watch other Earth Wrights work, especially those trained differently to what I was. I meant it when I called it a privilege."

She held his gaze for long moments until her fluffy grey cat sauntered in and rubbed against his legs, purring.

"Balthazar does not approve of many from the Guild." The cat sat on his haunches and cocked its head at her, tufted ears twitching. Her posture softened. "I suppose I can let you into the back room for a little while."

He stooped and petted the long-haired grey feline. The cat rubbed his head into David's hand and chirruped. Silly creature, but if that was what it took to curry her favor, so be it.

The cuckoo clock clicked and whirred, and the little door popped open. Shrieking, the black spectral bird jutted out, threatening to take flight, perhaps ready to attack.

"Be quiet!" She raised her hand, grasping Air in her open fingers, then tightening them around it as though clutching an unseen ball. Silence swallowed the next shriek, and the clock thumped against the wall behind it. "Enough of your needless yammer. I swear that sound goes through one's very soul."

The bird forced its way out several more times, mouth opened in silenced cries. Pathetic this way. Better than the horrid screams, though.

What Skill she had with Air! There were rumors that there once had been Air Wrights who could steal the breath from one's lungs. There was probably no more credence to that than the stories of Earth Wrights that could speak stone into submission. But watching her Skill made one wonder how much truth there might be behind those stories.

She strode toward the back of the shop, an odd determination in her steps, and beckoned him to follow. "As you can see, the door is well and thoroughly locked."

"With no lock?"

"Try the door handle." She cocked her head, brows lifted.

He turned the heavy brass knob and it spun freely in his hand, casting a merry shadow along the pattern-stamped, polished brass plate.

"Open the door."

He pushed the door, but it did not move. He leaned into it with his shoulder, but it stood its ground.

"Go ahead, open it." She gestured toward the vexing wood door with an open hand.

"How do you have this locked? How will you open it?"

"You can figure that out, if you try." She glanced at the doorknob and crossed her arms over her chest.

Interesting. Challenge accepted.

He laid his fingers along the cool doorknob—nothing unique there. He pushed his senses into the doorknob, examining it from the inside. Oh, wait, that was novel. Clever. "The latch bolt, and a secondary bolt too, if I am feeling this correctly—you disconnected them from the knob?"

She nodded once. "Open it."

"You want me to alter your work?"

"How better for you to understand the security of the arrangement?"

"But it is well understood that—"

"You really believe that is sacrosanct? That one Wright does not meddle in the work of another?"

"That is the Guild's tradition."

"Tradition followed only when it serves their purposes and laid aside when it is convenient for 'the greater good'. I assure you, they will not believe you unless you try it yourself." She flicked both hands toward the doorknob. "Go, there is work to be done which won't happen on as long as I am on the outside of that door."

"Very well." He hunkered down to kneel by the door and pressed both hands to the doorknob. Reaching through the knob's shank, along the internal hub, he found the break between the latch bolt and the tumbler pins. She left the seam obvious, though, and it took only a moment to repair it. He stood and turned the knob. The latch bolt made a satisfying click, and he pushed the door.

It did not move.

"What else is holding the door?"

"You find it." She tapped her foot. Loudly.

He knelt again and felt along the elaborate door plate. A small hole in the wood behind it—the size and shape of a keyhole. "Another lock?"

She cocked her head and lifted an eyebrow.

Pressing through the plate, through the door, was more challenging. Hard to get a grip on anything through so many different materials. But there, tumbler pins and springs. He slid them into place. But he could not shift the bolt. What?

No wait, there was one pin awry. Clever, like the doorknob, it had been disconnected. And she had situated the break in a tricky spot to reach.

Sweat trickled down the side of his face, and he panted heavily as he corrected the break. He pressed the door again.

Damn it all! The bolt was still latched. And now that he had repaired the tumbler pins, the entire mechanism had to be manipulated to pull the bolt back from the door jamb.

This time, when he pushed it, the door inched open. "Very clever, Miss Fuller. And very effective. As effective as that Chubb detector lock you have, perhaps more so."

"But far more effort to use. So, it is not my preference, but needs must. Do close and lock the door behind you."

He bit his tongue against the temptation to ask how that should be done. Good thing, too, as there was a key on a string around the inside doorknob.

High transom windows, covered with sheer fabric, above tall, shuttered windows, filtered light into the back room, reminiscent of his own workshop. Slightly narrower, with a lower ceiling, the walls closed down on him, like watchful Masters waiting to critique an unwary apprentice.

"Are you satisfied with my security?" Her tone dared him to find fault.

"Indeed, I am, and I would be interested to learn more about how you managed that lock. I can see ready applications for my workshop."

"Not before I've sorted this mess." She flipped the dusty canvas tarp covering the mantel's remains on the scarred wooden worktable in the middle of the room. "Too dark." She lit several lamps around the room.

Was it possible for the damage to grow worse the more clearly one could see it? "So, how will you begin?"

She jumped and twitched her head. Probably lost in thought. "Forgive me. I am not accustomed to working with anyone else in the shop."

"None of us are. Unless we take an apprentice—"

"Which none but recognized Masters are permitted to do."

He winced. Stupid to have stumbled on such a reminder now.

"I planned to start with this." She handed him a folded paper from her pocket.

It had been taken from some magazine or other, but it was a reasonable watercolor rendition of the mantel in its original state, though definitely not in the room where he had installed it. Was this an advertisement, or had the mantel been depicted in some other fine house? Interesting.

He looked from the illustration to the rubble and back again. "You will be able to remake it into its original form?"

"Hardly. I can already see there was sufficient material lost in getting it here that I cannot completely replicate it. However, this gives me a starting point for the work. Fortunately, the picture also includes the basic dimensions, which I will try to replicate. That is the sort of thing that will matter the most to the Lackwoods, I should think. They are not exactly the kind who will recall if a flower was here or there, or of this type or that. But if it does not feel grand enough, tall and wide enough to impress, that they will quibble over."

"If you can get them something at all, they have absolutely no right to object," he muttered under his breath. The corner of her lips turned up, hinting at the potential for a dry smile. "I would imagine you could shave a quarter inch, maybe as much as a half from the depth of the entire piece, and it will not be noticeable if the decorative elements are sufficiently repaired. That would give you more material to work with for visible repairs."

"And you do not believe that will hamper the structural integrity?"

"That is always a worry. Have you considered reinforcements of iron along the back of the legs and shelf? You could also line the inside with iron, decorative, of course, that would blend into the firebox, which, in any case, will have to be adjusted for any changes in dimensions of the mantel."

"That is an interesting thought." She chewed the inside of her cheek. "Very interesting. You find that the iron and marble are compatible?"

"It takes a little finesse, but they do not fight each other, not like working with granite." He shook his hand, remembering the bite Penn's headstone had administered to him not so long ago.

"You have been having difficulty with granite?" She looked directly at his hand. Interest and respect, that's what was in her eyes.

"You work with it?"

"On occasion. It was one of the materials Father first taught me to work." She bit her upper lip and turned away, as if sorting through old memories.

No apprentice Earth Wright worked with granite. "My Master did not allow me to touch it until I was a journeyman."

"As you know, my father's approach was different. But it had its advantages."

"You do not find it troublesome, then?"

She fiddled with her dress's high collar and sidled to the opposite end of the worktable. "It can be a bit fiddly when the quartz component gets its back up."

"That implies you've found a way to manage that."

Her eyes narrowed, and she glanced around the room. Looking for a trap? "You are first an Earth Wright. You would take instruction from me?"

"Madam, I am not an idiot."

"What is that supposed to mean?"

"I have seen your work, and it speaks for itself. I am happy to learn from anyone who can produce the hourglass I just saw, or the Wardian case displayed in your shop, or any of a number of things I observed this afternoon. Pray tell me, what is your technique to prevent granite's bite?"

"I will explain, teach you if you like, but for a price."

Of course, that was only fair ... "What sort of price?"

"I will need help with this mantel. Placing the iron supports and managing the large pieces of stone is too much for one body. Assist me with that, and I will teach you what my father taught me."

"Only if you allow me to observe the rest of the process, as well. The opportunity to watch another ... proficient ... Wright work is too rare to ignore." He dare not admit he was beginning to enjoy her company as well.

She studied him a long time, until he squirmed and tugged at his collar, a schoolboy accused of mischief.

"All right. I need to acquire the iron. I will start tomorrow after I close the shop."

# Chapter 11

Rebecca rose especially early the next morning, not because she wanted to, but Balthazar decided it was necessary for her to tend his empty belly, reminding her that her own was also in need of attention. She slipped out of bed and swooned as soon as her feet hit the floor. Apparently, the annoying feline knew something she didn't. Repeated late nights were adding up and not in her favor. Even with Birdy's steady supply of hand pies and puddings, at its tightest, her corset shifted loose around her ribs these days.

Not a situation she could sustain in the long run.

But she wouldn't have to. Once she got the mantel finished, then things would be different. She could slow down. Maybe even ...

No, she shouldn't dwell on that possibility, that the Guild would consider her for Mastery, much less grant it. That hope had been dashed so many times before. But maybe, if Mr. Enright saw her work, he might plead her case to them, insist that they give her a fair chance. That wasn't so much to hope for, was it?

Yes, it really was.

His dedication to his principles did not change that. Nor did his willingness to learn from her. Neither did his kindness and courtesy make a difference, even if it made her like him, just a little. Hope itself was too dangerous and the possibility of disappointment too bitter.

Enough. Best focus on the matters of the day right now, before it all got away from her.

She dressed and trotted along the mews with Balthazar to break her fast with Birdy. The pub had experienced a particularly challenging night, somehow involving the rail hands, a loose pig, and the constables. Birdy seemed as reluctant to share the details as Rebecca was to ask. But since the extra-large box of repairs brought with it an overflowing basket of victuals, what need was there to pry? A slab of ham, another of cheese, and a double-sized loaf of fresh brown bread, beyond the usual pies and puddings, to take home made questions a very low priority.

The ironmonger wouldn't be delivering the iron rods until after the shop opened. That would give her a few hours to start in on Birdy's work before the day got busy. And it would prove a welcome distraction from worrying about the mantel and Mr. Enright.

Condemn it all, that she had to ask for help to fix the blooming mantel, though. Condemn it all that she was in such a position that she had to take on the work, to keep not only the shop, but body and soul together. And condemn it all that he was proving himself to be not just a decent man, but a likeable one as well.

Her life was too complicated for that sort of distraction.

Enough woolgathering! Paying work awaited.

After the cuckoo clock screamed out the passing of enough hours, she ushered out the last satisfied customer. How they had marveled at her repairs to an heirloom clockwork toy—dancers on a tiny stage that performed to a music box under their stage—the one the clockmaker had declared impossible to repair. If everything with the Guild went pear-shaped and she had to leave Brighton, perhaps she could take up as a clockmaker. Something to put a bit more thought into later.

Mr. Enright arrived as she was pulling the blinds.

His suit hung off his too-long limbs like a cheap castoff from an older brother, shorter and fatter than himself, reinforcing his signature birdlike image. A long-legged whimbrel he was, down to the dun tones of his coat.

"Is there anything I can help you with?" He looked around the shop, pushing a shock of unruly dark hair away from his eyes. Windblown, he always seemed windblown.

"Broom's in the corner, near the clock." She paused from cleaning her glasses to point toward it.

He headed for the broom. Interesting. He was actually going to sweep. Few Masters were willing to do such work in their own shops, much less someone else's. Interesting.

She turned her sign to *Please Knock* and locked the door as the cuckoo screamed its hourly alert.

With a quick motion of her hand, she grabbed the Air around the black, scraggly bird and stilled it, silencing the bird after the second squawk. Mr. Enright nodded appreciatively, grey-green eyes crinkling at the edges. That clock...

She fetched a dust rag and wiped down the shelves and the largest items. A quarter of an hour later, the shop was tucked in for the night.

"Before we begin, we should eat." She beckoned him upstairs, where Birdy's offerings waited.

"Most thoughtful of you, Miss Fuller." He climbed the narrow stairs behind her, his footfalls heavy and loud in the confined space. "I'm embarrassed to admit, I didn't consider the matter at all. I should have and will going forward. Might I be trusted to provide a hamper of victuals for our next appointment?"

Next appointment?

Yes, there would have to be a next appointment, and the amount they would have to consume to accomplish the task would not come cheap. Very thoughtful. "I'd appreciate it."

She led him into the tiny kitchen. Birdy's basket waited on top of the worktable that occupied most of the room. Once pulled out, the two wooden stools under the table would take up most of the remaining space. "Please have a seat while I make up some tea. Forgive me for not using the dining room—"

"Not to worry, I understand—so much work to be accomplished tonight, the time and all that. Might I be of some use? Setting the table, perhaps?"

"The dishes are in the rack by the sink if you like." She filled the teapot while he edged around the table and managed to set it without knocking into her.

Street noises filtered up through the open window, the sounds of early evening, as people transitioned from day to night, between the work that could be done in the daylight and what must be done in the privacy of nightfall.

She cupped her hands around the teapot, heating it, as she brought it to the table. He had done a credible job setting the table, something Joseph had never managed. Not that Father had allowed her to assign her brother such a chore often. Women's work ...

She set her mother's floral teapot on a woolen pad and added tea leaves to the simmering water, then pulled the napkin off Birdy's basket. "It is not fancy, but it will do." She placed a hand pie on his plate. "The pub next door keeps me supplied with victuals and the repair work by which I pay for them."

He waited for her to pick up her own, then took a large bite from his pie. Crumbs tumbled from the flaky crust. "By Jove, these are much more appealing that what my landlady provides. Does the pub have rooms to let?"

Rebecca devoured half the savory hand pie, which had just the right amount of meat for the thickness of the crust, before replying. "A few, but mostly for those who cannot make it home under their own power after closing. Her customers are some of the roughest in town. They want tasty food, plenty of it, and no questions asked. I get quite a bit of repair work from her. I expect you prefer more genteel surroundings."

"I'll keep that in mind. Still, this is the kind of cooking for which a man would tolerate a great deal." He flashed his eyebrows as he popped the last of the pie into his mouth and glanced at the basket. She nodded, and he filled his plate. "What do you plan on accomplishing tonight?"

"Foremost, to craft some sort of plan of attack." She chuckled as she loaded her plate. How rare and pleasant to eat with a companion from whom she did not have to hide her appetite. "After you suggested the iron reinforcements, I drafted this." She pulled a sketch from her pocket.

He studied the pencil sketch and ran his fingers along those lines, a faraway look on his face. "The style is very much in keeping with the original, so I expect the Lackwoods will approve. I would recommend, though, that you move this bar down to here, it will yield a stronger result. I cannot tell from the sketch, but do you intend to include additional, visible reinforcement along the back? You might find your customers appreciate seeing some clear evidence of your work, even if it is not necessary for the repair. Indications of your 'trade secrets', as it were."

"I hadn't thought of that, as I prefer invisible repairs myself, but for these customers, you make an excellent point."

The corner of his lips turned up as though relieved that she might actually listen to him. "I will not tell you your business, but if it were me, I would add additional internal reinforcement here and here as well." He traced two imaginary lines along the drawing with his fingers. "I have found when repairing marble, it is a mite more fragile than in its natural state and working it around iron bars returns it to almost original strength."

"You repair marble?"

"I said I could not do repairs on this level, not that I did not work with marble at all. Marble monuments are not uncommon." He cocked an eyebrow at her, vaguely arrogant, but not undeserved.

"Of course, I should have thought." Dash it all. Why were her cheeks burning? She poured the tea, relieved to break eye contact. "Tonight, I would like to create the iron framework for the mantel and plan the next steps after that. Also, I acquired a piece of granite to help answer the question you posed to me."

He smiled brightly. "Excellent. I am all anticipation. Shall we get on with it, then?"

"Indeed."

As amusing as it had been to watch him fumble with her security, now that Mr. Enright believed the back room secure, there was no need to waste time having him open it himself again. She opened the lock, stepped in, and paused.

Working in the back room was—uncomfortable. For so long now, everything she did had been confined to her workroom in the cellar. This felt wrong, exposed, rebellious even. And unprepared. The Elements seemed scattered here, like disobedient children, running through the last rays of sun filtering through the transom windows, ignoring the calls to come under proper regulation.

"Where do we begin?" He locked the door behind him and glanced around the long, narrow room, eyes settling on the pile of iron rods on the floor beneath the shuttered windows. "I see you have laid in quite a stock of iron."

"Yes, it is there, but I am not ready. The room is not ready. I need to focus, to feel all the Elements." She closed her eyes and drew a deep breath. Hopefully, that would settle the disorder swirling through the room.

"I do not understand. We are doing Earth work. Do we need other Elements at hand?" Despite the stupidity of his question, his expression seemed genuine.

"Perhaps this is not a good idea." She waved him off with open hands. "You should go."

"Why? Have I offended you somehow?" His face fell and shoulders sagged like a kicked puppy.

Why did he have to look at her that way? She slipped back half a step. "I am not certain I can work with you watching me."

"I understand it's hard. Master McIntire, my Earth Master at Cambridge, insisted on watching everything I did until I made Master myself. Constantly breathing down my neck, and I mean that quite literally, making me second-guess everything I did. Hated every second of it."

"My father could be like that." Was that just the way Masters were with their journeymen?

"Would it help to remind you that I am here to learn from you, not to evaluate you? Helping you with the mantel project is how we agreed I would pay you for teaching me how to work with granite." He glanced at the bread-loaf-sized pink granite chunk on the worktable.

"I don't think that's a good idea, either." She closed her eyes again, back stiff against the quiet chaos swirling about.

What was happening? The Elements were not sentient, did not respond to personalities or emotions. They did not care for people. They simply were what they were, inherent in the physical world around them. Was something whipping them up? Yes, that was possible.

She closed her eyes and reached out. There should be a telltale signature in the Elements and the energy that moved them. All Wrights left a mark whether they intended to or not.

There, in the heavy, stifling Air.

She gasped. It was hers! Was she indeed so unsettled she had done this? It had happened before, reaching out to the Elements when she was agitated, nearly out of control. But not for years now. Was it Mr. Enright himself, or the presence of an audience that had her so stirred up?

Did it make a difference, though?

Not really. She exhaled and allowed her chin to fall to her chest, easing the tension in her shoulders. Slowly spreading her hands, she gathered each Element, soothing it, and herself, until the unrest settled.

When she opened her eyes, he was staring at her, not like some circus freak, but rather a museum piece to study. What had he seen—could he tell what she was doing?

Or had he felt it with his Wright senses? "You quieted the Elements in the room?"

"Sometimes my flame-tamer's temper gets the better of me, I am afraid." She dabbed the sweat from her forehead with her sleeve. "Allow me to bring my thoughts into order and touch the Elements properly, then we can get started."

He stepped back, allowing her access to the bench near the iron bars, where a basin and candle stood. With careful, measured steps, she brought them to the table and placed them on either side of the granite.

"Crack open the transom over that window, please." She pointed at the middle window.

Thank goodness he did not ask for explanations as he did so.

She snapped the candlewick through her fingers, and it burst into flame. Oh, that helped. So warm, so soothing. There were moments when it was hard to believe working any other Element was worth the bother. Fire was so perfect.

No, focus. Glancing over her shoulder, she caught a handful of Air and tugged it into the room. A soft whisper of Air teased the candle flame into dancing.

So beautiful when they cooperated thus. Just as Father insisted they were meant to.

It took both hands to wring the ambient moisture out of the Air today, forming a dainty pool in the bottom of the basin that reflected the dancing flame. With two fingers, she stroked the granite, leaving a smooth polished trail in their wake.

Now. Now, everything was in order. Now she could focus and work.

"That was incredible," his voice, a reverent whisper, just over the gentle breeze.

"What do you mean?"

"They way you pulled in the Elements with such ease and grace. I've never seen any Full Wright with such faculty."

She shrugged, but it was reassuring to hear confirmation of her skill. "Now it is time to work. Help me light the lamps." When they returned to the worktable, she handed him the granite. "You see how this piece is riddled with large quartz crystals? I chose this one especially because the flat face would be the most troublesome to work. Show me how you would treat it."

A bead of sweat appeared on his temple. "I suppose it is only fair that you see me work if I am asking the same of you." He ran his hands over the stone, examining it from every angle. "I would not work from the flat side, too many disruptions. I would take the opposite side and smooth it and go from there."

"Reasonable, but unnecessary." She turned the stone in his hand so the flat face looked up at them. "Carve a simple line on this side of the stone."

He nodded as his face wrinkled into something thoughtful, probably quelling the desire to argue. She had made that expression often enough when working under her father's instruction. Mr. Enright's eyes took on a faraway look as he adjusted his grip on the stone. A sharp, beveled line appeared under his fingers. Such precision, definitely the work of an Earth Master.

"Damn!" He jumped and dropped the stone. It bounced on the table, almost laughing at him. "Bloody thing bit me!"

"As we both knew it would." She pushed the basin toward him, encouraging him to dip his fingers in the cool water. "This particular stone has the temper of a mad dog. But it can be tamed."

"How?"

"By biting it first."

"What does that even mean?" Oh, the look on his face! Half rebellious apprentice, half slack-jawed journeyman baffled by his Master. And something else hard to define, rather soft and warm.

"That is why these are here." She gestured at the window, basin, and candle.

"You need to bring in all the Elements?"

"Need is a strong word. I do not require their presence, but the ritual soothes the nerves and is a reminder that every Element is present in every piece of work. The key issue, though, is that limiting yourself to a single Element in your work is what prevents you from being able to work granite. In fact, it's what keeps most Wrights limited."

He parked his hip on the corner of the worktable and twitched like a chill was running down his neck. "But our Skill is limited, at least for most. We do not cross the Elements in our work."

"No, that is simply wrong and shortsighted. Or perhaps it is just lazy. I haven't quite worked that out, though my father was sure it was laziness." She folded her arms over her chest. "Any Wright can work every Element, if they understand their Skill correctly. Fire Wrights have the easiest time of it—something about the nature of Fire, I believe—Earth, the most difficult, but the possibility is in all of us."

"Let me be sure I understand you. Are you saying our inborn affinity for a particular Element is not a limiting factor?" His eyes bulged and jaw gaped like a trout out of water.

"Yes, I am saying the traditional Aristotelian model is wrong. There are not four distinct Elements, there is only one, though it takes different forms. It's the form of the Element—solid, liquid, gaseous or raw—that we find easiest to work. We get into the habit of treating it in only that way and that is what limits us. Once you realize there are only different aspects of the single Element, you can bring together all variety of techniques into places that did not make sense before."

He leaned on the worktable as he rubbed his chin. "Do you realize what you are saying? That is—"

"Revolutionary? Or perhaps you think it heresy?"

"Yes, that, the former, I mean, not heresy." He covered his mouth with his hand, the crease between his eyes deepening.

Good, that was something.

"I can hardly believe it, though."

"Of course, I would expect little else." She held the granite at eye level. "What do you do to create the lines in this stone? How would you explain that to an apprentice?"

"It is a matter of pushing the stone into the shape you want it. Is that what you mean?"

"It will do. But what if you considered this not as simple stone, but as an Element containing Fire as well?"

"That is absurd. It is Earth, not Fire."

"Humor me, Mr. Enright."

He grumbled. "I would meet the Element with its own. If there is Fire, then I would press Fire into the stone. But any Earth Wright knows—"

"That the stone will reject it and spit it back out at you." She probably should not have rolled her eyes, but too late to now worry about that now. "Yes, that is true, if you force it on the stone like a police officer with a baton."

"How else does one apply a foreign Element, then?"

"By understanding that it is not foreign in the first place. Place your hands on the stone and observe." He laid his hand on the opposite side of the stone. She felt him reach into it but nearly dropped the granite. Father's Skill was the only other Skill she had ever touched before. The intimacy— "Pull back. I do not want to touch your Skill, only the stone."

He withdrew his hand completely. Clenching his fist, his cheeks colored. He'd felt it, too! "Forgive me. I have never done something like this before. I'll be more cautious." He rested his fingertips against the stone and reached again.

Better. Still close, but tolerable. "Now, can you feel the quartz crystal in the stone, near my touch?"

"I think so."

She pressed into the quartz crystal. "Can you feel how it resists me, threatening to 'bite', as you call it?"

"Yes."

"Understand, quartz is a conduit for Fire, closer to Fire than most things we consider being Earth. If you press Fire into it," she released the slightest bit of flame into the stone, "you see how the troublesome bit now conforms under your touch?"

"Zounds! It is exactly as you say!" He took the stone with both hands. "I have never seen granite worked in that way."

"The idea that there are separate Elements and that we are limited to engaging one at a time makes it difficult to conceive. My father was the only one to teach that technique." She harrumphed and tossed her head. "And the Guild rejected it."

"This is astounding. The implications are—" He stared agape at the stone as he drew a clean beveled line through it. Then another and another, until a simple frame traced the edges of the granite.

Such skill and so quick to adapt to the new approach! "Almost too much to consider? I know. Is it any wonder that my father's relationship with the Guild was so uneasy?"

"That explains a great deal. I'm astonished. You've given me a great deal to digest."

"Perhaps you'll deign to contemplate it another time. The deadline to finish the Lackwoods' commission is fast approaching."

"Indeed, indeed." He set the stone aside, but his tone promised that he would contemplate what he had seen tonight for a long time.

# Chapter 12

Work at Fuller's Fix-All continued into the wee morning hours. David dragged himself back to Belle Vue House, limbs leaden and stomach gnawing at his ribs. A post wright-work meal would have been nice, but too much to ask for.

And he needed space.

Space to consider the new ideas that had dropped in his lap like some revelations from on high. Space to consider their implications for himself, his work, and for the Guild at large.

And space from that woman. He needed that most of all.

He dropped onto his bed, head in his hands.

Better judgment insisted he run as far and fast from her as he could, and never look back. Underneath her hard exterior and fiery temper was a refined, disciplined Skill, the likes of which he had ever known before. And a passion for her work, and for the Skill, like calling to like within him, in a way no other woman had. Intelligent, sensitive, and strong. All the things a woman should be. All the things he wanted one to be.

That was dangerous. He had work to do, a guild to save, and yes, even ambitions to fulfil. She would only stand in his way. He had wasted enough time with Uncle Cresswell's failures as a barrister and couldn't afford to waste any more if he was to realize his desires.

How could he risk associating himself with one who threatened to upend the entire Guild with her—more accurately, her father's—ideas and her unparalleled use of Skill as a Wright? Risk his own good standing with men of importance and influence?

His stomach rumbled, and he raked his hands through his hair.

Then again, how could he not? Especially when his goal was to save the Wrights from the obscurity—and eventual extinction—that their hidebound traditions ensured.

How indeed?

Hunger pangs stabbed his gut. Wait, Miss Fuller had tucked something into his pocket just before he left. He pulled out a napkin-wrapped bundle—a hand-sized fruit pie left from their dinner. Bless her! He wolfed it down in three bites.

By Jove, that Birdy was an excellent cook!

He kicked off his shoes and fell, still dressed, into bed. Deep, if uneasy, sleep claimed him.

"Mr. Enright? Mr. Enright, sir!" That was Mrs. Gaskill pounding at his door.

David bolted upright. Great Scott—nearly eleven o'clock! How had he slept so late? "Yes, Mrs. Gaskill, what is it?"

Late-morning light streamed through the window, past the curtains he had neglected to pull, to glare off the whitewashed walls. Too bright! Searing through his eyelids, piercing his skull.

His clothes lay in a drunken trail from the door, past the lopsided press, across the windowsill, ending on the small blue carpet at the side of the bed. Yes, yes, he had gotten up at some point—his coat had been binding under his armpits—that's right. Somehow, he'd shucked his clothes and pulled on his nightshirt, but only because it was hanging on the bedpost, ready at hand. Drunken nights after dinner at the Inn of Courts had left him less hungover.

"A message just come for you and it looks important. I'll just slip it under the door—don't mean to disturb your privacy." A folded message, sealed with what appeared to be the Guild signet, appeared under the door.

Good heavens, she thought he was keeping company in his room, something Belle Vue House rules forbade! Not the sort of reputation he needed right now. "No worries, madam. Under the weather this morning, nothing more."

"Shall I send up a tray with tea and toast, then?"

"That would be most appreciated." He padded to the door and picked up the note with Cinderford's spidery handwriting scrawled across the front.

"Very good, then. I will be right back."

Best be presentable when she returned. David laid the message aside. At least he had not lied about being under the weather. His head throbbed, the room spun, and his knees quivered with the effort of dressing.

He knew working with Miss Fuller would be taxing, but this? Unprecedented. Was this the cost of using her father's methods? That seemed to make sense, that such revolutionary improvement would come at a great price.

He opened his door a mite and staggered back to the bed, landing on it just before his legs gave out.

"Stars above!" Mrs. Gaskill bustled in. "You look a fright!"

"I mentioned being under the weather." He leaned back on his hands, panting.

“To be sure, but this is several shades farther under that I expected. You look like you had a proper bender last night. You need a course of the anti-tox to set you to rights? I don’t advertise it, but I got some if you need it.”

“Very kind, very kind, but I was out late working the stone last night, not the pubs. A commission’s coming due, and I can’t be late with it.” He clutched his throbbing temples.

“Can’t say I’m disappointed to hear that. Not like you to be out getting drunk as a boiled owl.” Was it possible for her smile to be bright enough to hurt his eyes? “What you need, then, is a proper meal. I have a pot of stew on. I’ll set you a bowl in the dining room.”

Bless her.

Half an hour later, with a bowl of hot, hearty stew in his belly, headache subsiding, and strength trickling back, David opened Cinderford’s message.

Dash and damn it all! How could he have forgotten the welcome reception for the Royal Court Guild representative was today? So much for tending to those other complaints against the Guild. If he ran most of the way, he just might get there in time.

The doors of the meeting hall, on the third underground level of the Guild Hall under Ames’ house, opened as David burst into the corridor from the staircase, breathless and sweating.

“Glad to see you made it, Enright.” Master Water Wright Ephraim Fitzsimons, the Guild treasurer, wandered David’s way and nudged him with an elbow. Short, hunched shoulders, pointy nose and beady eyes. The man looked more like a rat every time David encountered him. His office resembled a rat’s nest with collections of this and that littering every flat surface, none of which he could be persuaded to part with. A bit like the money he counted for the Guild, which he would rather hoard than spend in payment of Guild obligations. "Was beginning to worry you might miss the reception. Would not be a good look for our undersecretary, you know."

"Your confidence in me is such a comfort." David strode past Fitzsimons, into the meeting hall. Best not give the little rat-man further invitation to converse.

The Guild assembly hall engulfed him in a cool, stoney embrace, soothing every ragged fiber of his being. The perfection of pure Earth, strong, firm, steady. Was there anywhere else so sublime?

The vaulted ceiling, carved into the bedrock, rested on intricate columns, each one different to the others. It was said a different Master did the decorative carvings on each of the pillars, placing his signature on them. A legacy to future Wrights. Gas lamps, brass fittings shaded with intricately crafted glass, lined the walls, lighting the room bright enough to read, but not so much as to hurt his eyes. A dazzling dance of shadows crossed the room's many angles, and slid along the polished limestone floor tiles.

Companionable clusters of comfortable chairs occupied the far half of the room, more than enough to seat every one of the two dozen attendees, with extra besides, so one could move from one conversation to another without the awkwardness of not finding a seat.

Sideboards laden with sufficient food to cater to two dozen Wrights' appetites lined the walls near the door. David's stomach rumbled. Good heavens, it smelt amazing. Fresh bread and pies, cold ham and more. No Guild gathering could happen without an abundant spread. No doubt every man in the room had at least one eye on the food.

A crystal bell rang and conversations stilled, turning all attention to Guild Master Allbright, standing in the center of the room, near a pillar he was said to have carved. "Your attention, please." The way the shadows fell across his face and long beard somehow reinforced the wizardly aspects of his person. He gestured to his left.

A sinewy man of medium height, with the lean, hungry aura of an actively practicing Wright, stepped to Allbright's side, leaving a conversation with Cinderford, who seemed offended.

Allbright paused for a moment, allowing the gathered Wrights to admire their guest. "Thank you all for joining us today, to honor Master Earth Wright Sir Wilbert Cullington-Price's arrival. He is the visiting representative from the Royal Court Guild in London."

Polite applause followed, a mite too polite to have been genuine, especially when the room's mood turned guarded.

"Thank you for your warm welcome." Sir Wilbert tipped his broad shoulders in a small bow. "I bring greetings from the Queen and the Royal Court Guild. As much as I would like this to be a trip of pleasure to your fine city, the business of the Wrights does not allow such luxuries."

A wet-blanket hush descended, silencing conversational sparks across the room.

"Let me ask you a question, Master Wrights of Brighton. How many of you are training a full complement of apprentices these days? A show of hands, please." Sir Wilbert extended open hands.

David glanced around the room. Not a single raised hand.

"How many of you are training any apprentices at all?"

A few hands went up, but far less than a majority.

"You've made my point for me, gentlemen. Our numbers dwindle while this new, modern era threatens our very existence, not from witch hunters of yore, but because of the subtle changes that infuse every facet of our lives. With factories and machines replacing craftsmen and apprentices, we cannot identify young Wrights, and their

Skill fades into obscurity. In another generation, if things continue as they are, Wrights might fade away entirely."

Angry murmurs of 'alarmist' and 'fearmonger' erupted throughout the room.

"I brought with me the numbers from our last census and I will show them to any who want to examine them. Those numbers do not lie. We are a dying breed."

More murmurs, maybe slightly less hostile. Only slightly.

"If we are to change that future, the time to do it is now. It is my hope, and that of the Crown, that the Brighton chapter of the Wright Guild might take a role of leadership and see the Wrights into the next century."

"What have you in mind?" someone from the far side of the room asked.

"What is to be demanded of us?"

"How much money do they want from us?" Was that Fitzsimons's voice?

Grunts of assent followed.

"Patience, my good Wrights, patience." Allbright lifted open hands. "Sir Wilbert plans discussions with each of you over the course of the next seven-day, culminating in a formal proposal that will be fully explained at our Assembly, next week. In the meantime, let us show our Royal Court guest true Brighton hospitality and partake in the spread Master Ames has arranged for us." He bowed from his shoulders and beckoned them join him at the sideboards.

David hurried toward the food, stomach rumbling and headache threatening. Politeness and good breeding must give way to desperate need. He grabbed a plate and heaped several pork pies on it.

"You've got enough there for three men. Working on a big project?" Allbright nudged David with his elbow as he served his own plate.

"I am. With a tight deadline as well. Even a Master must bow down to his customer's requirements." David forced a laugh.

"It wouldn't happen to be something for the Lackwood family, would it?" Sir Wilbert lifted an eyebrow and nodded to Allbright.

"Sir Wilbert, David Enright, my undersecretary." Allbright nodded at them, then wandered off into the crowd. Like many fellow Wrights, Allbright never was big on social niceties.

David watched Allbright's retreat, not because it was so interesting, but to buy time to work out an appropriate response.

"So, I am right, then." Sir Wilbert laid a generous slice of ham on an equally generous slab of bread, then spread mustard over the lot.

"How did you know?"

Sir Wilbert laughed and signaled David to follow him to the far corner of the room. "Have you ever been around servants? The pantry politics they share will tell one everything they want to know, and then some."

"You are acquainted with the Lackwoods?" David leaned against the wall and took a bite from the topmost pork pie. Dry but decent, not as appetizing as what Miss Fuller had offered him from Birdy's kitchen, though.

"Afraid so. Staying with them, in fact. They are throwing a dinner party in honor of my visit, to boot." His thin upper lip curled in a little sneer. "I expect it will be some dreadful, posh affair with every attempt being made to impress me."

"Forgive me for asking, and no offense intended, of course, but since they are not Wrights and know nothing of your affiliation with the Royal Court Guild, why would they be keen to impress you?"

"Not one to mince words, are you, Enright?" Sir Wilbert laughed, both amused and almost bitter at the same time. "You don't think

Sir Wilbert Cullington-Price, tutor to the royal family, is enough to impress anyone?"

Oh! Was he to have already known that? "I meant no insult—"

"None taken, none at all. I appreciate someone with that sort of perspective. Quite refreshing, considering the circles in which I am forced to circulate. And you are quite correct, for myself alone, they have no reason to curry favor with me. For that, you can blame my friend."

David took another hearty bite of pie, lest he put his foot in it instead, and waved Sir Wilbert to continue his story.

"My friend Baron Wareham is without any get. None on the right side of the blanket nor the wrong. Not that he didn't try, mind you. He's outlived three wives and now is getting up there. He needs to settle upon an heir."

"And the Lackwoods are hopeful he might look their way?"

"They are related to him in one fashion or another, though I've never bothered to sort out how."

"So am I—if one cares to travel along the family tree in a convoluted and mind-numbing fashion. For a man with no offspring, he still manages to have many relations." David chuckled. It was a connection through his father's side, one of many that Father seemed at odds with.

"Ah, but has the good baron given you a gift? As I understand, he gave the Lackwoods a piece of marble of some sort, giving them the notion that they might be a favorite. I am not sure that is the correct way to understand the gift, considering it was something Wareham was happy to be rid of. But far be it from me to involve myself in what is sure to be a disagreeable affair." Sir Wilbert raised his sandwich to David and took a Wright-sized bite.

Interesting. That explained a great deal about the Lackwoods and their desperation to repair the mantel. What people would do in hopes of an easy fortune. Odd how they would rather try to repair damage than have prevented it in the first place. But that was how people were.

"Speaking of relatives," Sir Wilbert licked a dab of mustard from his upper lip, "I saw your Uncle Cresswell the other day. Told him I expected to meet you while I was in Brighton."

David snorted and rolled his eyes. No, it was not polite, but neither was Uncle Cresswell. "I imagine proper manners prevent you from conveying the message he would send to me?"

"Let's go with that."

"He hasn't changed, then. How well do you know him?" David leaned away. Any friend of Cresswell was no friend of his.

"Well enough to agree that his character hasn't changed. His situation has, though, and not for the better. You are aware of his dire straits? I imagine your mother or sister has said something. Certainly, they keep you abreast of family news, no?"

"Most of the time." They knew better than to offer him news of Cresswell unless he asked, though. And he did not ask.

"It is a shame it all fell apart with him, and he sent you packing off to find your own way in the world. Keeping you in London would have been a boon, bringing you up through the ranks of the Royal Court Guild. You would have been more than a mere junior officer in that Guild by now, had you stayed."

"I doubt it. Between the gin and the French disease, he's alienated every solicitor from Manchester to Lyme. No one in their right mind wants him to press their case at the bar. Staying would only have painted my name with the same brush. That would have hardly propelled me up the ranks of the Royal Court Guild." Nor would getting arrested for coming to blows with the drunkard, which surely would have happened if David had worked even one more day with him. "Besides, no London Wrights were waiting in the wings to take me on after Cresswell washed his hands of me."

"True enough, I grant you. Still, though, for a clever, hardworking man like you, there are ways for you to stand out to the Crown, even here." Sir Wilbert glanced over his shoulder, as if checking for eavesdroppers. "Have you an office where we might talk?"

"We should take the back stairs." David jerked his head toward a green baize door in the wall behind them. Servants' stairs, but also convenient for making a quick escape when socializing became too much.

Two flights of stairs and a brief trip down the corridor took them to the barely-larger-than-a-closet space that bore "Full Wright David Enright, Undersecretary" on the door.

He unlocked the door and reached in to light the nearby gas lamp. It would have been polite to usher his guest in ahead of him, but David needed to clear the way first.

A tall stack of files on his desk, a recent addition, left the narrow room smelling vaguely musty. The full bookcases looked over the disarray in irritable judgment, but at least they did not throw things at him. He shoved the piles to either side of his desk, so that he and his guest could look between them whilst they talked. At least the rest of the room was tidy and dusted. There was that.

"Sit, sit, it's not much, but it is private. I imagine what you hinted toward has something to do with the reason you are in Brighton?"

"I do not suppose that was difficult to guess." Sir Wilbert settled himself in the spartan wooden chair and shut the door without having to reach very far. "Are you familiar with the state of the Brighton chapter of the Guild?"

"Not much different than the English Guild overall, I should think." David edged his way around his desk to sit.

"Random sporadic training, no consolidation of information. Fewer and fewer apprentices applying every year. Widespread fears that we are losing out to the growth of science and industrialization, heightening the fascination with mysticism, spiritism, and all that mumbo jumbo, all the while refusing to consider any meaningful change? Would that be what you mean?"

"Are things that bad everywhere?"

"I have spent the last year traveling the kingdom to understand the state of the Wrights and yes, it is probably even worse than I depict it." Sir Wilbert laced his hands behind his neck and pressed his temples with his elbows. "And the Brighton chapter adds to that a special level of disregard for even its own rules, as though trying to accelerate our way into oblivion."

"I have been working to address that later charge, but there is only so much one man can do, I fear." David grimaced and rubbed his temples. "You have come all this way to tell me, not the Guild Master? I do not understand."

"You may not realize it, but you have a reputation for being forward-thinking and flexible, and one of the few officers who might embrace the changes needed to keep us going forward."

Who would have said such things about him? Not Cinderford or Fitzsimons, certainly. Allbright? Possibly. "It sounds like you have a plan."

"At least the start of one. Naturally, the shortcomings of the Brighton chapter must be addressed before we can make too much progress. But that is not where you fit in. The Crown seeks to identify young Wrights and establish a proper school for their training. We cannot continue to rely upon apprenticeships any longer. Eventually, that school will become a repository for the Guild's formal body of knowledge. The Brighton Guild has long had a connection with

Brighton College, which employs a few Wrights as instructors. The effort to use that as a substitute for the old system of apprenticeships has been underwhelming, to say the least. But the principle is sound, just needs to be taken a step further."

"What has this to do with me?"

"You are the youngest Full Wright in this generation. You have something to offer to the future training of new Wrights. You have complained more than once about the shortcomings of your own training." Sir Wilbert raised an unruly eyebrow. "You're lucky Master McIntire is not the resentful sort."

"I suppose I am." David rubbed his palms together, staring at them. "Are you truly looking for new and different approaches to wright-work?"

"I am afraid so. I do not like change more than the next man, but facing extinction does change a man's mind."

"Then there is something, someone you must hear about."

"Tell me more."

# Chapter 13

BALTHAZAR LANDED ON HER chest with a lung-crushing thud, but did not insist she get up. Strange for him, since he was always as hungry as she was in the mornings. He curled on her chest, nose to nose with her, purring, insisting she stay in bed a little longer.

Who was she to argue?

Last night was so strange and tumultuous, despite being productive. And exhausting. She had staggered upstairs, barely conscious of removing her corset, and had fallen into bed face-first. She needed the sleep, to be sure. But now, with so many thoughts left unaddressed, her mind churned in a jumble not much different to the piles of rubble on her worktable downstairs.

The entire iron scaffolding for the mantel was assembled and the first two marble pieces attached. Coaxing the marble and the iron to come together had been more difficult than she expected. Mr. Enright was generous with what he knew, though, and showed her a few new techniques. While she might have figured them out on her own, it was so much faster learning them from someone who knew them well.

What a rare opportunity to work with, learn from, another Wright, someone skilled and sure of himself, not intimidated or resentful of her Skill. To be respected as an equal, with value to contribute alongside of his work. Strange, heady stuff.

Did he feel it too? The peculiar intimacy of sharing their Skill together. His touch in the stone was different to hers. Different and compelling. Did he realize Wrights pushed something of themselves into the Elements as they worked them, leaving traces of themselves as clear as the signs businesses painted on the sides of their buildings?

Probably not. According to Father, only the most sensitive—actually, he said oversensitive and distracted, but still—the most sensitive Wrights could feel another Wright's signature in their work. It wasn't a common ability. Likely for the best.

But he was an unusual man, to be sure. As strait-laced and rule-bound as Father had been freethinking. It showed in the regular, even ways his work was ordered. He brought the Elements into near-perfect military formation, without thought or effort to get them that way. That was simply how they lined up under his hands. Probably had to do with being an Earth-mover first in life. They preferred staid order.

While it was a sharp contrast to her more exuberant treatment of the Elements, it provided a structure, a foundation for her own work, something she'd never experienced before. Father had always sought to make her work like his, ordered and perfect. Mr. Enright—how different he was. He acknowledged the project as hers and instead of forcing her hand, he deferred to her Skill, finding ways to work around it, support it, strengthen it in ways she had not dreamt possible.

Perhaps that was his unique Skill, molding his work, adapting it to what best fit the situation. Humble instead of prideful, not insisting his own way. A proficiency she had never acquired.

What was more, he had whispered words last night that he thought her the better Wright, but perhaps it was that admission that made him the better Wright.

Did it really matter who was better? The opportunity to work with a peer was heady, intoxicating stuff.

And not a little dangerous.

Confusing.

Unsettling.

Her feelings? What were they now? What was the euphoria of the work and the thrill of new learning, and what feelings were connected to the man himself? He never said it, but he clearly shared the elation in the work. Heights no drink or drug could match. But was there something else, too? Did he feel anything beyond that? Anything for her?

Did she want him to?

Balthazar patted her nose with barely-sheathed claws and meowed plaintive cries of starvation. There would be no arguing with his stomach, nor hers. How had she failed to notice the gnawing, even dangerous grumblings of her own belly?

Birdy's back door stood open, waiting for her as she staggered in. Exhaustion turned her limbs to lead, and her head pounded with the intensity of cannon fire. She should have taken time to eat before bed last night. She would have to remember to do that in the future. Joseph had died from ignoring this sort of warning. If he had not been so depleted, Air would not have slipped from his control. Suffocation was not the way an Air Wright should perish. She needed to learn from his mistake.

"You look a fright 'dere! What happened?" Birdy caught her by the arm and helped her to sit at the worn worktable. "I ain't never seen you like dis." She pressed the back of her hand to Rebecca's forehead.

Rebecca parked her elbows on the table and supported her face in her hands. Delicious, intoxicating smells surrounded her. Her stomach growled loud enough for the entire pub to hear. "Up too late, doing too much."

"I'd say. You got to be takin' better care of yourself, girlie. When a woman got no one at home to do the job for her, she's got to do it for herself, ya know?" Birdy trundled toward the hob.

"I am in no condition to argue with you."

"Here, you start with dis while I fix you up a proper plate." Birdy pressed a bowl of perpetual stew in her hands. A pot of the brew always simmered on the hob. Birdy threw odds and ends in as she went about her other cooking. It boiled down into a mash of indistinguishable bites with a flavor that varied from time to time. But it was hot, and it was food. And it was available now.

Rebecca's hands shook as she raised the bowl to her lips, almost sloshing the viscous liquid down her chin. It was rude to down it all in a single breath. Rude, but completely and entirely necessary. "You are a lifesaver, my friend."

"So it would seem. Here, eat." Birdy slid a plate in front of her, piled with all the good things that made the Bird's Nest the most desirable —and profitable—working-class pub on this side of Brighton.

Rebecca grabbed the pork pie precariously balanced on the top of the pile and tore into it with all the grace and etiquette of a starving wolf.

"You ought to see a doctor. I swear you have a tapeworm or something. Dis can't be healthy."

Rebecca shook her head, her mouth too full to speak.

"Maybe they can help, yah? I hate seein' you like this." Birdy added a large tankard of milk to the table.

"My whole family was like this. It's normal for us. Speaking of being worried, you look run hard and put up wet yourself. What's that on your face?" Rebecca should have noticed sooner. What a fool she was for allowing herself to get into this condition.

Birdy's hand went to her dark cheek, not quite covering the even darker bruise spread across her high cheekbone. "Nothing, just clumsy, these days." She returned to kneading bread. "Eat your fill. I got another full box for you by the door."

Indeed, she did. Rebecca took a huge bite to occupy her as she stared at the box. A full box wasn't entirely surprising, but the contents were. Usually it contained plates and cups, items that got a great deal of use. Not figurines, a wall shelf, and another mirror. Things that were kept out of reach of Birdy's rowdy clientele. What was going on here?

"I have an enormous project due at the end of the week. Will it be a hardship if I am a little later than usual getting these back to you?"

"Do what you can, not to worry. Don't go killing yourself on that big project of yours, y' hear?" Birdy laid another plate on the table.

Rebecca returned to her shop an hour later, Birdy's words echoing in her ears. There was no way for her to have known the accuracy of her warning, which made it even more chilling. Finding the withered husk of her brother's body after he had ignored the need to sustain himself was not an experience she wished on anyone. Nor was failing to manage the Elements she worked on, as he had. So, she forced herself back upstairs as she downed a sausage roll, licked her fingers, and fell face-first into bed.

Finally, screams from the dashed cuckoo clock roused her. At least she felt more human and less like something Balthazar dragged in now. Best open up the shop and try to salvage what remained of her workday.

By the time the clock shrieked again, she had managed a few mundane repairs, recorded them in the ledger, and had enough wherewithal to silence the screeching bird before the third wail. Not as productive as she liked, but it was something.

The next item on her docket, an inlaid jewelry box with the lid torn from the hinges, would take a little thought. She could replace the hinges with new, but the wooden base was also damaged. She could replace it with fresh boards, staining it to match, or she could use her Skill to repair the original wood itself.

Her fingertips tingled where they came into contact with the box, and it molded beneath her touch. Heavens! That wasn't what she intended to do. She dropped the jewelry box.

Fire and Earth! She was far more spent than she realized if she was losing control like this.

The brass doorbells rang, not their happy little sound, but something harsh and rough, more warning than song.

Condemn it all! What was Mallory doing here?

His clothes were pressed and his tie properly snugged to his collar. Steps firm and purposeful. This wasn't Mallory the Drunk, but Mallory the Moneylender.

"Constable Moore told you to stay away from here." She scanned the shop for escape routes. Dash it all. The door to the back room was locked, as was the one to the upstairs. Reaching under the workbench, she pulled her favorite wooden mallet closer. Could be useful if things came to it.

"He cannot keep a man from his legitimate business." Mallory marched across the shop, past the shelves and glass-fronted display cases, toward her.

She lifted her hand as she pushed a subtle wall of Air toward him with one hand and pulled Air toward her with the other. He paused, a bewildered look spreading across his face. Another step forward into another wall of Air. He stopped.

"What is your business?"

"We are both aware of the business between us." Such loathing in his sneer.

"The payment is not due for several more days yet."

"Payments are so often missed. It is a good thing to make sure there is a reminder."

"I have never missed a payment. I do not need reminding. Get out." She pointed toward the door.

"Be careful of the tone you use with me, Miss Fuller." He pulled back his shoulders and parked his hands on his hips, elbows wide.

"Be careful of the tone you use with me, Mr. Mallory." She matched his posture.

"Is that a threat?"

"Are you threatening me?"

"No threat at all. Merely offering a reminder of a significant clause in the contract your father signed."

"And what clause would that be?" The words nearly caught in her throat.

"The consequences of a missed payment. You are aware of that, certainly."

"What are you talking about?" She gripped the edge of the workbench, her fingers threatening to dig gouges in the malleable wood.

"I thought you might have a hard time remembering." He smiled the kind of smile that begged it to be wiped off his face with a sharp rush of Air. Or better, Fire. He reached into his pocket and pulled out a set of folded papers. "Here." He slammed them on the workbench and shoved them toward her.

She willed her hands not to tremble and unfolded them.

"Here." Mallory stabbed the paper with a meaty finger. "Read that clause. Very carefully."

The coldness of his tone forced chills down her spine.

*In the event of default in the payment of any of the said aforementioned installments or interest, when due as herein provided, time being of the essence hereof, the holder of this note may, without notice or demand, declare the entire principal sum then unpaid immediately due and payable.*

She adjusted her glasses and read it again. "What is this? I have never seen this before."

"You see here, your father initialed this particular paragraph. Those are his initials, are they not?"

The scrawling letters did indeed look like Father's initials. She ran her fingers over the marks. The ink—that was not the ink from Father's fountain pen, the one he always used to sign such documents. "I have my suspicions."

"Are you calling me a liar?" Mallory leaned his hands on the workbench to tower over her.

"Is your conscience bothering you?" She rose on her toes.

"Are you calling me a liar?"

"I believe there is something irregular about this contract."

"How dare you!" Mallory slammed his fist on the workbench. "Don't you think you can bat those pretty eyes of yours and get out of a legally binding—"

"Legally binding?" Mr. Enright sauntered in, surrounded by an aura of professional calm and competence.

Why had she not noticed the bells ringing?

"None of your business, monument man. Run along and chip your stone." Mallory waved him away.

"I think not." Mr. Enright strode to the workbench. "I am Miss Fuller's legal counsel, and as such, it is exactly my business."

Mallory's eyes bulged like a pug choking on a bone. "Is that true? You've gone and gotten yourself a solicitor?"

"A barrister, sir, not a solicitor." Mr. Enright thumbed his lapels and rocked back on his heels.

"You're a stonemason, not a damned Chancellor's Egg." Mallory spat at his feet.

"There is no need to be insulting. Sir. I am hardly a newly-made barrister." Mr. Enright smiled. Was Mallory smart enough to recognize the danger behind that expression?

"Then mind your own business."

"This is my business." He shouldered Mallory out of the way and examined the document, tongue clucking under his breath. "Is this your only copy?"

"No, there is another in my office."

"Then you will not mind leaving it with me." He slapped his hand on the contract and pulled it away from Mallory's grasping fingers. "Miss Fuller, have you a copy of the contract your father signed?"

"Certainly, but I do not keep it in the shop."

"Of course, of course. Run along, Mr.—"

"Mallory." Rebecca spat the name.

"Mr. Mallory. I will examine her copy of the contract and the one you have produced. I will discuss any discrepancies I find with you later in the week. Run along now. Your business here is finished. I imagine you have other work to manage, yes?" Mr. Enright took Malloy's elbow, escorted him to the door, opened it, and propelled Mallory out. The bells jangled as Mr. Enright shut the door and bolted it in place. With an exhausted huff, he fell back against the door. "Pray forgive me, Miss Fuller. I'm sure I've overstepped all boundaries of decorum and good taste, stepping in like that."

Indeed, he had—but that wasn't why her heart was racing and pulse pounding in her temples. "Mallory's contract is a lie." She forced her fingers loose from the workbench. Dash it all! She had left marks, after all.

"I have seen his kind before, and I do not doubt that." He approached her, head hung slightly. "I fear I overstepped, declaring myself your legal counsel. I am the Brighton Guild's legal counsel, though. It is my role to help local Wrights with legal matters. Even so, if you wish me to step back and allow you to handle matters, I will do that."

She stared at him, searching for words. Yes, he had been overbearing. She was not a helpless princess waiting for a shining knight. But, what tools had she to combat this latest assault from Mallory, save those the law provided? And who better to wield those than a master in them? It was his official role with the Guild, so it was not so much... oh, for pity's sake, what was it? A personal favor, or what the Guild actually owed her this time? "I am not sure what to say."

"I saw that look in your eye. Perhaps you just realized this is some of the assistance the Guild owes you?"

"Quite."

"Then accept my help in managing that blackguard." He walked toward her, calm and confident. But was that a touch of hope in his eyes?

"My copy of the contract is in a lockbox upstairs."

"I brought a proper meal." He gestured to a large hamper near the door. How could she have missed that? "Perhaps we might examine it whilst we eat?"

"Only if you allow me to provide for a meal after we finish working tonight. I can only guess that you felt the aftereffects as much as I."

"When she saw me this morning, Mrs. Gaskill was certain I went on a bender to end all benders last night."

"You were bending metal..." she covered her mouth as she giggled.

His eyes grew wide as he laughed. "That is a terrible joke."

"I know, but how could I resist?" She held her sides and her breath, but the laughter would not be contained.

He covered his mouth and snorted. "I suppose that means I have lied to Mrs. Gaskill. She does not approve of that at all."

"No worries, I will defend your honor to her, sir." She leaned over the workbench, face in her hands, tears running down her cheeks.

He wiped his eyes on his sleeve, pulled his handkerchief from his pocket, and handed it to her. "... and here is my token to bear with you on your quest."

She took it and pressed it to her heart. "Forever shall I treasure this."

He caught her gaze, and they dissolved into a consuming paroxysm of laughter.

The cuckoo screamed, but she could not pull herself from their mirth before it finished its appointed calls.

"I suppose that means we should get on with things." He pushed himself upright, sighing so softly, she almost missed it.

She left Mr. Enright in the kitchen to set up their repast while she went to her room for the old contract, but she also needed a moment to think, assuming her racing heart and all the fluttery feelings would allow that.

What a rare and precious thing to share such a moment. Perhaps, just perhaps, there might be more like it. Someday.

But for now, he was waiting for her to bring that contract. Yes, that. That was what she was here for.

She knelt beside her bed and groped underneath. Dust and cat hair, so much cat hair. How many times had she forgotten to sweep under the bed for it to grow to such proportions? Thankfully no one but her need know.

It should be right there, near the bedpost ... But it wasn't. Perhaps it had been kicked further underneath? Or Balthazar had nudged it whilst on his rodent patrols. That had to be the reason.

Only one thing for that. She shoved her skirts out of the way, lay flat on the floor, and pulled herself partway under the bed on elbows and toes. Clods of cat hair flew in her face. She sneezed, once, twice, thrice.

There. What was it doing under the middle of the bed? She grabbed hold of the corner and dragged it, and herself, out.

Fire, Earth, and Air! "No!"

She rocked back on her heels, staring at the battered metal lockbox, the lid half-open, resting askew on the base. A brush of her fingertips revealed it had been viciously beaten with something that left traces of iron ... the poker from the fireplace?

"What's wrong?" Mr. Enright stood, breathless, in the doorway.

She pulled the lid back. The box was empty. "It's been broken into. Everything is gone."

"The contract?" He knelt beside her and took the box from her trembling hands.

"Yes, and cash. I should have kept this in the workshop, but it was so distracting—"

"When did this happen? Was there a break-in? Do you have any idea who could have done such a thing?"

She covered her face with her hands, rocking as she thought. "I always keep the stairs locked. Only I have a key... wait. Dash and damn it all! That wicked creature. Both of them."

"You know what happened, then?" He laid the box aside.

"Mallory burst in with his son several days ago, threatening to beat the boy for coming to me for help. The boy got upstairs while I was dealing with Mallory. I thought he was simply hiding. I would have never guessed he was in cahoots with his miserable father. How could I be so stupid?" She clutched her shoulders and collapsed into her lap, the room spinning around her. "Without the old contract..."

"One thing at a time. You need to eat. Right now." He took her elbow and helped her—really, more hauled her—to her feet.

She staggered and panted. Dash it all, he was right!

"Can you walk?"

Apparently, the answer was barely, but she could not attempt that and talk at the same time.

With an arm around her waist, he half-dragged her to the kitchen and put her in a chair near the table. Instead of handing her the nearest meat pie, though, he grabbed a spoon and a jar of jam.

"Don't argue with me, trust me, this is what you need first." He dug out a large spoonful of jam and pushed it toward her mouth like some sort of patent medicine.

She would have taken the spoon from him, but her hands shook too hard. She leaned forward, mouth open. Her body seemed to recognize the wisdom of his choice without mind to the indignity of it all.

Sweet, thick, cherry and apple, perhaps? A touch tart, and so very rich, filling her senses, like air to a drowning man. Jam, she must always have jam in the cupboards from here on out.

Three spoonfuls later, he stopped. "Breathe for a few moments. You should start feeling stronger soon. I would scold you more for allowing yourself to get into this state, but—" he chuckled under his breath, "I have done it myself more often than I care to admit. There's something about the Skill, isn't there?"

She swallowed hard and nodded, reaching for a slab of buttered brown bread. When had he prepared that? "Yes. I had not meant to do wright-work this morning. Mundane repairs, but sometimes the Skill just slips into my work, and I don't even realize it has happened."

"I promise not to tell anyone you said that. There are those who would have you declared a danger to yourself and others if they knew that, and that would limit you to being a perpetual journeyman." He pulled a stool close and sat beside her.

So close their shoulders nearly touched.

He leaned toward her to complete the connection.

Tears welled up and poured down her cheeks. How could her emotions betray her like this now? In front of him? She had not meant to push herself so hard, but the bills ... and now that her savings were gone ... She choked back a sob.

"I agree. Pronouncing you a journeyman for the rest of your life would not be fair, not in any sense of the word. You have greater control than any Master I have met. Than I have myself. Not just unfair, but it would be a tremendous loss to the Guild and to the Wrights of England." He handed her a meat pie and jumped up to pace across the tiny kitchen.

"Has ... has the Guild ... will the Guild ... agree to consider my application for Mastery?" She swallowed another spoonful of jam.

"Guild Master Allbright has still not given me his decision on that matter." He snatched the contract from the table. "This is the last straw. Any Wright facing such a loathsome creature needs the Guild's full support, and the only way that is going to happen is for you to have the status you deserve."

"Which is not likely to happen—"

"Which is why I am going to sponsor your application for Mastery. I will push for your recognition as a Full Wright. And, once I am done examining this contract, I will use every tool in my reach to put a stop to Mallory. Enough is enough."

# Chapter 14

THEY WORKED LATE INTO the night and the meal they shared after working left him walking back to Belle Vue House just after the bloody cuckoo clock screeched four times, as dawn painted the sidewalk with its rosy rays. He left through the back door, through the mews, lest anyone be able to observe him leaving Fuller's Fix-All at such an untoward time of day.

She had seemed relieved when he suggested it himself. But of course, what else could he do? It would not do to risk Miss Fuller's reputation so carelessly.

Sad that she seemed so unaccustomed to what should be basic courtesies. Especially after she had repaired his torn jacket seam—not with needle and thread, but she had wrighted it whole. So effortless she had made it appear, though they were both tired and worn from the work on the mantel. Was she so generous to everyone, or just to him?

A warm, fuzzy sensation gathered in his chest. One he had best ignore and get on with the business of the day.

First, another meal.

He strode into Belle Vue House as Mrs. Gaskill was setting out the first round of breakfast. Lovely fragrant platters of ham, fresh brown bread, some fancy buns, meat pies. He licked his lips.

"Another late night working?" She cocked her head, arms folded across her chest, and lifted an eyebrow.

"What else would I be doing covered with stone dust?" He brushed the dust from his pants. It floated down to the well-swept wooden floor, and she winced.

"It's odd for you to be out late so often." She handed him a chipped porcelain plate, plain white and serviceable.

He bit his tongue. Best not remind her that she was not his mother. "A family has commissioned a monument for a beloved relative who is lingering at death's door. I am trying to finish it for them so they will be able to lay their loved one to rest in the style they feel most appropriate."

Her expression brightened as her brows climbed up her forehead. "They are paying you extra for finishing in time, eh?"

He nodded and slipped in past her to retrieve several pork pies and a Chelsea bun for his plate. He trudged upstairs, eating as he went, ignoring her protests that food was not to be taken from the dining room. Her voice faded away by the time he reached his room. Tossing aside his coat and shoes, he was asleep before his head hit the pillow.

Sometime near noon, hunger pangs forced him out of bed. Annoying, but useful as well, considering the work he had yet to do. He paused at a bakery on the way to the Guild Hall, polishing off a slab of cheese between two hearty slices of bread as he walked. Some days, it felt like all he did was eat.

He allowed the noisy horsecar with its gaudy gold trim to pass, then ducked across the street in its wake. How would Allbright react to the news that he was sponsoring Miss Fuller? It might please the Guild Master that he no longer needed to decide the matter, or render him livid that the decision was taken from his hands. One could never be certain with men in positions like his. Especially when they affected such a cheerful mien most of the time.

At least this way Sir Wilbert could assess Miss Fuller himself—what happened after that would be out of David's hands. But if the baronet could not see the value Miss Fuller brought, then perhaps the Wrights deserved to die out for their sheer stupidity.

Certainly, she was fiery and unconventional, even a bit unladylike in her expression and demeanor at times. But what she created had a magical quality, and it had been a rare privilege to witness and even be a part of her process. More than that, it was transformative to work with someone whose basic understanding of everything he thought he knew was fundamentally different to his.

The freedom it gave her—and him, when he attempted to use her methods. Yes, his was a crude apprentice's effort next to hers. But with practice, he could, he would, become proficient. He would never be able to work the Elements in the same old ways again. And he would be better for it.

But there was more than that. Unfortunately, confusingly, and with so many complications, there was more.

He had once thought her plain, but it had been because he had never seen her, not until she was deep in her craft. And then, oh stars above, the transformation. Never, never had he seen a woman so ethereally beautiful as Miss Fuller at her craft. Beauty should not sway him. It was a temporal thing, to be sure. But in this case, there was no arguing, it was a reflection of something deep, even profound, within her, something that compelled him to know her more.

But would she allow it? Every inch of her was guarded. Guarded in ways he could not blame her for. There were excellent reasons, but they only drove him to explore the mystery further.

If for that reason alone, he had to shake sense into the Guild and see her granted at least Master Fire Wright status, if he could not sway them to grant her Full Wright status. If that didn't happen, she would disappear from Brighton, and from his life. And he could not have that.

And he was getting ahead of himself. One step at a time. And that first step started with a conversation with Allbright.

Down two flights of stairs, in the carpeted stone hall, lit by gaslamps and clever mirrors, Allbright's door was closed, as usual. David knocked.

"Come in, come in." The door opened and Allbright shuffled back to permit him inside. "I am glad you are come. Saves me the trouble of sending for you. Take a seat. We have much to discuss." He turned toward his desk, pumping his arms in a purposeful stride.

David sat in the chair Cinderford liked to use.

Allbright smoothed his grizzled beard and settled himself behind his huge Tudor-decorated desk and chuckled. "Don't think I missed that. The Secretary is a bit territorial, but it is a typical trait of flame-tamers. They all do it. Don't take it personally."

"I will keep that in mind, sir." David pushed back strands of hair that Allbright's wright-crafted breeze had tossed into his eyes.

"It is good to have a solid, steady stone-man to balance him out." Allbright folded his hands on his desk. "I saw you leave the reception with Sir Wilbert. Is there anything I need to be aware of?"

So many things, but not all of them would Allbright either comprehend or embrace. "I am sure he has told you that the Crown is interested in establishing a more formal educational process for Wrights.

Our work with Brighton College seems a logical place to begin the process."

Allbright stroked his long beard. "What is your opinion of his ideas?"

The hair on the back of David's neck prickled. "I believe they are the opinions of the Crown and the Royal Court Guild."

"Be that as they may, what do you think?"

"Does it matter?"

"Humor me, Enright. Answer my question." Allbright leaned in, brows drawing in, forehead furrowing.

"He seems to have progressive thoughts toward all matters pertaining to our Skill and our Guild." Must not fidget or appear flustered.

"I noticed as much." Allbright pulled back a fraction.

"You seem ... reserved."

"That is a fair assessment." Allbright tapped his fingertips together in an ominous rhythm. "What he seems to hint at would involve a great deal of change. What is wrong with the old and proven ways?"

David resisted the urge to look for something large and toothy, lying in wait for the Guild Master's signal to devour him. "Nothing has to be wrong with them, sir, in order for new ways to be considered. Was there anything wrong with the old ways of doing so many things that factories now do faster and more easily? I would argue, not. They were not wrong, but the new ways might have advantages that make them worth considering."

"Spoken like a true politician, Enright. A true politician." Allbright's snort suggested that might not be a compliment.

David squared his shoulders and let his expression drift towards a scowl. He might be the most junior officer and Full Wright in Brighton, but enough. "Is that a compliment or an insult? Sir."

Allbright crossed arms over his chest and laughed. "I knew you would be good for the Guild."

Odd. "I'm not following you."

"Change is hard for people, and it seems even more difficult for those who feel threatened."

"Threatened, sir?"

"Yes, threatened. You know as well as I, we are at risk of going the way of the dinosaur—whether or not we talk about it, every Wright is well aware that we are a dying species. But we react to it differently. Some among us," Allbright glanced at the chair David occupied, "want to dig their heels in, while others, like the Royal Court Guild, are desperate to try new ways to save ourselves."

"And you, sir, where do you stand?"

"Where do I stand? That is an excellent question. I suppose, while I am not as radical as you—who it is widely believed, will do anything to save our kind—I am open to some change and new things. Like Sir Wilbert's desire to expand our efforts to identify Wrights in Brighton College. It is an apt notion, and one that might even be expanded upon. Have you any idea how many institutions calling themselves schools there are in Brighton alone? Well over one hundred."

Remain neutral, do not let on surprise. "I had no idea."

"The majority of them are boarding schools for young gentlemen and young ladies. Those are the kind of young people least likely to encounter a Master Wright who might identify any Skill they would have."

"That's an excellent point. Those who can afford education like that aren't looking for apprenticeships where Wrights might encounter their offspring. If we were to have access to such schools—"

Allbright slapped his desk. "Think how many more Wrights could be brought into the fold. A promising notion, eh?"

"Very much so, sir." David stroked his chin. "You say half the schools are girls' schools, though?"

"There are those who argue wrighting is a uniquely male endeavor, but desperate times require desperate actions. And checking for the possibility of females with the Skill seems prudent."

"I agree. Perhaps it might be easier to gain access to those girls' schools if a woman were sent in."

"Male masters are employed often enough, so I am not sure how necessary—"

"Hear me out, sir." David leaned his elbows on Allbright's desk. "Would not the school mistresses and parents alike be much more amenable to a woman entering their midst? It would raise fewer eyebrows and be of far less concern, no? And if we are truly committed to finding new Wrights—"

"Yes, yes, I know, there must be due consideration given toward the fairer sex. The problem is—"

"There are few female Master Wrights." David's heart raced. Could it be this easy? "If I might—"

"You're going to bring up that Fuller woman, aren't you?" Allbright sighed and squeezed his eyes shut.

"It seems a logical consideration."

"We have noticed you spending a lot of time in her shop recently."

"I have nothing to hide, sir. The project she is working on is a complex piece of damaged marble that I previously installed in a client's home. That client engaged me to deliver it to her shop. She has permitted me to watch her work in exchange for assistance lifting and placing some of the heavy stone."

"I see." Allbright drummed his fingers, a thoughtful look crossing his face. "You earlier argued for her application for Mastery to be considered. Now you have seen her work. What is your opinion?"

"I will step in as her sponsor if that will facilitate the process." David held his breath.

The look of surprise on Allbright's face was almost comical. Almost. "Sponsor someone who did not apprentice with you? That is almost unprecedented."

A fact hardly lost on him, or on Sir Wilbert, when they had discussed the same thing. "Yes, sir, I am aware."

"That is a real risk to your reputation, especially considering you suggested she be examined in public."

David winced. Maybe that would teach him to think through his wild ideas a bit more carefully first. "I realize that, sir."

"And you are still determined to sponsor her?"

"Entirely. It would be our loss not to count her among us, especially considering what the Crown wants of us."

"Cinderford isn't the only one who is going to be unhappy with this. Her father ruffled quite a few feathers around here, and folks have long memories. You never met Morris Fuller, but even you would have found him a contentious old curmudgeon who cared only about being right. Even all these years after his death, few have forgiven that arrogance. His daughter hasn't helped herself either—she has her mother's flame-tamer temper and her father's pride."

"You knew about her mother? I had thought—"

"The Brighton Guild did not recognize her, if that is what you are asking. And a good thing it was, too. A woman with that sort of temper is a liability."

"And that is being held against Miss Fuller as well?" Of course, there had to be another obstacle.

"People have long memories."

"Does that mean, sir, that you will not approve my sponsorship?"

"Denying her with an active and influential sponsor such as yourself would be a difficult position to defend. I wish you had asked me about it first, but I suppose there is little choice but to allow it. However, your suggestion that she demonstrate her Mastery to the Guild Assembly later this week is definitely appropriate under the circumstances. No insult to your ability to identify Mastery, mind you, but, as you so aptly suggested, it seems the best way to satisfy everyone, all around."

David drew several deep breaths. "Do you question her capability, sir?"

"It is my role as Guild Master to question many things."

# Chapter 15

REBECCA REMOVED HER GLASSES and closed her eyes, breathing deep of the cool, damp, and stone-smelling air of the cellar workshop. Safe. Quiet. Alone.

She'd spent too many hours working in the back room with Mr. Enright, where everything still felt unsettled, unstable. Here things seemed normal, uncomplicated, at least as much as anything ever was. She knelt near the wall to the left of the stairs, near the stone arch, and stroked the wall.

Funny how much easier stone had become to manipulate since working with Mr. Enright. Not that it had been difficult before, but having now seen the staid beauty of the Element, appreciating its strength and stability through his eyes, it was far less effort to coax it into complacency. She pressed into the wall, hollowing out a niche the size and shape of her not-yet-repaired lockbox. No more keeping it under the bed. The workshop was far safer.

She rocked back on her heels and examined her efforts. Plain, simple, serviceable, hardly something she could be proud of. One day she might pretty it up a bit. But for now, she needed to save her energy for the work on the mantel.

The work that could solve so many of her problems.

The task was nearly completed, thanks to Mr. Enright's steadfast help. And if he was able to fulfill his promises, either one of them, then ... oh, what would happen then? She wrapped her arms around her chest and held her breath.

Was it really possible they would recognize her as a Master Wright of any variety? As a proper member of the Guild with all the rights and privileges she had been paying her dues for? Heady, heady stuff indeed.

That would mean she would finally be able to price her work appropriately, pay her bills, and fend off rabid dogs like Mallory. Not to mention proving the worth of her father's legacy. That would be something.

Would he have been proud of that? Probably not; not unless she attained the status of Full Wright.

If she were made a Full Wright, though...

No, dare not consider that. That would be too much. All of this was too much to consider. Too distracting. If she simply got paid for her work when the mantel was delivered, she would be free of her debt to Mallory—who might even be convicted of forgery and who knew what else, if Mr. Enright kept his other promise—free to make her own choices.

Choices like leaving Brighton if the Guild rejected her.

It would be difficult, leaving the shop Father founded. But what option would there be if that happened? Pride alone would demand it.

But what about him? Mr. David Enright?

Was there anything more than professional interest there? Maybe simple friendship? That was possible. That was good.

But was it enough?

She laced her hands behind her neck and pressed her elbows to her ears. What did enough even mean?

Nothing for the moment. Just a distraction she did not need. There were important things to be done.

It did not matter that he was the one to suggest that she visit the constables to report the theft and suspected forgery. It was the right thing to do, regardless. One she might not have had the courage to pursue, but for his insistence. But still, it made sense.

She marched upstairs, tucked her battered lockbox in a canvas bag, locked up the shop, and headed for the police station.

Three broad limestone steps led a steady stream of traffic up to the imposing police station door. The sort of place she avoided whenever she could. Not the police; constables were neither here nor there. But the crowd, the traffic, the jumble of so many things, jammed together, tied together with tension and frustration that inspired loud, angry words, and sometimes weeping. The thought alone threatened to produce an epic headache that could span days.

In the most technical sense, she had done what she had been asked and visited the police. Granted, that had not been what he hoped she would do there, but that was a technicality, wasn't it? She could go now and avoid the sensory storm waiting within. That was a good notion, yes?

No, no, it was not and not a way to help herself if the Guild would not. So, in she would go.

One, two, three deep breaths. One more and she would flee, so she yanked on the door.

The heavy door swung open, revealing a bright, busy landscape of uniformed men bustling about, dodging people, desks, and chairs as they went, and citizens in their street clothes, sitting or standing about as though waiting for something to happen. So many people all talking at the same time. The sounds, sharp buffeting waves of Air assaulted her, unrelenting.

A uniformed man directed her to a chair with instructions to wait to be called. Seems like he should have asked why she was there. Would that not help to get her to the right person sooner? Release her from this awful place more quickly? From the look of it, that didn't seem to matter to anyone but her.

She sat back and pulled her senses inward. There was so much happening around her. So much movement, so many materials, fighting one another instead of working in harmony. Why could not mundane craftsmen recognize when two materials did not harmonize? Find a way to coax them into cooperation, rather than allowing them to declare their disunity as they struggled in a battle only Wrights could detect? The sensory cacophony—she might crawl out of her own skin if she did not escape.

This, this was why she kept to herself and away from the public sphere. Nothing was worth this torture!

She sprang to her feet, bag clutched against herself. The door—only a few steps away...

"Miss Fuller?" She turned and stared into Constable Moore's concerned face. "Are you well?"

"I...I am sorry. The noise... it caught me off guard." She winced and pressed her temples.

"It can be a bit much. Would you like to come to my office and tell me why you are here?" He took her elbow and guided her toward the back of the building, to a small room with a door that blocked out so much of the commotion.

Plain furnishings outfitted the office. A wooden desk, two chairs, two bookcases flanking a window opening onto a narrow alleyway, a wooden chest of drawers, and a brass gaslight. Each piece was simple, well-made, and in harmony. The sensory pressure lifted enough for her to remember why she was here. Weight slipped from her shoulders, and she could breathe again.

"Much quieter in here. Please, sit down. Can I get you a cup of tea?" He pulled a chair away from the desk.

"Yes, thank you. That would be very helpful." As would a few minutes alone to gather her wits.

He strode out.

She needed to word all this carefully if she wanted to be taken seriously. Everyone knew hysterical women got a pat on the head, a cup of tea, and were ushered out the door without so much as a note recorded of their visit. Given that she had already been offered tea, she had to conjure a calm, factual presentation that would keep this from being a useless effort.

Constable Moore returned with a steaming cup of tea. "I added a spoon of sugar. Seemed like the sort of thing you would like."

"Thank you, that is most kind." She sipped the watery brew, the sugar being the only thing giving the hot water any flavor at all.

He sat behind his desk, lacing his hands and leaning on his elbows. "So then, what brings you here? Have you had another encounter with Mallory?"

She took another swallow of tea and breathed a deep gulp of air. "After a fashion. I know you told him to stay away from my shop. But he came by to remind me of my upcoming payment."

"Did he become violent?"

"Not precisely."

"Did he make threats, then?"

"Yes, but not in the expected way." Her voice thinned. No. Control. She would maintain control.

He pulled a notepad and pencil from his drawer and poised himself to write. Thank heavens! He was taking her seriously! "Tell me exactly what happened."

"While I am very well aware of when my payments are due, and have never missed one, he felt the need to appear in person to remind me, which is odd. He has never done that before. Moreover, he referred to a clause that I have never seen in the loan contract he signed with my father."

"What manner of clause?"

"It is called an acceleration clause. One that said if I missed a payment, the entire amount would become due immediately." The teacup clattered against its saucer as her hands shook, threatening to spill the remaining tea. She set the cup on the desk.

"While unfortunate, it is not an unusual provision in moneylending."

"So I understand. But the problem is not the clause, but that it was not in the original contract."

He laid down his pencil and pushed the notebook aside. "Then all you need to do is go to the magistrate and produce the original contract. It is not a police matter."

"That is the problem. When I went to get my copy of the contract, this is what I found." She dropped the battered lockbox onto the desk. "This is the box where I kept it, in my room, under my bed."

He lifted the box and turned it round in his hands. "A right fine job of this, no? Must have taken quite some force to open it. But what makes you think Mallory was involved? Was your home broken into?"

"No, there was no break-in. But when I found it, I remembered that, on the day you found Mallory trying to beat my door down, his son, the boy who wanted my help, escaped from his grasp and ran upstairs. I usually keep the stairs locked, but somehow had forgotten that day. The boy came down while you were taking my statement in the shop. Do you recall?" His dark brow knotted, and he looked away for a moment as though watching the scene in his mind. "Yes, yes, I recall seeing him come out of the stairway."

"Since there was no break-in, and he is the only person who has been alone in my home, I have to think the boy was working in cahoots with his father, that this was a plot by Mallory to change the contract in his favor."

"The assault on this box would have been loud. Would you not have heard it happening?"

"I expect the boy was at work on my box at the same time his father was trying to beat down my door."

"I see. It makes sense. And it seems the kind of shenanigans his sort of man would be up to." He chewed the end of his pencil. "Was there anything else taken?"

"There was cash in the box, set aside to pay Mallory."

"I am sorry to hear that, but it provides greater impetus for me to investigate, so that is something. Back to the contract, though. Did Mallory try to provide any documentation for his claim?"

"He shoved a contract under my nose, with what he purports to be my father's initials beside the clause. But it was not the original, nor was that my father's handwriting."

"Do you have a copy of that document?"

"It is with Mr. Enright, the barrister, who has offered to act on my behalf in this matter." Her cheeks flushed as though she had just confessed to some illicit affair with the man. Heavens!

"You hired legal counsel?" His rich, nearly black eyes widened—strange for a man who claimed to be rarely surprised.

"He ... he owed my father a favor, and on that basis, offered to help me." A slight stretch of the truth, but hopefully not one too noticeable.

"I see." He chewed his lower lip and shook his head.

"Is there something wrong?"

"Nothing I can speak of. Please, ask no more." He lifted an open hand.

What other sorts of complications did Mallory present?

"I will pay Mr. Enright a visit soon. Also, Mallory and his son." He scribbled a few more notes. "I expect that will only make Mallory even angrier, though. It is possible the boy might come to you again for help. It goes without saying that you should not interact with either of them, no matter what their story is. If the boy is a pawn in this, you cannot trust any story of woe that he tells you."

"I would like to think I am better than to fall for such a thing. But I appreciate the warning, nonetheless. I will keep away from the boy. As for his father, that might prove more difficult. I expect him to come calling to collect payment in a few days. What do you recommend I do?"

"Pay him what you owe and do not make him angry."

"And if I cannot?"

"I strongly suggest you make arrangements to be away from Brighton. Leave your direction with me, and I will let you know when you can return."

# Chapter 16

THE NEXT MORNING, DAVID pulled back the cover on the granite monument in his workshop and settled onto his work stool in front of it. The low stool put his knees nearly into his armpits, but that was the price one paid for being long-limbed. Sunlight through the frosted windows bathed the white granite and glinted off the mica flecks near the surface. He laid his fingertips on the cool, smooth surface. So steady, so reliable. How could anyone miss the many perfections inherent in this bit of Earth?

Steady strength and peace flowed into his soul. As much as his fanciful mind would believe these feelings came from the stone itself, they did not. Stone had no feelings, but its nature was solid, orderly. Perfect. And such stability, that was soothing.

He traced the angel carved into the monument. After applying Miss Fuller's techniques, the stone was as docile as limestone, malleable as clay in his hands. What a profound difference. He could craft a level of detail he had never attained. The Penn family would get full value for their pound. And he would have an exceptional bit of workmanship to point future clients to, even if they had to go to a cemetery to see it.

Future customers.

When had he started seeing himself as a stoneworker? It had been so long since he had "plied his trade" as a barrister—almost another lifetime ago. Even stranger, that of all those in the Guild, Miss Fuller would be the one to call him back to it.

Granted, it was his idea to take up her cause. And he had to argue with her a mite to allow him to do so. Even so, it was on her behalf that he could finally demonstrate himself as Guild Legal Counsel, perhaps paving the way for the Guild at large to view him in that light and return him to his first passion, the law. If that happened, he would owe her more than she understood.

His heart raced and breath caught in his throat. Finally, to step into the role that Uncle Rutter had hoped he would fulfil when he left David the shop, one that might allow him to help shape the future of the Guild.

He raked his hair out of his face. All right, that was getting ahead of himself a bit, not to mention tending toward the dramatic, but once in a while, it was not a terrible indulgence, was it?

And perhaps not the only indulgence to which he felt entitled. That blasted mantel was nearly complete. Finishing a work of that magnitude warranted a celebration, even if Miss Fuller considered that far too indulgent for her lifestyle.

How best to celebrate? Sharing a glass of wine would certainly be appropriate, but a mite unsatisfying. No, a proper meal, at one of the dining rooms, perhaps the ones at the Continental Hotel. That would be far more fitting.

But what would she say to it? Obviously, he would pay for it. But might that make it sound like more than it was—

Which was exactly what?

What would the invitation be? Two colleagues celebrating an accomplishment? Yes, it would be that. But there was more. Once the business of her Mastery was completed, then in the Guild's eyes, they would be equal. And he wanted to meet her as equals.

Never had there been a woman he had truly considered his equal. So never had there been a question of matrimony or any of the homely things that went with it. But she changed it all. The possibility of home and family seemed different now. Less drudgery and more comfortable, was that the right word for it? Going home each night to someone who understood everything about him, something appealing in that.

Yes, it was far too early to talk about such things out loud, but in the privacy of his thoughts, it was pleasant to contemplate.

Pleasant, if complicated. Very complicated.

She was complicated.

In the end, Allbright seemed relieved that he would not be deemed responsible for bringing the daughter of Morris Fuller up for consideration as a Master Wright. He expressed concern that it could become a blight on David's reputation if things went badly for her, which Allbright feared they might. Did he have as little faith in her skills as he made it sound, or was that a mere political cover, presenting what people wanted to hear rather than what he actually believed?

No way to know yet, but something to figure out. David needed to understand not just where Allbright stood, but how he played his hands.

Cinderford, of course, put up a jolly show of objecting to her, all the while winking at David as though they shared some special confidence between them. It was tempting to explain to him how little Cinderford actually understood, but prudence suggested revealing that truth just now was not the best way to play this game.

It shouldn't have been surprising that Treasurer Fitzsimons was the one to raise the biggest stink when the news made its way through Guild Hall. Of course, he objected to considering anyone who had not paid proper dues. That was the kind of thing a treasurer would squawk about. But Allbright overrode the objections, suggesting that it was more important to focus on the overall good of the Guild than to obsess with account balances. And he hinted that all the accounts would be made to balance, in ways which he did not explain, which was rather concerning, especially when Allbright did not deign to discuss the matter further.

For now, though, the issue was tied up in a neat little bow, and David could deliver the news and the formal request to demonstrate her work for evaluation at the next Guild Assembly. He patted his pocket. Yes, it would be nice to deliver good news for a change.

News that deserved celebrating—oh, there was a thought. Yes. That might be a way to present his invitation for dinner. It was traditional for sponsoring Masters to celebrate their journeymen that way...

Thud!

Damn. That would be the shop door, making a dent in the wall behind it.

He threw the cover over the granite and hurried out of the workshop, locking the door behind him.

"There you are." Mallory swaggered toward him.

The smell of cheap gin circled Mallory like a mangy vulture shedding loose feathers through the shop. There was a man who'd been on a proper bender, not the sort he and Miss Fuller had joked about. When had Mallory's drunken escapade started? His clothes seemed too fresh for him to have spent the entire night drinking, so he must have met sunrise with a pint or a bottle in his hand.

What chance that this wouldn't end in confrontation?

David tugged his coat straight and drew in a deep breath. Low at his sides, he opened his hands, gathering Air in his spread fingers. More difficult to control than Earth, but less likely to inflict mortal damage—at least without intentionally trying.

"You have some nerve, Enright, some nerve." Mallory balled his fists as he took a swaggering step closer.

"I've no idea what you are talking about."

"That trollop, Fuller. You 'ad her set the police on me and the boy. I got that straight from the constable's secretary. She saw Miss Fuller bending Constable Moore's ear yes'erday."

"What has that do to with me?" David drew his hands up and elbows out, pulling Air toward him in a ready pool.

"You don't think I know? It were your idea, no doubt, that she do it. She would never come up with such a thing 'erself. Never done such a thing a'fore."

What manner of harassment had Mallory subjected her to before? "You think her so cowed, so frightened of you she would not turn to the law for protection?"

"I ain't done nothing, just seeking what I'm due for the injustice she dun ta me." Three steps across the shop and Mallory was so close that his gin-soaked breath tickled David's face. "I's only gonna warn ya once, yeh? Don't put your nose where it don't belong, stonemason." Mallory stabbed a pointing finger into David's shoulder.

David held his ground. "In this context, I am a barrister. I would remind you to refer to me as such."

"What kind of barrister gets his hands dirty with work? You can't be no proper one, eh? What respect can be due you?" Mallory spat at David's feet.

David pushed Air at him with one hand and pulled with the other.

Mallory spun, tottered, and stumbled back. "What'd you jes do?"

David lifted an open hand. "Nothing. I laid no hand on you."

Mallory's brow furrowed, his slurred, drunken thoughts almost visible in the air before him. He shuffled forward, reaching toward David.

David flicked his fingers, and Mallory stumbled back, pushing at an invisible wall.

"There! I saw you! Your fingers moved. What'd you do ta me?" Mallory shook a pointing finger toward David.

"You're drunk. Go home, and I won't call the constables to deal with your sorry arse."

"I know what I saw. You did something to me. You're like her. That's why you're stepping in with her. You're a witch like her!"

"That is enough, Mallory, quite enough. Stop your raving and get out of here before I press charges against you." David grabbed him by the elbow and smoothed the floor under his feet. Mallory skidded and stumbled as David dragged him across the shop and shoved him out the door.

David threw the bolt with Mallory pounding on the other side, shouting stuff and nonsense about witchcraft, until he staggered away.

Damn drunken sot.

David leaned his back against the door and wiped the sweat from his forehead into his already sweaty hair. Though they were well past the days of witchcraft trials, it was not as though the Wrights had not suffered under them. Even from a drunken fool, the cries 'witch,

witch' were enough to freeze a Wright's blood in his veins. One might hope the modern age was beyond such things.

But it wasn't wise to trust in that too much.

One more reason Miss Fuller needed the Guild's backing. Stupid and alcohol-soaked as Mallory might be, a man like that could do her—and the rest of them—real harm.

Late that afternoon, the Fuller Fix-All cuckoo clock shrieked two of its required five times before Miss Fuller stilled its voice, and they headed down into the back room to finish their work.

"I cannot believe we are nearly done." She locked the door behind them, her voice less weary than it had been in days. Her cheeks had some color now, and the shadows had left her eyes. Eating before and after their work had improved their constitutions, just as he had hoped. "I would have been slaving over this until the last possible moment had it not been for your assistance."

He circled the mantel that stood proudly in the middle of the floor, balanced on legs now made more substantial than in its original incarnation, to accommodate the iron structure hidden within. It seemed to puff its chest out, pull back its shoulders, and demand attention paid in its honor.

Lovely, fine veins ran through the entire piece, uninterrupted, unscarred, a touch of detailed craftsmanship that would have been lost on most. Scrolls, leafy vines, and flowers climbed up the legs, reached toward the inner panels, and stretched to the shelf. Two plumb cherubim, with hands raised overhead, supported the shelf, flanked by more scrollwork. Delicate flowers lined the shelf's front edge, a detail that had not been present in the original, but should have been.

Underneath and unseen, an iron skeleton spanned the shelf's breadth, joined to the struts in the legs, stabilizing and lending strength to the wright-wrought amalgam of marble dust and stone fragments. A work far beyond the capability of all but a very few Master Earth Wrights.

He ran his hands along the entire piece, reaching deep within. Everything was exactly where it should have been, no gaps, no irregularities, no flaws. "It is truly a masterwork."

"Coming from a born Earth Wright, that is indeed a compliment. Thank you." Was that a blush blooming on her cheeks? So lovely.

"So then, what is left to do?"

"Not much. I would like to blend a few of the vines together better, and I am still not satisfied with the cherubs' faces. I still think they look more mischievous than angelic, don't you?"

He chuckled as he studied them. "Perhaps, a bit. But I like them better this way."

"As do I, but it is not ourselves we must please, but Mrs. Lackwood. And I am certain she has no tolerance for mischief."

"True enough—I swear she has no sense of humor at all."

"Absolutely none." She pressed her hands to her cheeks and drummed her fingers along her cheekbones. "I'm not exactly sure what needs to change on those faces."

He leaned in a little closer. "I think it is the turned-up noses and the shape of the eye, not quite round enough. Perhaps a bit fuller in the cheek and less in the chin as well."

"That makes sense. I should try that."

"Might I show you how I do that? I've done my fair share of cherubs on all the monuments I've worked."

"I hate to take up more of your time. You have more than paid your debt to me."

"Not a bother at all. It is rather fun. If you will lay your hands alongside mine near the face, you can feel what I am doing. The proportions are much easier to experience than to describe." Granted, there were other way to demonstrate, but none that would have her so close to him.

She arranged her hands, barely not touching his, on either side of the cherub, so close their warmth reached out to him. "I will start at the center of the face and work my way out, trying to avoid changing the actual head shape. That way, the whole composition will not have to be adjusted."

"That is worth remembering." Her breath tickled his ear.

Focus, focus. Now was not the time to lose himself in the distractions of her presence. "Reach into the stone with me."

The facial features required only the lightest touch, the slightest pressure to shift under his fingers. Her Skill was right there, hovering beside his, not quite touching, but fully present at the same time. He drew her Skill in, like taking her by the hand, and used it to shape the stone.

She gasped, but did not pull away, receiving his tutelage, welcoming it, embracing it as she claimed the knowledge as her own.

The experience—one he would remember for a lifetime—was over almost as quickly as it had begun.

"That was astonishing," she whispered, edging half a step back.

Just enough to leave a cold void where her presence used to be.

"You have taught me so much. I don't know how to thank you. I am quite certain our bargain has been unfair to you." She peeked up at him through her eyelashes. On anyone else, the expression would have been coquettish, but on her, it was cherubic innocence.

"Not at all. That block of granite has been clay in my hands. Easily the finest work I have ever done. Do not underestimate what you have taught me. I feel like all I have done was lift heavy objects, but, in light of that," he patted his pocket, "I have brought something else to the table."

She leaned back against the workbench, hands braced against the edge. "You spoke to them?"

"Yes, I did."

"You are smiling."

He was probably smiling like an idiot at this point, but did that really matter? Was it wrong to demonstrate how much he enjoyed his success? "Yes I am."

"So, what are the conditions of my acceptance? Who is aggrieved that I will be presented at all?"

"It was as you would expect. Allbright was not opposed, Cinderford, of course, was, and Fitzsimons was worried about unpaid dues."

"But he didn't refuse on that basis?"

He shrugged. "Allbright stepped in and decided to overlook the matter. However, if you have an opportunity, I would suggest you pay the current installment on your dues. I am sure the Lackwoods' payment will go far in making that possible."

"I hope so." She leaned back and sighed, a bit of the weight returning to her shoulders. "I've learned never to count money that wasn't already in my hands." She stared at the ceiling. "What sort of obstacles are they putting in my way toward getting accepted?"

"That is rather cynical, don't you think?"

"Am I wrong?" She challenged him with a cocked head and a raised eyebrow.

"It is nothing that will present you any difficulties."

"I am glad you think so, but perhaps, I should be the judge of that."

"Given the unique challenges of your situation—"

"Don't try to justify them. You sound like a politician."

"Given the unique challenges, Allbright thinks it would be best to go back to some older formalities."

Her eyes widened and her face turned white as the mantel. “That old blowhard wind-bag! He wants a public demonstration, doesn’t he?”

David gritted his teeth. Hopefully, she would never hear of his hand in the matter. “Assuming you are granted Mastery status, he believes that you will receive greater acceptance among your peers if they can observe your skills firsthand. I know it is not comfortable, but surely you see there is something sound in what he says.”

She stalked several circles around him and the mantel, shoving her glasses higher on her nose, and muttering under her breath things like ‘no one in recent memory’, ‘probably because of Father’, and ‘what do have they against females?’ He clenched his jaw—those words were not an invitation to discourse.

Finally, she turned on him and threw her hands in the air. “Fine, fine, if that is what it takes to please their sorry arses, then so be it. They will be pleased.”

“I feel the same way. But that is for tomorrow. Perhaps we should finish the job at hand before worrying about that.” He gestured toward the mantel.

“True enough. All that is left now is a thorough dust and polish. Has Mr. Lackwood tasked you with returning this monstrosity to his home and installing it?”

“Yes, just as we expected. My plan, pending your approval, of course, is to load it into the cart tomorrow and deliver it early the following day, while the street is mostly clear.”

“That seems reasonable. It will be odd, not having it to work on anymore.” There was something wistful in her tone as she retrieved a dustrag from the workbench.

"I agree. I had rather grown to look forward to the project." He pulled back his shoulders. "I wonder ... that is, I have been wondering ... we seem to work together very well."

"I had noticed the same."

"Would you consider, that is, are you amenable ... would you consider working together on some other project?"

She stared at him a moment, blinking hard. "That is an intriguing notion."

She did not deny him outright. That was positive. "Perhaps we might, if you are willing, discuss the matter more over dinner at the Continental Hotel dining rooms tomorrow. It is customary for sponsoring Masters to celebrate a journeyman's accepted application that way, so it seems appropriate."

She blinked more rapidly, as though trying to comprehend what she had just heard. "Dinner, tomorrow?"

He nodded, catching her gaze.

"I ... well, it never, I never ... all right, yes, thank you. It sounds pleasant."

Pleasant? That was a bit underwhelming, to be sure. But then again, from the lovely, hot-headed flame-tamer who stood, mostly wordless, before him, it was compliment enough.

REBECCA FINISHED POLISHING HER glasses and perched them on her nose to inspect the finished mantel. The wright-work done, morning sun filtered through the back room's open windows, sparkling off her finished work. After keeping the room shrouded from prying eyes for the entire course of her labors, revealing it now was like walking out in only her unmentionables, raw and exposed.

Which was an entirely too silly and sentimental a way to regard something designed and intended to be viewed and admired by important visitors. It was time to let it go—after one final examination.

Truth be told, it looked better than the image she had been given to work from. The subtle changes made all the difference, adding grace and elegance that had been just barely lacking before. Someone who knew it well would notice the differences.

The Lackwoods themselves might or might not. Or rather, Mrs. Lackwood might. Mr. Lackwood would simply be pleased to put the whole affair behind them and get on with life. He would be the easy one to deal with. She, on the other hand, would find some fault to nitpick. That was her way, impossible to satisfy, part and parcel of maintaining the upper hand.

As long as Mr. Lackwood paid her, his wife could—and would—say whatever she wanted.

Sighing, Rebecca gave the mantel one last swipe with the polishing rag and an affectionate pat, then scooted out of the way to make room for Mr. Enright and his crew to build a traveling frame around it. The temporary wooden cage would, according to him, give the men a safe set of handholds to lift from, and buffer it from bumps and jars in the process of transport.

Much as she trusted his expertise, and even more, his own investment in the project's success, the thought of transporting the cumbersome article turned her stomach. Though not more fragile—and probably less so, all told—than the original, undamaged mantel, after investing so much time, energy, and feeling into it, the possibility that anything might dare harm it again was nigh on unbearable.

And the thought that a drunken Lackwood might have another go at it with a poker—she shuddered and left the workroom. That would not, could not, be her problem.

Besides, she had other important issues to focus on. In a few days, she would demonstrate her mastery of Elements to the Master Wrights of Brighton. And her fate would be decided. So many things would be decided.

What chance that they would judge her fairly? Was there any safeguard in place that would ensure bearing the name Fuller alone would not condemn her? Mastery projects were traditionally judged after their completion, often with the name of the applicant not officially known. That kept the judging fair and unbiased. At least in theory.

No position of prestige and power was ever untouched by bias. Bribes and favors often influenced the promotion of Master Wrights and the promotion of Full Wrights. Especially with Full Wrights.

That was another point upon which Father earned the Guild's ire. He had no use for Full Wrights without the Skill to back up that name. Father called them pretenders and posers, unafraid to call out their deficiencies at Guild Assemblies. Not a great way to make friends or allies. Something else Father cared little for, but probably should have.

Mr. Enright would not pave her way with blackmail or other inducements. Nor would she have wanted him to. She needed respect as much as she needed the status, and that had to be earned. The old-fashion way. The hard way.

By impressing the everliving souls out of them.

She ran her fingers hard along her temples and onto her scalp. What could she do? What performance in front of an audience would clearly show her mastery over all the Elements? Or should she concentrate on a single Element, and settle for the title of Master Wright?

It would be easy to prove herself a Master Fire Wright. But her faculty with the Element could be her downfall there. Although the Guild claimed otherwise, people feared Fire Wrights, and were sometimes afraid to name the most powerful flame-tamers as Masters in the hope of keeping better control over them by limiting them to perpetual journeyman status. If she appeared more skilled than any of the current flame-masters—might be best to avoid the issue all together. Master Cinderford seemed the type to be easily threatened.

Dash it all! They all needed to grow up and stop being such fragile flowers who ignored the coming winter.

But that was the way things were. She didn't need to like it. Work with it, around it, yes, but not like it.

Perhaps she should seek standing as an Earth Wright. Her stonework was impressive, at least according to Mr. Enright, a native Earth Wright himself. Father would have thought that ironic. He always found fault with her stonework. Maybe it was Mr. Enright's tutelage that refined her Skill. But there again, if she were to show too much skill, the jealousy of the established Masters could work against her. Especially because she was already known to be a Fire Wright.

She could create a wind and rain storm within the Assembly Room to prove her mastery of Water and Air, though they might not appreciate having to clean up from the downpour afterwards. And no doubt, someone would start muttering some nonsense about weather control—a pipe dream for many Air Wrights, and it would not go well for her.

In that light, proving herself a Master in any single Element would not be difficult. Spreading her demonstration out among all the Elements, with no single one demonstrating excessive Skill, would be her best chance to prove herself without offending those prone to offense.

A Full Wright had to unify all the Elements in a single project. Like Father's clock, powered by fluid movement, enhanced by a touch of Fire, with Air-driven sound and housed in a case of Earth. Annoying as it was, none could deny the genius in the mechanisms.

There was a thought. A clock. It would be a fitting nod to her father's work, the kind of thing the Guild tended to appreciate. But no, the work was too fine, and too time-consuming for a roomful of cranky men to observe easily. She needed something still subtle in its demonstration that could be executed in a timely manner.

Her Wardian case had taken months to create and balance. Not the sort of thing an audience could appreciate from afar or with a brief glance. And she could not replicate it in a single evening, under observation, making it useless as a presentation of her mastery.

Bollocks!

The cuckoo clock overhead shrieked ten times, brazen as it mocked her dilemma.

Dash it all! Coming up with a proper task was every bit as difficult as actually creating the article itself. She might as well go back to bed, pull the blanket over her head and—

Oh, wait! Yes, that would work!

She dashed to her workshop, locking the door behind her. There was enough time to test the idea before getting ready for dinner with Mr. Enright.

The clock had just begun to shriek seven o'clock when Mr. Enright appeared at the door. Instead of silencing it, she slipped out and locked the door, leaving it to scream at an empty room. That should not have been so satisfying. After all, it had, indirectly, given her an excellent idea.

"I hope I am not out of place if I say how lovely you look this evening, Miss Fuller." He bowed from his shoulders.

Was it her imagination or had his dark suit been pressed and his shoes recently polished? Though still lank and lean, the suit hung in such a way as to emphasize his broad shoulders and fine posture. And a haircut? Yes, definitely. Gracious! How well it framed his even, pleasing features and earnest grey-green eyes.

Taking the time to curl the tendrils around her face and press her ruffly fluttery pale blue gown, the one that made her feel fanciful and fairylike, had been worth the effort. How embarrassing it would have been to be underdressed beside him.

"Thank you. That blue jacket suits you very well." Was he blushing? That was a first. And a bit sweet.

"Mrs. Gaskill insisted on pressing it for me when she heard I was going out to a dining room tonight. She wheedled that much information out of me, but no more. Fear not." He chuckled. "The horsecar will arrive soon. Shall we head to the stop?" He offered his arm.

Should she take it? What would he think if she did? What if she didn't?

He cocked his head and raised an eyebrow.

Yes, she was overthinking. She tucked her hand in the crook of his elbow as they walked to the horsecar stop.

Halfway between Fuller's Fix-All and the fashionable Montpelier Crescent, the Continental Hotel catered to a clientele somewhat less wellheeled than the Lackwoods, but more affluent than Rebecca had ever been—or hoped to be. How heartening that there were a few among the dining-room who looked like they were there, like her, to celebrate a special occasion with a rare treat. Comforting to know she was not entirely out of place.

Twenty or so small tables for two or four filled the dining room that took up most of the ground floor. Rich, warm wood paneling anchored the lower part of the walls, while fussy pink peonies climbed the wallpaper, buoyed by broad green leaves. Occasionally, a yellow bird peeked out behind the blossoms, as though playing hide-and-seek in a summer garden. Within the dining room garden, tables dressed with crisp white cloths and elegant crystal and china waited for occupants; maidens at a ball, hoping for partners.

Men in crisp, dark suits darted between tables, cloche-shrouded silver trays held shoulder-high, balanced on one hand. Hushed conversations lingered in the air, well-mannered and modest, not the assault on her ears that she had feared. Even the tempting scents from the kitchen wafted in, polite and well-behaved.

She sighed as some of the tension left her shoulders.

"You didn't expect the din of a pub on payday, did you?" he whispered in her ear.

She smiled weakly and shrugged as they were led to an empty table near the far corner.

"I asked for the quietest table. I would not have minded being seen with you in the middle of the room, to be sure, but I thought—"

"No, no, you were right. I much prefer someplace with less noise and bustle." She folded her hands in her lap and closed her eyes for a moment. "Are you not sensitive to such things?"

"I am, but not to the same extent you are. For me, it is light. Standing out in bright sun is like driving a knife through my temples." Such a look of understanding in his eyes.

It was the kind of thing she never shared—people thought her strange enough as it was. How astonishing that someone else knew the same torment.

"I have been told there is a theory that such sensitivity is directly linked to one's sensitivity and Skill as a Wright. A penance that balances the Skill we have."

"Interesting. I can't say I ever considered the possibility that I'm not simply a difficult soul." She looked away.

"I heard that same comment myself. My father thought that of me on many occasions, complaining to any who would listen about the trials of such a son." He shrugged as he glanced at the menu. "Do you find the same issues with respect to food and flavor? The evening special looks very good, by the way."

"Roast chicken with herbs and potatoes? Yes, that does sound appealing. When not half-starved from wright-work, I have been accused of being a picky eater. Although, everything from Birdy's kitchen has been acceptable. Perhaps because it is simple food. I have never given it much thought."

"The hunger is quite the occupational hazard, is it not?" Mr. Enright laid aside the menu and signaled to one of the waiters, who took their order.

"Indeed, it is." She plucked at the waist of her gown that was less fitted now than the last time she had worn it. "Is it only me who is regularly accused of having a parasite or a disease?"

"Hardly. Mrs. Gaskill is ever on about that, recommending one doctor or another. I wonder that people feel so free to comment on things of which they know nothing and are absolutely none of their business." He tugged at his too-roomy white collar. "Have you considered what your demonstration of Mastery will be? It is a shame your Wardian case is—"

"Far too subtle and sophisticated for a group of skeptical old men to appreciate?"

"That isn't the way I would have put it, but since you have said so, yes. Quite." He wrinkled his nose and glanced at the ceiling. "I suppose the question then is what would impress them, no?"

"I had a thought, and I would like your opinion on it." She peeked down at her tightly clasped hands. "Though, if you tell me it is a terrible idea, I am not sure what I shall do, as I have no other solid possibilities."

"I am intrigued. Tell me." He leaned forward with boyish anticipation.

Hopefully, she would not disappoint. "When I fixed that seam on your jacket, you mentioned how fabric is a notoriously difficult material for Wrights to work our skill upon."

"Indeed. There are few who will even bother trying. Are you considering doing a garment?"

"Not in the traditional sense, no, but rather treating a fabric to give it useful properties like—"

"Enright? David Enright!" A lean man of medium height, with heavy mutton chops and a shaggy brow, sauntered in toward them from near the center of the room. His fine black suit and crisp white shirt had been tailored to drape perfectly over his just-bordering-on-gaunt form, and his shoes polished to a blinding shine. More than his garments, his posture and carriage declared he was a man of some consequence, likely with a title and connections to prove it.

Mr. Enright stood so abruptly he nearly yanked the tablecloth off the table. "Sir Wilbert! Fancy seeing you here."

A title! She was right.

"Yes, yes, I know. My hosts find it disconcerting that I would choose this place, but I have a weakness for their roast chicken. Best I've ever encountered. Far better than what my live-in-Seven-Dials-in-a-fancy-crescent-townhome hosts are trying to ply me with." He glanced over his shoulder.

"Are the Lackwoods dining with you?" Mr. Enright peered across the dining room.

Great heavens! That man was connected with the Lackwoods? She half rose in her seat.

"Good Lord, no! They were happy to have me out of their hair tonight. Something about preparing for work done in their blasted drawing room before their twice-blasted dinner party. Dashed inconvenient timing that they schedule it on the same day as the Guild Assembly."

Mr. Enright's eyes grew wide, his voice dropping to hear a whisper. "Sir, should you not be more circumspect?"

Sir Wilbert snuffed. "I can see what she is. Surely, she is already aware of everything I have said. Are you not?" He bowed toward her.

She stood, gulping, searching for the nearest path of escape. "Just how do you know what you think you know, sir?"

"Young Enright here thinks far too well of himself to be out in company with a woman not his equal. That alone is sufficient clue. But with your petite frame and the way you flinch at every clink of fork on plate in the room, of course, it is obvious. Over time, one learns to recognize their own kind." Sir Wilbert cocked his head, a shaggy eyebrow raised high.

She exhaled heavily. It was a reasonable explanation, but one she would have to give a little more thought to later.

"I expect you are Miss Fuller, no? He mentioned your application to me."

She cast a quick glance at Mr. Enright. What inspired that guilt weighing on his brow? "Yes, sir. I am. You are familiar with my father, perhaps?" Granted, she probably should not have baited him with something so controversial, but if this Sir Wilbert was going to be so bold as to interrupt them, then she could meet him on an even field.

Sir Wilbert laughed as he pulled chair over from an empty table. He sat with them and signaled a nearby waiter that he had changed his seating. Mr. Enright apologized to her with his eyes.

Bold indeed.

"Quite so, Miss Fuller, quite so." He reclined back in a posture more appropriate for a wing chair in the parlor by the fire than a fancy dining room; so entirely comfortable, like he owned the hotel. "In fact, I have spent some time studying up on him over the last few days."

Mr. Enright cleared his throat. "Is that appropriate dinnertime conversation, sir?"

Sir Wilbert brushed aside the idea with a flick of his right hand. "Quite uptight, isn't he? But then again, you legal types are by nature. Have a little faith. If the Crown trusts me, I am sure you can, as well."

The Crown? Connections, she expected, but not of that sort. Who exactly was he? What connections did this man enjoy? Whose ear did he have?

Best keep a rein on her tongue.

"I found your father's theories quite interesting. Novel, to be sure, but not without some sound grounding. Especially considering some of the newest scientific research. Do you keep abreast of the research journals much?" Sir Wilbert leaned in on both elbows. Funny how those highest in rank could so readily ignore the bounds of etiquette, doing things which those lower in the social order would be excoriated for.

If his question had not sounded so sincere, she would have rolled her eyes, but she gave him the benefit of the doubt and restrained herself. "I do not enjoy the privilege of access to such things, I am afraid. It is not the sort of thing the local library is apt to carry."

"It is easy to forget how few have access to such publications. Once I left Cambridge, I found it difficult to stay current," Mr. Enright said.

"True, true. No offense intended, of course. You know that, eh? It is all so exciting to see how science, not that mystic mumbo jumbo, could lead us to a better understanding of what we are and what we do. Your father's theories are positively brilliant in light of that. Assuming you prove yourself at the Assembly the way your sponsor expects you will, I expect those same theories will experience quite a revival."

The hairs on the back of her neck rose and her skin prickled. "You are joking? No one has taken him seriously after—"

"Yes, that accident your brother suffered was unfortunate, but I cannot see how it had anything to do with your father's theories. If you ask me, it was more laxity in his oversight than a problem in his methods."

Had she heard him correctly? She pressed a hand to her chest and dragged in a deep breath. "I happen to agree with you, sir, but I am astonished you would have examined their reports so closely. Unfortunately, the local Guild authorities were quite convinced otherwise. Father was, politely put, unpopular among the local Guild members."

"Men believe what they want, particularly when it is convenient to what they already believe, eh?" He snatched a glass from the nearby empty table and held it out for a passing waiter to fill with wine, gesturing for their glasses to be filled as well. "But, be assured, they can be persuaded to change when the wind shifts, especially when it shifts from certain directions, if you know what I mean." He took a deep draw from his glass.

"You believe the wind might be beginning to shift?" Mr. Enright asked.

"Not yet, I don't. But after the Assembly, between your demonstration and what I have to say," Sir Wilbert looked at her, eyebrows inching up his forehead, "after that, it is possible everything that we thought we knew could change."

"Surely you exaggerate." She barely forced the words through her tight throat.

"No, I think not. But it comes down to what you make of the opportunity."

# Chapter 18

David stood in the mews behind Fuller's Fix-All as the sun peeked above the horizon. Just barely enough light to see. The streets, the mews, still serene, waiting for the day to begin.

Such a day it would be, following such a night. David raked the hair out of his face with his fingers.

Had meeting Sir Wilbert at the dining rooms last night been a good thing or not?

In many ways, it had not.

Sir Wilbert had made himself at home with them for the entire meal, including dessert and more wine afterwards. He had paid for the evening, which was the least he might have done, but considering the reputation many titled men had, David hardly took it for granted.

Still, Sir Wilbert had commanded the conversation and nearly all of Miss Fuller's attention. Granted, his stories about his role as royal tutor were fascinating. Who was not interested in a look into the workings of the royal court and all the personages involved there? And Sir Wilbert knew the Queen herself! Apparently, she was among the few individuals without Skill who had intimate knowledge of Wrights and the Guild. Of course, it was to be expected, but not something David had ever considered.

David had never been so close to someone who regularly rubbed shoulders with royalty. Without a doubt, a valuable connection to have when one hoped to serve as an officer in the Royal Court Guild one day.

But the timing! How pleasant it would have been to spend time and converse with Miss Fuller, apart from the work that they shared. Surely, they could talk about something more than Fire, Earth, Air, and Water. How else would he ever ascertain if she had an interest in him apart from the professional business of being Wrights? It was not the sort of thing one came out and directly asked. It should be, but it was not.

Or at least it seemed so. Where did one go to understand such things, anyway?

She had taken his arm on the moonlit walk to the horsecar and back to her shop, though. She had told him her favorite flower was a hyacinth, and he had told her he had probably never seen one, as his mother had a peculiar hatred of all flowers—they made her sneeze. She laughed and promised to teach him everything he should ever want to know about flowers.

That should indicate something, should it not? How was one to be certain? Perhaps, after she was awarded Master status, he might suggest a congratulatory dinner—at other dining rooms, far from Sir Wilbert. Yes, that seemed like a sound approach.

Assuming, of course, the Guild did as they ought and admitted her as a Master.

Despite the generous breakfast he had eaten, his stomach turned over in knots.

What if the Guild proved themselves hidebound imbeciles? What would happen then? He had already heard rumblings from Cinderford, who quietly insisted that they should fail to acknowledge mastery. She would then be classed as a perpetual journeyman and be left at that. She would be silenced and placed under permanent oversight that way and their problems would be solved. Done and done.

Ignorant, shortsighted, prejudiced flame-tamer who'd rather burn out an irritant than understand it.

Then what?

Could he afford to continue to associate with her if the Guild cast her aside? Could he achieve the sort of positions he sought while connected to someone declared a useless pariah—though nothing was farther from the truth!

Would he ever find an acceptable woman if he cast her aside, especially for something not her fault? No. Such an act would render him unworthy of an acceptable woman.

He had, long ago, come to grips with the notion that he might be a lifetime bachelor, and it was tolerable enough. Most of the time. But now that the possibility of something different dangled in front of him, it seemed the height of cruelty to have it torn away. On the other hand, giving up everything he had been working for all these years had a definite air of cruelty to it as well.

Dash it all! What he would give for a bit of clarity. He would have to work all that out later.

"Mr. Enright, you wanted to check out the wagon before we left?" Dillon Hughes, a gentle, lumbering giant, tapped his shoulder. The scars down his grizzled face and bulging muscles barely contained in his worn clothing gave the impression of a violent man, but no description could be more inaccurate. For all his great strength, he had a gentleness of touch and attention to detail that made him the perfect partner to move delicate stonework.

"I'm sure you've done your trademark excellent job, but I will give it a look simply to be able to tell customers that I've done so when they ask—and they always do." He ambled to the modest wagon and climbed in with the cargo.

The mantel sat nestled in its wooden frame, a marble caterpillar done up snug in its cocoon. Taut ropes and straps held it firm in every direction, with redundancies so if one gave way, another would seamlessly fill in for it.

"Excellent, as always. Fasten the canvas over the top, and we can be underway." David clambered across the wagon and over the back of the seat to sit beside the driver. The steady grey cart horse glanced over its shoulder, then turned back to the small pile of hay the driver had scattered to occupy it while the mantel was loaded.

Miss Fuller peeked from the back door, biting her knuckle, as she had been the entire morning. Who could blame her when so much was riding on this piece? He had tried to talk with her as Hughes' team was transporting it from the back room, but, wide-eyed and pale-faced, she couldn't manage her usual bright banter and seemed less agitated when he left her be.

"S'all ready, Mr. Enright? Shall the lads and I jump up?" Hughes asked, patting the side of the wagon.

"Up, the lot of you, and we'll get this done and dusted before the streets get busy." David waved them up.

Hughes' team arranged themselves at the four corners of the wagon, ready to lend stability to the mantel if needed. The driver clucked his tongue and urged the horse into a plodding motion. David gave Miss Fuller a confident salute as he settled in for what would be at least an hour's ride. She waved weakly and shut the door.

What should have been an hour turned into three. Long, worrisome, anxious hours.

A fire in one of the outbuildings of St. Nicholas Church called out the fire brigade, their horse-drawn engine, and a crowd of onlookers. The hand-pumped engine failed, leading to a bucket brigade, which Hughes' transport team felt obligated to join, leaving him alone with his driver to protect the wagon. The mantel was too heavy to be easily stolen, but some enterprising soul might have absconded with the horse and wagon. And there was always the possibility of damage, malicious or otherwise.

If only the fire brigade had a Master Water Wright available to manage the pump. How much inconvenience and destruction could have been avoided? Even if David could have made his way to the pump himself, his Water skills were no match for the task.

Few would have been. Even Miss Fuller.

What would it take to install a Water Wright of that caliber in such a position? Or perhaps a Fire Wright would be better suited? Could one snuff a fire on that scale? He never developed the skill in his own flame-training. Starting a blaze was far easier than extinguishing one.

Finally, finally, finally, the blaze and the crowd sputtered out. His team mounted the wagon, ashy and wet, but satisfied they had done their civic duty. Good citizens though they were, Mrs. Lackwood would hardly permit them into her house in that state to complete the delivery, so he sent them to clean up and meet him at Montpelier Crescent as soon as possible, while he and the wagon continued on their way.

There went another hour.

As the sun approached its zenith, the wagon pulled up to the Lackwoods' tradesman's entrance behind Miss Fuller, tool bag bouncing at her hip. Though she wore her usual drab workaday dress, with her hair pulled back in a plain knot, she was every bit as pretty as she was last night.

"What happened? Where is your team?" She gasped and stared at the sooty canvas tarp obscuring the mantel.

"So much for proper care and planning, I suppose. Did you, perhaps, hear of the fire at St. Nicholas Church? If not, I am sure you will soon. The team felt compelled to join the bucket brigade. I expect they will be here soon."

"The horsecar takes a different route, so no, I had not yet heard. But I am certain it will not be long until word spreads. Was anyone hurt?"

"As far as I could tell, no, only property damage." He jumped down from the wagon and joined her near the steps. "Are you here to check up on my work?"

"No, not at all. I am here to collect payment. Mr. Lackwood was quite clear that he would not pay me until the piece was installed. Of course, he only informed me of this after the work was nearly complete. I probably should have refused to continue at that point, but..." she shrugged.

Was she implying something about their working together and not wanting to disrupt that? The blush on her cheeks suggested it. Dash it all—now his cheeks were glowing as well. Hopefully, she wouldn't notice—or maybe it wasn't so bad if she did. "I am sure there will be no issues. Ah, yes, there's Hughes and the lads now! You are most welcome to observe, if you like."

"Your team will not be uncomfortable? I would hate to do anything that would impair their concentration."

"If anything, they will be more careful. Nothing'll ruin one's pride quicker than to stuff up in front of the one who's work one is moving."

"If you are sure then, I would find it reassuring to watch, so that if the Lackwoods find fault with anything—"

"You will be able to properly assign blame?" He chuckled and beckoned Hughes' team to release the ropes.

"That was not what I meant." Her brow furrowed. "Don't you know me better than that?"

"I am sorry, I am a terrible tease—"

"You were to have been here hours ago!" Mrs. Lackwood flew from the back door, screeching like a tiny angry raven. She sounded like the blasted cuckoo clock, all done up in blue ruffles and lace! "When someone says first thing in the day, I do not expect—"

"Is Mr. Lackwood here?" Miss Fuller looked over Mrs. Lackwood's head and into the house.

"You may deal with me." Mrs. Lackwood twitched her shoulders. So reminiscent of a scolding hen, David coughed into his hand to avoid laughing.

"No, madam, I will not. I believe I made that quite clear. If he is not available, then I am sure Mr. Enright and his crew can wait until he is in to conduct the installation." She glanced over her shoulder at the crew.

Hughes' jaw dropped and molded into a wide grin matched by the rest of his crew. Most of the working folks in Brighton would have liked to watch anyone standing up to the harpy, and seeing fiery Miss Fuller do so was a special treat.

"How dare you! They are not in your employ, but my husband's. Commence your work—"

"I am afraid not, Mrs. Lackwood." David stepped forward. "My arrangements are with your husband—"

"Who delegated to me—"

"No, madam. I will deal with him, or not at all. Get this cart turned around, boys, we'll take it back—"

"You will do no such thing. Wait here." She stormed into the house, slamming the door behind her.

"Now you've done it, gone and gotten the missus all up in a lather." Hughes ambled up, sniggering under his breath. "I'd just as soon not cart this bloody article full circle, but it'd be worth it to see her turn red as berry jam."

"Unfortunately, that will not pay the bills," Miss Fuller muttered, crossing her arms tightly over her chest and drumming her heel on the cobblestone.

She had so much riding on this. Who could blame her for being tightly wound right now?

The back door swung open and portly Mr. Lackwood emerged, pinching his temples and looking down a nose so sharp as to make him a caricature. "What happened to first thing in the morning?"

"Fire at St. Nicholas Church. Closed the road. Onlookers and the bucket brigade hemmed us in. Could not be helped." David stepped closer, scratching his cheek. The itchy soot on his face ought to carry his point.

"I suppose, I suppose. Get it on in. Mind the house and the furniture as you go. I will not hesitate to dock you for any damage done along the way. Miss Fuller, what are you doing here?" Was that a sneer curling his thin lip?

"I had been led to believe the mantel would be installed by now, so I am here to collect my payment."

"Of course." Lackwood rolled his eyes, as though expecting payment for her work was utterly unreasonable. "After it is installed, you may return—"

"No, sir. I am not paying for another horsecar ticket home and back. Unless you care to pay for it, I will wait."

Lackwood snorted and snuffled and blinked rapidly, as though he had never been contradicted and had no idea how to respond.

"Would you help me oversee the installation, Miss Fuller? That way, if there are any problems, you can address them right away." David gestured toward her tool bag.

"That does seem efficient. Excellent suggestion." She tossed her head, daring Lackwood to argue.

"Just get the bloody job done." Lackwood trudged back into the house.

"You heard the man, boys. Let's do the deed." David pulled back the canvas cover and Hughes' crew scrambled into action.

Several hours later, David and Miss Fuller stepped back to admire the newly installed mantel: clean, sparkling white in the midst of the toxic green wallpaper. While it was too pretentious for his tastes, exquisite craftsmanship was hard to overlook.

Mrs. Lackwood fluttered about, complaining about a bit of dirt here and there, a vein through the marble she did not like, and what she claimed to be a chip on the edge, which David had seen her create herself. Devious little shrew.

To her credit, Miss Fuller, though a bit pale and her color starting to match the walls—how could people live in this atmosphere?—cleaned off the dirt, explained that the vein was a natural feature of the marble and could not be altered, and ran her hand over the chip, repairing it as she did, with none the wiser for her efforts, and invited Mrs. Lackwood to examine the spot again. How perplexed and disappointed she was not to be able to find the damage she herself had wrought.

Shame that he could not enjoy that little show properly. He would congratulate her privately later, though.

"Have you any further concerns about the mantel?" Miss Fuller asked, voice so sweet it set David's teeth on edge.

"No. It is adequate."

Adequate? Insulting at best.

"Shall we proceed on our own to your husband's office, or do you prefer to escort us there?" David struggled to keep his voice and features neutral.

"Come." Mrs. Lackwood lifted her nose into the air and marched from the drawing room, down the green hall, to her husband's office, heels clacking on the polished wood floor. "There, he can deal with the likes of you both. And do not be surprised if I neither use your services again nor recommend you to my friends in the future." She threw the door open.

The woman thought far too well of herself. It was not the first time David had heard threats of that nature from cranky clients, and yet, word of quality work still circulated.

David ushered Miss Fuller in ahead of him.

"Miss Fuller?" Lackwood glanced up from his desk. Somehow, even while seated, he still appeared to look down on them. How? Probably something to do with the enormous chair he occupied. "Allow me to deal with Mr. Enright first. I do not conduct business with an audience."

"What are you trying to hide?" Miss Fuller demanded.

"Nothing. I have nothing to hide," Lackwood spoke through a clenched jaw.

"Nor have I. I have no objection to being paid in front of Miss Fuller. The price we agreed upon is fair, and I am not ashamed for it to be known."

"Here." Mr. Lackwood harrumphed and handed him an envelope. "As agreed. You may go."

What had there been to hide in that transaction? David checked the envelope and glanced at Miss Fuller. "I can have the wagon wait for you, if you like, Miss Fuller. Save you the fare of the horsecar to get back to the shop." Not to mention it would allow him some additional time with her.

She blinked, hazel eyes widening as the faintest blush rose on her cheeks. "I ... I ... that would be most considerate, thank you."

"Close the door on your way out, Enright." Lackwood waved him out, and this time, he would not be gainsaid.

David walked out, fighting the instinct to stay with every step.

A quarter of an hour later, Miss Fuller stormed from the back door, eyes blazing and heat radiating from her being. Great Scott! David helped her into the back of the wagon, her hand so hot she might have been dying of fever. If she did not calm down, she might light the straw padding in the wagon ablaze. Did she even realize? He gestured for her to sit with him near the driver's seat.

"What did he do?" he asked.

"Not what he did, but what he didn't." Miss Fuller clenched her fists so tight her arms shook.

"Didn't do?"

"As in pay me."

"What do you mean? He paid you nothing?"

Hughes' crew stopped talking and leaned in closer.

Miss Fuller stared straight ahead, eyes shimmering. "He cannot afford the entire sum, so has given me a small initial payment, and claims he will continue to pay installments." She swallowed very hard. "As he can afford to do so."

"He can't do that." David slapped the side of the wagon.

"That ain't right." Hughes grumbled.

The crew grunted sounds of agreement.

"Little matter. It is what he has done. I can hardly grab him by the throat and demand he pay, can I?" Given her expression, she might have done just that if David but nodded.

"The constables frown upon assault." David ran his knuckles along his chin. "We can simply march back in and remove the damn thing—"

"Aye!" Hughes pumped his fist.

"Yes!"

"Turn us about, he ain't—"

Miss Fuller lifted open hands. "I wish we could do such a thing. But he has already bolted the door and has a runner ready to fetch the constables and have them arrest anyone who attempts such a thing for burglary and theft."

"That by-blow of a Pimlico whore! He cannot get away with this." David snarled. "I will take the matter to court for you myself. This is unacceptable. He will be made to pay."

"That'll take a while." Hughes scooted closer to them. "But me and the lads will make sure they feel it starting today, won't we?"

The others laughed under their breath and began to whisper among themselves.

"Word that they shafted one o' our own out of fair wages won't take but a day or two to go 'round. Everyone to whom he owes money to will be at his door by the end of the week, demanding full payment. And there ain't one who'll be taking his credit no more. He'll be knowing the error of 'is ways right quick. God, what I wouldn't give to be a fly on the wall when 'is fine wife has her order turned down at the butcher when she don't 'ave ready coin to pay. That'll be a jolly sight."

"That is kind of you but—"

"But nothing! It's in our best interest not to extend credit to those who would do a turn like that. Every working bloke'll be interested in news like that. What's more they need to know. Self-interest, it is. It ain't no favor that need be repaid; though, if it were, you've done enough good turns to deserve it."

She managed a weak smile, then lapsed into the loudest silence David had ever heard.

# Chapter 19

THE MEN IN THE cart behind her muttered and planned, chuckling darkly as though enjoying the excuse to take a stand against those who had readily treated them as lesser creatures. To be sure, it was comforting to enjoy such support. And Mr. Enright's offer to represent her case against the Lackwoods—it was difficult to ponder what to make of it. It could mean so many things. He was a fierce advocate for fairness and justice, that alone could explain his zeal. But there also seemed to be something more personal ...

But none of that would solve her most immediate problem. Dick Mallory was coming tomorrow to collect on Father's debt, and, with the loss of her strongbox funds, there was not enough to meet her obligation. That alone was bad enough, but the acceleration clause... How long would it take for him to rip the shop, her home, from her hands?

And then what? Would the Guild step in to help? Surely not. They would more likely be happy to turn their backs and ignore her, to finally be done with her. Where could she go? Without family, would anyone take her in until she could get on her feet? Perhaps, since she didn't have the full amount for Mallory's payment, she shouldn't pay him at all, keeping that little bit she had to live from while she sorted out what to do next. Not that it would go very far—

"Miss Fuller?" Mr. Enright tapped her shoulder. "We're at the shop."

She jumped. Already? How was that possible? And so late. The afternoon sun struggled to climb over the roofline and into the mews. "Oh, yes, we are. I'm sorry, just a bit sidetracked." She needed to get a rein on her thoughts. Such distraction never served her well.

He jumped down and offered a hand to help her. Did he realize how much she needed it, or was he just being gentlemanly?

He patted the side of the wagon. "You boys get on. I'll find my own way back."

Mr. Hughes waved and jumped into the seat beside the driver, who signaled the horse to move on.

They stood side by side, watching as the wagon turned and returned to the street, the echoes of clopping hooves ringing achingly through the mews.

Now what? Where to even begin? Rebecca stepped toward the back door.

He followed. "May I come in for a bit?"

The last thing she wanted was conversation or company. To have to fix tea and engage in small talk? No. "If you wish."

Why? Why had she said that? She should have told him to go on, catch up to the wagon, and allow her to dwell in her own misery.

He followed her in and upstairs, their footsteps the only sound between them.

But what was there to say? Yes, he was the only one with whom she could discuss the situation, but what was there to say of which he was not already aware? What point in going over it all again? Nothing would change.

Surely, he would be compassionate and kind, but that felt too much like pity. He might be angry and vengeful, but she did not need an avenging angel. That sort of shows usually amounted to a great a deal of posturing and preening and expectations of appreciation, none of which she had time or energy for. She paused at the top of the stairs, clutching the stair rail for strength.

She needed to think, to sort out her options, to plan, not entertain.

"I can fix you some tea if you like." He slipped past her to the kitchen.

Dash it all. He was so determined. She pointed vaguely toward the teapot. At least he was offering to do something useful. There was that. How odd it was to watch someone else—a man no less—make tea. What man made tea? She sank down on a stool near the work-table.

At first, he tried to heat the water as she did, with his hands around the teapot, but, to his credit, gave up before he hurt himself or damaged the pot. He lit the hob, filled a kettle, and set it on the fire to heat the ordinary way.

"That little trick of yours is harder than it looks." He pulled out the other stool and sat down beside her.

She stared at the flames under the kettle on the hob. How long had it been since she had heated it there? Years. Yes, it had been years. "There is a particular knack to it, I suppose."

"Will you teach me?" The kettle whistled, and he went about making tea.

Truly, that was his concern? "At some point. You will forgive me if that might not be my top priority right now."

"I quite understand."

Arrogant, insufferable! She slammed her hands on the table and stood. "Do you? Do you really?"

He handed her a cup of tea and sat down again. "Perhaps a little more than you realize."

She sat down again and dropped several sugar cubes into her tea. "Do tell. When have you ever faced being cast from your home, without resources or friends?"

He glanced at her, then turned his gaze out the window. "I parted ways with my Uncle Cresswell under terrible terms. Not willing to endure another broken bone, I ran from the house with a blackened eye and a bloodied nose. I wandered the streets for a few hours, returning to find my bag packed on the back doorstep, with a note telling me in colorful terms where I could go with it. I had not a penny to my name."

That was unexpected. "You returned to your parents' house?"

"That was not an option either." He shrugged in a way that suggested those details were too painful to speak of, even now.

"What did you do?"

"Wandered. Did odd jobs as I could find them, living hand to mouth. Slept in alleys, attics, outbuildings, and barns, until I could save enough for train fare to Cambridge, where I looked up an old teacher of mine who set me on my current path."

"I would never have guessed. You clean up rather well." Why did that bit of history render him even more attractive?

"Master Earth Wright McIntire was a taskmaster, to be sure, but he connected me with the Cambridge Guild chapter, convinced that I could be a Guild Barrister, or more. But more would require becoming a Full Wright, which he also convinced me was possible."

"It must be nice to have such friends."

He turned and caught her gaze, his grey-green eyes more intense than she had ever seen them. "You are not without friends, Miss Fuller."

"That is kind of you to say, but—" The words caught in her throat. No, she would not cry. It would do no good and only complicate matters further.

"It is the truth. You heard Hughes and his men. They are happy to spread the word of Lackwood's deeds. I would not be surprised if he somehow finds the money he owes you when he discovers how hard his life becomes."

"One might hope so, but I doubt it will be in time to be of any real use to me. Mallory will be coming for his pound of flesh before any court or terrible gossip can have effect." She covered her face with her hands. It was bad enough to know it was coming, but to endure the pity on Mr. Enright's face ...

He touched her hand. "They are not your only allies in this matter. First," he reached into his jacket and withdrew the envelope Mr. Lackwood had given him. He counted out the bills and laid them on the table. "I want you to take this."

She stared, first at his face, then the money, then at him again. "I cannot take that from you. You have obligations of your own, and I don't know when I'll be able to pay you back. No. Debt has caused me enough problems. I will not add to it, hoping to improve the situation."

"You must." He pushed the bills toward her. "I do not immediately need this sum, and I am also confident you will pay me back."

She crossed her arms over her chest and pulled them in as far from the cash as she could. "How can you be certain?"

"Lackwood cannot avoid paying you what he owes."

"Mr. Hughes' intended gossip campaign is well-intentioned, but hardly assured. And, while I appreciate your offer to take him to court for payment, there is no telling how long that might take. And, to be honest, I have little faith in the courts on my behalf."

"I understand. But there is one more thing I will bring to bear on the situation that will play Lackwood's own greed against him. Men such as that will often be moved by their own interests even when justice does not appeal to them." A satisfied little smile played at the corner of his lips.

"What do you mean?"

"I will have a conversation with Sir Wilbert. He is staying with the Lackwoods, but more importantly, the Lackwoods dearly wish to impress him. His visit was the reason the Lackwoods were so desperate to have the mantel repaired. As I understand, Sir Wilbert is in a position to influence a certain childless baron to name Mr. Lackwood his heir. Learning of the damage to the mantel—which was a gift from said baron—was caused by domestic disquiet in their home, and that they failed to pay the craftsman who repaired it, could influence Sir Wilbert's opinion of them, potentially thwarting their ambitions. I think he would be able and most willing to exert some influence upon them in your favor."

That explained a great deal about the project. Great Scott, as insufferable as they were as ordinary rich folk, what would they be like if they acquired a title? But that was hardly her problem right now. "What makes you so certain Sir Wilbert would do such a thing?"

"As a member of the Royal Court Guild, he is most interested in protecting Wrights from exploitation."

"Even lowly journeymen?"

"Despite my deepest conviction that your status will change soon enough, yes, even for those of your current status."

His arguments made sense. They should. He was a barrister, after all. "And you are certain?"

"As certain as I can be of another man." He took her hand. His own was calloused and firm, from working stone, and yet so warm and strong. "Please, consider yourself released from any obligations associated with the money. If you can pay it back, so be it, but if not, then I will regard the matter as closed and of no further consequence. It is a loss I am willing to risk. I cannot tolerate the injustice I am seeing here... " He gazed deep into her eyes, "... and I cannot abide what I see happening to you."

She swallowed hard, gripping his hand, closing her eyes through a wave of lightheadedness. When was the last time someone cared about such things? Had it ever been so? "I do not know what to say."

"Thank you would suffice. That, and would you do me the compliment of calling me David?"

***

Now they were on a Christian-name basis. David and Rebecca. How strange that seemed. Strange and delightful. To have a friend now, one who would inconvenience himself on her behalf. Such a heady thing.

He stayed through a plain, but tasty, dinner from Birdy's kitchen. No doubt tomorrow she would be demanding all the particulars about this young man Rebecca supped with. She would deal with that tomorrow.

The evening, lingering in her kitchen and parlor, proved far more agreeable than the one they had spent at the Continental's dining rooms listening to Sir Wilbert's adventures. Sir Wilbert was a decent enough man, and an influential one, to be sure. But not worth giving up the opportunity to spend time with David. So, making up for it was necessary.

Where would this go, though? Was there any hope, any future there? Did she even want the future that might be? Maybe, perhaps. It had never been an option before.

At the least, it was a good question. One for which there were few answers. One she fell asleep pondering.

The next morning, she sprang from the bed before Balthazar bothered prodding her. Tomorrow was the Guild Assembly, the day everything could, probably would, change. For better or worse, it would change. Today the sign on the front door would read *Please Knock* all day and she would abscond away to the workshop downstairs to practice the best way to show her mastery to the watching eyes. Her stomach clenched and threatened to upend. No Wright was ever watched save in the course of instruction.

Such a burden they placed on her.

And such opportunity.

David was right. If they saw what she could do, right there, in front of them, how much harder would it be to ignore her? It was hard to deny what happened before one's own eyes. She had to use this to her advantage.

She dressed and dashed over to Birdy's for a quick meal, a little warm comradery, and a few more pieces to be mended. A brief tour of the shop to ensure everything was in order and she would—

Apparently, answer the pounding at the door.

Dash it all! Dash and damn!

"Stop your pounding, I am coming." She trudged to the door to admit Dick Mallory, who staggered in, tie and hat askew.

"About bloody damn time, woman." Lovely. Drunk as usual, more gin than beer on his breath. "No wonder you can't pay the bills, closing up shop while decent folk are working for their livings."

She gritted her teeth. No point in rising to his bait. The sooner he was paid, the sooner he would be out.

"Why don't you be quick about it and give me the keys? I know you can't make your payment." He held out his open palm. A long-healed ugly scar ran from his wrist to his ring finger.

"How would you be privy to such information?" She stomped to the workbench, then whirled on him. "Unless you had something to do with creating the hardship you seem to expect."

He held his ground and leaned forward. "You got nothing on me."

"The police are investigating."

"They found nothing."

"I doubt they would inform you of a case they are building against you." She edged behind the workbench. Best have some distance, and preferably a solid object, between them.

"So, you admit to bringing false accusations against me and me lad?" He kicked the workbench's leg, knocking it into her side.

"I have led no one astray."

"You set those miserable constables on me, witch. They told me it were you. And a bit'o brass is the best cure for that kind of trouble. Be sure they'll be seeing it my way when all is said and done."

Bribing the police. Lovely. Was it true? And if it was, had Constable Moore found out? The others might be open to bribery and ignoring crime, but not Moore.

She drew an envelope from her pocket and slapped it on the workbench. "Here's your payment. Now get out."

"What?" His look of astonishment might have been comical had it not been all but a confession of guilt.

"It is all there. Count it if you choose, then get out of my shop."

"It can't be." He riffled through the bills.

"Your business here is done. Go." She pointed at the door.

"Where did you get this?" He waved the envelope at her face. "What have you been doing—"

"I will not dignify that with an answer."

"There is no way, unless you've become some sort of strumpet."

"You have your money. Now get out."

"You think this is over? That you can get away with this?" He staggered around the workbench.

She darted to the other side, keeping the bench between them. "With what? Paying you what I owe you?"

"After what you did to me, you don't deserve this place."

"Did to you?" She raised her left hand. "I'm the one with the bone scars and cold weather ache. You did that to me!"

"You were da one dat made me angry. Deserved what you got, woman. No one crosses me."

Bile rose in her throat, but it explained a great deal. "Perhaps you shouldn't have celebrated our engagement by bedding another woman."

"If you'd been more amenable, I wouldn't a'had to. Ya can't blame a man for dat." He reached for her. "I ain't gonna let you get away with rejecting me."

She slipped past the bench and headed toward the door.

"You best not fight me. I deserve recompense for da' injury to me pride, me reputation." He followed.

"A long rot in gaol is what you deserve."

"No one treats me dat way. You're going to get what's coming to you." He stumbled as he leaned in close to her.

"Go and take your lunatic rantings to someone who cares to listen. I have work to do." She threw the door open and pulled a wall of Air from the back of the shop to shove him in that direction as she pushed more Air out the door.

"Don't think I don't know what you're doing, witch. I felt that. You'll regret raising your hand against me."

"Out!"

He snorted and swaggered toward the door. "I got things to do meself. It ain't you who has me going." He sneered and stumbled out.

She bolted the door behind him.

The cuckoo clock screeched. She nearly knocked it off the wall, trying to silence it. Vengeful, arrogant, blackguard...

Maybe drink wasn't the only thing addling Mallory's mind—coca was becoming quite popular. Could that explain his near-delusional obsession with punishing her?

Either way, Constable Moore needed to know about this latest incident—after she finished practicing for the demonstration tomorrow.

# Chapter 20

"GREAT SCOTT, YOU SHOULD have seen Lackwood's face!" Sir Wilbert laughed, blue eyes crinkled beneath shaggy brows. He slapped his thighs as he tipped back in his chair. He caught himself on the wall and pushed himself upright once again. How could a man of such dignity be so utterly amused by the diversion permitted by a tiny room? "Priceless, I tell you, priceless. You've made my trip to Brighton quite worthwhile."

"I am glad to hear it, sir. Very glad." David leaned forward on his elbows.

"You shouldn't be, I'm afraid." Sir Wilbert's mirth drained away and his expression froze, somber and severe.

Had the temperature in the room dropped as well, or was it David's imagination? "What?"

"Despite facing consequences for nonpayment that left him pale and stammering like a schoolboy caught cheating, I'm afraid Miss Fuller will not be seeing her money anytime soon."

"He is hard up?"

"He's lucky his creditors don't form a mob to dun him good and proper. He owes so much." Sir Wilbert leaned back in his chair again and rocked several times.

"Despicable vermin," David slapped the desk. "Making promises to Miss Fuller he well knew he couldn't keep. I hope Hughes and his boys are successful at alerting every shopkeeper from here to Hove of Lackwood's tricks."

"As it should be, son, as it should be. I appreciate credit as much as the next man; I don't want to see it threatened by snakes like him. Speaking of snakes, that money-lender, has he—"

"Mallory's the reptile's name. I imagine he's already been to call upon her. I did what I could to ensure she met her payment this month—after that wretched boy of his robbed her."

"Oh yes, it was a rather complicated situation. The police are looking into the matter?" Sir Wilbert ran the back of his knuckles along his mutton chops.

"I am following up on that as well. I'm sure Mallory has already tried bribing anyone whose palm might be greased. Constable Moore—who everyone in Brighton knows cannot be bribed—is managing this case, though. So, there is that."

"I'm glad you are on top of it, Enright. The local chapter has failed miserably. Miserably, I say. And you can be sure I will take word of it back to London with me. This cannot continue. Between you and me, the chapter here is on thin ice with the Royal Court. This won't help their cause any." The creases on Sir Wilbert's forehead emphasized his was no idle threat. "How long do you think it will take to find a resolution in the court?"

"It'll come up for trial soon, but will be a hard one to win, for sure. The evidence is not as strong as I would like it to be, and there's so many owing him money, finding an unbiased jury will be nigh on impossible." David fisted the hair on the back of his head with both hands.

He should have considered that possibility before releasing Miss—Rebecca—from her need to repay him. No, no, the truth was, he was well able to absorb the loss, and doing her a favor was worth it. Not only because it helped correct a grievous injustice.

That look in her eyes, the beginnings of warmth, and regard—or at least he hoped so. Yes, that was entirely worth it.

"You helped her make this month's payment, no?" Sir Wilbert studied him, like a father scrutinizing a son.

"I was able to help her make up the difference between what she had and what she required."

"Good on you for not offering to pay the whole sum. Respect her dignity and all that. She is that class of modern-thinking woman who would appreciate that sort of thing." Sir Wilbert stroked his chin. "You ought to just marry her."

"What?" David sat up ramrod straight, his tone a mite more forceful than it should have been.

Sir Wilbert shook his finger at him and laughed. "You've gone sweet on her. I knew it."

"That is no concern of yours."

"I beg to differ. It is of great concern to me."

"And how do you figure that?"

"The fate of our kind hangs in the balance. We are a dying breed if something doesn't change." Sir Wilbert pulled back his shoulders and settled into an expression that could only be called severe. "I am sure you are aware of the work of Gregor Mendel, are you not?"

"The principles of inheritance?"

"Precisely."

"The man studied pea plants!"

"That does not invalidate his findings. In fact, after Mendel's publication four years ago, the Royal Court Guild formed a team at the Royal College to study the phenomenon among our kind." Sir Wilbert pulled back his shoulders and folded his hands atop the desk.

"Are you suggesting Wrights are like pea plants? Our height, color, and born Elements can be predicted from our parents?"

"No, we are hardly that simple, and the principles of inheritance are still being debated, but one thing is clear. A Wright father is more likely to produce a Skilled child. And the stronger the natural Skill of the father, the stronger the Skill of the child. Think of what might happen with two Wright parents!"

"Are you suggesting—"

"Two Full Wrights stand an excellent chance of producing more Full Wrights. If you are so committed to our cause—"

"I should put myself out to stud as I were a prize bull and she a cow?" When had he gotten to his feet?

"Calm down, young man, calm down. Nothing so crass as that. Do release some of your bluster and sit down. I merely suggest good breeding should be one consideration in making a match. The upper class has considered such things, though not in a Mendel sort of way, for ages. You must agree, she is an exceptional candidate in many regards. I will leave you to consider that. I need to have a few words with Allbright before the Guild Assembly begins." Sir Wilbert chuckled to himself and ambled out.

The unmitigated gall of the man, suggesting such a thing! So full of himself! Wrights were not livestock to be bred! Heaven forfend Rebecca got wind of such a notion! She would probably never speak to him again, merely for listening to Sir Wilbert's prattle—and he would hardly blame her for it.

With any luck, Sir Wilbert would keep such ideas to himself and word of it would never get to her. But that was a problem for later. Much later.

Right now, there were more important matters in the offing. The Guild Assembly would be called to order in less than an hour and no matter what happened, his world would change.

A delicate knock at the door.

Rebecca.

He pulled the door open and ushered her in. "I can't say how glad I am to see you here." And for the fact the tiny room forced him to stand close to her. Close enough to hear her more rapid than usual breathing, and was it?—yes, he did feel the increase in her pulse. Rarely was he able to sense Water so clearly.

"I could not stand the scolding of my father's clock anymore. I left early simply to be away from it." She laughed and sat in the chair Sir Wilbert had just vacated. "Is everything ready?"

"Yes." He edged around his desk and pulled out a neatly folded length of fabric from the drawer. "Will this do? Guild Master Allbright himself acquired it. He thought that would mollify those who would complain if you supplied it yourself." He handed it to her.

She closed her eyes, stroking the creamy folds, then ran a single thickness between her thumb and finger. "Gracious, he settled on the thinnest cotton the linen draper carried, did he not? I can hardly fathom the expense."

"Everyone knows fabric is difficult to work and the finer the weave, the more difficult the process. The best way to demonstrate your Skill, in his words." David eased into his chair.

"He isn't wrong on that point." Rebecca bit her lip and stared at the cotton. "One might even be tempted to argue he is setting me up for failure."

"Or making your success more notable. It is difficult to read Allbright's motives, to be sure. You can manage it, no? Do we need to find another—"

"No, no, I can handle it. I need a few moments to get the feel of its character, though." She ran the textile through her fingers and against her cheek, eyes closed, breathing deeply. "At least there will be no doubt on its own. It possesses none of the qualities I intend to impart to it. Will it be a dramatic enough presentation?"

He shrugged and nodded. "I have given that some thought. The wrighting itself is not terribly dramatic, but the demonstration you suggest will be. That should be sufficient."

"May I count on your help for that?"

"If necessary, but it would be better if you selected assistants from the attending members. That way, there will be less suspicion that your sponsoring Master is interfering."

"I hate that you are right. Dash it all. I hate this!" She jumped to her feet and paced the few steps across the room and back. "You who are so moved by injustice, how can you tolerate—"

"Unfortunately, the best way to change this nonsense is from the inside. Meet them on their own terms now, and then once inside, we can work to ensure fairness and justice for future Wrights."

"And if the attempt fails? If I fail?" Her air of confidence fell to the ground, shattering into tiny, sharp shards that pierced his soul. Never had he seen her so vulnerable.

He slipped around the desk and took her warm hand in both of his. "You will not fail. But if something does go wrong, I have been giving that some thought, too. We can talk about it later, if things come to it. But it would only be a distraction now. We ought to take this one step at a time."

Her head drooped, and she pressed it into his shoulder. "I know that is sound advice, but I don't much like it."

"I can't say I blame you."

A brisk knock on the door, and she jumped back from him.

"Enright, are you there? Is Miss Fuller about?" Guild Master Allbright called through the door.

"Come in, sir, she is here with me." David hurried back to his side of the desk.

Allbright strode in wearing his formal black robe and Guild Master's gold silk stole. Embroidered in red with the symbols of all four Elements, and trimmed in royal purple braid, the stole made him identifiable in a room—handy when proceedings had a way of becoming contentious. "It is a pleasure to see you, Miss Fuller. I haven't seen you in quite some time." He offered a small bow from his shoulders. His frizzled mousy brown hair was pulled back into a queue and his long beard had, somehow, been tamed into submission, to lie obediently across his chest.

Tightness in Rebecca's jaw suggested she was biting her tongue. Little surprise, as there were numerous tart responses to be made to Allbright's remark. "I am honored to be invited to the Assembly this evening." She managed a slightly out of practice curtsey.

"Master Enright has all the paperwork in order, so I anticipate things shall progress smoothly. I apologize for the irregularity of the circumstances under which your application for Mastery is being handled." His words might have been proper, but there was little sincerity in his tone.

She quivered, probably with the effort to control a sharp remark. "My father's death following the initial application makes things rather irregular, does it not?"

He knew it! He knew it! She had the capacity for politic answers when necessary. But he would probably get an earful later, when they enjoyed their celebratory dinner.

"I am glad you have persevered." Allbright handed Rebecca a small sheet of paper. "This is the order of events for the evening. Have you any questions?"

She turned it so David might read with her.

*Roll Call*

*Minutes of the last meeting; vote on minutes*

*New Business:*

*A message from the Royal Court Guild presented by Master Earth Wright Sir Wilbert Cullington-Price*

*Demonstration of Mastery, Journeyman Rebecca Fuller ...*

"There is no designation of Full Mastery on the agenda, sir." David took the paper from her and held it out to Allbright. They had spoken about that just this afternoon, and he had been assured—

"As to that. There was some objection to the notion of a journeyman who has been without a Master these several years, progressing directly to Full Wright, when the usual process is to attain one Mastery at a time." Allbright pushed the paper back at David.

Rebecca's jaw clenched, and she deep a long deep breath. "The demonstration I have planned will cover all four Elements, sir."

"So I understand. There is nothing to prevent the Assembly from voting to admit you to Full Wright status if they are suitably impressed with your work. But it is far more likely to be approved as a Master of a single Element. In that case, which Element would you prefer to demonstrate Mastery of?"

Cinderford, it must have been Cinderford who insisted. David would have words with both of them after this. "If I may, sir, her first Element is Fire, but since we have arranged the cloth for the demonstration, perhaps Earth would make the most sense? What do you think, Miss Fuller?"

Oh, the glare she gave him, but it wasn't for him. She could not risk glowering at the Guild Master right now. "I will defer to my sponsoring Master's recommendations."

"Excellent. That is always a mark in a journeyman's favor." A bell in the hallway chimed. "I hear the quarter-hour announcement for the Assembly. Shall we proceed to the assembly room?"

Somehow, the chime seemed so out of place. This was the sort of event that the dratted cuckoo clock should be screaming about.

# Chapter 21

REBECCA SLIPPED ON THE dark grey journeyman's robe that David handed her and followed behind him and Guild Master Allbright, who carried the fabric for her demonstration tucked under his arm. How different, and a little unapproachable David seemed in his black robes and white and purple stole, marking him as Undersecretary of the Guild chapter. She had never seen him in that guise before, and depending how things went, might not want to again.

Through the corridor, down the cold, stone steps to the third level, with no conversation. Just as well, though. Nothing she had to say would be considered fitting conversation. It was quite like the Guild to agree to examine her for Mastery, but minimize what they would allow her to achieve.

She should have expected that, prepared herself more for the possibility. Still, though, to be acknowledged as a Master of any Element would be enough—for the moment, at least, it would be enough. David was right. Focus on that now, and deal with the rest later.

They joined a trickle of members into the exalted Guild Assembly Hall, a room to which she had never been invited.

Father had always thought it a grand place. But he was an Earth Wright and found comfort in being surrounded by the embrace of stone. The vaulted ceiling, carved out of the bedrock, hung overhead, looming, quiet, and threatening. She touched one column as she passed, reaching through the pillar to the ceiling for assurances it was stable. It was, exactly as David had assured her it would be.

But really, there was something wrong about being surrounded by an Element as impenetrable and cold as stone. Unlike the other Elements, stone declined to yield whenever it could, hard and stubborn to her touch. How could one feel welcome in a place constructed of such stuff? The gas lamps whose Fire brightened the walls, and ventilation shafts bringing in Air ,helped stave off the sense of suffocation, of being trapped as the walls closed in around her.

Just enough that she did not run screaming from the assembly room. Not that she wouldn't have to do that at some point tonight, though.

On the positive side, the space itself was so dreadful that the milling Master Wrights, most dressed in somber dark suits, seemed downright friendly by comparison, even with their veiled stares and outright glares her way. No, they did not welcome her, none of them did. But it wasn't simply her they did not welcome, but her father's legacy.

She could blame Father for this.

Later, she would do that later. For now, she needed to focus on the reason she was here.

They had built a dais at the far end of the Assembly room, with wooden chairs laid out in a semicircle several rows deep around it; enough for all the Masters in attendance. More like a stage for some kind of dramatic performance than the place where a business meeting would be held. She frowned.

Did this strike the right notes, or was it already leading those who would judge her in a distinct direction?

So difficult to tell.

And nothing she could do about it.

An elaborate wooden podium, not carved, but wrighted by Earth Wrights, shared the dais with a plain long table. That was where her fate would be decided. Each of the table's corners held the accouterments to summon a different Element, a bowl, a candle, a piece of limestone, and a tiny wind chime mounted in a standing frame. An unusual way to summon Air, but it would work. Several tall candelabras stood behind the dais, raising long candles that added their flickering glow to the dark shadows. Fire. Close enough to feel. Yes, that helped.

Hopefully, no one would remember that she was first a Fire Wright and try to take it away.

Enough already! Stop! Feeling sorry for herself accomplished nothing but distraction.

Interesting, though, they set the table up the way a Full Wright might require. So perhaps—no, best not worry about what it might mean.

Her stomach grumbled. She had forced herself to choke down some of Birdy's delightful bread and jam before she came, but it would hardly be enough to sustain her.

David assured her that a meal would be laid out for the entire assembly afterwards, when business was complete. The food would be too distracting otherwise. Wrights were always hungry and could never concentrate when food was available. Or so it was said.

But she and David would only stay for that as long as courtesy required. He promised her a proper dinner, away from the judgment and prying eyes of the Guild, to celebrate her achievement.

If that happened at all.

Guild Master Allbright directed them to seats at the far end of the first row, nearest the back wall of the hall. Convenient to the dais, but unobtrusive and out of the way. Probably for the best. He ambled off to greet and make small talk as his position required. Was he as calm as he appeared? Did he even care that her life would never be the same after the next few hours?

Why would he? What difference would it make if he did?

She eased into place beside David, back rigid, eyes fixed on the candles behind the dais. Each flame seemed to reach out with warmth and strength, a meager promise of support. The only ones in the room. Other than David, of course.

Everything inside her shook.

"It's all right to breathe, you know." He elbowed her gently.

"So you say. I'm not so certain."

"I have faith in you."

"It is nice that one of us does."

The noise level in the room rose as Master Wrights flowed in, rising to a crescendo that marked Sir Wilbert's entrance, and fading again as the Royal Court Guild representative took his seat on the other end of the first row. David acknowledged him with a nod, but Rebecca dared not face him.

Master Cinderford, a candle stub of a man with a greying black wick to complete the image, trundled to the center of the dais, his black robe and officer's stole flowing around him, and rang a crystal bell. "All rise to honor the Guild Master."

Guild Master Allbright stepped up to the dais, somber as an aged wizard presiding over arcane rites, and took his place behind the podium. He removed a scroll from underneath the lectern, unrolled it, and read a list of names. Each Master stood as he heard his name until Rebecca was the only one left seated. Guild Master Allbright gestured for her to stand. "Master Wrights of Brighton, we are assembled. You may be seated."

Master Cinderford returned to the dais to read the minutes from the prior meeting. Rebecca tried to pay attention, but lapsed into reviewing what she would be called upon to perform. Fabric was both a difficult and an unforgiving material to wright. She could not afford mistakes.

Votes were called on the minutes, results recorded, and Guild Master Allbright returned to the podium, pausing until the group settled, then beckoned Sir Wilbert to join him. "May I introduce Sir Wilbert Cullington-Price, representative of the Royal Court Guild, here to address us on matters of particular importance to the Crown."

Polite applause and curious murmurs followed.

David leaned down and whispered, "He's been here all week, meeting with most of the Masters individually. What can he possibly have left to say?"

"Given dinner the other night, I can't imagine that would ever be a problem." She could not risk looking at David as he pressed a fist to his mouth and quivered.

"Thank you for your warm welcome, Wrights of Brighton. Thank you for inviting me to your homes and offices and workshops. The problems we face, as you well know, are many and varied and will require all of us to pull together to ensure our survival."

A somber blanket, damp and cold, descended upon the audience, hushing what few whispers remained.

"Since the Great Volcanic Synchrony of 1680 that conceived our kind, there have never been many of us. No other coincidence of volcanic eruption and visiting comet have produced such a change in mankind, so those who are learned in such things have concluded that our inception was a unique, one-time occurrence in the annals of human history. Since then, we have survived trial and famine as we have struggled to identify who and what we are, to nurture our Skill, and, someday, find our place in society." Sir Wilbert let his words fade away, and the meaning take hold.

No Wright was entirely comfortable about being both human and somehow separate from the majority at the same time.

"Now society is changing around us, and to survive, we, too, must change in deep and fundamental ways that will push us all to our limits." Dissatisfied grumbles circled the room; Sir Wilbert lifted his hands. "No, no, this is not a matter of discussion or debate. It is a fact, whether you care to accept it, that does not change the reality of what we face. To that end, the Crown is reluctant to lose such a rare and valuable resource as the Wrights of England. The Royal Crown Guild has been instructed to call upon each of its chapters to institute sweeping changes to ensure our survival. Beginning tonight."

Grunts and shuffles replaced the earlier dissatisfied whispers. It would not be a straightforward thing to change the ways of Masters.

"Wrights have a long tradition of training young Wrights up in our ways. Masters take on apprentices who progress to journeymen, become Masters themselves, who train new apprentices. In this way, we have kept our history alive. Our legacy of training must continue. It must also change to fit the times. Even to the point of looking to those ignored by traditional approaches to training. Before I continue discussing the new Crown initiatives with you, I invite you to take part in the first of what I hope to be many demonstrations of these new views toward developing Masters of our Skill." He gestured for Rebecca to join him beside the podium.

This was not in the plans!

David grabbed her hand. "No, he did not discuss this with me, but go, it will be fine. He is on our side."

She stood, convincing her feet to move toward the dais, not the inviting green baize door which dangled escape before her like raw meat to a starving hound.

"Today, we offer for examination a journeyman Wright to progress to the status of Master. Miss Rebecca Fuller."

She straightened her spine and pulled back her shoulders. Despite whatever else they would find fault with, she would show them no weakness as she took her place before them.

"Miss Fuller is the daughter of Full Wright Morris Fuller and Fire Wright Marguerite Fuller, both now lost to us. Her brother, Air Wright Joseph Fuller, has gone the way of our ancestors as well, leaving her the last of a family of Wrights."

Why had Sir Wilbert presented her pedigree? What had that to do with anything? Why did he have to remind everyone of her father?

"Her application for Mastery was submitted three years ago, just before Morris Fuller succumbed to a heart attack." He emphasized those words. "Her application has lingered in an unsponsored state since that time. Our own undersecretary, Full Wright David Enright, has taken up her sponsorship. It is under his oversight that she is presented to you today. Due to the irregularities all round, she will confirm her proficiency for all of you, here and now, to assure you our new approaches will not bestow honor to the unworthy."

She stepped onto the dais. Murmuring and pointing circulated throughout the room, settling into a general sense of ill-ease at the deviation from well-established patterns. Not the ideal start to things, but it was what she had to work with. And if David believed he was an ally, then perhaps this was for the best.

Guild Master Allbright stepped up beside her and gestured toward the table. "Call upon the Elements, Miss Fuller. Once you are ready, I shall provide you with the material you requested for your demonstration." The edge in his voice suggested he was as surprised by Sir Wilbert's actions as the rest.

Not an auspicious way to begin.

Rebecca took her place behind the table, closed her eyes and drew a slow, deep breath. Don't look at the wolves lying in wait. Focus. This was the easy part. Reaching out to the Elements was second nature, like breathing itself. The question was, how much did she want to show off?

She opened her eyes and swept her gaze across the audience. Disgruntled, judgmental, disapproving. If there were ever a time to make a show of things, it was now.

Very well, then. She raised the candle before her, holding it chest-high. She stroked it upwards from the base, barely brushing the wick with her fingertips. A gentle flame flared in the wake of her touch. Tradition said she should set it aside and move on, but she paused, drawing the candle close, and stared into the comforting Fire, allowing it to assure her she could do exactly what she had set her mind to. Yes, that was what she needed to hear.

Placing the candlestick back in its place, she walked around the table to the bowl. She gathered her hands above it and squeezed the Air until Water dripped into her upraised palms, overflowing into the bowl. The crowd gasped. Even Master water-wringers usually began with an already full vessel. Who had chosen that for her? Master Fitzsimons, no doubt. It was the sort of thing a rat would do.

Earth was next, with a lump of grey limestone. Limestone was tricky at times. It often liked to collapse into dust instead of molding to a desired shape. And, of course, this stone seemed especially chosen to be of the crumbling variety. But David had selected it for her and had warned her about it. He intended for her to show off.

But Father had taught her well. With one hand she raised the limestone toward the crowd, with the other, she pulled Water from the Air, crafting a tiny, gentle shower over the stone. She rolled the stone in her hands, like a ball of dough, rounding it into a ball, then pulling a hole in the middle, creating a ring torus, one of the most difficult shapes to achieve in stone. As she raised it overhead, the crowd's eyes fixed on it, jaws agape, exactly as it should be. Now, only Air remained.

Three dainty steps took her around the front of the table to the delicate framed wind chimes, colored glass rods hanging from a wooden crosspiece. Of course, they would be glass. Easy to shatter, resistant to Air, like the limestone, chosen as a subtle test, worthy of the Guild Master. She dropped her hands to her side and opened them, palms toward the chimes. A little Fire to warm the Air, and she pushed a gust to swirl through the chimes. Gentle, bell-like tones filled the room. Rather pretty. Their simple song belied the difficulty of the feat.

From the corner of her eye, Sir Wilbert nodded and forced back a smile. At least one man in the audience was on her side. Two, including David. That was enough.

"Now that the Elements are all accounted for, Miss Fuller will demonstrate her mastery. I have acquired these yards of ordinary cotton and jar of wool grease, and attest to their unaltered state." Guild Master Allbright handed her the folded cloth and a ceramic jar, stoppered with a wide cork. "Pray explain what you plan to do."

"It is well understood that cloth is among the most difficult items for a Wright to work with, and thus usually left to the craft of mundane tailors and seamstresses. However, it is a useful material that can be made more useful by the efforts of a Wright upon it." She lifted the edge of the fabric and waved it. "As it is now, the cotton is soft, but fragile and susceptible to the ravages of Air, Water and Fire. I will remake the cotton fibers, with the addition of the wool oil, into a wholly new fabric, designed, with the use of Air, Water, and Fire, to resist the effects of those Elements."

"It can't be done." A man in the front row sneered. Several more loudly agreed.

"This is a waste of our time. Why bother with it?"

"Our dinner is being held up with the slip of a girl showing off—be done with it already."

Sir Wilbert clapped and raised his hands. "Silence. You discredit yourself and our Guild with these insults. If she fails, she only humbles herself, but if she succeeds, think of what innovation can come from Skill at this level. There will be no doubt she is a true Full Wright."

He said it! Sir Wilbert intended for her to be made a Full Wright. Her heart swelled so much she could hardly breathe.

He would not be disappointed.

"Order! Order!" Guild Master Allbright waved the dissenters down. "This talk is unbecoming and an insult to her sponsor, our undersecretary. Miss Fuller, pray continue."

Her cheeks and her hands blossomed with heat. Little did they realize their taunts only bolstered her resolve. "First, I will soak the cotton with the wool oil. It is not enough to saturate the cotton with the oil, though, it must be bound by Fire to the fibers as I reshape them to resemble the fibers of natural wool." She unstopped the jar and poured the viscous, sheep-y, grassy-scented oil over the fabric, working it in along the textile. For several minutes, she passed yards and yards of cotton through her hands until she had thoroughly worked the oil throughout.

"You can see it is now saturated." She held up the somewhat translucent cloth to her audience. "Now I need several extra hands to hold it open so that I may reshape the fibers. Guild Master, would you please call upon the assembly for assistance?"

Guild Master Allbright pointed out the loudest, crankiest of the audience members, six of them, to join them on the dais. Grumbling all, they stomped up to the front and held three poles over which she had draped the ends and middle of the fabric.

"As I reshape the fibers, the cloth will thicken and tighten." She spoke more to the audience than the assistants.

This part was for show. She could have managed this from the table, but it was far more dramatic to do it this way, and it put her biggest detractors in close proximity to observe what she was doing. David had suggested it, and as much as she disliked it, it was a good idea.

"You're as crazy as your father," one of the men holding the middle of the cloth hissed.

"The Wright who could do what you suggest's never been seen. You'll make a fool of yourself, lass," another murmured, with only slightly less hostility.

"Hurry up, so's we can get on to dinner," a third muttered.

Heat built in her chest. She placed one hand above the other below the middle of the cotton. "First, I will use Fire to open the fibers to accept the oil, then Water-wrighting to move the liquid oil into the fibers. As I do so, I will also reshape the fibers and use the pressure of Air to lock them into shape."

It was a highly simplified explanation that did not even begin to address the intricacies of understanding the complex shape of wool fiber or the painstaking process of replicating it in the cotton. But explaining it in that depth would be the wrong sort of showing off and win her little support. Later, if asked, she could further detail the process.

Building a controlled ball of flame in her palm, she worked the oil into the cotton. Under her hands, the translucent quality faded, exactly as it should. Her stomach grumbled. Dash it, she should have had a more substantial meal before she came. But the small changes required by the fibers should not demand too much.

"Now to reform the cotton fibers to mimic wool." She grasped the center of the cloth in her fist, crushing it together, blending thin fibers together into creating thicker ones with the tiny scales and the crimp characteristic of wool. The cotton shrank and thickened under her fingers, taking on a faint grey cast, and the slightest fuzz to the surface.

The man nearest to her work gasped. "By Jove!"

Focus, focus. Now was not the time to succumb to distraction. So easy to lose her place and craft an inconsistent product that would fail when tested. Focus.

Inch by inch, she worked her way out from the center, the length puckering and tightening down as she went. Somewhere in the distance, the gasps and whispers continued until she reached the last corner. The men holding the draping poles now stood within arm's reach of one another.

"Look how it has shrunk." Who had said that?

"Yes, it is much smaller and far denser than it had been. Guild Master Allbright, Master Cinderford, Master Fitzsimons, would you please help me demonstrate the changes?" She gathered the length from the poles and gestured for her assistants to return to their seats. Born an Air Wright, a Fire Wright, and a Water Wright, all officers of the order. Who better to help her?

“What would you have us do?” Guld Master Allbright asked, with all the deference he might extend another Master Wright.

“Allow Masters Cinderford and Fitzsimons to hold the fabric while you establish how it responds to Air, please.”

The two grumpy Masters held out the altered cloth, facing the audience while the Guild Master stood in front.

“I have infused the new fabric with tiny pockets of Air, which allow it to perform more like wool. Would you examine the cloth to verify this?” she asked.

“Infused with pockets of Air? Intriguing.“ Guild Master Allbright ran his hands along the length and breadth of the sheet. He blinked in surprise and repeated the action. “Master Fergusson, pray join me and confirm what I have found.”

A hunched and wizened Wright, leaning heavily on a walking stick, tottered up to the dais. Guild Master Allbright took the cloth from the others and brought it to Master Fergusson, who examined every inch, even rubbing it to his face. “I’ll be. It is as she said!”

“I’ve never seen the like.” Guild Master Allbright scratched his head. “How does it react to Water?”

“Would you change places with Master Fitzsimons? Pray, someone provide us with water?” She was tempted to hand him the almost-empty bowl and dare him to wring his own Water from the atmosphere, but spite would not help her cause.

Several men from the back of the room leapt to assist.

“Pray, Master Fitzsimons, would you please do whatever you deem appropriate to saturate the fabric?”

Such a smug little smile the ratty little man wore. For now.

A full washtub appeared on the dais, placed by smiling men who were obviously anticipating her failure.

"Do as you will, Master." Rebecca stepped back as the Guild Master handed him the textile.

Master Fitzsimons smirked as he wadded up the sheet and plunged it into the washtub, water sloshing along the front of the dais. He stirred up a whirlpool that seized the sheet and dragged it down. Apparently, he wanted to show off, too.

"And here you have..." he pulled out the cloth.

Water sheeted off the surface as though it were glass.

"That can't be." He grabbed it and wrung it hard. "The bloody article is dry! Impossible" He handed it to Master Cinderford.

"Completely dry." The admission must have cost Master Cinderford dearly.

"I concur." The Guild Master ran his hands along a loose edge.

"Master Cinderford, if you will assist me." She draped it over the table. "Pray burn it."

"I do not recommend that. It could be very dangerous." Master Cinderford backed away.

"We have a tub of water waiting to quench any flames." Guild Master Allbright nudged the washtub with his foot. "Do it."

Huffing, Cinderford snatched the candle from the table, gathered the flame into his hands and swelled it into a double handful. "Stand away."

Rebecca and the others jumped back as a ball of flame flew at the cloth-draped table.

Flames danced along the surface, withering and fading, until nothing remained.

Master Cinderford growled and grabbed the flames from the nearest candelabra and threw a double-sized flame ball at the table. It danced a little longer, but waned as the first had.

"Great Scott!"

"She's done it."

"I've never seen the like."

"That's Master Wright work, no doubt."

Sir Wilbert approached the podium. "As you can see, Miss Fuller has convincingly showed—"

"Wait just a moment." Master Fitzsimons shouldered Sir Wilbert away and waved his arms.

"What are you talking about?" Sir Wilbert demanded.

"Enough of this farce. This entire show has been a moot point. She cannot be recognized as any sort of Master."

"Why not? You've seen what she's done." Sir Wilbert stomped toward Master Fitzsimons.

"Ask Undersecretary Enright to check the Guild's charter. You will find there is a very clear rule forbidding the advancement of any journeyman who has failed to pay their dues. Moreover, she is so far in arrears as to be suspended from active membership and declared a lifetime journeyman. With all due respect to the Royal Court Guild representative, this has been a waste of time."

# Chapter 22

WHAT HAD FITZSIMONS JUST intimated?

David's pulse thundered in his ears. His face chilled, and he jumped to his feet.

Angry shouts exploded across the room as the audience sprang up, rushing toward the dais.

"Why was she even considered if she is in arrears?"

"Look what she's done, though!"

"What was the point of this exercise? Get her out of here."

"You can't ignore that cloth-wrighting—it's unprecedented!"

David leapt up to join the other officers near the podium, away from all the crush. Rebecca backed toward the far wall, the look of horror on her face—no, he could not focus on that yet.

"Why allow her as a journeyman at all? Dismiss her and be done with her trickery. You can't trust anything that Morris Fuller touched."

"Trickery? Yes, this must be some sort of trickery. Everything about Fuller was a lie."

"What she claims is impossible."

"But we have seen—"

"Nothing but Fuller having another go at us from the grave. Get 'er out!"

David nearly slipped in the puddle around the washtub as he turned his back on the angry swarm of Wrights. Flutters of Air and flickers of heat raced through the throng. Not a favorable sign. "Treasurer, there is no such clause in the Charter."

Fitzsimons shoved an old, worn piece of paper into David's hands. "Check for yourself, Undersecretary. It is all in order."

An original charter document? The faded ink and tattered paper suggested it. Was there a date? Yes, there. It was from the early days of the Brighton Guild. One of many scraps that made up the patchworked affair that served as Brighton's Charter, as piecework as the common law that governed the land. One more thing David intended to clean up, but had not yet accomplished.

"There, right there, you can see—" Fitzsimons jabbed his gnarled finger at a line near the bottom of the document.

Scribbled in a different handwriting, but still old and faded, an addendum which indeed stated what Fitzsimon claimed. "However, sir—"

Fitzsimons tore the paper out of his hands, snarling like a cornered rat. "Don't you try to contradict what the Charter clearly states. The rule is clear, and none of your slippery words can change that."

"Be that as it may, you are ignoring a more recent document, which states that a quorum of Guild officers may waive all but the performance requirements for advancement."

"I've no idea what you are talking about." Fitzsimons' face flushed a dangerous red.

"Your familiarity with the document, or lack thereof, has no impact on the application of that clause."

Fitzsimons' beady eyes squinted, and he snarled. "When was that official vote taken?"

"It was not." Cinderford shouldered his way between them, far too much satisfaction on his face. "There was no formal vote taken."

"We discussed this in my office over a week ago." Allbright stepped in close. "I remember it clearly."

"Exactly." David said. "That makes this—"

"I was not present for that meeting." Fitzsimon stomped.

"Yes, you were." David pulled himself up tall and glowered, usually an effective way to cow rodent-men like Fitzsimons. "You were there at the start, declared that it had nothing to do with you, and told us to carry on without you. You had more important things to do. That constitutes—"

"You did not alert me that there would be a vote of any kind. I demand to have my say in this matter."

"You should have considered that before you wandered off to find lunch. You cannot come in now and overturn—"

"Who are you to say that? As Treasurer, it is my right and responsibility to prevent harm to the Guild by freeloaders—"

"You have a right and responsibility to ensure that the Guild is upholding its promises to its members. Which you have failed." Dash it all. Now he was shouting, too. That never helped one prevail.

"Of what are you accusing us?" Cinderford stood shoulder to shoulder with Fitzsimons. The candle stub and the rat. How did such men come to be leading the Guild?

"The records accuse you, not I. You have ignored appropriate requests for Guild intervention. And yes, it occurred during the time dues were being fully paid. When you are finished embarrassing yourselves here, I will happily show you."

"Business is not complete. This candidate for Mastery must be voted upon." Cinderford turned to the audience, arms upraised. "A vote must be taken."

"Gentlemen," Sir Wilbert marched to the dais, chest puffed, shoulders back. He faced the throng with open arms held high. "This is all must irregular and unbecoming the dignity of the Guild. All of you take your seats and return to order."

"Who do you think you are?"

"You're not an officer here. What business is this of yours? Go on—"

"She has no business among us cheating the Guild of its dues!"

"Get her out of here!"

"You get out!"

"As the representative of the Royal Court Guild ..."

The shouts drowned out Sir Wilbert and a subtle transformation from audience to mob rippled through the room.

"This is a travesty, and I will not stand for it." David looked straight at Allbright, "You know this is wrong, and it is time to do something about it."

Allbright clapped; thunder rippled from his hands and silenced the room. Interesting Air Wright's trick, that, one he needed to learn. "Silence. Enough. This meeting is adjourned. Out! Every one of you, out!"

Unfortunately, that was not the something that actually needed to be done.

"Miss Fuller," Allbright shoved her Mastery project at her, "it is best that you remove yourself as well. You will be notified of the Guild's decision. Do not return here unless you are summoned."

She snatched the fabric from his hand, jaw gaping, but without words.

"Guild Master, I must object," Sir Wilbert rushed toward Rebecca.

David stepped aside as street-dogs, Cinderford and Fitzsimons, dove on Sir Wilbert, cutting him off.

Fire, Wind, and Earth! Had they no regard for proper procedure and adherence to ... anything?

Stupid question.

Sir Wilbert glanced over his shoulder at David, bulgy pug-eyes staring over flaming red cheeks, and waved him away. Lovely way to dismiss the junior officer, so that the adults could talk about family matters.

Enough!

Let them argue themselves hoarse. Once they were tired of the game, he would come back and set down the rule of law. Wouldn't they be surprised for him to have the last word on such matters?

Or they still might simply ignore him and force him out of office. Given the things Sir Wilbert had been saying about the Brighton chapter, that was a strong possibility.

Crusty, hidebound, power-hungry...

It would not be the first time someone more powerful forced him away; Uncle Cresswell had done his worst and look where he landed. David would survive. There were other Guilds, maybe even the Royal Court Guild itself, who needed his services. He could sell the shop and move on.

Rebecca caught his gaze. Never had he seen her unsure or frightened... until now.

What about her? What was she going to do after this debacle?

He hurried around the arguing officers and caught her arm. "We need to get you away from here. I dislike the tone of the men out there."

Gasping, she clutched his arm and leaned into his strength.

Damn it all, she had overexerted, and now with no meal provided— He slipped her arm over his shoulder and hurried her to the narrow, dim servants' corridor behind the dais, pulling the green baize door shut, blocking out the noise and mayhem behind them.

She leaned into him, shaking and panting. "I don't ... I don't think I can walk back."

"I should have thought, made sure you prepared properly. I'm sorry."

"Not your fault. I know better. I should know better. Just so distracted..." Her voice trailed away.

"Come. We will leave by way of the kitchen." He guided her along the long, unadorned corridor to the kitchen, a space that strictly forbade Guild Members from entering.

But gossip was a high-value currency, always welcome below stairs in any establishment. All the kitchen staff knew was that they had not been called to set out the meal. They hungered for clues as to why, falling on them like starving hounds as soon as the door opened.

Only a few well-chosen words were required to procure a pot of jam–which he insisted she consume immediately—and several well-stuffed meat pies, sausage rolls, and other victuals that could be eaten while they walked. For the price of another juicy tidbit, the kitchen staff allowed David and Rebecca to leave via the kitchen stairs, exiting into the moonlit mews.

# Chapter 23

THE SWEET-TART CHERRY JAM helped quell the worst of the trembling, shoring up her jelly knees. It had been damfoolishness to skip that meal before she came. At least as stupid as attempting to force the Guild to recognize her, when all they could see was her father.

What a legacy he left her.

Wrapping a strong arm around her waist, David helped her out the door and into the tepid, humid night air. At least she was no longer surrounded by stone.

Stupid! Foolish! Father always said she would ask for too much one day and learn of her folly too late.

He was right. About everything. Like he always was. He was right.

Now what? What was she going to do? A perpetual journeyman? That would only increase the Guild's scrutiny on her and decrease what she could earn. Exactly what she needed most.

Every Master Wright in Brighton would consider it now his sworn duty to protect the Guild against her abuse, dogging her every step, intruding on her shop and work. It wouldn't be below them to drive away her most lucrative customers, to teach her not to intrude on their little fraternity.

How would she pay Mallory and...

Her knees gave way. David supported her until she stood again.

This wasn't at all helpful. She shook her head hard—perhaps that would dislodge the overwhelming thoughts. But no, it only dislodged her glasses.

Leaning on his support, she trudged along the mews, until they opened into the street. They stopped in a patch of gaslight from the streetlamp. She leaned against the side of the nearest brick building to catch her breath. Moonlight beyond them painted everything it touched a gaunt silvery grey, lifeless and cold. Never would she skip a meal like that again. Assuming she could afford to eat in the future.

He pressed a fat sausage roll into her hands. "Eat."

She might have argued—she knew what to do with a sausage roll, after all—but her stomach rumbled too loudly for it to have been a convincing effort. It took both shaking hands to get it to her mouth. Firestorms! Maybe she needed his instruction after all.

To their credit, the Guild kitchen produced a decent enough sausage roll. Their flaky pastry was tasty, but tough and dry compared to Birdy's. They did use a better quality of sausage, though—must be nice to afford such luxuries off the backs of journeymen who would never see the Guild's advantages for themselves.

"Can you make it back home now? Or shall I borrow your cloth and set a picnic for you here?" The light of the streetlamps caught his expression just so—such a striking profile. But what did that look in his eyes mean?

She popped the last bit of the sausage roll in her mouth and dabbed her lips on her second Mastery project—perhaps that made it a little more useful than the Wardian case that had been her first.

"I think I can make it back now. I certainly do not want to stay here." Nor ever to see the place again, but she didn't need to say that. She pushed herself off the wall. The world spun for a moment, but settled back quickly enough.

He offered his arm. She took it, mostly because she still needed the support. Later, she would ponder what those emotional entanglements might mean. First, she had to get home.

A pair of lamplighters, now finished with their nightly mission, whistled as they strolled back to return the tools of their trade until they were needed again at morning. How different the street's night dwellers were to those who made their way in the day. What a different world.

"I hardly know what to say." He held her hand against his forearm, looking up into the stars as though there might be answers written in the sky.

"I admit, I was prepared for things to go wrong, but not in so spectacular a fashion as this." She tried to laugh, but it sounded too much like a choked sob. Perhaps now was not the time to prove she still had a sense of humor.

"What you did with the cotton..." He glanced down at the thick, light grey cloth now draped over her arm. "It was spectacular. I have never experienced anything like it, never conceived something like that could be done. Reshaping each fiber ... what that requires ... the mind boggles."

"Clearly, it stupefied the Masters, so much so that they lost all ability to think rationally at all." Yes, sarcasm dripped from her words, like venom from a snake's fangs. Hopefully, he would not take offense. And if he did—well, tonight he would have to deal with it.

"That would be one way of putting it."

"It was foolhardy to expect them to behave otherwise."

"No, it was not. There were those among them who were duly impressed by your work, ready to admit you to the status you deserve. I heard their voices distinctly, among the others."

"And those others will now believe themselves at liberty to hound me at their convenience, demanding I satisfy their curiosity and divulge my 'secrets' to the Masters because I am their junior, and evermore will be so." Her vision fuzzed and blinked away the burning.

"No, that isn't going to happen. Fitzsimons is wrong on so many levels. Dead wrong, and I will not let it stand."

Good that he could not see her roll her eyes. "You believe you can do that?"

"He is wrong about the Guild charter, wrong about procedure, wrong about the way he registered his objection. So many violations of protocol and rule, he has not a leg to stand on."

"Assuming you get anyone to listen to you. Master Cinderford is aligned with the treasurer. I've no clue where the Guild Master stands, but given that he dismissed the meeting rather than bringing it to order, I have my doubts about him, too."

He sighed, scuffing his foot along the cobblestones. "I thought I did, but now I am not so certain."

At least he was being honest. Whether or not she liked what he had to say, it was best he spoke the truth.

"I am so sorry. This was not at all what I expected. Not with Sir Wilbert firmly in our camp."

"You still believe that?" She chanced a peek up at him.

"Absolutely. Without a doubt. When he waved me off to help you out, I am certain he was pulling Allbright, Cinderford, and Fitzsimons into a meeting." He pursed his lips into a wrinkled frown as he walked three more steps. "But you are right. He is not part of the Brighton Guild, so I've no idea how much authority he has over what this chapter does. Dash and damn it all, I am so sorry. I could have—should have—"

"Pray do not go there. I do not blame you. Granted, I would very much like to do so. It would be satisfying to have someone to spew vitriol upon, to be sure. But it would not be fair. You took a significant risk in sponsoring me in the first place, and I appreciate it. I hope it doesn't work against you."

"But it wasn't enough. Dash it all, it wasn't enough." He met her gaze for a long moment, probing, asking with his eyes.

"Pray, don't ask me what I am going to do now. I don't know."

"Promise me you will wait until I have confronted the—"

"No, please. David, no. No more confrontations, no more trying to force stodgy, self-absorbed old Masters to consider any new ideas. Let them all die out and fade into obscurity. It's what they want. Let them have it. In any case, Dick Mallory won't come knocking at my door for another month. So, I have a little time to sort out what to do, where to go. Unfortunately, Brighton is no longer an option. I can't live or work under that sort of constant scrutiny."

"Have you any family to help you?"

"No. My father was alienated from his people, and alienated us from my mother's. I do not know their names, much less where they might be. Even if I did, having never met them, I can hardly show up on their doorstep hand outstretched, can I?" Even if she could, she wouldn't.

"Friends, then. Surely your father had teachers in the other Guild chapters, Masters who would assist you?"

"You underestimate my father's ability to disenfranchise himself from polite, and potentially helpful, company."

"He sounds like my Uncle Cresswell."

"Tell me about him." Anything to keep him from asking more questions she didn't want to answer.

He studied her for a moment—what was he looking for? "Uncle Cresswell is—or was—he could be dead by now and no one would have informed me—a syphilitic drunk who gave the pox to his wife, and accused her of unfaithfulness. He sent her away, pregnant, claiming the child was no spawn of his. It was probably a mercy that she and the child died shortly after the birth. It sounds horrible of me to say such a thing. But Uncle—" he shuddered. "He had a promising career as a barrister, but that is all gone to Pimlico now. Good folk don't want to be represented by a barrister too drunk to know the law. He's lost more friends than I will ever have, and tarnished my reputation more than a mite."

"That makes us kindred spirits, I suppose?" She stared at the street, not daring to meet his eyes right now. Whether she was right or wrong, it would be too much.

"I suppose that means we need to—"

"What is that?" She stopped short, shut her eyes, and concentrated. That faint sound. It was familiar. And yet wrong.

"What? Wait." He stopped, too, and turned his body to face the sound. "I swear, it sounds like that bloody cuckoo—"

"Yes, it does. But it has gone on too long, too many times. There is no reason for it."

"You told me your father was ever fiddling with the clock. Is it possible—"

"That he made it to screech for some other reason than to sound the hours?" A shiver slithered down her spine. "I suppose. Yes, that's possible, but it's never done that before."

"What could trigger it?"

That smell. She parted her lips and drew in a deep breath, tasting, rubbing her tongue against the smoky flavor on the roof of her mouth. "Fire!"

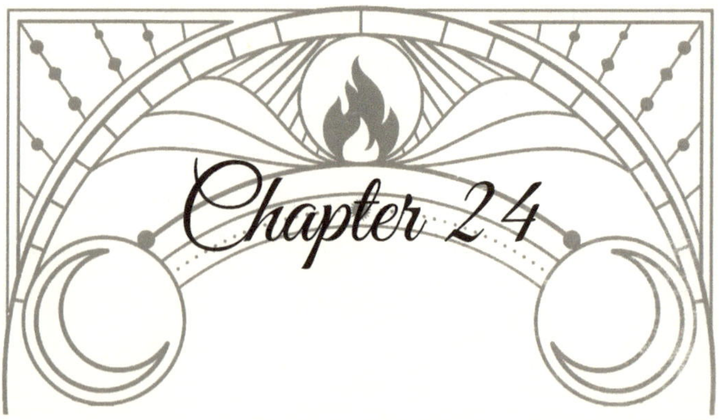

# Chapter 24

SHE JERKED HER HAND from his arm and ran for the mews behind her shop. David followed closely, pulling ahead in the last hundred yards. The faint odor of smoke swirled about him, growing more potent with every step. Still too faint for the mundane to notice, but it wouldn't be long before the curious would be peeking out their windows.

Pray not let it be the Fix-All shop. Maybe the shed in the mews? Something that could be contained easily ...

Damn and bloody hell!

Smoke curled from the shop's open back door that sported damage unrelated to any sort of flame.

Rebecca paused a dozen steps from the door, panting, eyes wide. "We've got to spread the alarm—the fire brigade... wait, do you hear that?"

The cuckoo clock continued screaming from the shop. But there was another voice shouting with it.

"Someone's in there? Whoever broke in is still there?" Fire-Wind-and-Air!

"Most likely. It sounds like the boy—"

"Mallory's boy?"

"He sent Fletcher to rob me once. Why wouldn't Mallory use him again?" She pressed her fist to her lips. "I can't—I can't leave him in there." She wrapped her project over her shoulders.

David caught her hand. "You can't, you're still too spent." He snatched the cloth from her shoulders. "Raise the alarm. I'll try and get him."

She looked from him to the open door and back. "Condemn it! I hate that you're right. Go!" She ran for Birdy's back door.

The cuckoo and the boy screamed again. If the clock survived the fire, he would have to figure out how Fuller had created it...

He wrapped Rebecca's project over his head like a cloak, ducked low, and rushed inside. With one hand ahead of him, he pushed smoke up and out of his way, with the other, he pulled Air in through the open back door. Not much, just enough to keep around him so he could breathe.

Creeping through the back room, he could make out flames beyond, on the shop floor.

"Help!" A boy's voice. Rebecca must be right.

If it had been Mallory, he would leave the blackguard to his fate, but a boy? Even if he had been the one to set the fire ... no, he could not turn his back on a child.

He crawled toward the door, smoke heavy above him, heat increasing against his face. Somehow, though, it seemed Rebecca's project blocked the hot air from reaching him. Poking his head inside the shop, his eyes burned with smoke and fire. A pile of ... something... in the center of the shop burned like a Guy Fawkes bonfire.

Clearly deliberate.

"Where are you?" David shouted, rising up, only to be blinded in the haze.

"Help me, please, help me!" The plaintive words came from the back corner behind the workbench.

"Get on your belly and come to me!"

"I can't! I can't see you!"

"You don't have to. Follow my voice."

"I'm scared! The flames will get me. I can't control them!"

Control them? Did the child have some kind of Skill?

"They aren't alive, son. They aren't after you."

"Yes, yes, they are! You don't understand. They are angry at me for doing this! They're going to kill me!" the boy shrieked. "I ain't never done nothing like this before. Ain't never tried to hurt nothing with fire. I made sure no one was here—I thought ..."

"Stop your blithering. If you don't listen to me, the flames will kill you. Do what I tell you, and you'll live. Now, get on your belly and crawl."

The boy wailed. "No! No! I can't!"

Stupid child deserved his fate. The flames popped and sent burning embers flying. They landed on Rebecca's cloth on his shoulder, glaring and hissing at him. He felt only their weight through the fabric, no heat. With a flick of his shoulder, the embers dislodged and bounced along the floor, smoldering.

David coughed and readjusted the cloth over his head. Still, he couldn't leave the boy to it. And if he was an undiscovered Wright, all the more so. What were they going to do with him, though? How could they get him away from his father and train him? Was he already so bent in criminal ways that they should allow his Skill to fade away lest he become a rogue?

All things which didn't need to be determined now. Survive first.

Pressing his shoulder along the back wall, he belly-crawled toward the boy. "I'm heading your way. Come to me if you can."

The flames in the center of the room snapped and a fiery bit of wood flew toward them.

"It's attacking! I told you. I told you! It hates me!"

David pulled Air away from the flaming bit, smothering it to a hot coal. "Don't be daft, boy. Fire isn't a living thing. Now come."

A shadow from the corner inched closer.

"That's it, keep coming. I'm heading your way." Flames from the central fire licked at the ceiling. Once they caught overhead... "Hurry! There's not much time."

# Chapter 25

"Birdy! Birdy!" Rebecca pounded the back door. "Fire! Fire!"

The door inched open and Balthazar poked his head out, Birdy close behind. "What? What're you talking about?"

"The shop, there's a fire. You need to clear your building."

Birdy stepped into the mews, saw the smoke and gasped. She dashed inside, crying, "Fire! Fire!" She must have grabbed a pot and spoon to bang as she ran.

Rebecca ran on to each house along the mews, raising the alarm. She ducked down the alleyway to the street and found the fire bell near the streetlight and rang it with everything she had. "Fire! Fire!"

People, most in their nightdresses, trickled, then poured out into the street.

"Where?" a whiskered man with an old-fashioned banyan tied over his nightdress asked.

"My shop." She pointed. "I was out and came back to..."

The man grabbed a nearby boy's shoulder. "Run to the fire station—go quick, lad, run! Buckets! Find buckets!" The boy dashed off, and the man trotted into the crowd.

How long would it take for the fire brigade to come?

She rushed back to the mews, slowed by the crowd and the questions. So many questions. Almost all well-meaning, but with no useful answers, they were pointless distractions.

Another crowd gathered in the mews, blocking her view of the shop. "Excuse me. Please, let me through ... Pardon me ..."

Finally, she shoved her way to her shop. "David! David!"

Several milling people turned toward her

"Have you seen him come out of the shop? There was someone inside. He was trying to rescue them."

Blank looks, shaking heads, shrugs.

"I ain't seen him." Birdy laid her hand on Rebecca's shoulder. "I heard something fall inside."

"No!" Rebecca turned toward the door, but Birdy grabbed her arm.

"Don't go in there, lass. You can't help none."

She yanked her arm away and ran for the door.

Heavy, acrid smoke dropped her to her knees a step inside. "David! David!"

"Here! Don't try it. It's too much."

"Where are you?" Dragging clean Air from the door and pushing smoke aside, she crawled in through the back room.

"Don't come in. You can't."

Nearly at the door into the shop now. "Don't tell me what I can't do."

"Stay back!"

The cuckoo screamed, weaker than before.

"You're near the clock, aren't you?"

"Don't come in!"

She peeked into the shop—yes, she could barely make them out, huddled near the wall under the clock. A mass of flames—hot, blistering hot—between them and the doorway. "Cover your faces!"

She lifted her hands and wrung the Air near the flames. A small shower rained down, dampening, but not quite drowning them. "Along the wall, you can make it now! Quickly! Quickly!"

A cloth covered mass lumbered her way.

"How'd you do that?" Fletcher stared at her.

"I did nothing. You're smoke-addled. Run for the door." She grabbed the boy's arm and shoved him toward the back room. He scrambled away.

David took her upper arm. "You too, now. We've got to get out."

"No. I've got to save this. It's all I have." She tore away from his grasp.

"You can't do this alone. Let me help."

"How?"

"Take my hand. Remember when we worked the stone and our Skills touched? If we do that again, join our strength ... I'm not skilled enough with Fire to put it out directly, though."

"Don't need to be," she panted hard. "Use Air, not Fire."

"Push the Air from the shop and suffocate the Fire?"

"Yes."

"Together ... no one has ever tried that before ..." She grabbed his hand and they faced the flames. "Can you feel my Skill?"

"Can you find mine?" He squeezed her hand hard.

"Yes, yes, it's there." Heavens, what were they doing? How was this supposed to work? They might well bring the building down atop them.

"Gather Air with me. I know this is utterly daft, but we can't get distracted wondering how this works." He squeezed her hand again.

He was right. Hot Air, writhing with the flames, gathered between them, more than she had ever attempted to control on her own. "With this much, I think we can do it."

"On your mark, then." He glanced at her, nodding, face covered in soot and ash, sweat trickling down his cheeks.

"On three. One ... two..." Was it even possible? "Three!"

Strength, far more than her own, more than his alone, more than the sum of their strength, surged through her veins, her bones, to her hands, now tingling, burning with surging power. Almost too much to control. If they lost hold, it could pull their breath away, like Joseph. Kill them both. Control, find the control. Hold on to the Air...no. Not hold it, can't hold Air. Raise up a wall around them. Divide them from what they pushed away.

A wall of Air swept out from a foot ahead of them, over the flames, shattering the front windows in a violent explosion. As the glass fell around them, the breath tore away from her lungs and blackness descended.

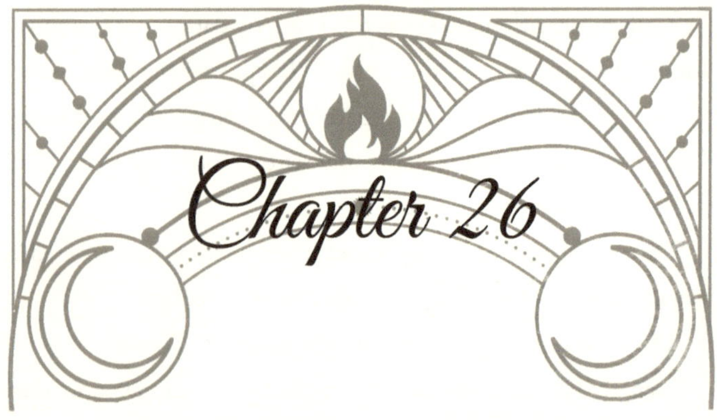

# Chapter 26

REBECCA COLLAPSED INTO HIM as the fire's glow snuffed out. He fought against the dragging forces, threatening to pull every last bit of Air from his body. Gasping, he clawed breath into his burning, aching lungs. Breathe, he had to breathe!

Heat ... light ... gone. Cool air pouring in. No strength, exhausted. Falling, no, could not fall. He fought to stand on his knees. Escape; must get out ... he forced his eyes open.

Ash and charred remains everywhere. So much dust hanging in the air. A few glowing embers, yes, but no wall of heat, no flames.

The fire was out. He sagged back on his heels.

They had defeated it! He would have whooped, had the breath to speak.

Somehow, they had managed the impossible.

"We did it! It's over! You were right." He croaked out the words in a ragged whisper. Slipping an arm around her shoulders, he supported her, but her head lolled like a broken doll's.

No!

He pulled her closer and pressed an ear to her chest. There, yes, a flutter of heartbeat. A tiny rise of breath. She lived! But barely. Spent beyond measure, she needed help.

He planted a foot hard and pressed up, staggering to his feet. Not much better off than her. Bloody hell! No way he could carry her out.

Men, firemen, rushed in.

"You there! Are you hurt?"

"We need help. Can't..." he collapsed to his knees again.

Firemen swarmed around them, manhandling them out the back door into the mews. The horde dispersed, leaving them on the cold ground, surrounded by a milling crowd. David staggered to his feet.

With a loud cry of thanks, Birdy rushed over and took charge of Rebecca. Good, good, she would be in safe hands. Safe. Cared for. Perhaps he should ...

A man in a Fire Captain's helmet charged in and blocked David's view. "What happened? What were you doing in there?"

"A boy, Fletcher Mallory ... trapped inside. He started the fire. He confessed. Had to get him out. Got him, before ... explosion." David wheezed; no breath left to speak. He cupped his hands to his face, discreetly pulling Air to him, reacquainting his lungs with their Element.

"Sit." The captain waved for someone to bring water.

"Anyone else hurt?"

"No, it doesn't seem so. The explosion put out the fire. Damned lucky, all of you. Don't know why the explosion didn't level the building." He dragged the back of his hand across his forehead. "So lucky."

Yes, they were, but not for reasons the Fire Captain understood. "The boy?"

"That's a matter for the constables. I'm sure they'll be here sooner or later. Sit tight. Gotta make sure there're no more active fires about." The captain trotted off.

Should find Rebecca, tend to her. He craned his neck, searching the crowd for signs of her or Birdy. There, not too far. Dash it all! His legs refused to cooperate.

At least she would be cared for properly with Birdy, if he couldn't see to her himself.

He covered his face with his hands. The surrounding chaos ... too much right now.

What had they done? Such a thing wasn't possible, or at least he would have been certain of it until just now. Wrights worked alone, in private. Their Skills could not fuse that way.

But they just had.

They just had.

The magnitude of the task they had accomplished, it was the sort of thing whispered by apprentices and journeymen still day-dreaming of what sorts of magnificent powers they would learn to wield as Master Wrights. Of fairy tales of old that all true Masters knew were simply flights of fancy.

Until now.

How had their Skills come together, blended, magnifying until the whole was greater than the sum of the parts?

What was more, neither of them was born an Air Wright. Even a Master Air Wright could not have done what they had. How was it possible? Was Morris Fuller right? All the Elements really were one?

She was the one who had done it all, though. She was the one who had directed their joined Skill. It was her expertise, her strength, her understanding that made it all feasible.

Expertise and understanding that the Brighton Guild was ready to throw away over a foolish, irrelevant technicality.

"You there? You all right?"

David peeked over his hands.

A man in a constable's uniform approached. Constable Moore. "The Fire Captain said you had something to tell me? Something about the fire?"

Oh bollocks! The boy! "Yes, yes. The reason we were inside."

Moore pulled a pad and pencil from his pocket. "Why don't you start from the beginning and let me get it all down, then I'll find someone to help you back to your lodgings."

# Chapter 27

THE CONSTABLE THAT HELPED David home also informed Mrs. Gaskill of David's heroic actions, rescuing a boy from certain death in the fires. Mrs. Gaskill was so pleased to count a hero among her boarders, David didn't have the heart to disabuse her of the notion by telling her of the boy's role in the fire. Having survived a housefire as a girl, Mrs. Gaskill dreaded them like nothing else and had little sympathy for those who would set fires.

She helped David to his room, fussed over him, dressed the wounds he hadn't even realized he had, and made up plates of his favorite foods to keep in the kitchen for him until he was ready to eat.

Largely because of her smothering attentions, by the second day after the fire, he was up first thing in the morning and on his way to the Guild Hall. It was time to prove he actually was a hero by saving the Guild from itself. Hopefully, with Sir Wilbert's support, he could wrest success out of the debacle of the Assembly.

Come to think of it, it was rather odd no one from the Guild had called upon him after the fire. It was the type of information that got around town quickly enough. Surely, they knew of it. Given he was an officer of the Guild, they should have shown some concern.

Strange.

Ames opened the cellar entrance door for him. "Welcome, Enright, do come in." His somber tones hung in the air like a low cloud, palpable and heavy, taking up the entire doorway. "What brings you in this morning? Haven't seen you since the Assembly."

David edged past the heaviness, into the cool, gaslamp-lit hall. "I should have thought the reason would be well known, at least here at Guild Hall."

Ames blinked several times, head turning this way and that, like a confused crow. "No idea what you are talking about. Did something happen?"

David slapped his forehead. "Truly? You have no idea?"

"Fitzsimons has suggested you were keeping away, pouting over the outcome of the Assembly."

David snorted—or it might have been a snarl. Ames could decide that for himself.

"Don't get me wrong. I could hardly believe you would stoop to such unbecoming behavior, even in light of a disappointment." Ames peered into David's eyes, unkempt brows drawing low. "Say, what did happen?"

Gossipmonger. "Have you seen Sir Wilbert? Is he about?"

Ames stopped his frown almost as soon as it had begun. "'Fraid not. I heard he packed up and left Brighton the day after the Assembly. There might have been some unpleasantness with Cinderford or the Guild Master himself, or perhaps a falling-out with his hosts. But I wouldn't know much about that. Though those folks he was staying with, Lackwood's the name, I think, there's quite a buzz going about today. Some say merchants won't take nothing but cash from them.

Quite an ugly thing, to be sure. Can't imagine why working folks would turn on a nice family like that. You did some work for them recently, no?" Ames thumbed his lapels and rocked back on his heels.

Did Ames believe himself subtle or clever? "Not something I would know much about. Do you know anything about Sir Wilbert's plans?"

"No idea if he has concluded his business here, or if he intends to return at some point. No idea at all."

"I see." Clearly Ames knew more than he let on, but David would not take the bait. Such games the man played. "You will excuse me. I have a great deal of work to catch up on." Ames' disappointed stare bored into his back as he sauntered off.

Why would Sir Wilbert suddenly take off? That could not be a good sign. A representative of the Royal Court Guild should be in possession of more spine.

Ah, well, he had one less ally today. Disappointing, but that hardly altered his course. But it changed where he would begin. He ducked down a narrow side corridor that contained both the ghastly file room and what passed for the Guild Library.

Library first.

The most impressive thing about the library was the striking door marking the entrance. Elaborate oak, wright-carved with the traditional symbols of the four Elements. A bit of gold paint embellished the carving, lending a regal sense to the otherwise arcane symbology. It used to remind David of the basic foundations of the Wright's Skill. But now it seemed silly and old-fashioned, covered in marks of a world gone by.

Perhaps, if he succeeded, he would not be the only one to think so.

Shameful that the library behind such a door could fit in only a few bookcases, in a room barely larger than David's office. Shouldn't there be countless tomes of wisdom and great weight contained here? A desk and a chair might also be welcome additions, but were only necessary if someone intended to make use of the library's works. Considering the amount of dust on the shelves, that rarely happened.

Master McIntire had often described the Guild Library in London as a repository of wonder. Shelves reached to high ceilings in bookcases that lined the walls and in many rows beyond. Many desks with scholars pouring over wise tomes, sharing ideas with one another.

When all this settled, David would explore the London Guild Library for himself. So many things he needed to better understand in light of all that had happened.

For now, though, he had to find the volumes with all the bylaws. Naturally, they were not on the shelf set aside and labeled for such works. Bother it all! As Guild Secretary, the library was Cinderford's purview. Come to think of it, so was the file room.

Neither coincidence nor comforting. Bah!

There! Tucked away in the most difficult to reach spot of the most difficult to reach shelf. Probably intentional, but perhaps that was a touch more cynicism than was deserved.

Or not.

He shimmied between dusty bookcases to scale the farthest one back. Yes, it felt like sacrilege to be using the lower shelves like ladder steps, but with no ladder present, what choice had he? Interesting, the dust hadn't been disturbed on these shelves.

Just as he'd thought. Bloody little rat Fitzsimons hadn't even bothered to check if the rule he was relying upon was still in force.

Once he'd wrestled the books down, David sat on the floor near the shelves. With his clothes already full of dust and cobwebs, why bother dragging in a table and chair at this point? He spread the books on the floor before him.

Two issues to sort out. First, the voting rules, which should be simple and straightforward. Those should be set down as amendments to the bylaws, laid out with little ambiguity. Best start with the most recent volume and work backwards. Old rules were ever being rewritten and superseded by new ones.

Of course, the volume was handwritten by a man who clearly did not benefit from the kind of penmanship instruction David had. He rubbed his knuckles. How beating his hand black and blue had improved his penmanship, he'd never understood, but his fine penmanship suggested it had worked. Perhaps.

Ah, yes, there! Difficult—no laborious—to make out, but it was there. Elucidated in spidery scrawl, the official rules of attendance and voting. Exactly as he told Fitzsimons it was. Wouldn't he be pleased to hear that? Best try not to gloat whilst shoving the bylaw amendments under his nose. Better that than down his throat.

No, he would not follow that train of thought, tempting though it might be. His tools were laws, rules, and procedures. Not his fists.

Now regarding dues. It should be enough that they voted to overlook the dues rules in Rebecca's case. But it would be more convincing if he found some precedent for doing it. But that wouldn't be in the bylaws and charter. For that, he would have to tackle the impossible-to-describe-in-polite-terms file room.

He tucked the useful volume under his arm and trudged to seek his fortune in the chaos next door.

Three hours, three bloody hours, marked by the polite ticking of his pocket watch, not that wretched cuckoo in the Fix-All shop. Odd, how accustomed he had grown to that ghastly thing, even missing it now. Who would have thought? At least it would have kept him company as he sifted through notes and receipts and scraps of paper he could not quite categorize.

But he found it! He held his prize aloft, biting back the urge to whoop with glee, or at least gloat loudly. A note from the Guild Master before Allbright, granting an exception to Fitzsimons' convenient rule. And it was in regard to that Guild Master's own journeyman! Exactly the kind of precedent David needed. If it had been done once, then there was no reason it couldn't or shouldn't be done now, for the journeyman of another Guild officer.

Marking the place in the volume of bylaws with the relevant note, he dusted himself off, straightened his coat, and steeled himself to deal with what would be two perturbed old men. Best chat with Allbright first, though, and prepare him for the storm.

David peeked in Allbright's partially opened door, the tidy, spacious office such a contrast to the cramped, chaotic rooms in which David had spent his morning. "Might I have a word with you, Guild Master?"

Allbright set aside his pen, gesturing for David to enter, and shut the door behind him. "Yes, yes. I was wondering when you would come around."

"You are aware of what happened, are you not?" David sat in Cinderford's favorite chair, back straight, shoulders pulled back. The wright-crafted breeze that seemed to blow from the false windows dislodged a clump of dust from his lapel and it wafted gently onto Allbright's massive desk.

"I trust you were not injured in the fire, no?" Allbright shut the ledger he had been writing in and leaned forward on his elbows.

David deposited his book on the edge of the desk. "I am rather surprised you would have taken no pains to find out more directly. Sir."

"You are a grown man, are you not, Enright? You don't expect mollycoddling from the Guild, do you?"

"Certainly not. Still, I was under the impression it's considered common courtesy."

"I suppose courtesy is sometimes lost amidst other, higher priorities." Allbright stroked the length of his beard.

"Higher priorities, sir? Since I have been unavailable for several days—and on that matter, yes, I am recovering suitably, thank you for inquiring—would you bring me up to date on these high-priority Guild matters?"

"Oh, do not be such a prig, Enright. It is unbecoming. You know as well as I, the trouble you stirred up for the last assembly."

"I stirred up, sir? I must beg to differ. Have you forgotten, my part was done in accordance with our charter and bylaws, with the support of the now conspicuously-absent Royal Court Guild representative? It was Fitzsimons who caused the disruption, and I dare say he did so in the most inflammatory way possible. Do not place that on me."

Allbright's eyes narrowed into a fierce glower. "You were the one who sponsored Miss Fuller."

"As one of our local Masters should have stepped up to do some time ago!"

Allbright muttered something under his breath.

"You fault me for stepping in to right a wrong that had been committed by the Guild?"

"You were the only one who noticed." Allbright spoke through gritted teeth.

"No, Miss Fuller did, as well. And in truth, what matters who noticed it? We were not being faithful to our own principles. Does that not bother you?"

"Does it not bother you to have caused chaos and division within the Guild?"

"That was Fitzsimons. How can you not understand?" David's pulse pounded in his temples. "The meeting was calm until he erroneously brought up a rule—"

"Yes, about that. He has an excellent point. It seems prudent—"

"Prudent? Pray excuse me, sir, did you say prudent? How can you consider that behavior prudent? There was plenty of time for him to register that objection well before the Assembly."

"As I understand, it took him some time to find the documentation—"

"Which is another issue that needs to be addressed, but that is for a later time." David drew a deep breath. Calm, he needed calm. "Regarding Fitzsimons' argument, there are two significant issues. First of all, you can examine the exact rule of order he objected to and to which we adhered when taking the vote." David turned the volume to face Allbright and shoved it toward him, opened to the correct page. David pointed at the relevant paragraph until Allbright put on his glasses and squinted at the page.

"That does not—"

"Yes, sir, it does. If you would take the time to read the text, you would—"

"Are you lecturing me, son?"

David banged his fist on the desk. "Do not condescend, sir. It is my job to assist you in such matters. If not as Undersecretary, then as the Guild Legal Counsel. If we do not adhere to our own bylaws, such as is the case now, according to our own charter, Miss Fuller has legal recourse—"

"Only if someone will take on her case." Allbright scowled his silent accusation.

"Are you suggesting I should not do the job to which I was appointed?"

"I suggest you should consider carefully how that task should be accomplished. Your future with the Guild might well depend upon it."

"Is that a threat?" David stood, braced his hands on the desk, and leaned toward Allbright. "Are you suggesting I violate the rules of my office, the rules of principle, of decency to deny a member of the Guild what they are entitled to?"

"A member who is in arrears on their dues."

"In response to the failure of the Guild to uphold their duties to that member. One might argue the Guild is in arrears to the member in question."

"Absurd, you are twisting words to suit your ill-informed opinions."

"Ill-informed, sir? Are you suggesting I do not know how to read the law?" At least Allbright's opinions of him were clear now. Rebecca's suspicions were right.

"I am suggesting you are trying to advance your particular agenda without respect—"

"Are you not supporting that very thing with Fitzsimons?"

"I am merely appreciating his attention to our charter."

"And what about that of your Legal Counsel—or have you forgotten my role? You can see here, in a clause which supersedes his references, a legitimate vote had been taken that day in your office. Also, here is precedent, provided by the Guild Master whose post you assumed, where that exact thing was done for his journeyman who was behind in his dues."

"So, it has been done before? What has that to do with the situation today?" Allbright shoved the book toward David.

"I cannot believe you even ask that question!"

The door flew open and Cinderford and Fitzsimons burst in. "Guild Master!"

David jumped to intercept them. "Excuse me, but this is a private meeting. How dare you burst in like that?" How had they known about this conference?

Probably Ames. So, he was in on this, too. Lovely.

"No, no, this is my office, not yours. It's fitting that they be part of this discussion." Allbright stood and waved them in. "Enright, do be good enough to show them what you have shown me."

The rat and the candle stub crowded close, hovering over David's shoulders like schoolmasters eager to find fault. He read each of the relevant documents aloud, pointing to each word as he read it. He could also play the role of a schoolmaster.

"I still do not approve of your so-called vote." Fitzsimons folded his arms and huffed. Did he stomp his foot as well?

"It does not appear to matter if you approve or not. The rules state you were in attendance at the meeting and a binding vote was taken." Allbright's mild tone only seemed to increase Fitzsimons' agitation.

What side was Allbright on? What manner of game was he playing?

Fitzsimons' nose twitched like a rat's as he snorted. "Be that as it may—"

"And you can be assured we will be drafting a proposal to change that rule—" Cinderford interrupted, glaring directly at David.

"Be that as it may, it does nothing to change this. A rule is a rule." Fitzsimons slammed down his copy of the charter addendum, crossed his arms, and tossed his head as though to declare victory.

"I am sorry to disagree with you, but this might." David laid the file room note top Fitzsimons' scrap. "Not only was the vote taken within the rules, there is precedent, recent precedent for such an action. In fact, the Master in question is still a member in good standing among our ranks today. Perhaps you would like to speak with him?"

"No, I would not. I care not who he is, nor what he might have to say." Cinderford sputtered. "You cannot agree with this, Guild Master. You simply cannot. That woman and everything she stands for is a hazard to our existence."

"Do you mean to say the woman, who stood before the Masters of Brighton and demonstrated Skill we would have considered impossible, is some kind of threat to us all?" David folded his arms across his chest and stared down his nose.

"You saw for yourself the chaos she caused in our always peaceful assemblies." Fitzsimons threw up open hands.

"The chaos came when you stormed in with your ill-founded accusations. You can't shift the blame on her for that."

"Not since her father's days have we seen such discord in one of our meetings. It was her presence that sparked the strife. Simply because you have feelings toward her ..."

"Do not conflate issues. It seems the issues you have are with her father, not with her," David said.

"It started with Morris Fuller, but what he began, she continues," Cinderford said. "She is every bit as much trouble as he was."

"Each Wright is to be judged by their own merit. That is our way." David pinched the bridge of his nose. "Or have you forgotten our fundamental principles?"

"Why wait for her to continue the destruction her father began? The writing is on the wall. You were not here to experience the havoc Morris Fuller wreaked, Enright." Cinderford stepped closer. "But we were, we all were. None of us will forget how he threatened the traditions, the stability of the Guild."

"And you truly believe she should be judged for his transgressions? Is that any way to manage our membership? There's not one of us without some dodgy relative to be held against us." David turned to Allbright. "Sir, this comes down to you. You see the precedent, clearly you can make allowances for the situation and remain well within established practice. You must take a stand, sir, for the sake of the Brighton Guild chapter. You must take a stand. How is this branch of the Guild to be run?"

"You have a point there, Enright." Allbright clasped his hands behind his back and paced the length of his office. "The good of the Guild appears to be the prevailing concern here."

"The Wrights at large, not just the local Guild. There is a broader picture as well. Pray remember that." David said.

"But that starts with the local Guild, does it not?" Cinderford paced alongside Allbright.

What was Cinderford going to do next, kiss Allbright's feet?

"There is much to consider, much to consider."

"The matter is relatively clear and uncomplicated. I encourage you not to allow sentimentality to confuse matters." David clenched his jaw.

"Yes, yes, you make a good point. An excellent one." Allbright returned to his desk and sat down. "This is a serious matter, and I must consider the best course for the Guild at large."

Thank heavens he would put an end—

"And for that reason, for the sake of the unity of the Brighton Guild, and the integrity of our philosophy and teaching, I must deny Miss Fuller's application for Mastery, and in accordance with long-accepted rules, assign her the status of perpetual journeyman."

"You have made an excellent choice, for the sake of the Guild and all its members." Fitzsimons and Cinderford crowded in to offer congratulations.

"Excuse me, but did I hear you correctly? In what way is this for the good of the Guild? Do you not recall anything Sir Wilbert told us? How he spoke of dwindling numbers, failing apprentices, and a threat of extinction on the horizon?"

"And that is the reason why we must stick to the principles and philosophies that have carried us so far. Surely you can understand—" Allbright said.

"Nothing of the sort. This is shortsighted at best. Ignorant and fearmongering at the worst."

"How dare you speak to your Guild Master that way!" Cinderford shoved himself between David and Allbright.

"My Guild Master? I am ashamed to be associated with such a foolhardy decision."

"Ashamed to be associated? You are undersecretary here. You might want to rethink your words," Fitzsimons said.

"Hardly. What I need to rethink is my association with you." David slammed his hands on the desk. "I am done with this nonsense. I resign my office and my loyalty to the Wrights of Brighton..."

"If you do that, you can no longer practice your Skill among us." Cinderford's sly smile suggested he thought he'd played a trump card.

"I am well aware, Master Cinderford. I am well aware. I will be happy to leave you to your own practices. And let you inbreed yourselves into extinction. Good day."

# Chapter 28

REBECCA DRAGGED IN A sandpaper breath—when had Air become so rough it tore her throat on the way to her burning lungs? At least the thundering in her head had subsided to the point she could hear something other than the dull drumbeat pulsing in time with her heart.

When had she gone to bed? She wasn't wearing her corset, so she had changed at some point. How could she not remember putting on a nightdress? What a strange thing to forget. What had happened...

... wait, yes.

The Guild Assembly.

The fire!

Fletcher Mallory. David!

David!

What had happened to him? Where was he?

Rebecca fought layers of sheets and blankets, clinging like live animals, determined to keep her in place, as she struggled to sit up and force her eyes open.

Oh, bright! It was too bright! She shaded her eyes with her hand.

Mrrrow. A paw batted at her foot. Balthazar, there at the foot of the bed. How thoughtful of him not to have slept on her chest. It probably would have been the death of her.

She sucked in another arduous breath. What was that, riding on the air? Food; hot, fresh food. Her stomach clenched as though she had never eaten before and might not survive if she didn't soon.

Unfortunately, that might be true.

"I thought I 'erd you stirrin', lass. Don't be getting' up yet, ya know. I don't think you be up to that, yet." Birdy's soothing island lilt, everything wise and warm and soft and good, filled the room

Rebecca squinted and peered toward the voice. Birdy, in her familiar worn apron and warm smile, trundled toward her with a tray of mouthwatering smells.

"Jus' you lay back dere now, and have you somethin' ta eat." Birdy laid the tray on a small table next to the bed and helped Rebecca prop herself up on a mound of fluffy pillows.

"Where am I?"

"Dontcha remember? You're at me place. The firemen helped me bring you up here after they took you outta da fire."

"I ... I don't remember." She glanced around the small, white room with exposed beams and a plain wood floor. A worn, ragged curtain struggled to shield a roughly-framed open window that cast sunbeams on the lopsided press and equally crooked chair in the far corner.

"I can't say as I'm surprised." Birdy sat at the side of the bed and placed the heavy tray in Rebecca's lap. "You barely been awake a'tall since it happened."

"How long have I been here?" Rebecca pressed her temples with the heels of her hands, trying to force Birdy's answers into her sluggish mind.

"Three days, now, lass, three days. I been able to rouse you enough to get some hot soup in you, maybe some porridge and some jam, but then you go right back to sleep. It's a relief to see you finally comin' round to yourself again." She handed Rebecca a knife and fork. "Eat now, talk later."

"The fire? The shop? What happened?"

"I can't say I knows exactly." Birdy folded her arms across her chest and waited for Rebecca to take several bites.

How was it possible to make ham and roasted apples taste this delightful? Surely if magic were real, it was resident in Birdy's kitchen.

"I heard a young boy ran out of the shop's back door not long after you went in. Then there was this gawdawful explosion spewing glass everywhere. Then the fire brigade came along and pulled you and your young man out. They said the explosion snuffed the fire somehow, but had no idea how that could have happened. It was the darndest thing, they said. The constables came 'round looking for the boy." She leaned close and dropped her voice to a whisper, "Word has it the scamp might o'had something ta do with the fire. Trouble seems to follow that one."

Rebecca fell back against the pillows. Eating should not be so exhausting. She swallowed another luscious mouthful. "So, he's all right then?"

"The boy? As far as I heard, he scampered off, though he might a'been found by now."

"Not the boy, David."

Birdy chuckled. "Ah, him. He's fine, not to worry."

A worried knot in Rebecca released so abruptly she nearly sagged like a rag doll. "He's been by every afternoon to check on you. I imagine he'll be here before long. He's been quite insistent."

She tried to force her smile back, but it was a pointless effort.

"You should be smilin'. He's the kind one marries!" Birdy grinned. "I'll send him up to call when he comes by today."

How utterly improper—though Rebecca would have it no other way. "Did the fire spread? Were any other buildings—"

"There were a few small fires, a little damage, but not much. Nothing that people cannot take care of on their own." Birdy patted Rebecca's arm.

"And the shop? Is it lost?"

"I can't say. I've seen some men looking at the building, but I haven't been able to get much out of them. From the look of it, though, the t'ings on your displays are pretty well lost, but that damned cuckoo clock is still screaming every blessed hour."

Of course the clock survived. How fitting. And hopeful. "And my rooms above?"

"I have no idea, none at all. But not to worry. You can stay here with me as long as you need—"

"But—"

"No, I won't hear none o' dat. You always been there for me, no questions asked. It may not be much, but the room's here for you as long as you need. Now, eat up. I need to tend the kitchen. Call out if you have a need." Birdy ambled out.

David was safe. Thank heavens for that. But the rest? She threw her arm over her eyes.

What was she going to do? Even if the structure was sound, how was she going to repair the shop? Without the shop, there was no income to pay for repairs. And the Guild—no point in even thinking of that.

She had a place to stay for now, though. There was that. She didn't have to run away in haste. Perhaps she might be able to help Birdy out to cover her room and board for a bit. If her basement workshop was still accessible, perhaps she could still use that. As soon as she was strong enough—who knew when that would be? And if the Guild permitted her to continue her work and did not shut her down out of spite.

Merciful heavens, it hurt to breathe. She pulled her arms in tight against her ribs. How close had she come to sharing her brother's fate?

In the back corners of her mind, she had blamed Joseph for his fate, criticized him for shoddy wrighting, but how wrong that judgment. No one had ever warned them about how depleting using Father's methods could be.

Was Father even aware of the dangers inherent in the methods he'd taught them? Certainly, he had never seemed to take any safeguards...

A sharp rap on her door. "You up to seein' the constable, lass?"

She gulped and grabbed the dressing gown lying across the foot of the bed. That was probably better than being left alone with her own thoughts. "Yes, I suppose that would be all right." She nearly put the dressing gown on upside down, but somehow, she shoved her arms in the sleeves, and tied it.

The door swung open and Constable Moore strode in. "Thank you for seeing me, Miss Fuller." He tipped his hat and pulled the lopsided wooden chair from the far corner of the room close to her bed.

Birdy propped the door open and backed away.

"You gave us all quite a scare, there. I'm happy to see you've finally woken up." His earnest smile crinkled the edges of his dark eyes.

"Thank you for your concern. I pray you don't have too many questions for me. I fear I hardly recall anything that's happened." She pressed up on her elbows and inched higher on the pile of pillows.

"Not a surprise, to be sure. Lucky thing, I'm not here to ask questions. Mr. Enright, who was pulled from the building with you, has provided us with most all the answers we needed."

"Then, might I ask, why you have come to call? Surely this is not a social visit. I am far too informally dressed for that."

"I wish I could say that it was, but you're right." Chuckling, he crossed his legs and clasped his hands over his knee. "Still, though, asking after your health is a business matter."

"I'm not sure I understand."

"Arson is considered a crime. The degree of your injuries determines what additional charges we might press. The boy is sitting in the gaol right now, just determining what is to be done with him."

"Fletcher Mallory? But his father—" Her voice hitched in her throat.

"Not to worry. Dick Mallory is sitting with him. It seems there is a great deal to sort out there. That little trick of theirs, having the boy rob establishments whilst Mallory kept them busy, has been going on for some time. You were the first to register a complaint. Since the fire and word spreading of the boy's involvement, several more have come forward. We've got quite the investigation going on. I expect a long prison stay for them both."

"I suppose it was naïve of me to assume I would have been the sole recipient of his attentions." She bit her lower lip. Was it better or worse to believe that they had not singled her out? Odd thought, that. "But how revolting to use a child like that."

"He would not be the first, and certainly won't be the last. I'm sure you won't be surprised to learn we are also investigating his money-lending practices. Apparently, you're not the first to have concerns about his contracts. Those may take some time, and there's no telling the outcome, but I don't expect his wife will be trying to collect on those debts in the meantime. As of right now, she's not considered part of his schemes, and she would like to keep it that way."

"I can hardly believe that he is being held accountable."

"You and most everyone else in the neighborhood, I would say. I had three random people stop me on my way here, asking if the rumors of their incarceration were true. Seems that boy has a history of mischief—"

"I'm astonished. Dick Mallory has always evaded consequences before. Is it possible he won't this time?" Rebecca rubbed the bone scars on her left arm.

"I hate to predict the outcome of a trial, but the evidence is piling up."

"Speaking of piles," she forced a little laugh—quite a pathetic effort. "You wouldn't happen to know the state of my shop, would you?"

"After the explosion, there isn't much left of the shop interior. Experts in such things are being called upon to determine whether the building is safe, though. I can't say when there will be a firm answer as to that. Wish I could tell you more, but it would be hopeful thinking. Still, it would be best if you stay around Brighton. When the cases come to trial, we will need you to testify."

"Is that really necessary?"

"Absolutely." David peeked through the open door. "May I come in?"

Haggard. He looked haggard and windblown, and thinner than he had been before. Cheeks sunken and face pale, his coat hung loose around his shoulders, but his voice was sure and strong.

Heavens above! Had a voice ever been more welcome? "I suppose we should ask Birdy to bring in a settee and convert this to a sitting room."

"I hope I am not intruding," David grinned as he sauntered in. "I hear the words 'trial' and 'testify' and, well, you can imagine what that does to a barrister."

"Naturally." The constable tipped his head to David. "I assume you agree on the importance of Miss Fuller's testimony in this case."

"Indeed, I do. It will be crucial."

"Then I will do my best to make myself available." Rebecca smoothed the blanket over her lap, grateful for the pretty dressing gown covering the plain and rather worn nightdress.

"Then my work here is done, and I shall leave you to more pleasant company. Good day." With a flash of his eyebrows, Constable Moore showed himself out.

Rebecca's cheeks prickled hot. It was not as if Constable Moore would ever tell anyone she was entertaining male visitors in her bedroom, in a dressing gown. But still, it felt so scandalous!

Birdy peeked in, "It ain't strictly proper, but I'm gonna close this door. Me regulars will be comin' soon for dinner and they be a noisy lot! I'm sure you need some quiet for your conversation." She pulled the door shut.

So much for any objections. Not that she didn't want a little privacy for their conversation, but how shocking it would be to be caught like this!

Who would catch them, though? Birdy kept the pub-side stair to the upstairs locked and guarded the kitchen-side stair herself. Intruders to her kitchen found themselves banned from the pub, and no one who had ever tasted her food would dare risk such a fate.

"It is delightful to see you looking so well." David pulled the now-empty chair closer and sat down.

"Well? Perhaps you should reconsider your standards." She pressed her hands to her cheeks. "Even I can tell my face is gaunt, and I cannot imagine the rest of me looks much better. I found my brother after he overexerted, and I will never forget—"

"There is no need to go there." David lifted his hand and shook his head. "You are alive and mending, and that is enough. Can we agree on that?"

"Yes, I suppose that is the crux of the matter." Gracious, he was handsome when he smiled like that. "I find there is a great deal that I don't remember about what happened that night."

"That is no surprise, for so many reasons. What we accomplished was unprecedented. To my knowledge, there are no records of Wrights working together, joining strength and Skill as we did. I would have called it impossible, but clearly, I would have been wrong."

"Just because it is possible does not make it wise, though." She drew and exhaled a long breath. "I understand my brother's death much better now. Perhaps they were right. Father's new ideas were, are, too dangerous."

"Dangerous, absolutely, in ways that we couldn't have imagined. But they cannot be ignored." David took her hand in both of his, so gently, so tenderly, but still firm and strong. "But we don't have to consider that now. When you are stronger, there will be much to discuss. Perhaps this is simply silly and selfish, but for now, I'd like to enjoy the fact that we are both alive."

"It is rather something to celebrate." She laid her other hand over his. Did he realize how his Skill warmed his hands, made them tingle in hers? Did he feel it, too?

He lifted her hands to his face, pressing them to his cheek. Eyes closed, he simply breathed, the stubble on his cheek rasping gently against her fingers. The feel of his very being pressed against her hands, open and trusting, vulnerable as no one had ever been toward her. Asking nothing, but somehow everything. Hoping, not demanding.

Her eyes burned, and hot trails coursed down her cheeks. He caught them with his finger, then cupped her cheek with his hand.

Tears were silly and foolish and pointless, but where else was the overflowing feeling to go?

"It is very, very good to be alive." His soft voice turned the words into a caress.

"I am certain about nothing else right now but that." And maybe, just maybe, about him.

A soft knock and they both jumped, but David did not release her hands. Birdy shouldered the door open and presented a modest wooden tray with a teapot and two cups. "Thought you might be needing some tea about now." She handed David the tray and shut the door.

"I give her credit for an attempt at subtlety." He chuckled. "Would you care for some tea?"

"That would be nice, thank you."

He checked the steep of the tea and poured two cups, adding a liberal amount of sugar before handing it to her.

Birdy always made a fine cup of tea, properly sweet and strong, even if her timing was less than perfect. "I have a question about the fire, now that I think about it. The boy—am I remembering correctly about his role in the fire?" Pray those were fever dreams.

"He confessed to setting it, both to me, and as I understand, to the police, as well. His father, of course, influenced him to do it ... but the manner in which the deed was accomplished was left to the boy's imagination."

"I see." She pressed the heels of her hands to her temples. What a complicated mess this was! She had never suspected Fletcher to be anything but a clumsy young boy. Was it possible?

"That is another issue that you should not trouble yourself with right now." He set his teacup on the now-crowded side table, eyebrows knitting together.

"It does not sound like you are about to share good news." She bit her lower lip and pulled her knees tight to her chest.

"No, that would make things too easy." He stared at his hands in his lap. He often did that when matters of the Guild came up.

"Old, grumpy men don't like new things, do they?"

"No. No, they don't. Especially when they convince each other that they are right." He raked his hands through his hair.

Her tight chest forced her voice to a bare whisper. "I suppose that was to be expected. The possibility was too much to hope for."

"I hate that you were right. I hate it enough to have done something about it." He took her hand again. "I am not sure you will approve, though."

"What have you done?" Could he feel her racing pulse in her hands? She gripped his hand a little harder and held her breath.

Staring into her eyes for three long breaths, he seemed to steel himself. "I ended my association with them; resigned my office and my affiliation with the Brighton Guild branch."

"You cannot be serious! Consider what you'll lose."

"All I can think of are the principles I will have to set aside if I don't."

"But your uncle's shop, you will not be able to work stone—"

"I suppose that puts us in similar circumstances." He scrubbed his face with his hands. "All I know is that I am certain it was the right thing to do ... No, there is one more thing I know. Somehow, we will get through this. Together."

Together, what a lovely word that was. "What does that look like?"

"No idea. But I am willing to work that out as we go if you are."

"I am."

# Chapter 29

THREE DAYS LATER, DAVID polished the Penn headstone one last time. Thankfully, the final polishing was a step he preferred to do the mundane way, so being barred from wrighting had not affected this final project. A fact that seemed to disappoint the three different Wrights who had conveniently come to call as he was finishing his project. If only they would put as much energy into developing new Wrights as they did into ensuring he did not practice his Skill, then maybe the Guild would not be in such a muddle.

He opened his workshop windows, allowing the morning sun to glint off the granite, sparkling and shining as only stone could. How he would miss the feel of stone under his hand. He dragged in a deep breath of salty sea breeze, cool and so heavy he could almost taste it.

Hughes and his team would be here shortly to pack the headstone up for a trip to the cemetery. Later that afternoon, Mr. Penn would be laid to rest before a flock of family anxious for the reading of his will. And David's life as a worker of stone would be as dead as Mr. Penn.

What next?

Several solicitors, representing local merchants, had approached him about bringing their cases before the local bar. That was a start. Perhaps, if he rented out the shop to another stonemason, or some other business entirely, that would be enough to survive in Brighton for a bit. Enough to give him a little time to figure out what was next.

There, done. He threw the polishing cloth aside and covered the headstone with canvas. He would miss working stone, to be sure. But a temporary hiatus did not mean forever. One thing at a time.

He locked up his workshop and headed into the shopfront as the front door opened.

"Afternoon, Mr. Enright." Hughes sauntered in and tipped his hat. A scraggly beard now covered the lower half of his round face, making him that much more intimidating as he towered over David. "You have the headstone ready for us?"

"Preparing for winter, there? Seems a mite early for that." David stroked his chin.

"Ya well, it takes a bit to grow in proper. Why wait to the last minute?" Hughes rubbed his patchy cheek ruefully.

"I like a man who thinks ahead. The monument is ready for you. Let me unlock the back door, so your men can get to work."

Hughes stuck his head out the front door and called to his team. "The boys'll be round back presently." He removed his hat, his broad smile lighting his eyes and beyond as he followed David to the workroom.

"You seem pleased with yourself today."

"Ain't often that a plan comes together so well as this one."

"I'm not sure I follow." David stopped and turned to look up at Hughes, whose dark eyes twinkled.

"You've heard of Lackwood's troubles, yes."

"Not really. Been occupied with other things at the moment."

"Understandable. Such a shame about Miss Fuller's workshop. Good thing they got the blokes responsible for it locked up nice and tight, though. How bad off is the building?"

"Inspectors have not made their full report, so I can't say. And there's no telling how long they will take making their determination—lazy blighters."

Hughes folded his thick arms across his chest, leaning back on his heels with an air of satisfaction David could almost feel. "Makes us all the 'appier that the ugly Laclwood bugger is gettin' his due. Every day there's a new world of trouble they be facing with one merchant or another. And today I 'eard that two more of his staff walked out. Young maids, hired at the Lammas quarter day. They didn't want to wait about only to find out they weren't gettin' paid for the quarter. O'course the upper staff isn't so flighty, but it sure is hard for a grand house to run without the lower staff."

"Are you saying the word's gotten around that fast?"

"It has—who isn't interested in knowing who ain't paying their bills? Though I will say, the talk got louder after that row the mister had with the fancy man staying with 'im. The fancy one's valet started talking to the staff and then around town—not sure what 'e said, but there ain't no one willing to work for 'em now, nor sell to them unless they see 'is cash in hand."

Sir Wilbert had a hand in that? "I am astonished."

"There's better yet!"

"He's found the money to pay Miss Fuller?"

"Well, as me boy Ernie 'eard this morning, it seems that our Lackwood fellow has found a deep pocket somewhere to start paying thems he owes!"

"He has, now?" If that had been Sir Wilbert's plan, despite abandoning them at their darkest moment, perhaps he was a better chap than David had credited him for being.

"Miss Fuller is said to be among the first he's going to make amends to." Hughes grinned like a dog with a bone as he rocked back on his heels. "I wish we could take all the credit, but my Freddy 'eard that it were because that fancy guest of theirs knows a highfaluting relative of some variety and is bringing him to visit right soon, and o'course Lackwood can't properly host some hoity-toity without food or staff, now can he?"

"Assuredly not. I have it on good authority that guests like to eat and have their rooms made up." Was it wrong to smile so at Lackwood's misfortune?

Hughes laughed heartily. "Justice don't 'appen often, but when it do, it's sweet, no?"

"I never would have expected such a thing, but—well, that is excellent news." Especially since it could have a significant impact on Rebecca's future decisions.

"Perhaps you might tell Miss Fuller, lift her spirits while she recovers, yeah?"

"That is an excellent notion. As soon as you and your boys have the stone settled, I'll do just that."

Birdy greeted him as he walked into the Bird's Nest's front door. "I imagine you're here to see her, no? She's in the small room to the side dere, but I'll warn you, she is taking company there with a Mr. Lackwood. As I understand, she had some awful business with him not long ago." She winked.

"Lackwood is here?"

Birdy pressed her finger to her lips, eyes twinkling with mercenary glee, and beckoned him to follow. She led him through the kitchen, filled with bubbling pots and tempting smells, and pointed to the scullery. "You might find the view from that room interesting." She pointed to her ear.

David nodded, forcing his smile back, and tiptoed into the scullery. Dimly lit by one narrow window facing the alleyway and smaller than his former Guild office, it barely held the sink and tables for dirty and clean dishes. A gap between wall and ceiling hinted at the room beyond. Convenient, that; was it built that way intentionally or only a convenient happenstance Birdy was in no hurry to repair?

Yes, eavesdropping was improper, so he grabbed one of the pans soaking in the sink. If he was here, helping Birdy out a bit and overheard something, that was different. At least, technically, it was. He began scrubbing very, very quietly. The water was still warm—they had not been here long- perhaps Birdy had been tending to a similar task just before he arrived.

"Was the repaired mantel well received at your dinner party, Mr. Lackwood?" Rebecca asked. Her tight voice was probably mirrored in a stiff posture and a thin smile. She was expressive that way.

"Indeed, it was. None had any idea that it had been damaged at all." Did offering a compliment hurt as much as Lackwood's tone suggested?

"Then, if you have not come by to complain about my work, I hardly understand why you have come to call."

"I ... I have a favor to ask of you." The audacity of the man!

"A favor? A favor? You truly wish to ask a favor from me?" Was it David's imagination or did a wave of heat pour through the gap in the wall?

"I realize it is irregular—"

"Irregular is not the word I would use under the circumstances. Audacious, insulting, impudent, but not irregular." Her voice tightened and thinned to razor-sharpness.

"I understand the circumstances are less than ideal..."

"You have refused to pay me despite our contract, despite my work having been 'satisfactory,' despite all common practice and decency. Now you wish to ask me a favor? In what way can you consider that appropriate or proper?" That creaking—was she leaning on the table?

"I am desperate, Miss Fuller."

"You are desperate? You? I doubt you have any idea of what that word means."

Lackwood snorted. "My staff is leaving my employ; merchants will not sell to me without cash in hand—"

"That seems most unfortunate for you, but hardly what the rest of us would consider desperate. What has that to do with me?"

"Feigned ignorance does not suit you. You need not pretend when I know it was you that set the gossip—"

"Stop right there. You are mistaken." She slapped the table. Hopefully, she was not upset enough to leave a handprint behind. "I have spoken to no one about the issue. If there is any gossip going around, it is not from my lips. I have been rather indisposed, or were you not aware?"

"Quite unfortunate, that. You may not have done the talking yourself, but you have those gossips off to do your—"

"No, sir, I have not, and I would thank you to keep such accusations to yourself. That is not how I do business." If her words grew any sharper, Lackwood would bleed soon.

"Do you mean to say that you don't know what is being said?"

"Birdy, the owner and innkeeper here, mentioned that she had heard something to the effect that you were not good for your obligations. She also warned me that she was only allowing you in for the purpose of speaking to me. She planned to ignore any order you placed rather than put me in a position to have to pay for it when you reneged on your obligations."

"This is what I am facing all over town. It is both unfair and intolerable. Call them off. This must stop."

"You believe I can do such a feat, or if I could that I am under any obligation to do so?"

"Call them off so my life can return—"

"Why should I do that?"

"Because that baronet who is so enamored of you—"

A fist landed hard. The table screeched across the floor and David jumped, nearly dropping the pot he scrubbed. "Stop right there. The baronet is my barrister's friend. I barely know the man and resent your accusations of impropriety. It is bad enough you refuse to pay your debt to me, but now you seek to ruin my reputation? If that's all you have to say, it is best you leave now."

Oh, to see the expression on Lackwood's face! "He seems to admire your work, Miss Fuller. That is all I meant. And he was insistent that you be paid and did not accept my explanation that we had worked out—"

"No, nothing was worked out. You refused to honor your obligation and dismissed me with a pittance of what you owed me, with little further hope of seeing the remainder."

"You know I will pay—"

"We had a written contract, which you have ignored. What assurance have I that it will not remain too inconvenient to pay me forever."

"It's unfair of you to judge me so. I have—"

"A great number of individuals to whom you owe money. That is not an excellent reputation to draw upon. Do you take me for a fool, sir?"

"If you will cooperate with me, I expect to be in a position to remedy that." Foolish man, how could he think anyone so stupid?

"And how exactly do you expect that will work?"

"The baronet has decided to bring my relative, a baron, to Brighton to shame me for how I run my household. A horrid judgmental act if I have ever heard of one. But if I can find favor with my relative, I expect—"

"Your financial situation to be improved?"

"Without going into detail, yes."

"You want a favor from me, to improve your situation, and still I have no assurance that your debt to me will ever be recompensed? What sort of imbecile do you take me for?"

A chair squealed along the floor and heavy footfalls plodded back and forth. "What will it take for you to call off your dogs?"

"Do not refer to the honest workfolk of Brighton either as 'mine' or as 'dogs.' I can assure you, nothing I say to them will alter their current opinion of you, which has a great deal more to do with their experience of you than it does with anything related to me."

"You are refusing to help me?" Could Lackwood possibly be surprised by that?

No, probably not. The man was shrewd and manipulative, but not stupid.

"I am saying that you are the only one in a position to help yourself. At this time, there is nothing I can say to them that will change their judgment of you. It is out of my control."

"What is that supposed to mean?"

"Pay me what is my due, and I am willing to let that fact be made known to any and all who are interested. I imagine that seeing you pay your debts will go a long way in reestablishing your credibility. Certainly with more authority than what mere words could accomplish."

"You would be so self-serving, so unfeeling, so mercenary?"

Another faint wave of heat radiated through the gap. Did Lackwood not feel it?

"If you think wanting to be paid is mercenary, then I believe this conversation is over. Pray, see yourself out. I am not yet strong enough to escort you."

"But I need—"

"I assure you, in every respect, my needs are greater and far more important to me."

"Fine, then." Something dropped onto a table.

"What is this?"

"Go on, look at it. Count it. You'll find it's all there."

Paper rustled and flipped as Rebecca muttered under her breath. "It would appear to be in order. I do not understand. You insisted you could not pay me."

"I hope you're satisfied. You have cost me nearly the entire contents of my wine cellar."

"If this is all you got for it, it seems like it was not much of a collection to begin with. Or are you planning to go to all the trades and merchants you owe and have the same disgraceful conversation with them as you just had with me?"

"That is none of your business, you greedy little—"

She slapped the table with a thunderclap—she must have figured out Allbright's little trick for accomplishing that. "I am sorry for your discomfort, sir, but there is no need to blame me or begin shouting insults. It was you who entered into agreements with everyone you owe. That is not our fault, nor should we be punished for it. Perhaps in the future you will be more prudent—"

"I do not need financial advice from you!" A chair scraped on the floor, then toppled over. "And you can be sure that neither you, nor those miserable dogs you've set on me, will ever work for me again." Heavy steps stomped away.

David carefully set the now-clean pot aside and turned to see Birdy in the scullery doorway, hand over her mouth, laughing softly. "Served da dog-cheap blighter all proper. She did a right nice job of holding his feet to da fire, didn't she?"

"Absolutely. Can you escort me to her?"

"My pleasure. And I'll fix us some tea to celebrate as well." Birdy offered her arm and guided him through the pub to the small side room.

The low, exposed-beam ceiling almost grazed the top of David's head. Tightly packed tables and chairs littered the path from the doorway to her. Faint heat shimmers warped the sunlight that struggled in from the window behind her.

How did one congratulate another on something he never should have discovered in the first place? Should he give her some time to regain her composure?

"Come in, both of you, and quit pretending. I heard you in the scullery—don't deny it. I must say, you scrub a good pot, David." She winked and waved them in. "And no, I am not upset. I rather like it that I have two witnesses to that conversation in case the esteemed Mr. Lackwood tries to twist this encounter into something not in my favor."

"Was right nice to hear 'im put in his place. I'll go fetch us some tea and biscuits—gotta celebrate such things when they come." Birdy turned away, a skip in her step.

"I am sorry for eavesdropping," David righted the fallen chair and sat across from Rebecca.

"In this one case, I do not mind, but I hope you do not intend to make a habit of it." Her tone was light, but her narrowed eyes—best not ignore her words.

"I most assuredly do not. I am not sorry for what I heard, though. He paid you the full sum?"

"With this," she tapped the envelope, "his debt to me is fully settled."

"Perhaps Sir Wilbert has proved his good intentions after all." David shrugged. "That will pay off Mallory?"

"According to my records, yes. With a bit left over as well. No telling what his records might say, though."

"But what then? Will you try to repair the shop?"

"I'm not sure what the point would be." She pressed her elbows on the table and leaned her face into her hands. A cloud of defeat hung over her. "As a perpetual journeyman, I still won't be able to charge enough for my work for it to be worthwhile."

"I wish I could suggest otherwise, but no. While there may be a few sympathetic Masters in Brighton, the official Guild position will be—"

"Hostile. You don't need to soften it. They will be hostile." Her hand fell limp to the table.

"Unfortunately, true. But at least this gives you some time to sort out what to do next." He edged his fingers toward hers.

"Have you thought about what you will do now that you cannot work stone here?"

"I'm considering renting out the building and pouring myself into practice as a barrister."

"That seems reasonable. Perhaps, if my shop can be repaired, that is an option I could consider. I am acquainted with several women who keep body and soul together renting out property."

"That's the spirit! There is a way through this for certain." He squeezed her hand. "I wonder though, Lackwood said, or at least I thought he did, that Sir Wilbert was coming back?"

"He did indeed. And bringing the baron with him. That seems awfully strange, don't you agree? I understand Sir Wilbert was supportive of me, of us, but that is a great deal of trouble to go to, isn't it?"

"It strikes me that way, too. It would be interesting to find out what he intends by it." Interesting, indeed.

# Chapter 30

FOR THE FIRST TIME since the world turned upside down, inside out, and backward, Rebecca stood in what was left of Fuller's Fix-All. After the encounter with Lackwood, Birdy insisted she spend the next day recovering her strength before facing the destruction. She had been right.

The odors of smoke, charred wood, and burnt leather hung in the air, heavy and dark, foreboding. Though it was not possible, somehow it felt like the ghosts of flames still danced on the floors and walls, reminding her of how she could not control them, only defeat them with great violence. And with the reminder, great sadness, as if she had betrayed a dear friend.

Fire had always been her friend, her comfort, an Element she trusted and understood. But that night, it had turned against her. What choice had she then?

Did it have something to do with the boy? If he was a Wright and had started the fire with his Skill, had that made a difference in the way the flames responded—or failed to respond—to her? Could such things even be possible? If anyone would know, it would be David, and if he did not, he would record the matter in his notes to pursue later.

So many things he wanted to study and learn. That was one of the most likeable aspects of his character. Unlike the other officers of the Brighton Guild, he was curious and not biased, willing to learn, rather than try to force facts into the theories that already existed.

The sort of person she could relate to. The sort she might have a future with. And he seemed to want that, too.

Was it enough to keep her in Brighton?

Until they stood shoulder to shoulder in the fire—oh, how dramatic that sounded; how dramatic it had been—she had not been sure. But when their Skills touched, and they joined forces against the world ... no, she could not turn away from the possibilities such a partnership held. She would stay and wait for what came next.

No matter what that was, she would have to deal with the shop, so here she would begin.

The wind that suffocated the flames had shattered nearly every bit of glass in the shop. A great blackened circle stretched out from the middle of the shop, reaching halfway to the front door and perhaps a third of the way to the back and sides. At least half the shelves and glass-fronted cabinets stood in ruin. A few nearest the walls might be salvaged. That was something.

The front of her worktable bore scorch marks, one corner mostly charred, but not too far for restoration. That was positive—

*Caw ... ca-caw ... caw...*

She yanked a stream of Air and silenced the clock—the clock! Father's Gothic horror still hung on the wall, covered with soot, more than slightly askew. But it remained. With a quick flick of her hand, she released the stilled Air and allowed it to cry out to its heart's content.

Somehow Father had crafted not just an irksome timepiece, but some sort of fire alarm in that clock. When she took it down to clean it, she would inspect it and try to figure out how he had managed that. How much damage had been spared, even lives saved, because of its warning? If she could replicate that—

But she could not, not in Brighton, with the Guild's prejudice against her.

She pressed her temples with both hands. No, not right now. That was a problem for later. Other things needed to be dealt with first.

Other things like sorting out if the building was as structurally sound as the inspectors claimed it was.

While she had no specific reason to distrust their analysis, and they had no reason to approve efforts to repair it if it were indeed too dangerous, still she needed to confirm its strength with her own senses. Then take the next steps, whatever they were.

She crouched down, closed her eyes, and laid both hands on the floor, reaching deep into the hardwood boards. It ached with the injuries inflected upon it, groaning, whining its outrage at the insults offered to it. But the damage had been contained in the uppermost layer of the flooring, not in the supports beneath. Those remained sound.

The tension holding her together washed away in a nearly audible 'woosh.' Her strength gave way, and she caught herself on her hands before she toppled over. Her workshop below was sound!

As she forced her eyes open, she caught sight of her Wardian case, hidden behind a toppled display. Soot and ash covered the glass—but the structure held! A green fern frond waved at her from behind the dirty glass, assuring her the little world remained.

It was there, it was there! What she crafted stood! She covered her face with her hands as great heaving sobs surged through her, like waves buffeting the shore. If that case could stand through the fire, through everything that had been thrown against her, then so could she.

"Rebecca?" That was David's voice, not much more than a whisper, near the door to the back room. "Are you all right?"

She dragged her sleeve across her face. "Yes, yes, I am fine. Thank you. The city inspectors were correct. The floor is sound. I have not confirmed the rest, but I suspect they were right about that, too."

David approached and crouched beside her. "The boy had no idea what to do with Fire."

"If I had my guess, he may know how to start a fire, but nothing more, not its nature, and especially not how to control it. I mean, he piled a mound of old rags and paper in the middle of the room and expected it would catch everything else ablaze."

"It would have, but for that." He pointed at the clock. "Which I'm somehow not surprised to discover survived, and in reasonably sound condition to boot."

"I intend to figure out how Father crafted it as soon as there is time."

He helped her to her feet. "Are you all right on your feet, or do you need help?"

"It sounds like there is more than mere courtesy behind that question."

"You are most perceptive." He rubbed the back of his neck. "I'm afraid so. I received a rather urgent message from Guild Hall. Sir Wilbert is back in Brighton and has called us to an urgent meeting."

"Us? You and I, both of us? Together?"

He pulled a hastily folded piece of paper from his coat pocket. "Here, written in what I suspect is his own hand."

"Immediately? What could be so important?" She dusted off her skirts. Botheration, her glasses were filthy!

David handed her a handkerchief as she yanked them off her nose. "I suppose he didn't conclude his business with the Guild? I really don't know, but it seems we should go there directly."

"As soon as my glasses are clean. I should like to see clearly the bearer of what I can only expect is more bad news."

Was it possible that Master Ames had been standing by the door, waiting for their arrival? The quick way the door opened to them suggested it was so, as did his barely contained curious expression as he led them to a large meeting room on the first level of the Guild Hall. Though, his round face and the equally round rest of him seemed formed for the jovial things of life, there was something about the way his little eyes turned squinty and creases lined his forehead when he looked at her.

No, he was not as jovial and guileless as he liked to appear.

Inside the meeting room, a scarred oblong table took up most of the space. Gaslights lined both long walls, casting mellow light. A pair of slightly worn sideboards at either end of the table might have been used to hold the victuals ubiquitous at Wright gatherings, but today they were bare.

That seemed telling, but of what?

At the head of the table, Sir Wilbert waved at them and beckoned them to take seats opposite candle-stubby Master Cinderford and ratty Master Fitzsimons. Both men shared the same look of insulted obligation. Guild Master Allbright sat at the table's foot, every inch a grumpy old wizard contemplating crafting a curse, but Sir Wilbert seemed unmoved by it all. What was one to make of that?

"I am glad you have come. Miss Fuller, pray sit here," Sir Wilbert gestured at the seat nearest himself.

David held her chair, a mite protectively, and helped her arrange herself as comfortably as might be possible. Then, he sat beside her, sidling his chair a little closer than considered proper. "Your summons did not include a reason for this meeting. Perhaps you will enlighten us now?"

Sir Wilbert reached under the table and pulled up a neatly folded, somewhat dirty cloth. "I believe this is yours." He slid it along the table to Rebecca.

"I had wondered what had happened to it." She drew it to her. The familiar order within the fibers soothed her, reminded her that, regardless of whether the men in the room recognized it, she was an equal among them.

"I imagine it got left behind when the firemen hauled us out of the shop." David said. "I went back later to look for it, but assumed someone must have had a rummage about and picked it up."

"Thank you for returning it." Rebecca ran the thick, comforting fabric through her fingers.

"It is Guild property, as the Guild bought and paid for the supplies to make it." Fitzsimons muttered under his breath, not deigning to even look at her.

"Of course." Rebecca stood and half-shoved, half-threw it at him. "I hope it does you as much good as it did us. Oh, and you may pay me for the work I did on it, because that does not come free."

"At a journeyman's wages—" She fought the urge to shake the glee from Fitzsimons' voice.

"Yes, about that," Sir Wilbert rapped the table with his knuckles, plucked the cloth out of Fitzsimons' reach, and folded it neatly. "I would like to offer you an exchange, Miss Fuller."

"Of what kind?"

"This," Sir Wilbert held her mastery project out toward her, "for this." He held out a black satin stole, the kind worn with formal robes for official Guild events. Red embroidery formed the ancient symbols for all four Elements down each end, connected by a chain of gold thread.

"That is—"

"Yes, the mark of a Full Wright."

"What is this?" Fitzsimons pounded the table.

"The assembly summarily voted to apply the rank of perpetual journeyman. You cannot do that." Cinderford shouted, leaning in on his elbows.

"That decision has not been recorded in the minutes of the last meeting." Wilbert laid a heavy tome on the table with a purposeful thump. "I checked. The meeting minutes are not recorded at all. As if it had never happened."

"I have not gotten around to it. I will address it right now." Cinderford pushed back in his seat and reached for the volume.

Sir Wilbert pulled the book away. "I am afraid you cannot."

"What are you talking about?"

"I will get to that in a moment. First, Miss Fuller, would you accept the rank of Full Wright as recognized by the Royal Court Guild?"

She glanced at David, who nodded, jaw agape. He would be the one to warn her if there were anything untoward about this. "I am honored, sir." She took the stole and sat down before her knees gave way. "Pray forgive my asking, though, but how?"

"After hearing about the fire, I went to check on you. Your friend Birdy assured me you were safe, but would not permit me to call upon you while you were still unconscious. I stopped to examine the scene of the fire and found your project left there, with no trace of damage. Forgive me for borrowing it without your permission, but I hope you will agree, presenting it as a Mastery project for judging before the Royal Court Guild was a worthwhile cause. On the strength of Master Enright's petition as your sponsor, a Master's panel examined it and found it worthy of the rank." Sir Wilbert almost, but not quite, controlled the satisfaction in his voice.

"The Royal Court Guild cannot overrule our decision. They do not have jurisdiction—" Allbright sputtered.

"Actually, in this case, they do. Since the official record of the meeting had not been entered before the ruling of the Royal Court Guild was made, they have the procedural right to name her a Full Wright, and to offer her membership in that branch of the Guild as well. Do you accept, Miss Fuller? You too, Enright, since, as I understand, you are no longer a member of the Brighton branch—which has been duly recorded, by the way. The Royal Court Guild invites you both to join their ranks."

David glanced at her with brows upraised, nodding.

Rebecca blinked and nodded once.

"We would be honored to accept affiliation with the Royal Court Guild." David took Sir Wilbert's outstretched hand and shook it firmly.

"Very good, very good."

Allbright pounded the table, a slight breeze coursing through the room. "No, it is not very good. The Royal Court Guild is meddling in business not their own, which will disrupt the operations of the Brighton Guild. I will go to London today and file an official complaint. As Guild Master, I cannot—"

"Wait to purchase your train tickets, Master Allbright." Sir Wilbert lifted an open hand, his tone so casual he might be speaking of the weather.

Master Fitzsimons gasped. "You will not insult our Guild Master—"

"About that. I suggest you sit down and listen carefully." Sir Wilbert rested his arms on the table and drummed his fingers as he waited until the Guild Master complied. "While in London, I also brought my concerns about the current state of the Brighton Guild to the Royal Court Guild Master, who you are aware, of course, answers directly to the Queen. In fact, Her Majesty was present at the meeting. It is at Her behest that I present this." He handed Allbright a large document bearing a royal seal, the barest hint of self-righteousness in his voice. "Go on, open it."

Allbright cracked the seal, his hands trembling. The color left his face as his lips moved, reading it. "No, this is not possible."

"What does it say?" Master Cinderford craned his neck, trying to catch a glimpse of the text, not even trying to be subtle.

"They cannot do that." Red-faced, Master Allbright pushed the document at Master Cinderford.

"Actually, they can. The Brighton Guild has many long-standing violations of their charter, and this latest irregularity was, as they say, the final straw. The Crown has dissolved this branch and declared that Brighton's affairs will be managed by the Royal Court Guild until such time as the Crown sees fit to change that."

David bumped his knee against hers under the table. She caught his eye for a moment, and he nodded. So this was real? Not some crazy imagination?

"The Royal Court thanks you for your service as Guild Master, and yours as Secretary and Treasurer," Sir Wilbert looked from one man to the next. "But, as of now, your services will no longer be necessary."

"How are affairs to be managed here, then?" Allbright spat the words, traces of wind swirling around him.

"They have assigned me responsibility for the Royal Court Guild's oversight in Brighton." Sir Wilbert's smug little huff was difficult to miss.

"You can't—they can't—" Cinderford stammered as though he couldn't bear to form the words, adding ambient heat to the swirling Air.

"The document is signed by the Crown. It is done. All that is left is for you to vacate your offices."

"Vacate our offices?" Fitzsimons eyes bulged like a pug that had been stepped on.

"I expect you should be able to be out by the end of the day. I will need that space to install my own assistants."

"And who might those be?" Allbright drummed his fingers on the table.

"Does it matter? How has that anything to do with you?" Did anyone else hear the warning that edged Sir Wilbert's voice?

"Let us say I am curious to whom the Brighton Wrights will be answering." Master Allbright said.

"We all answer to the Royal Court Guild and, ultimately, the Crown. Now be good fellows and pop off to take care of those offices. I'll send some boys around to assist you."

"What about ... them?" Cinderford's hand trembled as he pointed.

"What does it matter to you? Go on, now, I have other business to attend." Sir Wilbert waved them out.

# Chapter 31

DAVID FORCED HIS FACE into an appropriate, somber shape as the now-former officers stomped out. Their expressions were stony, but traces of heat and wind radiated from their departure. Those were some furious Wrights.

Chances were high that tickets to London would be bought today. Oh, to be privy to the conversations that would take place at the Royal Court Guild—if they were even admitted.

Whether Allbright and the others agreed or not, Sir Wilbert was correct in terms of procedure and protocol. The documents Sir Wilbert presented carried the weight of law, and no amount of complaining or conniving would alter the course now set. It wasn't often that David so thoroughly underestimated someone, but this time...

"May I offer my congratulations, Miss, ah, that is, Master Fuller? The Royal Court judging panel was most impressed with your work." Sir Wilbert bowed from his shoulders.

Rebecca seemed more wary than pleased. "Forgive me for asking, but what did they say when you revealed the identity of their candidate—or are they even aware yet?"

"You will be surprised to hear that Morris Fuller is not anathema in all quarters of the kingdom. In fact, there are those who are quite interested in learning more about his approach, especially having seen your work for themselves." Such a self-satisfied smile he wore.

"Truly? Forgive me if that is very hard to believe." Her eyebrow arched almost to her hairline.

"After having seen conditions here, I can understand why. A shame that the Brighton brand of the Guild was not held accountable sooner, but things are changing. And for the better. Speaking of change, Enright," he pulled out another sealed document and pushed it toward David.

David opened it, scanning the perfect penmanship. Seriously? Was that possible? He read it again. "Secretary? The Royal Court Guild wishes for me to serve as Secretary here, under your direction?"

"Upon my recommendation, I might add." Sir Wilbert folded his arms and rocked onto the back legs of his chair. "Between you and me, they are grooming you to take over as Guild Master once we clean up the mess here."

"But I resigned—" David glanced at Rebecca, who tapped her Master Wright stole and seemed utterly amused.

"So I heard. Are you surprised to learn that is a mark in your favor, clearly establishing your stance in the matters here?"

"Guild Master? Truly?"

"Not yet, son, not yet. You still have to prove yourself, but I have no doubt that will happen in the natural course of things."

David rubbed the back of his neck. Words should not be so difficult to find. "Thank you for your support."

"You showed yourself worthy of it. It won't be an easy ride, to be sure, but we'll make an honest go of it. And, of course, you will receive the stipend that goes along with your office to compensate you for the time and effort." Sir Wilbert brought his chair down with a soft thud.

"Stipend?"

"Why does that not surprise me?" Sir Wilbert rolled his eyes. "Somewhere deep in the Charter is a statement regarding a gratuity for the officers. You'll need to ferret that out so we can have everything properly stated and established. I suppose that ought to be your starting point, clearing up the charter and bylaws and what not."

Establish proper structure and procedure for the Guild? Had he heard correctly? "Having recently spent some time digging through the scraps and scribbles which have passed for governing documents, I would be pleased to do just that." David licked his lips.

"And you, Master Fuller," Sir Wilbert turned his gaze on her. "You have not the experience with the Guild to argue to place you as an officer—"

She lifted open hands and edged back. "You'll get no argument from me. It is not a position I want."

"Excellent, then you will not be disappointed by this—" He slid yet another document toward her.

"Me? What could the Guild want of me?" She eyed the sealed missive as though it might bare teeth and bite.

"The Queen is interested in the first female Full Wright in the records of the Royal Court Guild. You have confirmed her opinion that Guild tradition has caused us to overlook fully half the potential Wrights of England." He pushed the paper closer to her.

The door opened and a red-headed, freckled man, who barely looked old enough to shave, peeked in. "Shall I bring him in now, sir?" How did such a deep, resonant voice come from a chest so narrow?

"This is Jackson, my assistant. You will be seeing a lot of him, I am sure. Jackson, Master Enright and Master Fuller, both Full Wrights. Jackson here is a senior journeyman of mine."

"Another Earth Wright? It seems I will be surrounded by them." Rebecca laughed as she broke the seal on the document with trembling hands.

"Who better to stand steady when a Fire Wright's temper flares?" Sir Wilbert cocked his head and flashed his brows. "Yes, Jackson, do show him in now."

Rebecca scanned the paper; her jaw dropped and she blinked rapidly. Perhaps worried that the words might change as she did.

David held his breath to stifle a chuckle. Never had he seen her so caught off guard.

"A school?" She pointed at the beautifully penned page.

"I had mentioned the notion Enright here, but I'm not surprised he wouldn't have shared it with you, yet."

Not surprised? Sir Wilbert had specifically told him to hold his peace on that matter. Not the time to mention that now.

"You are, of course, well aware that the old apprenticeship system is no longer serving us well, especially if we are to find female Wrights. So, Her Majesty has commissioned the Royal Court Guild to establish a school dedicated to the discovery and training of female Wrights."

Exclusively for females? That made sense, if Rebecca was to be in charge of it, but still it was an interesting choice.

"They are asking me to lead it?" Rebecca pressed her hand to her chest. "I don't know how to do such a thing. My father's teachings were unconventional, not a proper apprenticeship by any form or fashion."

"Exactly. It is a wild experiment—desperate measures are called for these days. And you are the only living apprentice trained by a different school of thought. And as our only female Full Wright, we have no one else to train girls."

"And if it fails, it seems like there are many directions to point the blame. At my father's philosophy, at my teaching, even, perhaps, at the notion of female wrights in the first place." Her eyebrow arched in that shrewd little way they had.

"I understand why you say that, but the Royal Court Guild is fully behind the view that female Wrights are necessary."

Rebecca's eyes narrowed, a warning her temper might flare. "Was there any special favor given to my application for Mastery because the Guild needed a female—"

The door swung open and a short, stocky man in a very expensive suit strode in. His walk alone marked him as a member of the privileged class. His lean frame and rugged hands suggested he might be an actively practicing Wright. "As to that, Miss Fuller, I can speak to it directly. I was a member of the evaluation committee, and we knew nothing of your identity, even what branch of the Guild you came from. Your work was judged on its merit alone."

"Baron Wareham, Master Enright, Master Fuller." Sir Wilbert gestured accordingly.

David and Rebecca stood, bowing and curtseying.

"Sit, sit, we have too much to discuss for us to waste time on formalities." Baron Wareham dropped into the chair across from Rebecca and beside Sir Wilbert and pointed to David. "I understand you and I are related in some form or fashion."

"Through my father's line, as I was told." There was a vague resemblance around the eye and jawline, but not enough to make David wary.

"A breath of fresh air to know there's someone worthwhile down the line. A far cry from those Lackwoods." He snorted, the edge of his lip curling. "I hear he tried to cheat you out of your wages." He looked at Rebecca.

"The matter has been settled now. The debt has been paid." Her thin smile gave testament to all that was not being said.

"No need to be so nice about it, Miss Fuller. I have little connection and no affection for the family. But staying with them gave me a close-up view of the work you did on that piece of stone. Remarkable, utterly remarkable."

"Mr. Enright and I worked on that piece together, your Lordship—"

"Don't go off doing that play of modesty here. The workmanship is worthy of praise."

"Forgive me, your Lordship," David said. "And please correct me if I am in error, but Miss Fuller is not trying to be modest, but is speaking to the fact that quite by accident, we discovered that our Skills could be used together in ways that have never been explored before. That is the 'together' she spoke of."

Rebecca nodded.

Lord Wareham slapped the table. "You see there, Cullington, you see!"

"Indeed, I do." Sir Wilbert actually grinned.

"I do not follow." Rebecca's brows knit and she frowned.

"The school which Master Fuller has been charged with founding will need a source of funding. The Crown offered, but Wareham here has insisted on having the privilege himself. And apparently you have proven him quite correct." Sir Wilbert wagged a pointing finger at David.

"The Crown may want a school for girl-Wrights, but seeing your Mastery project, and the mantel, and now this—" the baron said.

"There is quite a story to be told about the fire as well." David jumped in.

Lord Wareham laughed. "That does not surprise me! I recognize a sound investment when I see it. It is my intent to be the first patron of the school, which I fully expect will expand to include boys in time, and will form a foundation for the future of Wrights themselves."

"I hardly know what to say," Rebecca gasped, eyes shimmering.

"Don't say anything. You, and I dare say Enright as well, are going to do all the work. I'm going to sit back, shell out the money, and be given far too much credit for the endeavor." Lord Wareham winked. "I had a look at your shop, and I am convinced that the building can be repaired. That seems more prudent than finding a new location, at least at this stage of the process. I will fund the repairs and necessary renovations, including making a proper extension out of that back room and fitting out the attics for student rooms. That, with what the Crown intends to provide to pay for student expenses and a stipend for yourself as headmistress and whatever additional staff you require—that pubkeeper next door, might want to tap her to provide the tucker for you and your charges—should keep you and your students quite comfortably."

Such generosity! Was it possible that there were really those who were as concerned with the future of the Wrights as David was?

"If it does not work out as you expect, what will I owe you for the renovations to my building?"

"She's a shrewd one, just as you said!" Lord Wareham slapped Sir Wilbert's shoulder. "Nothing, Miss Fuller. There is risk in all investments. I'm willing and able to bear the loss. But I don't expect it will come to that. And yes, you can have Enright put it all into writing to make it official."

"Why would you do this, take such a risk? You don't even know me and have barely seen my work."

"That one piece spoke volumes. More than you can understand right now." His tone shifted, low and somber. "There are some things that are bigger than a single man. I want our kind to outlive my generation, to thrive into the next century and beyond. That's worth taking risks."

"I don't know if I can do this." She stared at her hands.

"There's only one way to find out. And as to you, Enright," Lord Wareham turned to David. "No doubt you will have your hands full trying to whip this branch of the Guild into shape. But you intend to follow through with that Mallory chap, yes?"

"Absolutely. As I understand, the boy turned on him and has sung quite the song about the crimes Mallory put him up to. The police are building a strong case with Constable Moore at the helm. I don't think Mallory's got the sort of connections that will keep him from quite a stretch away from home and hearth."

"As it should be. I trust you will handle the matter, then? Now, about that boy of his, the one who set the fire—"

Rebecca gasped. "What have you heard, my lord?"

"This and that, mostly. But it seems the child has a reputation for playing with fire. Leads one to wonder, is it possible ..."

"We both suspect he may be a Wright," Rebecca said. "I could feel traces of another Skill in the flames."

"Interesting. I have a friend, Master Coulston, a Fire Wright—you remember him, don't you, Cullington?—who was something of a scamp as a youngster. He's taken on a few apprentices with troublesome pasts, made proper Wrights out of most of them."

"And those he failed to reform?" David and Rebecca shared a glance.

Lord Wareham shrugged. "I'll make Coulston aware of the boy. I imagine he'll visit. If there's hope to train the lad, he'll take him on as a ward—he's got the connections to make that work. If not, we'll see to it that's he's put away long enough for any trace of Skill to fade away. Can't risk a rogue Wright running about." He glanced at Rebecca. "Not to worry, though, Miss Fuller. I should think your students will come from better circumstances. Wouldn't do to start such an endeavor with established troublemakers under your wing."

"I am relieved to hear that." Rebecca said. "Who will identify the school's students? What about the lessons I am to teach them—I've no experience managing children or a school."

"Not to worry, the Crown and the Royal Court Guild are heavily invested in the success of this endeavor and will identify your first students and provide all the support you need."

Rebecca cocked her head and arched an eyebrow. "You mean breathe down my neck for results?"

"I like to think there will be greater subtlety than that. Yes, all parties involved expect results, to be sure, but they are realistic, considering the magnitude of the task. Would you be willing to walk down to your building with me? We can discuss the repairs and some of the other particulars of the situation."

"That seems prudent, if, of course, Sir Wilbert considers my business here complete?"

"By no means. There is a great deal of work yet to be accomplished. But getting repairs underway is a high priority, so we will continue again soon. And do be a good chap, Wareham, and don't scare her off with your fancy dreams and plans. We have only just got her to join us." Sir Wilbert stood.

David pulled Rebecca's chair out for her. "Good day, then, Master Fuller." He bowed from his shoulders.

"Good day, Master Enright." She curtsied and followed Lord Wareham out.

Sir Wilbert dropped back into his seat. "I wish you could have been in London with me, Enright. What a spectacle it was! Master after Master, trying to find some weakness in this deceptively simple little project of hers." He fingered the cloth of her project.

"Having worn it in the midst of a real fire, I can only imagine their frustration."

"She really is extraordinary." Sir Wilbert chewed his lip as he stared at the door. "So, are you courting her yet?"

David winced, a flush rising on his cheeks. "We are walking out together."

"Well, that's something. It is about time, you know. You best not make a hash of it." Sir Wilbert wagged a pointing finger at him.

The hair on the back of his neck prickled. "What is that supposed to mean?"

Sir Wilbert leaned in close, his voice lowering. "Every unmarried Wright in London is aware of her and considering the possibility of courting her themselves. Mendel's ideas are too compelling to ignore."

"Are you suggesting the Guild considers her some sort of fine breeding stock?" He forced the words through gritted teeth, his jaw aching with the effort not to voice his true sentiments.

"Hardly. We still don't know if Wrights can be bred. But the possibility is tantalizing and adds to her other desirable qualities."

"What do you mean by desirable qualities?"

Sir Wilbert frowned and tossed his head. "So, she has a flamer's temper. That is not enough to turn a determined Wright away. Some would consider it an agreeable challenge to conquer it. You must admit, her Skill is incredible. We must learn as much as we can about her father's ways. She is too much of an asset to the Guild to be lost to some mundane sort of man who cannot ever learn of what she really is. Enright, you must marry her and do it quickly."

"The Guild has no right to put such demands on either of us. It's positively medieval." He folded his arms over his chest, hopefully subtle in his effort to restrain his skill.

"Don't be a fool. You like her, don't you? You get on well, don't you?"

"Yes."

"Then where is the problem? It seems the intersection where duty meets desire is an excellent place to be. And if you hesitate, the opportunity might well be lost."

# Epilogue

"So here we are again," Rebecca said as David pushed her chair in at the Continental dining rooms.

He had requested the same corner table they had shared during their last visit. How warm and cozy to find the little yellow bird peeking at her from the pink peony and green leaf wallpaper, greeting her once again. Now that she knew what to expect, the clink of the china and low hum of conversation faded into the background rather than rasping her nerves raw. So much more pleasant.

"I have it on good assurance that Sir Wilbert will not be making another surprise appearance to join us." David chuckled and unfolded his napkin.

"Considering we have spent the better part of the last five days with him, I should expect him to be quite tired of our company by now." She picked up the menu, though she had already decided on the herbed chicken. Her mouth watered at the thought.

"I know I am tired of his."

"Is that the kind of thing you should say about the Guild Master?" She winked.

He peeked at her over the menu, eyebrows high. "Acting Guild Master. It is important to remember that."

"Because his position is only temporary, or because he has gotten under your skin like a bad itch?"

"Am I so obvious?" He set the menu aside and signaled the waiter.

"Perhaps I recognize that look."

"From where?"

She snickered under her breath. "You have to ask?"

A black-coated waiter paused at the table to receive David's order. "I admit, I occasionally got a bit short with you in your workshop."

"A bit short? On occasion?" She cocked her head and arched her brow.

"Fine. I often became crotchety and voiced my frustration. Loudly." He huffed, grey-green eyes twinkling. Gracious, he was handsome. "But only because I was annoyed that I had not learned such techniques sooner."

"Well, I suppose I cannot hold that against you. And I will concede Sir Wilbert is a demanding taskmaster. Reminds me a bit of my father that way. Wanting things done on time and right the first time."

"A far cry from working under Allbright and Cinderford, who seemed content to have as little done, as slowly as possible. I used to irritate them with what I wanted to accomplish, and now I can hardly keep up with Sir Wilbert's demands. I thought it would be a good thing, but now I'm not so sure." He reached for her hand across the table, laying warm fingers atop hers.

How delightful.

"He does seem determined to right all the wrongs of the last several Guild Masters as quickly as possible." She glanced over her shoulder.

No, Sir Wilbert was not supposed to be there, but still, it behooved one to be cautious. "He can be rather exhausting."

"That would be one word for it. And his assistant, Mr. Levy Jackson," he mimicked Jackson's trademark clipped tones and pushed an imaginary shock of red hair out of his eyes, "is cut from the same cloth."

Rebecca hid a chuckle behind her hand. For all his peculiarities, Mr. Jackson was not a bad fellow, just a busy one. "A journeyman usually is."

"What do you think of our new Guild Master?" Though his voice was still light, David's expression tightened just a mite.

"I have interacted with him more in the last fortnight than any of the other Guild Masters through the years. His energy is both contagious and exhausting." She sipped her wine. "I confess, it is pleasant to be in his favor. It is not a position that I am accustomed to."

"Compared to the utter neglect of the past, I imagine it could be disquieting." His nose wrinkled, and he sniffed.

That was one word for it, but not the one she would have chosen. "To be sure, I also take it with a grain of salt. It is quite clear that his good opinion toward me is with respect toward the Skill my father taught me to use. I could be the devil's own mistress, for all he knows, and he would still be content to count me among his acquaintance, and more significantly, his Guild."

David chuckled, but more because it was obligatory than that he meant any levity. It was nice to read his expressions so clearly now. "I would call you cynical, but that might imply I don't agree."

"You've seen it, too?"

"He is a man with a deep passion for his cause, that of saving his people. I respect and admire that. I share the calling, though perhaps not with quite the same fervor as he. I'm not sure that we would always come to the same decisions in pursuit of those goals."

"On another day, I would like to hear more about that—the issues, the challenges, the differences of opinion. I have a great deal to learn about the state of our kind. But that is for another day."

"What is for today, then?" He pressed her fingers with his. Such warmth in his fingers, his eyes, his smile.

Oh, that smile. She would never tire of that expression. "Celebrating, for one thing." She turned aside, her cheeks prickling.

"Yes, there is a great deal to celebrate, not the least of which is that the immediate future, as laid out for us by our acting Guild Master, will keep us both fed, housed, and together in Brighton for some time to come."

Together.

"Yes, it will. I haven't begun to understand how to feel about that. If I am honest, I can't remember the last time I didn't worry about how I was going to find the next day's supply." The niggling knot in her gut had eased, leaving an odd little void she didn't know how to fill.

"The question is, what are we going to do with that time?" Such earnestness in his eyes. And hope, there was definitely hope there as well.

Maybe hope was supposed to fill that void. It certainly seemed to fit in that space. What an interesting thought.

"It seems like Sir Wilbert has our time already quite accounted for, doesn't he?" She lifted an eyebrow, daring him.

"He has spoken to you?" He slapped his forehead, grimacing.

"No, not in so many words, at least. I give him credit for at least attempting to be subtle."

"Attempting? That hardly sounds like him. What did he say?" Every inch of David's exposed skin turned bright red. Not without reason.

"Nothing directly. He has asked several times about whether we have dined together since his intrusion, what is my opinion of you ... exactly the sort of things my father was apt to bring up when he was seeking to match me with Dick Mallory." She shuddered and swallowed back the rising bile.

"Forgive me, but I don't understand why he would have even considered that. To be paired with a mundane man—never mind of what moral character he might be—would be the end of your ability to practice your Skill. Why would he want that?" He squeezed her hand, protective and strong.

"I have wondered that, too." She sighed. "Toward the end, when he lost his teaching credentials and my application for Mastery was ignored, he lost hope that I would be given a proper rank and affiliation with the Guild. I think he feared what might happen if I were left to practice what he taught me without some kind of guidance or accountability. He was not the trusting sort. No telling what he thought I could become, with my mother's temper and his stubbornness. Better I trade my Skill for the safety of a marriage of any sort than risk—well, whatever he imagined the dangers to be. I don't like to think about it, but I fear he believed I would have gone rogue without the affirmation of the Guild."

"I am glad that you refused Mallory." David waved at a waiter to refill their wine. He squeezed her hand again, a quiet statement of his faith in her, the sort that she could fully believe. "Does it bother you, knowing Sir Wilbert's hopes for us?"

"Should they make me question your sincerity?" Should it be so hard to meet his eyes after asking such a question?

"No, no, they should not." He exhaled heavily, tension leaving his shoulders. "I would hope you know me well enough by now that—"

"That you are a principled man and that you will sacrifice a great deal to uphold your convictions."

"You are no sacrifice." He pressed her fingers to his cheek. "I suppose I have never told you. For a long time, I thought I would spend my life a confirmed bachelor. My work with the Guild is too much a part of who I am, and I thought there would be no one with whom I could share that. It is such a wonder to share that aspect of my life with another."

"I can see the appeal, especially since I once accepted that fate myself. Though, if one only has one choice—" She held her breath. It was stupid to tempt fate with statements like that.

"Please stop. My hopes and intentions are unchanged by Sir Wilbert's or anyone else's opinions. Except for yours. What do you think? Do we continue on the journey as colleagues ... or as something else?" He pressed his lips hard as if to stop himself from saying too much.

"I have no experience with either." Oh, that was painful to admit. Was her isolated life a character flaw to hide, or some sign she was insufficient for company? She had never thought about it.

"Colleagues can be quite dreary. Look at Sir Wilbert."

She snickered. "You make an excellent case. You are far better company than he."

He permitted a small smile, but not too much. "But am I sufficient company for you?"

She gazed at him. Oh, the feeling in his eyes. She did not even have the words for it. Was it possible? Was there even a chance of it working? "Yes, I think you are."

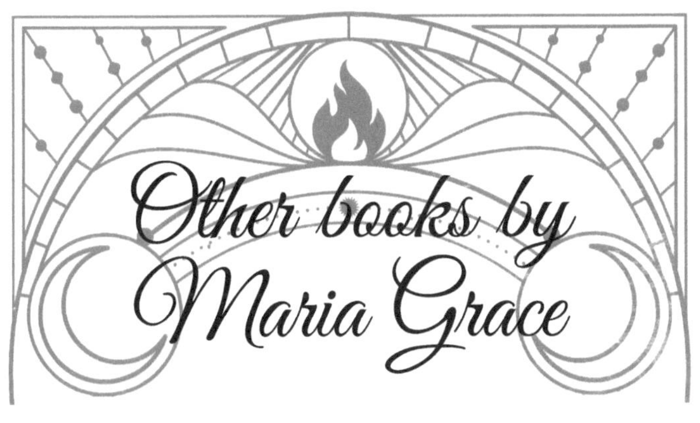


**JANE AUSTEN'S DRAGONS SERIES:**

*Pemberley: Mr. Darcy's Dragon*

*Longbourn: Dragon Entail*

*Netherfield: Rogue Dragon*

*A Proper Introduction to Dragons*

*The Dragons of Kellynch*

*Kellynch: Dragon Persuasion*

*Dragons Beyond the Pale*

*Dragon Keepers' Cotillion*

*The Turnspit Dragon*

*Dragons of Pemberley*

*Miss Georgiana and the Dragon*

*Here There Be Dragons*

***The Queen of Rosings Park Series:***

*Mistaking Her Character*

*The Trouble to Check Her*

*A Less Agreeable Man*

***Sweet Tea Stories:***

*A Spot of Sweet Tea: Hopes and Beginnings*

*Snowbound at Hartfield*

*A Most Affectionate Mother*

*Inspiration*

***Darcy Family Christmas Series***

*Darcy & Elizabeth: Christmas 1811*

*The Darcy's First Christmas*

*From Admiration to Love*

*Unexpected Gifts*

***Given Good Principles Series:***

*Darcy's Decision*

*The Future Mrs. Darcy*

*All the Appearance of Goodness*

*Twelfth Night at Longbourn*

***Fine Eyes and Pert Opinions***

***Remember the Past***

***The Darcy Brothers***

***Regency Life (Nonfiction) Series:***

*A Jane Austen Christmas: Regency Christmas Traditions*

*Courtship and Marriage in Jane Austen's World*

*How Jane Austen Kept her Cool: An A to Z History of Georgian Ice Cream*

***Behind the Scene Anthologies (with Austen Variations):***
*Pride and Prejudice: Behind the Scenes*
*Persuasion: Behind the Scenes*

***Non-fiction Anthologies***
*Castles, Customs, and Kings Vol. 1*
*Castles, Customs, and Kings Vol. 2*
*Putting the Science in Fiction*
Available in e-book, audiobook and paperback

# About the Author

Six-time BRAG Medallion Honoree, #1 Best-selling Historical Fantasy author Maria Grace has her PhD in Educational Psychology and is a 16-year veteran of the university classroom where she taught courses in human growth and development, learning, test development and counseling. None of which have anything to do with her undergraduate studies in economics/sociology/managerial studies/behavior sciences. She pretends to be a mild-mannered writer/cat-lady, but most of her vacations require helmets and waivers or historical costumes, usually not at the same time.

She writes Gaslamp fantasy, historical romance and non-fiction to help justify her research addiction.

Contacted her at:

author.MariaGrace@gmail.com

Find her on

her website Random Bit of Fascination (RandomBitsofFascination.com)

Facebook

GoodReads

# Acknowledgments

So many people have helped me along the journey, taking this from an idea to a reality.

Thanks so much to my beta team—your input is invaluable!

Friends of the Blue Order, your unflagging encouragement and imagination has been inspirational.

My dear friend Cathy, my biggest cheerleader, you have kept me from chickening out more than once!

Thank you!

Made in United States
Troutdale, OR
12/22/2023

16350637R00217